ALSO BY JACQUELYN MITCHARD

FOR ADULTS

Still Summer

Cage of Stars

The Breakdown Lane

A Theory of Relativity

Christmas, Present

Twelve Times Blessed

The Most Wanted

The Rest of Us:
Dispatches from the Mother Ship

The Deep End of the Ocean

No Time to Wave Goodbye

FOR CHILDREN AND YOUNG ADULTS

Look Both Ways:
A Midnight Twins Novel

The Midnight Twins

All We Know of Heaven

Now You See Her

Ready, Set, School!

Rosalie, My Rosalie

Starring Prima!:
The Mouse of the Ballet Jolie

Baby Bat's Lullaby

SECOND NATURE

SECOND NATURE

A Love Story

JACQUELYN MITCHARD

RANDOM HOUSE | NEW YORK

Second Nature is a work of fiction. Names, characters,
places, and incidents are the products of the author's imagination or
are used fictitiously. Any resemblance to actual events, locales,
or persons, living or dead, is entirely coincidental.

Published in the United States by Random House,
an imprint of The Random House Publishing Group,
a division of Random House, Inc., New York.

RANDOM HOUSE and colophon are registered
trademarks of Random House, Inc.

LIBRARY OF CONGRESS CATALOGING-IN-PUBLICATION DATA
Mitchard, Jacquelyn.
Second nature: a love story/by Jacquelyn Mitchard.
p.   cm.
ISBN 978-1-4000-6775-6 (alk. paper)
eBook ISBN 978-0-6796-4396-8
I. Title.
PS3563.I7358S43 2011
813'.54—dc22   2010048497

Printed in the United States of America on acid-free paper

www.atrandom.com

9 8 7 6 5 4 3 2 1

First Edition

For my daughter Mia,
my daughter Merit,
and my daughter Marta,
but, most of all, for my
firstborn daughter, Francie,
who wouldn't accept the end

God has given you one face,
And you make yourself another.

—WILLIAM SHAKESPEARE

Author's Note

Second Nature takes place in a possible but imagined future, in a Chicago that is more a product of my memories than a city that is on any actual grid. The events, procedures, and outcomes may one day be possible but now exist only on these pages. All the errors of fact or supposition are my own.

SECOND NATURE

This is what I know.

My father stood in the center aisle of the Lady Chapel—that hunched, hexed little building he hated as a father and as a firefighter—under the lowering band of sooty, mean-colored smoke, and he looked right at me. He understood what had happened to me, and although he couldn't tell me then, he was still happy. He thought I was one of the lucky ones.

I was.

This is what I remember.

There were fifty of us in the Lady Chapel that late afternoon, December 20, the shortest day of the year. Inside, in winter, it was always about as warm and bright as an igloo. Wearing our coats and mittens as we sang "O Come, O Come, Emmanuel," we could see our breath. As a place of worship and a historic structure, the Lady Chapel was exempt from all the building codes and conformed to none of them, which was why Dad despised the very sight of it. The mahogany pews, each with a different intricate carving, massaged for seventy years with layers of flammable polish, were nothing but tinder to him. Raw and reckless new structures, when they burned, were flimsy as tents. But the old chapel had stone walls a foot thick and had been reroofed so many times that Dad said that it could have withstood a phosphorus bomb.

It didn't take anything as potent as a bomb, only a small candle in a small draft.

That day, just as the choirmaster, Mr. Treadwell, brought together his fingertips and held them up to his delicate cheekbones, twinkly as a ballerina (looking back, I think Mr. Treadwell was twinkly all the time, what my mother called "a confirmed bachelor"), first one and then the other Christmas tree on either side of the altar went up like ten-foot sparklers. A few kids simply stood, flat-footed and amazed, as though the pyrotechnics were some sort of holiday surprise.

I knew better than to think that, even for a second.

It was only luck that I was in the last row of the choir's three-tiered semicircle, because I was taller and older, in eighth grade. I turned to run straight back, but the fire was more agile, leaping voraciously ahead of me along the strip of gold carpet between the seats. The Advent banners dodged and gyrated above my head like burning bats. I held my new purse, a birthday present from my Grandmother Caruso, up to my face, instinctively protecting my lungs. Then, I turned around to face the fire on the altar, which went against all instincts, except for someone raised in my father's catechism: Keep cool. Keep making choices. These rules were not second nature to me by then. They were first nature. I felt my way along the communion rail and then turned left at the wall, feeling my way along under the windows until I saw what I knew what must be the door—a ghostly flapping of white light that looked like a giant moth. This, I knew, must be the door opening and closing. When I got there, I reached for the big bronze curve of the door handle. I knew it must be there. But my fingers were clumsy in my leather mitten, and when I stopped to pull it off, other kids rear-ended me, knocking me sideways. I jumped up and grabbed for the door handle again, trying to ignore the escalating chorale of high-pitched screaming. Was there a moment of stupor? It could only have been a moment. The next thing I recall clearly was standing up, looking over my shoulder at the oxygen mask on the face of my father's rookie, Renee Mayerling, a grown woman who was not as tall as I was already at thirteen. She shoved me along with the exigent roughness of a rescuer, with her other hand dragging Libby Van de Water. Suddenly I was out, tripping and falling on my face in a foot of fresh, burning-cold snow, which probably saved my eyes. As soon as I could, I lifted my head to look around me. There was my friend Joey LaVoy and his brother, Paulie, who were not in the choir but had come running over from the school, yelling, *Help them! Help them!* That's when I really saw the other kids from the choir everywhere around me, some lying still as sleeping bags, closed and pale, others crawling half naked, because their clothes had caught fire. There were a few I didn't even recognize, because somehow their arms and faces were swollen as brown as the surface of caramel apples. Renee came out and I looked for my dad, who would have been right behind Renee—I just sensed him being right behind her. And then he wasn't. Instead, he stayed inside the door, while Renee crouched low, holding out her arms to Dad. I understood then. I should have known it, and somehow I should have done something, like kicked away that big doorstop. One side of the huge arched door was always kept locked, by order of the principal, Sister Ignatius Bell, so that students could enter and leave the Lady Chapel in single file only. But kids hadn't run for their lives in single file. In the smutchy darkness, they collided with the locked side and fell, and the kids behind them tripped and fell, and pretty soon the ones on the bottom must have been pinned down and the others kept on coming.

I turned over in the snow and scooted to a sitting position, then struggled to my knees. I could still see over my father's head, all the way to the altar. Sweet Mr. Treadwell must have waited until he could shepherd out all of the kids he could see. He stood on the altar like a living crucifix, his arms out and his head thrown back, the two flaming fir trees on either side of him, their skinny trunks gyrating like ink lines in the deep dirty yellow flames and then vanishing altogether. I cared about Mr. Treadwell but knew Dad would not be going back for him. It was already too late for my teacher. At last, Dad did come out and I exhaled a prayer of relief. The fire was taking on force: The whole chapel seemed to shudder, like a witch's oven in a cartoon, something the witch could command to do evil if she wanted to. But Dad was out. I could see my father's gray eyes behind his goggles, and it was almost as though he spoke to me: *Sicily. I'm okay! I promise! Would I let you down? I'm the Cap. I'm the Daddy.* Whatever else was happening around him, he reassured me. He never understated the dangers of his job, but he called them "manageable, with common sense." He made me think—long past the age when most kids stop believing in their fathers as mythic beings—that he was the barrier evil could not cross.

Dad must have heard a sound. He jerked and looked over his shoulder.

I think I saw skinny little Danny Furtosa at the same time my father did. Danny was standing about halfway between the door and the altar, with his hair on fire. This flat line of muddy smoke had begun to descend from the chapel's ceiling, layering down atop the glow of the fire—something I had seen only on my dad's five million or so accident-scene videos, which I was never supposed to watch but, of course, did. I knew that my dad was measuring that bank of smoke against the distance between him and Danny and hoping he had five seconds, which I knew even then could be plenty of time. And still, I tried to scream for him not to go. My mouth didn't open. My neck didn't lurch, the way it does when you gather your vocal chords to shout. I thought it was just smoke—and fear—clogging my voice, shoving it down.

It wouldn't have mattered. He would have gone anyway.

He got far enough to pick Danny up. And then there was a sharp musical burst as one of my dad's crew, Tom McAvoy or Schmitty, used a pike pole to slam in one of the old leaded windows. My father and Danny Furtosa disappeared in the unfurling red velvet of the flashover. It foamed toward Renee and me like the disgorged depths of a dragon's throat. My dad always said there was nothing so pretty as a flashover. Renee said to me, "Oh, my God. Oh, Sicily. Listen. Look at me." But neither of us could look away. Did I notice, like Renee, how majestic and lovely that flashover was? Of course I did. I was my father's daughter. He wouldn't have panicked. And I didn't panic either. There was still a chance that my dad had survived. He was a twenty-five-year veteran. People lived through flashovers all the time. I knew he would have bad injuries. But that was okay if I could keep him.

The sharp dread for my father was not my only thought in that fractured and fractional moment. Never had I perceived fire as other than mesmerizing—something to be respected for its power but not to be feared, something that my father routinely conquered. Everyone would see the transformation of my face. Everyone with eyes could understand what that did to me. Not even I would grasp how powerful was the simultaneous denaturing of my being, the part no one could see, and how that shift would shape my life as much.

More.

If it hadn't been for that ten minutes ten days after my thirteenth birthday, I would have grown up exactly the same as a million other kids just like me.

The fire happened during the last hour of class on the last day of school before Christmas vacation at Holy Angels Catholic School. My father was forty-four years old, captain of Ladder 19, Engine Company 3, in Chester, Illinois, just outside Chicago. At the scene, his primary role should have been making sure where everyone was, but he and Renee were first on scene and the fire was too bad to follow procedure exactly: There were kids involved, and one of them was me. Although Dad would have expected that the training would take over, smooth as a motor starting, and that he would act no differently than he would if his kid wasn't inside, I didn't believe that then and I don't now. Still, he and Renee carried thirty-four to safety out of that gruesome, impossible, inaccessible little place, and twenty-six kids lived. No one could have done more. My father was a hero because he was in the wrong place at the wrong time. I was in the wrong place at the wrong time too—damaged, but a survivor. But I was part of that fire too—and though I had nothing to do with it, I was in some measure responsible, just as you are in some measure responsible when a car rear-ends your car, because you're there. If you set a fire, even a campfire, the law says you're responsible for whatever it burns. If you could have put that fire out and you didn't, you're responsible. If I had been home sick that day—and I was sick, a little, and my mother wanted me to stay home, because she was wacky-protective if I even sniffled—my father still would have answered the three-eleven alarm. Would he have gone the extra distance? I used to toss that back and forth, thinking at first, maybe not; Dad was by the book. He said that his best friend, Schmitty, had "hero genes," but that he himself did not. What my dad would have wanted was to be with me at the hospital that night, holding my mom on his lap like a child as she cried.

To my best friend, Kit Mulroy, and me, my parents' displays were humiliating. They'd been married since they were twenty-three and he still called her "my bride." My mother was at the hospital that night, alone—with her sister and her parents and my friends' parents, yes, but entirely alone.

My father died where he stood, from his injuries. He would have been able to brace for it. He would still have been breathing air from his mask. When he put it on, I knew, he had twelve minutes, and the whole thing lasted no longer than six. When the hoses fought it all down—it couldn't have taken long, less than a minute?—leaving the chapel a thick, charred hulk, its medieval walls gruffly upstanding, the water along the roofline already slushing to a filthy glaze, I was still kneeling in the snow. It went that quickly. From behind me, I felt the urgent, gentle hands of the medics helping me onto a rolling stretcher. Everywhere, by then, were paramedics, from towns all over, their vans filling the circle and lunging up over the high curbs onto the lawn, rushing to the kids around me. Some kids the medics just knelt to touch and then quickly, softly, laid a blanket over them, as though tucking them in, and walked past. Of course I knew why. Other kids they grabbed up, starting chest compressions and shoving oxygen masks on, yelling like athletes breaking the tape when they got a breath. It took so long for me to get out of there, because my cart's wheels got stuck in the snow. Renee tried to stand in front of me, but I saw guys from my father's crew bringing him out—in their arms, not on a bed. Dad still held Danny Furtosa in his arms. Danny's face was pushed tight against my dad's chest. In the end, Dad was old-fashioned South Side Irish, a certain kind of guy.

Even if he could have ducked and run to me, he wouldn't have wanted a little kid to die alone.

CHAPTER TWO

What if I hadn't picked up the phone the night that Eliza Cappadora called?

I almost didn't.

It was the end of a long day—the longest day of what was, for me, the longest week of the year. I usually endured the anniversary of the fire by checking out—in a diagonal sprawl across my large and demulcent bed, sleeping fifteen hours at a stretch in the embrace of an indecent number of pillows. But this year I had to sock away money, money for a house, money for a week on Cape Cod. So I needed to work. Luckily, even around the holidays, there was plenty of work for a medical illustrator: doctors putting finishing touches on the papers they would deliver at conferences in the new year, lawyers preparing for personal-injury cases they would try when they could get enough people in town to seat a jury. And yet interacting even with clients I knew well enough to call friends was like wearing a cardigan made from fishhooks.

By the time I put my keys into the seventeen or so locks Aunt Marie insisted we have—despite the fact that Angel and Frank, the doormen, had the combined weight and heft of a bulldozer—my spine was so stress-pressed that I must have shrunk two inches in height. No sooner did I get inside and collapse gratefully against the door for the first long breath I'd taken that day than my cell phone began to vibrate against my abdomen. I'd stashed it in the front pack I wore when I needed my hands free and had turned the ringer off for the ballet class I took on Tuesdays and Fridays.

No, I thought.

No more people.

Days like today underscored what I already believed—that if humanity were a divine work of art, it would still be a work in progress.

I stepped around a dozen piles of clean clothes that I'd shucked and left arrayed around my living room in heaps, like cut-loose marionettes, then took out the phone and glanced at the message list. Four calls were from my aunt, who was leaving in the morning for England. All of them would say the same thing: *Are you sure you're going to be okay?* Four more calls were from a number I didn't know, and I was in no mood to blow off a solicitor. So I wrapped myself in my biggest cashmere blanket and slid back the heavy glass doors to my balcony. It was cold, well below freezing. The wind this far up bellowed off the lake. But I loved looking at other people's lives as defined by their balconies. In summer, some people brought out barbecue grills and kegs, as though these eight-by-four concrete ledges were backyards. Some grew climbing roses and tomatoes in thick tubs. Tonight, the penthouse three floors above me had three lighted Christmas trees—pulsing madly, white, silver, and gold, to syncopated rhythm. Diagonally and a floor down, Santa's sleigh sailed out from a space that wouldn't have accommodated even two tiny reindeer, unless they really were the size of Jack Russell terriers.

And there it was! What I'd been anticipating for days.

This one person—directly across and two floors below—never let me down.

At Christmas, whoever lived there always spelled out a greeting across her porch rail—and always, always always, got it wrong. One year, it was MARRY XMAS. One year the lights read NOLE, NOLE. This year—perhaps the best ever—PEECE! I wanted to call my best friend, Kit, but she'd gone with her family to their cabin in Vermont for Christmas.

But even the annual misspelling bee didn't dispel my gloom.

A few moments later, I was driven inside. I wanted to be out there, where the cold wind could give my thoughts a hard sweeping, but I couldn't tolerate cold. The best skin grafted onto your face still isn't facial skin. And no matter how well it's done, it's scarred, so it gets tight and dry quicker than normal skin. Torquing up my humidifier, I climbed onto my bed. Then I noticed my phone spinning around on my dresser like a live green beetle. I hated it (I still hate it) when people called back more than once in the space of an hour. If you don't answer, do they think they can goad you into it? Maybe it was my aunt, calling from some Christmas party at a condo in the clouds where there was a phone in every one of the five bathrooms.

"For Pete's sake, I'm fine!" I said. But the voice was young. Not Marie's.

"Sicily? Is this Sicily Coyne?"

"Yes?"

"Hi, Sicily. This is Eliza Cappadora." I let a beat of silence pass. Was I supposed to know her? The name was familiar, tied to something. But what?

The tentative, slightly lilting voice began again. "Hello?"

"Hi," I said. "I'm here. I'm so sorry. I thought you were my aunt . . . not that I always sound that hostile toward my aunt, but she's leaving for London tomorrow and she worries about me like I'm six years old."

"I watch your aunt on TV all the time."

"Well, this is the royal baby thing. Aunt Marie likes socially irrelevant news."

Eliza continued, "We met last summer. At the police against firefighters softball game in Hilldale? My husband was playing."

"Your husband is a firefighter?"

"No, my mother is the police chief in Parkside. My husband works at his family's restaurant. But my mom isn't the softball type. . . ."

"Oh, sure, no worries. Just, Eliza, how do you know this number? I don't mind, but—"

"Dr. Sumner gave it to me. David Sumner? Maybe he shouldn't have."

"Oh, David? It's okay," I said. "If it's okay with David, you must be all right."

David Sumner was one of my burn-surgeon brigade, extraordinary for many reasons, not the least of which was that he was a burn survivor too, his chest and upper-arm skin rippled by a pot of boiling jam he pulled down on himself when he was three. David Sumner had worked with me (well, *on* me) during my early trauma period. How long since I had visited him? Months? A year? There was no excuse. I was at the University of Illinois Chicago Circle campus several times a month. I hadn't been a patient for seven or eight years, but UIC was still my alma mater—in every sense. I'd graduated from there, the hospital was my greatest source of referrals for work, and it also was the place where I'd had all twenty-five of my reconstructive surgeries. Intuition would presume that a person would hate the sight of the place on earth where she'd endured the purest physical torment. But I felt for UIC the affection someone feels for a strict parent: The surgeons had fought to make my face at least work like a face—with, for example, a mouth that closed nearly all the way—even if it didn't look like a face.

"How is he?" I asked.

"He's well. But that is not why I'm calling. We actually first met a long time ago: I was with my mother at your father's funeral."

"Really," I said. *Where was this going?*

"It was around this time of year?" Eliza said.

I hated to have to say it. "Yes, it was. In fact, the fire was twelve years ago today."

"Give up!" Eliza said, and then . . . she began to laugh. To laugh! My first reaction was shock and dismay. "I'm sorry! I'm so sorry, I get stupid when I'm tense, and I'm just an idiot!" Eliza said, but she couldn't stop laughing. And then I began to laugh too, for no good reason except that Eliza's laugh was as irresistible as a child's. Only long after we became friends did I realize that Eliza meant to say, "Get out!" Adopted at the age of eight from a Bolivian orphanage, Eliza spoke perfect English, better than a good many American-born physicians of my acquaintance. Under stress, however, she tended to lose her grip on the idiom.

"You didn't know," I said.

"But I should have. There's always a story about it in the newspaper." Eliza was right about that. The Holy Angels fire was still one of Chicago's biggest collective heartaches. There would be some feature about where the survivors were now or a photo of the monument where twenty of the twenty-four children who died slept together at Queen of Heaven Cemetery—a green granite arch with their lyric names lettered in gold (Erin, Sofia, Malachi) and the dates of their births and deaths. A few of those dates—impossibly—were in the same decade. Even all these years later, someone always left a Santa teddy bear or a little potted tree with ornaments. The arch was green Italian marble because the colors of the Fighting Saints of Holy Angels were green and gold. It had been designed by my mother. Grandma Caruso said that's where I got my ability to draw.

Although I didn't tell Eliza, five nights earlier had been another anniversary—the tenth year since my mother's accident. My mother died two years after the Holy Angels fire.

Mom was on her way home from her part-time job at a vet's office when her car was T-boned in an intersection by a kid who'd gotten his driver's license that afternoon, one of about six pertinent ironies. My mom hadn't needed to work that day but had volunteered to fill in for the other receptionist, whose sister in Wyoming had been . . . in a car accident. My mom didn't need to work at all. We had my dad's pension, his life-insurance benefit, and gifts from the village and the benevolent fund, including my college scholarship. But Mom did need a way to divert herself from full-time hysteria over having lost in one day her first love and, if you will, her religion—which was me. I wasn't dead, of course. But at first I wished aloud that I would die under anesthesia during yet another hideous patch job. Then I would always wake up and slowly realize that I was not in heaven but in a hospital room overlooking a bakery on Taylor Street, and I would be fury itself. I upended trays of food and tore up the pictures of me, taken when I was little, that my mother kept in her wallet. "Why am I alive?" I would ask Mom. "Why did I live through that to go through this?"

That was what my mom got—two years of sitting at the bedside of her ranting, melted child. At first I was out of school most of the time, and tutors, like my dad's rookie Renee, who had studied to be an English teacher, helped me keep up. But why did I want to keep up? What was I going to do or be? I had been one of the cute girls in our small school. Everyone accepted that Marianne Modica and Jennet Liff would for sure grow up to beautiful. (They did.) But Tess Reagan, who died, and I might have turned out to be really pretty too. I knew this and I hated my mother for it, as I hated her for everything. It was the kind of nonchalant, dependable scorn that any ripped-off kid feels for the remaining parent, the one who isn't sainted and can't leave. My father was dead but still my hero and protector. I didn't care that my mother knew it.

I actually once told my mother that I wished she had been the one who died. And though I wept and apologized, and she wept and forgave me, it was true. We both knew it.

She died not quite nine months later.

That should have obliterated me, and it would have, except for Marie.

A private jet owned by a rich boyfriend had whisked her across the country from a Utah ski holiday. Once she arrived in the ICU for the second time in two years, she pulled me close to her and said, "You're like the patron saint of suffering." When a surgeon came out to quietly explain to the gathered family—my grandparents, their brothers and sisters, and my aunt Christina, who is a Franciscan nun—that there was nothing more they could do, that my mother's chest was crushed, I could not make my legs work to walk across the room and say goodbye to my mother. Marie stayed by my side even then, her adored big sister behind that drawn curtain. She did not leave Chicago, for business or pleasure, for the next three years. To adopt me, Marie gave up a job in the lofty six figures as an anchor on CBN News in New York, the rich boyfriend with the airplane, the beach house in Sagaponack—all in exchange for waking up every night to comfort a tremulous teenager who wouldn't eat and had begun to wet the bed each time she dreamed that she saw tiny flames on every flat surface. "It's not much," she told me the night Mom died. "But I'll never leave you."

I had forgotten I was even holding the phone when Eliza said, "Sicily, are you there?"

"I am. I'm sorry. Just spaced out for a moment."

"Do . . . do you think we could have coffee?"

"Well," I said. "Sure, okay . . . why?"

"I'm a first-year resident at UIC. Not on the burn unit. At the Center for Reconstructive Surgery. I'm only a resident, studying to be a doctor, but—"

I giggled a little. "I know what a resident is. I'm a medical illustrator. And I have spent a fair amount of time in the hospital."

"Of course. I know that. I'm going to be a reconstructive surgeon. And my mentor, Dr. Grigsby, pioneered full-face transplant surgery, well . . . years and years ago."

"Does she have a new technique? Does she need illustrations?" I asked.

"No. No. I . . . She just moved here from London, actually, to head up a team at UIC. And I told her about you. I told her about your career. I told her about your . . . face." *Huh?* I thought. Then Eliza said, "I was thinking you might be hoping for a face transplant."

"A what?"

"A face transplant."

"For me?"

"Well, yes."

"I don't need a face transplant." I almost laughed again.

"That's the thing," Eliza said. "If you thought you *needed* to have a face—that is, a new face—you probably shouldn't be considered. If you couldn't work or have a social life, for example, with your face the way it is, you really shouldn't be a candidate for a new one."

I sat down on my bed, flummoxed. "Eliza, this sounds like *Alice in Wonderland.* Like, if you're well read, you shouldn't wear red . . . or whatever. This is very thoughtful, but you know how many surgeries I've already had? Why would I do this? Not to mention, I don't have a million dollars or so sitting around."

"Whatever your insurance didn't cover, the hospital would. There's a fund."

"Eliza," I said, suddenly eager to be asleep, oblivious. "It's just really awkward. You might as well suggest I . . . hatch fertilized eggs from an alien. This is so not on my radar."

"I'm sorry. This was probably inappropriate. You must think I'm trying to score success points with my boss. It is not that. It was something my husband said. When he was in college, he thought he might be a teacher. He helped with summer sports programs at Holy Angels. He graduated from there."

"I played . . . uh, hoops, summer league." I didn't try to say "basketball." I didn't say "basketball" or any words that began with "B" or "P" if I could help it. Not having lips is a disadvantage with plosives. I'd avoided them for so long, I was virtually my own simultaneous translator.

"Right. Ben transferred to your school because there was too much attention at public school about him—but that doesn't matter."

Then I remembered where I'd heard the name Ben Cappadora: back when I was in first grade. He was the boy who was kidnapped and returned, whose parents once lived in Chester, where my parents had lived and where my Grandma and Grandpa Caruso still did. The Cappadoras were a sort of local legend, the unluckiest family around.

"Sure. Everyone knows about Ben. And his brother—didn't he make a movie?"

"Vincent. My brother-in-law. Yes, He did. He won an Oscar. But it was only a documentary, not like, well, *Star Wars*. He's a little famous."

"But how does this involve me?"

"I think Dr. Grigsby will probably kill me, also, in doing this," Eliza said, as though talking to herself. I was curious now. "Don't be angry with me."

"I'm not angry," I said. "What did Ben say?"

"How cute you were, and really tough too. He said you played to win," Eliza said. "Oh, dear. Dr. Grigsby seeks out patients who are tough. You have to be tough to go through this procedure."

"Well," I said. "I did always play to win, I guess. Maybe I still do. But I don't think I want to take this opportunity from someone else who really—"

"I get it. So, maybe just the coffee will be good."

"At UIC? Not a chance," I said.

"We'll go to Lotta Latte," she said.

"Now you've got a deal."

We parted with a promise to meet sometime. I wrote her home phone number on a piece of paper that I folded and tucked into a corner of the frame that held my mother's photo, one of three framed pictures I kept by my bedside—her, my father, and my own eighth-grade graduation picture.

In my photo, I was sitting on a rough wooden bench, outdoors, wearing cuffed jeans, my arms circling one drawn-up knee. My lustrous hair, shiny as a horse chestnut and exactly that color—a replica of my mother's—was drawn over one shoulder in a thick sheet. I recalled myself as a little girl, wearing a red taffeta skirt that spun out like the trumpet of a lily, at Grandma Coyne's house for some occasion, and her taking my chin in one soft, floury hand as I pranced through the kitchen. She told me that I had my father's face—not like that was a terrific thing. Along with dimples and some smashing cloudy eyes, Dad also had a chin the size of a quarry. *Ta, Sicily,* Grandma said. *Ta, don't you worry yourself. You'll grow into that chin.* Just that year, I finally had. The misty eyes inherited from my dad were set in high cheekbones, strong as a scaffolding, making that chin look not protruding but proud. I was playing flirt with the camera, gazing up from under abundant lashes, my smile both tolerant and mischievous, hinting at a knowingness I did not yet quite possess. An energy sprang from that picture—that of a girl who had begun to understand the joyous potential of her supple body and smooth skin.

I still had that hair. I styled it carefully and had two good inches trimmed twice a year. Mom had refused my demands to cut it all off. By the time my mother died, my many surgeries had left my face shaped roughly like the face of a snowman, if that snowman had been put together from bits of cheap plastic in slightly different colors. The strange contours had the effect of making it seem that I was wearing some kind of mask; this, in turn, had the effect of making my hair, which had escaped the fire with nothing but a frizzle here and there, look fake too, like a wig. It also itched like a hill of red ants whenever my hair touched the places where I was healing. Mom got it off my neck by plaiting it into a flat intricate braid she then looped up and pinned in a barrette. Half the time, I pulled it out, telling her I not only looked like a monster but a monster whose mother made her look like something that belonged in *The Sound of Music.*

I still had those eyes. They'd always been my best feature, and now they were my communication salvation. You'd be shocked by how much you telegraph with the tiniest smirk or pout. If you had to do it all with a wink or an eye roll, you'd increase your repertoire. I collected eye gestures from other people, like from the memory of poor, doomed Mr. Treadwell with his "twinkling." Now the repertoire was so much a part of me that I must look like some B actor trying to get noticed in the crowd scene. *Hey! I'm intelligent! Hey! I'm nice! Hey! That was a joke! Don't be afraid of me!* I fluttered my lashes so much I was surprised I couldn't lift small weights with my eyelids.

I used my hands too, and not just the way all Italians do but for what I came to think of as DSL (Disfigured Sign Language, as opposed to American Sign Language). I kept my hands soft and impeccably groomed so that I could mime everything from opening a textbook to opening the gut for an appendectomy.

The esteem that normal people get for nickels and dimes cost me thousands of dollars in sweat and effort, and even then sometimes it was denied me. People fled from me, psychically and in fact. Your face is your defining impression on the world. My job was to contradict that impression every day of my life. To do that, you have to be willing to scream, vamp, and pantomime.

I could no longer close my eyes and instantly summon the splendid young girl's face that once was mine. My own face, and my parents' faces, had begun to slur away, like ink drawings dissolving under a spilled glass of water. I was becoming one of my distant memories.

After I hung up with Eliza, I slipped out of my dance clothes, showered, and pulled on a triple-XL UIC T-shirt that brushed my knees. Then I stowed my leather briefcase—holding my laptop and separate folders in which I'd placed the notes and sketches from each of that day's appointments—in my office. My office was no more than an L-shaped niche under a northern skylight—two long banks of laminated ledge with generous decks of shelving above, arrayed with my two desktop computers, my pastels and ink pens, and my sketchbooks. But it was as immaculate as my personal space was a mess—even my pens gradated by shade, the rose next to the carmine, the claret deepening to the maroon. In my home life, because Aunt Marie spoiled me, I was a slob. The cleaner picked up after me.

The only personal space I would allow no one else to lay hands on was the little glass shelf in my bathroom, where my prosthetic nose reposed in its box. I loved my nose, which was truly a triumph of the anaplastologist's art, down to the minute wires that simulated the tiny veins you have on your nose but never even really see. Wearing it with a thick pasting of the kind of glop makeup that burn victims use, I could, from a distance, appear almost ordinary.

Useful as it was, putting on my face (no pun intended) was always an effort.

It was not one I would make tonight.

I thought briefly of my last appointment that day—with a new client, Dr. Sajid Joshi. When I was ushered in to his office, he had made no attempt to acknowledge my presence, beyond the involuntary spasm of shock no one (no one) could suppress the first time they saw me. Potential clients were all acquaintances of acquaintances: People knew to expect a scarred face, and yet I was always worse than what they could allow themselves to imagine. A handsome man in his forties, Dr. Joshi was speaking on the phone, in *Russian,* with a British accent.

"*Nyet, Nivilit cheyetah,* Irina," Dr. Joshi said. "*Gravo prieta tu pona.* Bloody hell, Irina." Smiling, he covered the receiver and glanced at me. "Canceling appointments is one thing. Canceling a surgery when you need it is quite another."

When he finally hung up but didn't apologize, I still had to be more than civil to him. I knew I had to sort of groom him, the way that runts, from wolves to chimpanzees, have to fawn over the dominant members of the group. So I said pleasantly, "You used Russian." I leaned over to place my digital tape recorder between us and checked the microphone. Dr. Joshi gazed frankly down the neckline of my sweater. He didn't think I saw him do it, and so tenuous is the bridge of credibility between a disfigured person and a normal one—particularly a dominant male—that I dared not call him on it. Dr. Joshi was a hotshot, a future gold mine of projects. "You spoke Russian," I said again.

"Why, yes." Dr. Joshi preened. "I speak three languages." And then he sniffed. If you ever sniff after you say something self-congratulatory, be aware that someone will notice it. It's an involuntary reflex for conceited people, and I had to be a student of behavior to survive, reading everyone else's glossary of expressions like a second language, although mine, to them, appeared blank—a pane of lead. Dr. Joshi said, "How is it that you understood?"

"I took a little in college. I just recognized a few words, that's all."

"You took *Russian*?" The surgeon couldn't hide his bafflement.

If you are a sympathetic, aware, and kindly person who would swear up and down that you don't judge people by their appearance, you still really do think, deep in the nucleus of your being, that someone with a deformity is dumber than you are (unless he's Stephen Hawking). You'll still do weird things unintentionally, like talking louder to someone who is perfectly competent but has cerebral palsy.

I had to prove all the time that the inside of my head was not as damaged as the outside. I expected it. Expecting it is not the same as accepting it, particularly if you got up that morning in a foul mood and the day went downhill from there.

I should have nodded politely. Instead, I saw him and raised him one. "I speak five languages. I minored in languages. Italian—my family speaks it a little, but I wanted to be fluent. Latin was required, of course, and I taught myself Spanish when I was in high school. I took Russian because the alphabet was a challenge. Like a game." I could see from his expression how Dr. Joshi felt about having a young woman with a face as alluring as a catcher's mitt try to best him, so I quickly added, "You speak it like a native."

"I was a boy in Moscow," said Dr. Joshi. "Then we lived in London, where I read at Oxford." Another sniff. "My mother is Russian, a farmer's daughter. My father was a Sikh, a surgeon like myself. Forbidden marriage. Much passion. Much quarreling. But five happy children. My mother has many grandchildren now."

"That's interesting," I said. "Unusual. Let's get started."

"Of course," Dr. Joshi said. "But . . . I would venture that it is you who is unusual in this work. You're forced to meet people. Is that difficult for you, given . . . ?"

"Given how I look?" I said. The guy was pure gall on a cracker. "It used to be. I do have to factor in that some people will believe things that aren't true."

"Such as?"

"That I'm kind of dim-witted and have no sex life," I said, and then couldn't believe I actually had.

My aunt Marie used to tell me that if it was socially acceptable to slug disabled people, I would have both eyes on the side of my head, like a painting on the wall of a tomb in Egypt.

Dr. Joshi was too dark-skinned to really blush, but he fumbled, dropping his laptop as he turned toward the projection screen. We both held our breath, but the unit was undamaged, and Dr. Joshi quickly—almost too quickly—marched through the succession of photos of the technique he had pioneered. The new procedure would allow surgeons to use a smaller cannula to implant genetically engineered cells into a herniated disc, making the repair a rather neat office procedure. This was only the first interview I would need. Later, I'd use my rough sketches to make finer sketches of the progressive steps I'd created from my own drawings and then with the drawing programs on one of my three Macs. My final sketches—the whole procedure minus the gore—were what a medical illustrator does. They would make plain and to scale, in the paper Dr. Joshi would present, what photographs could not show. I did drawings and even animations in the same way for professors to use in teaching. For lawyers, my drawings made injuries specific in court without causing jurors to throw up. As I sketched, though I was being careful, I also was thinking that when I got home I'd find a message blinking on my office phone, telling me that "Doctor" had decided to proceed another way. When I stood up to leave, however, to my shock and his credit, Dr. Joshi extended his hand. He said, "I'm sorry I offended you."

I answered, God help me, *"Dasvidaniya."*

Standing at the window before I climbed into bed, I studied the traffic out on Lake Shore Drive, the taillights and headlights strung in a curve like a necklace of bright amber beads. *Next year,* I thought, *I won't have to put myself through this.* My life was going to change. Next year on this date, I would be a different person, putting someone else's needs before my own. I would be truly grown up.

My phone *brrrred* and spun again. By the time I got to it, it had stopped.

The missed call was from Joey, my fiancé.

Yep, my fiancé.

I'd become engaged the previous fall to Joey LaVoy, the first kid I saw that day when I struggled to my knees in the snow still clutching my melted vinyl purse to my face. Joey and I would be married in August. Most people with a congenital deformity or a disability who thrive at all do end up with someone, but the someone is usually either another "special" person they met in rehab or is the kind of person who gets off a little on it. It was down to the way Marie had raised me that I was engaged to a bona fide hunk, who also was a firefighter like my dad, and in Chicago too, where only the best of the best worked.

My aunt was no psychologist. But she knew human types. She was a TV news chick. She could suss out the core of people like a hunting dog. A sassy, hyperactive flyweight, she reminded everyone of Audrey Hepburn, with her Peter Pan haircut and her short black dresses with tights and ballet flats. Marie's appearance was as deceiving as mine.

Even now, well into her fifties (how well, she never revealed), my aunt was the kind of woman people thought of as "kittenish," long after the age when a cat was a cat. In fact, not only was she no kitten, if she'd been a feline, she'd have been the kind with half of one ear torn, the kind that could bristle to twice its size in battle. You could ask anyone who'd been in Marie's sights, ever so trustingly unaware before she pulled the trigger in an interview. Or you could ask me. I think no one knows Marie better than I do, not even her sisters or her parents or her (kind of many) lovers. When my aunt Marie said that she would never leave me, that night at the hospital, she meant it. And in return she demanded absolutely just about fifty percent more in everything. Giving me a pass would have been the worst thing she could have done, but there's no instruction manual to tell you that. My aunt flew on instruments: *You can't be as good as; you have to be better than,* Marie said. Over and over. Day and night. It was her litany.

The first thing she did was get me to survivor-type groups—not to learn coping techniques but to see what I could become if I didn't choose to live life like it was a giant slalom. She was right. What I saw shocked me into fight mode. Mine might well have been that pitiable—but so much simpler—life, the twilight existence some girls endured, living on disability, sewing veils to wear to the mall, never driving, dancing, dating, or drinking. In burn groups and loss groups and body-image groups (I was good for any group), most people ran a continuum from depressed to suicidal. True, many of them adjusted, with time. Those who adjusted came to talk to those of us just starting down the road. Most were in the helping professions, counselors or nurses or teachers. Some were teachers because they embraced the common fallacy that children are gentler. In fact, normal children are ruthless little brutes, programmed to survive. Kids might be more honest, forgiving, and way, way cuter. But they're also hand mirrors of the selves those people would have been. Most of the people who visited to inspire us were living what was still a middle life, not quite this or that.

Marie wouldn't hear of that for me.

I was going to be the world-champion faceless person.

I had to do everything I could that normal girls did. I wanted to quit ballet after the fire, although I'd studied it since I was four. Nix. A year later, I was back at the barre. In junior year of high school, I was in a master dance class. Just before recital, several mothers of the other girls sent a discreet but firm note to the dance teacher, who made the big mistake of passing it on to Marie. While they entirely understood my situation, their daughters were unsettled by my appearance when they performed—ballet *was* intended to be an act of essential beauty. Marie's response was to buy every seat in the recital hall, so no one but our family could attend.

Marie was right. But there were times when I just couldn't do it: I balked at the threshold of the world. College interviews? Volunteer work? The harder she pushed, the harder I pushed back. There were times I was sure that the nonagenarian lady next door would stroke out from the sound of Marie and me screaming at each other. (Mrs. Rain-flow finally did die—not because of us. But *at the funeral,* Marie made the heirs an offer for Mrs. Rainflow's place, in order to knock out the wall and combine both apartments into two big studios linked by a massive kitchen and dining room.) Despite all her insistence that I make my own way in the world, without compromise, I know Marie really believed I would live at home but not quite at home, all my life. After all, I'd been given plenty of chances to attend conferences, juicy junkets, as part of my job. I'd even received two awards. But they were sent to me in the mail, because there was no way I would ever get on an airplane or even the el—planes sometimes burst into flames; the train gave off sparks when it braked. There was no way I would ever go up to a podium, in front of people, and let anyone snap a picture of me being handed some little bronzed statuette of a pen and a paintbrush.

And yet, probably surprised because I behaved as though I deserved my propers, people responded. I made friends beyond my tight high school circle (at Holy Angels, I got a kind of deferment as a fire survivor and a martyr's daughter). When Joey and I met up again in college, after he got out of the military, he asked me out—asked *me* out, me alone, on a date, not as part of a congenial group. While we had always been friends, I figured Joe was a pervert or had suffered some odd genital injury in the military. Marie thought that was nonsense. Still, we started slowly, with Kit and me joining a group of friends we had in common with Joe, for a movie, then a cookout; I always found a spot to sit far from the barbecue grill. He was sensitive to me: He never did things like ask me out to a bar where people would be dancing. Our first real date was a late afternoon of Christmas shopping downtown, which I thought was awfully romantic. Our second was a winter picnic at the harbor. When we went out to dinner, it was to small places on the West Side, where people had known my family, not to swanky spots, where even haughty waiters had permission to stare. Joey became the leading wedge that opened a way for me into the world of summer tavern volleyball and vodka frost parties and . . .

eventually everything. Still, the more comfortable I got, the more frightened I felt. When I confided, Marie urged me on.

"What if it doesn't work out?" she said. "It's not going to hurt less if you pretend you don't care."

Although I finally did let myself fall, ours would have been a very proper courtship even by eighteenth-century standards. Joe was awkward and I, nearly twenty-two by then, was still an exasperated virgin, although determined to correct that oversight. The lovemaking didn't happen for two years. And when it happened, it was never our best thing, although our bodies were built for sex—me a dancer, him a gym rat. Our intimacy never approached the total abandon of self you were supposed to feel. But it was good enough. It was one C in a garden of A-pluses. We were pals. We had history and hopes. Joey sheltered me. Joey set me free. When I was with him, I forgot that I was supposed to be an untouchable. With Joey at my side, I was at least as good as.

So if Marie was the sun and Kit the ground on which I stood, Joey became my north star.

I knew tonight he'd want to take me out, to distract me with bad jokes and good wine. I knew I should go. Tomorrow at 7:00 a.m., Joey would start his forty-eight-hour shift. But it would be even harder on me to be sociable than it would to eat pasta politely. Despite my inability to smell, I'd trained my brain to let my tongue do what little tasting I could do. But I couldn't train my mouth to act like a lady. And so I ate sparingly, and only when I needed to, a fact that drove my aunt Marie crazy, as she drank thimblesful of wine and worked out like a prizefighter to stay TV-lady skinny. Joey took an almost erotic pleasure in food, hence my working more hours and taking on new clients to help pay for the house with the fancy gourmet kitchen that we would buy one day. For Joey, I would even learn to cook. When I described the kneading and the thumbprint required for my grandma's homemade gnocchi, Joey said, "I love it when you talk dirty."

But even for sweet Joey, I wouldn't go out tonight.

For one thing, my beloved seemed to have a genetic inability to be comfortable in public without his lifelong friends. When we were alone, we didn't lack for things to say. In public, Joe liked people around, and I assumed it was to cover his own shyness. So Neal Polachek, Joey's best friend, would most likely tag along or meet up with us at some point. If it wasn't Neal, it would be Andy English or Adam Sawicki or Joey's brother, Paul. I tried to like Paulie, who'd dated Kit for a few months, prompting my best friend, who always took new romance far, far too seriously, to rapturous speculation about our being sisters-in-law. Now Paul was dating Jane, a high school teacher and tennis coach who was exuberant and fun to be with. But since the engagement, Paulie and Jane seemed almost to avoid us—I never knew why—while Neal, a loner, for whom three weeks with a woman was an enduring relationship, was always available.

So when I called Joey back and his phone went over directly to voice mail, I did a quick little *fouetté en tournant* of victory.

Honey, I'm pooped, I thought, but what I said, since it was even harder to understand me on the telephone, was, "Honey, I'm worn out tonight. I'm going to sleep. I'll come to the station tomorrow." It wasn't that I took Joe for granted: Having him was like being given a birthday present every day. I worried that I would let him down—that I was too self-centered for the patience and daily-ness of a married life. But there was nothing I wouldn't master for Joe, for the life we would have, the house we would buy, the children—rowdy little girls, tender little boys.

I would bring something nice to the station tomorrow. Cannolis, maybe. I liked Joey's fellow firefighters and felt almost more comfortable in a firehouse than anywhere else, since the days Kit and I used to ride bikes to my father's station after school and eat Schmitty's chili and corn bread. Joey's crew knew who I was and who my father had been, and they treated me like an ordinary woman. They were cocky, yes. But the Rogers Park territory they worked was among the toughest and busiest in the whole city. Joey had his own right to a little swagger. But that wouldn't have been Joey. He was always humble. Even when we were kids, he didn't seem to know how cute he was, nearly girlish in his good looks. He had been my first crush, something I never told him.

I left the ringer on in case he called back. At least we could talk.

Instantly, the phone rang. A special ringtone: "Big Girls Don't Cry." I would always answer the phone for my aunt.

"Sweetheart," Aunt Marie said. "Are you alone? Can I come over?"

"I'm having an orgy," I said, stifling a yawn.

"Oh, good, then I won't have to change."

Marie knocked. She always knocked. Doors locked primly on either side of the big kitchen. But when I let her in, she threw aside any pretense of respecting my space and climbed up onto my bed like a girl ready for gossip. Tomorrow, Marie would leave for London with a camera crew, to await the birth of King William's first child with the newly crowned Queen Katherine. The prince or princess would be the first baby in six generations born to a sitting English king. Instead of a deathwatch, she was going to a birthwatch.

"I never sleep before I go anywhere. Do you?" she said.

"I sleep beautifully. I never go anywhere," I said. All those blasts and sparks. Not me. I hadn't had candles on my birthday cake until I asked for them, when I turned twenty-one.

"Do you want to go to England with me? I can still make it happen."

"I'm not a TV news chick, Auntie. I work for a living. I've put up with a whole university of long-winded lawyers and doctors this week."

"Will you be okay?"

To tease my aunt, I made my eyes wide in a pantomime of fear.

"Sicily. Really! Come on!"

"I am. Really. Just. Tired," I said. The anniversary swung softly, like a dark cloth, between us. "I had the weirdest phone call." I told my aunt about Eliza Cappadora. Marie remembered interviewing Beth, Eliza's mother-in-law, after Ben's kidnapping—the mother's strange presence of mind, despite the fact that she was literally dirty, her clothing smeared and wrinkled, her hair in oily strings, her manner robotic.

"She didn't want to plead with the kidnapper," Marie said. "In fact, she said whoever did this was a heartless bastard and that anyone who saw her son should grab him, even if it meant killing the person he was with," Marie said.

"She was tough."

"She was not. Beth was so fragile she was almost transparent. I asked her, 'When did you eat?'" (This is Italian for "How are you?") "And Beth said, '. . . Eat?' Not like sarcasm; as though she really didn't know what I meant. I felt horrible."

"Something supersedes the nose for news."

"Yes," Marie said. "Many things do." She gave me the look that made strong politicians want their mommies.

"Did you know them?"

"I knew Pat, her husband, a little, growing up. Your grandfather played Pedro in the backyard with Pat's father, who started the restaurant—Angelo. Pat and Beth were a few years older than me." Everyone was a few years older than my aunt. "Beth and her family were at your father's—"

"I know. Eliza told me."

"She was out on the sidewalk, taking pictures, for *The New York Times* or something. She's a photographer. She said she felt lousy, having to do it. Just like I felt interviewing her, back in the day."

My aunt turned and picked up the photo of my mother, in its brushed silver frame. We both studied it.

"How happy would Gia be? You getting married, your engagement party in a few weeks?"

"Happy," I said. "But I wouldn't be getting married except for you, Auntie."

"Lachele LaVoy wouldn't be too pleased to hear that. Her golden-haired boy had something to do with it, too." Lachele was Joey's mother. And she worshipped the ground her elder son walked on. When Joey brought up having kids—which he did, often, and sometimes around his mom—I got this weird feeling that Lachele thought they would look like me, like me now, not like I would have looked before the fire. At first it annoyed me. Then I found her discomfort a bit amusing.

I said to my aunt, "You shoved me out of the nest. That's what good mothers do."

"Well, thank you," my aunt said, turning away so I couldn't see her eyes filling, although I did. "That makes me feel . . . great. And also really disloyal to Gia."

My mother's hands smelled of the old-fashioned cologne called Joy, which Dad gave her every Christmas. Mom said it was "the costliest perfume on earth," although that hadn't been true since she was a child herself. Because I was a kid, and kids adapt or die, I adapted. My mother never toughened. The scent of Joy, faint on the few sweaters I kept bagged in plastic, was the scent of her suffering. Long before she died, she grew old young, sinking like a kite bobbing at sunset, rising a little less each time.

Who would I have been if my mother raised me?

Marie said, "She was five years older. But I used to have to beat up boys who stuck the end of her ponytail under the ketchup dispenser."

"So that's how you got good at beating people up," I said. "You're still trying to start fights. I watch your show when nothing else is on. All you do is provoke people."

"That's what they pay me for," Marie said. Though she co-anchored the CBN News five nights a week, Marie Caruso was best known for *Two at Ten*, a scrappy Sunday-morning talk show that paired people like the founder of the Teeny Queenie Beauty Pageant with a spokeswoman for Mothers Against Sexualizing Kids. My aunt said then, "Gia was happy. Most people don't get what they want in their lives, ever. She had a great deal of joy, for a short time. And a great deal of grief. But only for a short time too." In the picture, my mother was pulling away from someone outside the frame of the snapshot, someone she was dancing with. At weddings—I remembered this—people would pull back into a circle to watch my parents dance with the captivating ease of people who'd more or less grown up in each other's arms. In this picture, my mother's black dress, with its plunging back, looked both innocent and sensual. After all those years, it was as though Gia's hips were still in motion, and you could tell the effect that powerful sway would have on other people—probably because my mother would have been the last person in the football stadium to consider herself sexy. Marie said, "Christina and I, we gave up our dolls when we were ten or eleven. But Gia kept hers. All she wanted was to be a mommy."

And she had never believed she would be.

My parents were still in love after twelve years of marriage, probably more so because they had given up, believing that they would always be each other's only family. They were the melancholy, doting, perpetually young aunt and uncle to all the kids on their street, most of them South Side Irish, like my father and his parents and their parents.

Only by chance had my father's best friend on the force, Pete Nicastro, taken him to the West Side for the Feast of Our Lady of Mount Carmel and introduced him to a cute little Italian girl named Marie. Only by chance, one night when he picked Marie up for a date, had Jamie met Marie's older sister, named Giaconda after the lady in the painting with the secret smile. Marie was a good sport. Mom and Dad were married six months later. One spring, twelve years later, when Gia began to feel truly sick, they were frightened, not hopeful: It was impossible. And yet their prayers had somehow melted the merest edge of a celestial glacier and loosed a single crystalline drop. I got my name because they used money saved for a lavish, long trip to Italy for a down payment on a ranch house in the suburbs, a nice solid red brick. A rising star on the Chicago Fire Department, Dad jumped at a spot in Chester, for less money and far less adrenaline.

All for me.

All for a dozen years, give or take.

I said, "Auntie, I don't really remember them." I thought but didn't say, *It feels as though I was born to you.*

Marie said, "Do you remember the year you ran hurdles?"

"I loved it. My ballet teacher had a fit."

"I was visiting one time, and you won your race. All of a sudden Jamie said he thought you'd be a firefighter someday. He told me never to tell your mom. She would have had a fit too. So would I."

"It'd be ironic," I said. "Or something. You die doing what you dream of your kid doing. But Dad worked with guys who came back after getting some bad burns. Even facial burns."

"They had to overcome the fear."

"Joey is scared of fire. He loves it. But he's scared."

Marie replaced Gia's photo. My mother was laughing, her thick hair, shiny as a horse chestnut, coming out of its pins and plaits, her bare back sumptuous as a cello, a straight spine rising from a narrow waist above womanly hips.

A lot of joy. For a very short time.

"You know why Eliza called?" I finally said.

"I forgot to ask!"

"She works for some doctor who did the first face transplant. She called to ask if I wanted a face transplant."

My aunt looked down at her perfect nails. "What did you say?"

"Auntie! I said no. Of course!" There was a long, viscous thread of silence. "What did you think I said?"

"You never say what I think you're going to say," Marie told me, leaning over to kiss my eyes, as she had done for ten years. "I won't wake you. I'll say bye now."

"God save the king," I said. "And all."

I fell back gratefully on my bed and tried to concentrate on the hum of the humidifier, the way you focus on a faraway sound when you're restless. But sleep shimmered like a star out of reach. Kit would be awake but probably out with the latest in her interminable string of loser boyfriends—the one she'd invited (too early on) to visit her family at their house in Vermont. She would talk to me in the nuts way Kit always did when she wanted someone to believe that she was getting way too many phone calls. It was comical and almost worth it, although I didn't like Alex any more than I'd liked Cam or Spencer or Ryan or Craig.

Instead, I dialed Joey again.

"Ah! See how it is when you try to do without me?" he said. "You're a wreck."

"No. Just can't sleep."

"Let me come over at least, Sis," he said.

"No, I'd be bad company. I'm sleepy and crabby."

"It's nine-thirty!" Joe said. "How tired could you be?" I could hear the jeers over some televised sport in the background, as well as all the other unmistakable creaks and clinks of a bar.

"I worked a long day. For you, mister. To get a Sub-Zero refrigerator for the poor, brave civil servant I'm marrying. I had the weirdest conversation ever too. With this young surgeon who called me."

"What?" Joey said. "Somebody called you about work on a Friday night?"

"No. Guess what she wanted."

"Sicily, you know how bad I am at stuff like that. She's getting engaged and she wanted you to draw her naked." An acquaintance of my aunt's had once asked me to draw a bust of . . . well, her bust, when she was facing cancer surgery, so that she could remember her body whole. Knowing what I did about the grief of mutilation, I did the drawing.

"She wanted me to meet her boss about having a face transplant."

"Huh? You mean it? You'd consider that?"

"No, Joe. I wouldn't consider that." Why had he said this? Why had neither Joey nor my aunt dismissed this idea with appropriate scorn?

"Where would it come from?" Joey asked.

"A person who didn't need it anymore, I guess, Joe. A dead person. An organ donor. I didn't even think about that part."

"You've had cadaver skin before."

"An inch long. Not a whole face!" There was a strange sensation on the line, like the auditory equivalent of the way people glance up and to the left when they lie. "Joe? Would you want me to do this? You know, people have to take drugs forever after they have a face transplant. Drugs that can cause cancer. It's not like a face-lift." A cheer rose. Someone had obviously nailed a bull's-eye on the electronic dart-board.

"Baby, I would never want you to consider doing anything you didn't want to do."

"So you would want me to consider it. That's what you're saying."

"I never said anything like that, Sissy," Joe told me. "Quit reading between the lines."

"But you're thinking it."

Joey sighed. "I just want what you want."

"I don't want a face transplant."

"So don't have one. Would you look like you?" I knew enough about anatomy to say that I would probably look like me and like the donor too, but mostly like me. Joe said, "I remember when they first did them. They were pretty gross."

"They're not now. That doesn't mean I should have a twenty-hour surgery so your mother can have photos of a church wedding, which I'm not having either."

Joe sighed again.

I hung up on him. Later, I texted: *I'm sorry. I love you.*

I punched my pillow and slipped a satin mask over my eyes.

Then I got up.

Since the fire, I had come to love the darkness. If I didn't love it for facile reasons you could unearth in any first-year psychology text-book—for invisibility, oblivion, all-cats-in-the-dark-are-gray—I loved it because, during the years of rehabilitation, sundown was my signal that the battle had ended for that day. For twelve hours there would be no stretching and prodding, no steeling myself to bear the singular dis-comfort, south of agony and north of pain, of the extenders inserted under my skin so that the scarring on my throat wouldn't drag my chin down into a turtle tuck. Twelve hours of respite. In front of my full-length mirror, I pulled off my sleep mask and my nightshirt.

When I came inside earlier, I hadn't pulled the shades. The aggre-gate glow from the tops of buildings and all those Christmas lights and the ever-present press of cars made the room noon-bright. I tipped the pier glass to put my face in shadow and tried to see myself as another would. I did have one hell of a body, made to show off. I shook my hair forward across my face and throat and stood still for a long interval. This is how Sicily at twenty-five should have looked. Sicily at twenty-five might have had a younger brother or two, gracefully aging parents, her choice of boyfriends.

I was an outpost from myself.

But I had so much more than most.

A life.

A love.

Even some ordinary people didn't have so much.

Why would I risk that? A face transplant would remedy only one thing and come with its own universe of unforetold complications. It couldn't bring my family back. It couldn't even restore my stolen identity. I could look whole, but I would still be mauled inside. I reached up and touched my face. Suddenly I was ravenous for the dinner I'd ignored. I'd have eaten frozen pizza—still frozen. I thought, *To have a mouth. To taste . . . a delicate cream sauce. A strawberry.*

To taste a kiss.

You can remember smell but not taste. Try it.

I would end up forgetting the coffee date I made with Eliza, of course, after what was to have been my engagement party. It was two months after she called when I again picked up the tiny folded slip of paper with her cell-phone number.

That night, though, I closed the shades, slid into bed, and reached up to turn on my police-band scanner.

"Ninety-one, are you available? Proceed to one thirteen Dearborn Street: a two-story inhabited dwelling with fire visible on the roof . . ."

"Ladder Ninety-one en route."

"Medic Eight, Engine Three. You have a call on North Union, possible Charley response. The cross street is Evelyn. The number is twenty-four North Union; a male subject bleeding freely from a gunshot wound . . ."

"Ladder Eleven is on the scene at a two-story uninhabited ordinary, three twenty-two Maywood Avenue. Nothing happening. Can you in-vestigate?"

"Ladder Eleven, one of our good citizens driving by said they saw smoke at Maywood, cross street LeMoyne."

"God bless 'em. There doesn't seem to be a problem. We're return-ing to quarters."

I fell asleep under the patter of mayhem that still made me feel safe.

CHAPTER THREE

"I'm not wearing any mother-of-the-bride gear!" Marie called to Sicily, who didn't answer. Just before noon on the day of Sicily's engagement party, Sicily had decided to make huevos rancheros. This marked precisely the third time in Marie's memory that Sicily had cooked anything—making it quite possibly the third time in history altogether. She had left the door to the kitchen open to Marie's side of the apartment so that Marie could offer encouragement, although asking Marie about cooking was like asking a devout Mormon the merits of Lemon Hart 151 versus Bacardi. Cooking, for Marie—whose kitchen, with its double refrigerators and triple ovens, could have been the TV set for *The Great Cake-Off*—involved lightly reheating the pad Thai after spooning it out of the trapezoidal white carton. Marie heard Sicily counting off the ingredients as she took them out of the bag from

Melissa's, the little market across the street that boasted selling ingredients so fresh that they did not have a refrigerator.

"Four eggs," said Sicily. "One small onion, diced. Tomatoes, fire-roasted. Auntie? How do you fire-roast tomatoes? One at a time on a fork? Or all of them at once on the stove?"

Okay, so she wasn't Sicily's real mother, Marie thought.

It was at times like these that Marie—who was careful to tell friends about her brisk plans for turning Sicily's half of the apartment into a combination home gym and office, who smiled in wry complicity when someone blatted on about how she and her husband couldn't wait to "get their lives back" after the last kid finished college—wondered what the hell she would do with her own life once she got it back. Marie hadn't seen Sicily take her first steps, or fed her pureed peas, or strapped her in to a papoose contraption so the dentist could yank out two-year-old Sicily's abscessed tooth, or cried herself sick, as Gia had, when Sicily screamed for so long that she passed out. So maybe it wouldn't be such a big dislocation as Marie imagined. Maybe after the initial jolt would come a serene immersion in long-renounced liberty. Marie wouldn't have to listen thirdhand to Kit Mulroy's minute and mournful dissection of her latest in a serial string of bad romances. She wouldn't have to have men in masks clean the mold off the ceiling of Sicily's rooms from the damned humidifier that ran day and night. She wouldn't find her own cashmere sweaters, casually liberated from her closet by her niece and stretched out of shape by boobs two sizes larger than her own, draped over a dining room chair.

She wasn't Sicily's real mother.

She was nobody's real mother.

A skillful doctor had taken care of the threat of that—on two occasions two decades ago—and left Marie none the worse for wear. When she listened for an emotion from those incidents, there was only a loud absence, like the void left when a siren stops. Or so Marie thought until she inherited Sicily, her daughter-by-dint-of-despair.

And still, it was not only for the sake of her niece that Marie had shoved anything out of her own life that would interfere with Sicily's. It was for Marie herself, compensation for the loss of her sister, and for both men she had loved enough to marry, and for the doctor who explained, as he cheerfully vacuumed away the products of accidental conception, that he'd had to give his own poodle an abortion ("Not here, Miss Caruso! Don't worry!") because it was too small to give birth to seven puppies. Sicily's blooming was recompense for losses and regrets that could still ambush Marie, especially late at night, in some unlikely place—in a tent city built by protesters in Washington, D.C.; on the eighteenth floor of the Four Seasons in San Francisco.

If there was an Olympic team for pragmatics, Marie believed she would have been its captain. She was the sprightly surrogate, the cheerleader and role model. Good at it. "Prop" was the word that occurred to her. Something fake but convincing enough for a good impression, like the olde-tyme lamppost they pulled out of some back room for her last publicity photo, making her lean against it with her arms folded and her smile a welcoming beacon—so she'd look all trusty-wusty and charmy-smarmy, instead of the brassy West Side broad she actually was. So she'd look like somebody's maybe-a-little-hipper . . . well, mother.

"Did you hear me?" Marie called. "I'm not dressing up in some celery-colored linen suit with a boxy jacket."

There was no answer, but the fierce smell wafting in from the kitchen didn't bode well for brunch. Sicily usually used the sink for mixing paint or cleaning pens and brushes. What would Marie do when there was no one to yell at about toxic chemicals not belonging in the same sink we used to wash lettuce?

Sicily had rewired Marie's heart as no adventure, no honor, no catbird-seat job had ever done. Marie was not Diane Sawyer, and she had gotten out of New York before it became clear to everyone but her that she never would be. Within a certain realm, she was a household name, with even more influence than affluence. Chicago native Warren Elizabeth Adams, the third Adams and first woman to be elected president of the United States, had chosen Marie to conduct her first on-camera interview. ("Are you named for Warren G. Harding, Madam President?" Marie asked. "I think so," President Adams said drily. "My mother hoped to keep me humble, but she did not succeed in that.") Not even Marie's Pulitzer for "The Madonna of Juarez"—the story of a Mexican teen who walked across the bridge to surrender her baby into the arms of bookend California physicians, getting five thousand dollars to buy a house, where first she sold coffee and pastries, then coffee and beer, then beer and herself—not even that could touch the hem of Marie's devotion to Sicily.

Sicily was Marie's reason.

How big would this place feel without Sicily's music, thumping like a kind of combat artillery, her ossified bowls of oatmeal, the spoons mortared in them like pop-art sculpture, the tubes of tinted moisturizer she left in the pockets of her jeans that showed up in brown streaks on Marie's silk T-shirts after they went through the wash? Like Central Park on a sunny morning with no earnest runners huffing their way around the reservoir. Like a beach without gulls. Like a long, vast parade with no marching bands.

Marie had never really expected Sicily to leave. She had not expected someone who needed her to accomplish so thoroughly what Marie had with such single-minded diligence set out to help Sicily accomplish.

Sicily is mine, Marie thought. *Not Jamie's anymore. Not even dear Gia's.*

Mine to give to Joey.

Of course, Sicily was beyond lucky to have Joey—one of a kind, maybe one half of one percent of one of a kind. Somehow, astonished by the pink sapphire on Sicily's hand and the small country wedding planned for August at Uncle Al Caruso's big stone house near Lake Madrigal, Marie had never fully registered that the poignancy of Sicily's past would rear up and demand its due. The times that Marie's own mother had remarked how like Gia Sicily was, in her every movement, now numbered in the hundreds. Patricia Coyne, Jamie's mom, had offered Jamie's slim wedding band for Joey, as well as the gold locket given to Gia by Jamie as a first-anniversary gift, to be the traditional "something old" for the bride's regalia. Martin Coyne, Sicily's paternal grandfather, would walk her across the lawn to the arbor. Marie would be the something blue, sitting there with all the other relatives. Sicily's parents had the advantage of being saints. And so, from now on, the thing to do, Marie thought, was to present that news chick's face, still downright perky, even though she knew—she could actually *feel* some days—that her very posture was eloquent with a hurt she had never expected to experience.

There was one more emotion, perhaps the one that caught Marie by surprise with the least warning. And it was her mourning for Sicily's face. Wearing their grandmother's ancient satin with one hundred and ten buttons up the bodice, Gia had been a bride fairer than the calla lilies she carried. Sicily was taller and stronger through the shoulders, but in a strapless sheath, that cascade of hair twined and tendriled . . . oh, Sicily would have been a stunner, a bride to outshine—no.

No.

The secret to living Marie's life was keeping it squarely in the present, not letting herself be borne back along too many rivers with banks shrouded in the softening fog of time.

"I'm not wearing any mommy-of-the bride gear," Marie repeated, letting her voice rise up to shrill on purpose, nudging-and-not-nudging, making an elaborate business of jangling through the wood-and-aluminum hangers she favored.

Her closet was "finished," as was Sicily's, with a ridiculous expanse of drawers, shelves, and grottoes. Sicily always said that the number of pairs of shoes Marie owned gave her the raw urge to rush to the Red Cross and donate blood. One pair was silver; the other forty were black. And of those forty, probably fifteen were ballet flats that would have been indistinguishable to anyone but Marie, distinct only by their labels, identifying them as having been made by different Italians.

When Sicily didn't respond, Marie went on, "I don't have anything like that, Sicily! Not for tonight, not for August."

"I can't fry an egg," Sicily announced. "I'm hopeless at huevos." She had come into Marie's room and was sitting on the round African bride stool that Marie kept in her closet so that she could slip her stockings on without running them. "I can draw a good greenstick fracture though. And I'm hell on a skull fracture. How many skull fractures will I draw in my life, you think? They're a favorite subject for lawsuits."

"I wouldn't underestimate a good greenstick fracture," Marie said. "Or a skull fracture either."

"You don't have to play mother of the bride," Sicily said.

"Well, good," Marie answered, biting her lip. "Fine. I'm glad it's not a big deal." So there. So what? Sicily was only acknowledging what Marie had already admitted. "I look like shit in lavender."

"Auntie, what I really mean is that you don't have to playact. It doesn't matter what you wear, because everyone knows you're mother of the bride." Sicily, twenty pounds heavier and five inches taller than Marie, grasped her aunt's shoulders and gently brushed her mouth against Marie's eyes, in a parody of Marie's ritual good-night kiss. "You're not the only mother I've ever had, Marie. But you're the only mother I ever will have."

. A great hollow barrel rolled through Marie's stomach, part sweet satisfaction, part desolate longing for Gia. Gia would have been the mother God created for ceremonies such as these. How she would have delighted in tiny flourishes—little place cards made by hand, each with a tiny ribbon dangling a fairy slipper and a teeny black tuxedo shoe, a cloud-shaped poster decorated with the collected evolution of Joey and Sicily, from gap-toothed moppets in Sister Colette Amici's second grade to the single prom photo Sicily had allowed Lachele LaVoy to take—a picture of Sicily facing away from the camera, her strong, resplendent back bare nearly to the hips, as she fastened a white rose to Joey's lapel.

Jamie and Gia had been remarkable parents, who had taken their job seriously and done it well.

When Marie was visiting, staying at her sister's house in Chester, the routine of Sicily's preschool days never varied: Gia kept a big roll of butcher paper disguised by a circle of garage-sale glass and a big old shawl, as an end table. Before Sicily sat down to a (cooked) breakfast, Gia laid out a full kitchen table's length of the butcher paper, taping it securely at both ends. As Marie sipped her coffee, Gia would sketch a castle with a tiny princess for Sicily to paint. On those visits, Jamie would come out into the midst of that domestic grandeur and kiss Gia in a way that made Marie's stomach contract. She had, if she was honest, wanted to be Jamie's wife—yes, a thousand years ago, but yes—not his pal, the "best gal" at their wedding. She had wanted to be Sicily's mother, not her godmother.

And yet she'd done her best. The charcoal-on-gray invitations for the engagement party tonight read only ME AND JOE, FOREVER AND EVER. But inside, under the date, time, and location, was a subtle (Marie thought it was subtle) hint that this event also was, de facto, a wedding shower. Not even Kit could convince Sicily to put up with an afternoon of silly guessing games (*Why does the groom throw the bride's garter? Why tie tin cans to the bumper of the new couple's getaway car?*) and to make a keepsake bouquet by pulling the ribbons from each gift through a hole in a paper plate. So Marie had penned in graceful Catholic-school penmanship, *Your presents will be your gift.*

Sicily pretended to be mortified. But no one on earth loved surprises more than Sicily did. And Marie had one tucked away right now in her enormous purse—a week at a lush tumbledown resort on Big Pine Key.

So maybe she was a parent after all. A hasp in Marie's spine slipped open and she relaxed. To Sicily, who had disappeared and returned, Marie said, "I guess you puking all over my three-hundred-dollar suede coat the first time you got drunk earns me my spurs."

"I only did what you told me. We had the never-get-in-a-car-with-someone-who's-been-drinking talk—"

"Cripes, Sicily. It wasn't even a week before!"

"I was being cautious," Sicily said. "I was thinking ahead."

"You weren't even sixteen."

"You literally kicked me in the rear when I was holding on to the toilet, remember? You told me to run away and live with distant relatives. And me, a disabled girl . . ."

"I didn't kick your butt until you told me—and I quote—to 'not make such a big effing deal about it.'" Marie didn't ever use hard-core vulgarity, a trait that was just about perpendicular to the rest of her personality.

"Well, this is all goddamned interesting, but tonight I'm wearing jeans," Sicily said. "And double cashmere. It's goddamned cold out there." Soon Marie had picked out her own variation of the same outfit; black Highbeam jeans and a ruffled Lenore Hannigan blazer. And then there was nothing left to do but wait for six hours or so until the car Marie had hired would come for them.

"I could work," Sicily said.

"You could sit," said Marie.

"I could try to wash the tomatoes out of that pan."

"Let it soak."

And so they sat. Marie made mimosas. "Do you remember making fake mimosas for me, with ginger ale and orange juice?" Sicily asked.

"I make them for myself still, all the time," Marie said. "Two real ones and I'm ready to dance on the table to old Blondie songs."

"I'd pay big for that," Sicily said. Before either noticed, they were both three mimosas in. "Auntie, will you get married after I move out?"

"I think I'm a little . . . uh, over the meridian for that, Sissy."

"People do it all the time at your age!"

"I didn't say I was never going to do it again. I expect to do it at least once more before I stop forever."

"Not that. You know what I mean. What about that guy you were with? I want to call him Moss or Gray . . ."

"Brown," said Marie. "Brown Stuart."

At some point, it became clear that Marie's life would be the chance to grab a carry-on bag, a long dress, some underwear, and a cab—headed for places girls who grew up in a two-flat at 79th and Kedzie Avenue rarely got to go, to the trials and the nuptials and the funerals of the famous and the infamous. She traveled light, literally and personally, with no strings. That wasn't to say she lacked for love. Brown Stuart, her counterpart at her first job, her lover for years, would have married Marie a thousand times. Bookish, boyish, a kid from South Boston, suddenly rich and visible, he had switched his first and last names to mimic the prep-school cred that Anderson Cooper owned the day he was born. When Marie was pushing forty-five—still young enough, technology being what it was, to have perhaps one child—she'd finally decided to take Brown up on offer one thousand and one. But Marie's decision to say yes to Brown's proposal coincided nearly exactly with her sister's death. Five or six years ago now, Brown wrote to say he'd married Melanie Towers, a D.C. bureau reporter not a day over thirty-five. In short order, Brown and Melanie had a little boy. Marie sent a baby gift, the most impractical engraved rattle she could find, in that bird's-egg-blue box that, even empty, firmly announced its status.

Tipsy now, Marie noted a perilous loosening of her tongue. "It wasn't Brown I really wanted," she said.

"Who, then?"

"It was your dad."

"Come on!" Sicily was clearly as puzzled as she was beguiled. "You had, like, what, five dates? Four? Who falls in love in a month? It's impossible, except maybe for Kit."

"It's not impossible," Marie said, a bit blearily, standing up as the doorbell buzzed. "I was crazy about him."

"Really?"

"No fooling," said Marie, and then spoke into the intercom. "Who is it, Angel?"

"Mister LaVoy, to see Sicily."

"He works until three," Sicily said as Marie pressed the button. "It's one o'clock. That's too weird."

"He got out early," Marie said. "Angel knows Joey. He isn't going to send up the Boston Strangler dressed as a Chicago fireman."

"That's what the Strangler counted on," Sicily said, and they both turned their eyes to the knock at Sicily's entrance—and it *was* weird, Marie thought, too soft, as if made by a handful of wet rags rather than a handful of knuckles.

"That's freaky," Sicily said.

Marie, only five feet one, stood on her toes to peer out of the security portal. It wasn't Joey, but she recognized the kid. Motioning to Sicily, Marie moved aside. It was Joey's younger brother, whom Marie had met maybe twice. His head bowed, Paulie stood holding a newsboy's cap in his gloved hands, his unzipped parka having slipped from his shoulders to the floor. Sicily stepped back, confused, pulling her shirt away from her stomach in a gesture Marie recognized as nerves. Sicily's throat and chest didn't sweat very much—too much skin had been removed for there to be a real pore structure—but when she was frightened, as she was now, sweat burst from her scalp and her stomach: Within seconds, a wet mark appeared on Sicily's silk undershirt.

"Joey's hurt," Sicily said. Marie thought exactly the same thing. Some lazy slate-eyed deity had heard Sicily disavow her angel mother for the sake of her crazy aunt and, with nothing better to do, decided to prove that Sicily was indeed her mother's child, replete with her mother's destiny. "It has to be Joey. I know it. Don't answer the door."

"Nonsense," Marie tutted, and pulled the door open.

Paul shuffled back across the hall to the elevator doors, his pallor greased with something else, perspiration like a shining scum despite the cold. He was crying. Voltage sped along Marie's arms.

"Do you know already?" Paulie asked.

"Know what?" Marie said.

"Where is Joey?" said Sicily.

Paul drooped, bending forward, like a man on skis. Crossing the hall in one step, Marie reached out and pulled him toward her. "Look at me," she said, holding his shirtfront in one small fist. "Do we know about what?"

"Neal is in jail," Paul said.

"Neal is in jail? Why?" Marie said. "Is Joey okay?"

"For DUI."

"Well, that's not good," Marie began, loosening her hand as the electrical impulses retreated, muscle upon muscle surrendering. "Joey's fine, though. Right?"

"And he told them!" Paulie went on. "Neal always drinks like a crazy man from that day to New Year's Eve, then he quits. So why was he drunk last night? I called Joe and I was, like, it's two weeks since New Year's! He's been picked up before, and why does he tell them now? And Joe's like, because of me getting married. It's the guilt. I guess he just felt sorry for Joe. And you too."

"Sorry for Sicily?" Marie asked. A realization was pounding at the back of her skull, where a headache set its pike.

Angel Flores, the doorman, appeared behind Paul at the open door, huge and somber in his burgundy livery. "I think I may have made a mistake, Miss Caruso. Can I help?"

Marie noticed now that, although there was a clear resemblance, Paulie wasn't handsome, as Joey was, but plain, as though made from scraps left over after his brother. Half the length of a thumbnail added on to Joey LaVoy's delicate nose made Paulie's face ferrety. The cleft in Paulie's chin was a gash that made him look deficient, where Joey's was distinguished, a hint of a parenthesis, the only offbeat note in a patrician face. It was as though the genetic code had been scrambled, like a handful of Scrabble tiles.

"Mr. LaVoy said there had been a family tragedy," Angel said. "I should have been specific. I didn't think that would be wise on the intercom."

"We're okay," Marie said. "It's okay to go, Angel."

"Frank is downstairs now. I'll just wait," Angel said softly.

Paul began to wipe his face, leaving a snail trail of snot across the suede cap in his hand. "Neal is friends with those police in Parkside. Half those guys he went to school with. Denny Schuman and Ryan Pray. Even that girl we all thought was a dyke, Clarice Dooley? Even some of the old guys his father played softball with."

"I don't get it," Sicily said. "Make sense. What's Neal got to do with Clarice Dooley?"

Marie did know Neal. You rarely saw Joey without the big thick guy who seemed to have no more brains than he absolutely needed, who sported a perpetually goofy smile and a cheesy sprayed tan. Neal worked with his dad, finding underbooked charters for small business groups. He was successful, but you knew he'd never do a thing on his own. Once again, Marie's forearms began to prickle. *Something is coming,* she thought. Paulie was not making sense.

He told them. He told them. He told them what?

"I said not to do it," Paul pleaded.

"You told Neal not to get drunk," said Marie.

"No! Oh, God, God and Christ. I said, *Neal, don't do that.* I was just a kid too and I didn't know from anything, but I couldn't talk him out of it, and, to tell you the truth, I didn't think there would be nothing but a little smoke. Neal was twelve. I was eleven years old. Joe was thirteen. Neal was like, we can get Christmas break extended to a month. Smoke damage. That's what he said. Smoke damage. It was this little candle like my mother would light for her miscarriages. One candle. He snuck it off the shelf in back, where they sold them for a buck to put up in that stand by the altar." The voltage came in waves now, up over Marie's shoulders to her neck. She hauled Sicily back into the apartment and plumped down with her onto the couch. Sicily's whole body was shivering. "Last night Neal was just driving too *slow,* not too fast. This has happened before. They let him sleep it off, the cops. But this morning he wakes up and goes, *I started the fire—*" Paul snapped his fingers. "It was like his brain just shut down. Boom! He confesses! Now!" Paul's eyes widened. *Go figure,* he seemed to be saying.

Marie was holding Sicily's wrist, stroking her hand, when Sicily sprang up like a dog at the end of a chain, nearly jerking Marie's arm out of the socket. Sicily leapt at Paulie, raking her nails along his cheeks until beads of blood burst from the marks. "No!" Marie cried. Angel had to help force Sicily back into her apartment, with Marie on the other side, holding Sicily as she had when Sicily fought her restraints to scratch at her wounds after a surgery, with a traumatic might. Angel boxed for exercise at Jim's Gym, where Marie also worked out, and his young face reddened with the effort. Marie would have bruises in the morning. Sicily's fingers were individual, powerful creatures, clamping and pinching, twisting away. At last, Sicily fought only in bursts and finally not at all. She went limp, then sat up and gagged, helplessly spitting into her hands—nothing more than a bit of rice and bread, but Angel looked away. Marie ran for paper toweling.

"Breathe out," Marie said. Sicily tried but kept gulping the air thirstily and hyperventilating. *Good grief,* Marie thought. *Let's not have a blackout too.* "Sicily, look right at me." Sicily did, her gray eyes nearly metallic. "Sicily, breathe out. Angel, there are lunch bags in that side of the pantry. Little brown bags . . ." As though he'd lived there with Sicily, Angel was back in two steps, shaking a brown bag out like a leaf. *How few people really listen,* Marie thought, trying to form the open end of the bag to accommodate Sicily's difficult mouth. Marie had high-strung friends, prone to designer drugs. She'd seen plenty of panic attacks and, on the night Jamie died, she'd had one herself, while waiting in the airport with Brown Stuart. The CO_2 never failed—that and the concentration. "Breathe. Fill it up like a balloon." When Sicily's breathing slowed to a shallow pant, Marie realized that she was gasping too. She motioned Paulie inside. They had no neighbors, but she would not conduct her private life in the hall.

As soon as the door was closed, Sicily, now hoarse, said, "You . . . you told Neal not to set the chapel on fire?"

"Yeah, I did," Paulie said.

They were interrupted by gentle knocking at the closed door: Mr. Sansone, the retired police officer who lived on three, with the other doorman, Frank Abuela. Marie hadn't even heard Angel call them. They stood with their hands empty and overlarge, shrugging and looking at each other as though it was their job to stand behind Angel and lift their shoulders up and down, backup singers in a silent performance. And yet their presence, as witness—the very bulk of men the age Jamie would have been—was of some passing comfort. But Sicily's eyes roved back and forth along a strip of wall over Marie's head. What was Sicily seeing?

When her niece tried to stand, Marie braced for more combat.

"It's a serious situation," Angel said to Frank and Mr. Sansone.

"Auntie, I won't hurt him," Sicily said. "Paulie. Listen. You are saying that Neal set that fire. That's what you're saying."

Paulie nodded. The tiny wounds high on his cheekbones had stopped bleeding and begun to swell and gel, as if the welts were stuck with dots of jam.

"Did you see him do it?" Sicily's voice now was cold as a coin, every syllable's timbre the same.

"I only saw when he came back out. The priest's door was open—like, not open, unlocked. But none of the kids in the fire came out that way."

Slowly, Sicily turned away, speaking to the broad expanse of window. "Joey always said the door was locked. He told my mother that the door was locked. But it wasn't. So Joey knew. Joey always knew. The altar was on fire. None of us would ever have gone toward a fire. Or through the priest's door. It would be like going backstage with God." She stopped. "Neal opened that door. That was why the fire went up so fast. That air from the door."

Paulie said, "Neal went back and closed it."

"If he closed it the first time, everybody could have lived," Sicily said. "At least, there was a chance."

Marie put her arms around Sicily. "Was it just you?" Marie asked. "Who was there?"

"Just me," said Paul. "Just me. Joey came later, after the bell."

"No it was not just you," Sicily said dully. "You're lying. Joey was there. Joey was the first person I saw after I fell down in the snow. He said . . . he said that was the first time he knew he loved me."

Marie rubbed Sicily's back. She was hearing nonsense. Neal Polachek had committed murder? Neal had killed twenty-two kids and two adults and brutally damaged six more kids for life, and the boy who put his body inside Sicily's body, his heart into Sicily's hand, he knew? He accepted and lived with this?

"He said that was *what made him love me*! You talked this over, didn't you? Neal told you ahead of time. You tell me right now."

"Only that day. It was a prank, Sicily. He didn't plan like . . . some school shooter. Neal is a good guy."

"Neal is a . . . good guy," Sicily repeated.

"A good guy?" Marie said. "You scummy little idiot! Look at my niece. Look at her! Neal and you and Joey knew those kids. Dominic Kelly can't walk without an oxygen tank. He's like eighty but he's only twenty-four. Sicily's father *died*. He died, at forty-four years old. All these families' lives—and you didn't tell."

"What good would that do, lady?" Paulie asked. "Joey wanted to make it right. He's getting married to her to make it right. He's the kind of guy who could do that. He's giving up the life he would have had to make her happy. We were only kids. Neal just couldn't stand to see Joey go through with this. . . . He's his best friend."

"Go through with it," Sicily said. It was as though they all had their parts but hadn't memorized them yet. "Go through with it. So it was mercy. Joe never wanted me."

"Get out of here," Marie said to Paul. "Go away." Angel nodded and began to herd Paul toward the door.

Sicily said, "Neal was old enough that he could do time. Maybe even now Joey and Neal could go to jail. They were thirteen. Letting someone kill someone else. Not prevent . . . standing still for a crime. That's a felony murder. You could do time too. Why does it matter so much that Neal was a kid? Shannon Finnucan was a kid. She's in Queen of Heaven now. Tess Reagan was a kid. Victoria Viola was my friend. Keely DiCastro was only ten. So were Emma Bakken and Simone Sinico and Gabriel O'Connor. Byron Lynch lived next door to you. My dad was holding Danny Furtosa when they burned! I was a kid. Why did you come here?"

"I didn't want you to hear it," Paul said. "On the news."

"It wouldn't be on the news," Marie said. "Not by name. We would have thought it could be anybody. There'll be an inquest."

"But there was going to be that party tonight. Neal couldn't let—"

"Shut up," said Marie.

The buzzer sounded. Angel looked questioningly at Marie, who leaned over and turned on a lamp. The room, which had grown murky and dim as cloud cover piled up outside, snapped back into focus. There was a sudden urgency.

Sicily said, "Did Joey send you? Did he want you to tell me?"

"No," Paul said. "Of course he didn't."

When Marie interviewed people, she studied their faces: The very vigor of Paulie's shocked expression was proof he was lying, and she knew that Sicily, who was acute this way as well, saw it too.

Angel spoke into his phone, then said, "Jerry Krause came in to help, Miss Caruso. And—" Angel jerked his head in Paulie's direction. Sicily's beloved had arrived.

"Do you want to see Joey?" Marie asked.

"I'm going to my room," Sicily told Marie. "He knows where it is."

Sicily removed her pink sapphire ring, dropped it on the carpet, and walked away.

Marie used the paper towel she still held to blot her forehead. Frank and Mr. Sansone mumbled a few consoling words.

"Helluva thing," said Mr. Sansone. "You call me."

Both of them left. What was the inspirational message? The Oprah moment from the dozen leftover gray cards, now destined for recycling, that read, ME AND JOE, FOREVER AND EVER?

Frank returned with Joey LaVoy, who acknowledged his brother with a blink. Paul and Angel waited as Marie followed Joey into Sicily's bedroom.

Joey fell to his knees and wept, beseeching her, "Please, Sicily, please listen. Maybe once it was feeling responsible. Maybe the first time we went out. But I love you, Sicily. I love you now. Please, God, believe me. Don't pay any attention to Paulie. Can't you think about it?

Try believing that? I love you, honey." Sicily lay facing the bookshelves, so motionless she might indeed have gone to sleep. Then Sicily turned, quick as a snake coiled in her comforter, crawled across the big bed, and thrust her face at Joey. Joey fell back, sprawling. "That's all for you," Sicily said. "Hell is all over you. Just follow Neal."

Marie drank a tall glass of water and a taller glass of Shiraz. Sitting on Sicily's couch, she kept vigil, turning the pages of Sicily's sketchbook. A drawing of Joey, decorously nude, his thigh drawn up, his face somber. Marie, burdened by flowers, copied from a photo Sicily had taken with her telephone the previous Easter, on the eighty-fifth birthday of Marie's mother, Annette Caruso. An elbow, a curved hand, a child's skate. Marie flipped on another of the standing lamps. This must be how meditation felt. She had passed one hundred minutes of time without thinking outside a space two by three feet.

It was dark, maybe eight o'clock, when Marie crept into Sicily's room.

"I'm awake," Sicily said immediately. "I didn't take an overdose."

Marie lay down beside Sicily, who allowed her aunt to curl close to her.

"I was thinking about those science-fiction movies where they put humans in museum cases so they can wake them two hundred years later?"

Marie nodded, inhaling the playful sweetness of her niece's Elizabeth Morrison cologne at the edges of a sharp, sour tang of sweat. Sicily never smelled dirty. Marie wanted to kill Joey LaVoy with her hands.

"You know, I would forgive Joey if I could. I would find a way to rationalize it. I would think maybe it was just pit—feeling sorry for me at first but later it wasn't faked. I believe him that he does love me, in his own way. If we got married and had a child, then it would be real. As real as anyone's marriage."

"Baby," said Marie. Although Sicily's form was indistinct, Marie reached up, found a strand of Sicily's hair, still damp with sweat, and twined it around her finger.

"I would if I could. But I can't. I just can't. Do you remember Mrs. Viola? From over on Easterly Boulevard?"

"I was in New York then," Marie said softly. "I haven't lived in Chicago since I'm twenty-five, honey. Well, back then, anyway."

"I forgot," Sicily said dreamily. "She would come to the door all the time, for a whole year, after the fire."

Abruptly, Marie did remember. Gia's face was as stiff and clenched as Marie had ever seen it when Mrs. Viola scratched at the screen one summer weekend. . . . Why had Marie been there? . . . Sicily's gradua-tion, her eighth-grade graduation. Sicily attended, although she told Marie she was glad that her face was bandaged after a recent recon-structive procedure. In empty chairs at the front, there were little white mortarboards, each accompanied by a spray of laurel, for the three eighth-graders who had died in the fire. One was for Victoria Viola, part of the group who hung with Sicily and Kit, not a best friend but definitely a second-tier sleepover girl. Marie remembered it well now: Gia quick-stepping to the door before Sicily could open it. Marie heard Gail Viola saying, *Oh, I—I'm so sorry to bother you, but you know, I can't sleep at all, even with the pills . . . I said to myself, Gail, you have to try once more. Sicily! You two was friends. Did you see my Victoria? Did she suffer? I know that Victoria is with our Lord, so all I want to know is, did she suffer? That's all . . .*

"She does this all the time," Gia had told Marie. "She comes once a week. I don't know who to call, Marie. The police? The school? If I'm down with the laundry or something, she'll come right in. And it upsets Sicily more than seeing Dennis Coyne, even though he could be Jamie's twin. She came in February when there was a blizzard. She stands in the rain. Oh, my God, I feel so sorry for her. What can I say?"

Mrs. Viola's face was not like skin but like soap, Marie recalled, as though white chips would break off. Marie told her sister, "You have to make her stop, Gigi."

But it was a year, another visit, before Marie finally heard Gia say, almost harshly, "Gail, I know how you feel, better than anybody, I know. But Sicily is hurt. She has had fifteen surgeries, Gail. You can't do this to her."

But all I want to know . . .

"What about Mrs. Viola?" Marie asked Sicily now. "Why did you bring up Mrs. Viola?"

"She got . . . okay. She sort of gave her life to taking care of the terminally ill. She still works at Sundial. The . . . you know . . ."

"Hospice, yes."

"Vicky's little sister was a year younger, and she still lives with her parents." Sicily paused. "Vicky's sister's life stopped. Right then. And Mrs. Christiansen, little Kieran's mom, she used to write to me too. She stuck letters in our mailbox that said the same thing as Mrs. Viola. I only saw one letter. Mom threw them out. Mrs. Christiansen drove off the road by Sherry Creek. Everyone thought she ran away with some guy. She was pretty, like Mom. They didn't find her car until the creek thawed. No seat—no restraint." Sicily sighed, her breathing rough. "If I could remove the section of my head that knows all that stuff, then I could forgive Joe, because, Auntie, it's not in him to do wrong. If I could remove the section that knows he was going to marry me out of remorse, I would. Because I didn't want to marry a special guy. I was too proud. I was a fool. I had a guy who looked like everyone else. But the joke was, why did I have him? He didn't love me. Not like I loved him. I still do. Why didn't I get the joke?"

Oh, Sicily! Marie thought. *It would have been better if Joey had set the fire—easier to dismantle this castle you built with your adoration.* Who else would want Sicily?

"Who else will ever want me?" Sicily said.

"Plenty of people," Marie said. She consciously made her arm relax, refusing its natural inclination to tense.

"Special people," Sicily answered. "And it's not how they look on the outside that makes me afraid. It's how they'd be on the inside. You made me into an ordinary person on the inside whose face is destroyed. I could love someone whose face is destroyed, or who has Tourette's or MS or anything else, if he was like me, raised like me."

"Huh," Marie said.

"To be able to be like what Michelangelo said about the statue in the stone."

"What is that?"

"Michelangelo said he could see clearly the statue he would make, in every block of marble and that all he had to do was to chip away the rough walls that kept it prisoner and there it would be—perfect. I fight to let people see through the rough walls to the real parts of me. But I don't think everyone else does that."

What could Marie say? She had read the books too. Case histories. Most people who prevailed and made real lives did find love. But it often was with "special" people, men with dangling little funnels for legs or who were big, blond, and blind. *God forgive me*, Marie thought. Her philosophy professor at UIC was an astute, witty, estimable man, with an adorable wife and two sons, despite his glazed eyes and his zippy wheelchair, courtesy of Vietnam. Why would a mate like Professor Kenny be anything but terrific? Who cared about looks? Who cared? Joey LaVoy, button-cute as an underwear model—sexy and full muscled, good smelling and strong—turned out to be a minor monster, the thing imprisoned inside him not beauty but a deadly secret.

Why hadn't she encouraged Sicily to befriend people whose experiences were like hers? Who else would not judge her? Why had Marie fought so hard for Sicily to be *like everyone else* and taken pride in it? A vicious thing, the boomerang of good intentions. Marie had done it wrong. She had raised Sicily to want not as good as—but better than. Now Sicily, who would always be damaged, couldn't teach herself to want anything that felt lesser. "Sicily, you'll start over. This was a hard lesson."

"You think?"

"Okay, more than that. This is a tragedy, and, yes, you've had a life filled with more of them than any ten people deserve. But if it's love you want, maybe you have to look behind the rough walls."

"Okay. Say I do," Sicily said. "How do I know they will?" Marie thought back again to the disabled people she knew and the stories she'd read. With the exception of deaf people, the mated pair rarely was made from two of a kind. "What if the other person in the stone wants a beautiful wife who has . . . one arm? Not many people want a girl without a face, Auntie. That's a really rough wall." Marie thought of Professor Kenny's dazzling blond wife. He couldn't see her, but sure as hell everyone else could. Sicily sighed and then drew in breath, as though it were a fluid that could nourish her. "It's a shame. I could be frozen, like in those movies. And come back later. Maybe there would have been an age of enlightenment and everyone would be kind. Maybe everyone who's damaged could be repaired. But I would still know about the fire. I would still know that, for Joe, it was an obligation. They couldn't cryogen my heart."

Both of them lay in silence, but not at rest, until the edges of the windows brightened. Another brand-new goddamned day.

CHAPTER FOUR

I barely got out of bed for five days.

My aunt begged me to take a walk outside, do some stretches, take a bath. She ran hot water into the giant triangular tub and poured oil of lavender into it. She told me that it would make me feel better. But I didn't want to feel better. I wanted to feel sick unto death, and it helped to smell and have greasy hair. Marie brought me broth and scrambled eggs I couldn't swallow. The salt and tang of beef broth nauseated me: It had the aroma of flesh. Eggs disturbed me—they've always disturbed me—because they're one cell. Everything, from sounds and textures to lights and sight, seemed malign, out of place, distorted, as though there had been a nail scraped across the surface of the natural world.

Juice and water. I had to drink, because I breathed primarily through my mouth, and it would dry up too quickly otherwise.

I wanted to die, but not from thirst.

In the first days after the fire, when I was newly undergoing the startling process of debridement, which is the slicing and scraping and picking away of dead tissue to hasten the growth of new tissue, I amused myself—if you can call it that—by planning my own funeral. Listen, everyone does this, even people whose faces aren't being literally skinned on a daily basis. Everyone who feels blue has the irresistible urge to think about how bereft people would be if you were gone, what those who came to mourn would say about you, and even what you'd wear. (For me, that wasn't an issue. Nobody would be opening *that* casket.) Before the fire, I'd known only one kid who died, and she died by suicide, the older sister of a girl my age. Shelby kissed her parents good night, and *brushed her teeth* and took a whole bottle of her mom's Valium; apparently she had intended to hang herself from a clothing hook on the back of her bedroom door but lost consciousness before she could. No one ever knew why. Shelby did not have a history of depression. She had a boyfriend, and they were happy together. She had a ton of friends and a full ride to Carleton College the following fall. Her funeral was the most heartbreaking occasion of my life to that point. Her parents had made poster boards of all her baby pictures and school photos and awards, and I thought, how bad could it have been if it looked not just good but *superlative* from the outside? Even if your father was a closet molester, even if he hit you, why not run away and change your name instead?

In college, a biology professor told the class that he had attempted suicide after his fiancée dumped him for the equivalent of a billionaire sultan. He also tried to hang himself (I don't know what the fascination is with hanging, except that it's like running, in that you don't need any special tools). My professor knotted a few of his neckties to make a noose and threw it over the shower rod. He probably weighed only about a hundred and sixty, but as soon as he stepped off the side of the tub, he realized that his toes touched the floor and he was going to suffocate instead of breaking his neck. Then the shower rod broke. So he went to the closest big box store, like a Savemore. On the way he picked out songs (I remember that one of them was the Beach Boys' "God Only Knows," which he thought would be guilt-producing). While standing in line with a heavy-duty shower rod, who did he see but his ex-girlfriend with her sweetheart, the Arabian prince. They were cuddling and didn't notice him, but my prof wanted to go up and show them the shower rod and say, *Look at all the trouble I'm going to so that I don't have to live without you!* At that moment, this store employee came up and gave my professor a sample of pizza on a little napkin. It was really good. He decided to have a slice of pizza before he killed himself and ended up buying a whole pizza.

"There is a moral of this story," he said. "It's that there's always pizza. And sometimes pizza is good enough for that day."

Losing your girlfriend to a handsome billionaire—especially if you happened to be a skinny amoeba nerd—is not comparable to losing your father and your face. And for teenage me, there wasn't even going to be the joy of pizza. I couldn't script the tributes, but I hoped there would be a goodly amount of them. I did choose Bible verses, like the one about the pillar of fire that gave us light by night. I chose my favorite hymns ("Were You There?" and "Jacob's Ladder"), and then I ran out of ideas for that portion of my afterlife.

After the first time I saw my face in a mirror, when my lips were peeling away like a rind, I figured patience was the ticket. No one who looked this bad got better. There would be some kind of overwhelming infection that would take me out. The fire had left a perfect map of its journey on my face. The burns on my neck and chest were (I would learn) relatively minor. They were caused by exposure to intense heat where my body wasn't covered by my clothing. I had left my coat open. But I'd worn leather mittens, and because I'd held the purse to my face with both hands, my ears were whole. There was a band of undamaged flesh about an inch wide, just beneath my hairline, V-shaped, between my eyebrows. The rest of my face looked like an undercooked rack of ribs, with some of the packaging still stuck to it. Those bits of plastic were vinyl scraps of my purse, fused to my face, that the medical team hadn't yet been able to tease out. I was sure I would not survive. But every day, my body persisted in restoring itself: I was strong and young and in rude good health. And though I tried to loose my grip on it, life would not release me.

At first, friends came in packs. There were so many daily pilgrimages to the hospital and then to my house that I was exhausted simply by the sheer magnitude of their voices. By early February, only three or four people showed up, maybe twice a week. So few, so soon? I had been a popular kid, with nine or ten birthday-party invitations under my belt every year. Had they simply forgotten me? Not until I was grown did I begin to understand that a crisis without margins is intolerable to the human temperament. People expect you to get better, and I wasn't going to. People expect you to have a fighting spirit, and I didn't. There's an initial contact high that comes from being part of something big and lasting and dramatic, from actually knowing someone whose name is synonymous with an event that will never be forgotten. But time passed. The stories on TV about the fire dropped down to short updates that followed the weather forecast.

The biggest tragedy about tragedy is this truth: It's tedious. People can't stand to feel obliged for a long time. If you ever have a lingering illness, try not to linger too long. You'll wear out your welcome. That's not bitterness talking. It's experience.

A few people hung in there and tried not to wince when they saw the newest surgical insult added to injury. Kit, however, never left, never blinked, never looked away but once. It was when I told Kit I hoped to die and waited for her to start crying and talk me out of it. Instead, she got up and left my room. I got up too and followed her out into the hall. She was putting on her parka and knit hat. "What are you doing?" I said.

"I'm leaving."

"We were talking. You're practically the only person who ever comes to see me anymore."

"Sicily, you're my best friend. But if you want me to sit here and listen to you talk about your funeral, you can . . . you can . . . blow it out your nose," Kit said. "I feel really sorry for you, but not as sorry as you do."

"Kit! If I don't have a right to feel sorry for myself, who does?"

"You do. But your dad wanted you to live, and you're all your mom has left. And why did I waste all this time on you? I'd still want to live anyhow. I know I would."

"Try it," I told her.

"I would want to live anyhow."

"You would not."

"I would."

"You would not."

"I would. I would find other things. I would try to have a way to be grateful."

"You would not. You're so dumb, Kit."

"I would."

"I'm not really going to kill myself."

"I don't care if you do," Kit said. "Why not, anyhow?"

"It would hurt, that's why. I couldn't face one more thing that hurt."

Kit took off her coat and crossed the room to hug me.

"You don't really hate yourself, Sissy. You hate everybody else. People who commit suicide hate themselves, but they hate other people too. If you were like that, you'd sit inside all day and watch talk shows and eat taco chips and weigh three hundred pounds and wear Hawaiian shirts with sweatpants."

We laughed.

Kit came to see me the day after I found out about Neal and Joey; Marie had canceled the party. Kit brought magazines and newspapers. She talked about the news of the world, which was not Kit's style—despite the things about her that I cherished, she could obsess all day about a zit or different brands of mineral-based foundation. Today, Kit didn't even mention the name of her latest beloved, the one I already called Evan-Until-Easter. He was handsome in a hotel-bar kind of way, employed in some job that depended heavily on commissions, played the guitar and wrote his own songs, was almost-but-not-quite divorced or still lived with his parents. She had envied Joey and me.

I didn't ask how she felt now.

After a few minutes spent on judicial misconduct and typhoons, she said, "Sissy, get up," with all the spirit of the Iowa Hawkeye cheerleader she had been. "They say it takes twenty-one days to get over a guy. I read it. Get a calendar. This is day one."

"This is day zero."

"Sicily, you've come too far now to let this be the thing that destroys you. Do you really want to give Joe LaVoy that much . . . power over you? Especially now that you know he was faking it?"

"He wasn't faking it."

"Okay. Why isn't he here now, then? Why did he give up so easy? Was it really loyalty to his retard best friend?"

Why wasn't Joe here?

Why had he given up after a five-minute sob session?

He had called. He'd left dozens of messages last night and today. But he hadn't come back to face me. Even the right to refuse was denied me: I would not have the satisfaction of spurning torrents of apology. Was this some backhand liberation for Joey? If Joey didn't really love me—if he hadn't grown to love me with time—what else about my life was a lie? I wanted to smack Kit. How big a calendar did you need for convincing yourself to give up on the guy you loved, your friend for life, who stood by and let his best friend kill your father— and still liked his friend? Ten times that day, I'd thought of calling Joey, constructing sentences with blanks he could fill in to win me back. *I didn't know until after you and I* _____. *I had to hang out with Neal because he* _____. *I thought I was gay but now I've changed and that's why I* _____. I would have accepted anything.

"Maybe you weren't meant to be with him anyhow, Sicily," Kit said. "There has to be something better for you than a guy like that."

"Are you kidding? For me? That's so entirely possible. I have my pick of guys."

"Why aren't you crying, Sicily? Why aren't you crying over the love of your life?"

"I don't cry," I said. "I just don't. Some things are too miserable to cry over."

I tried to remember the last time I had cried.

Everyone except Mom and me and the rest of the family, as well as Dad's brother-and-sister firefighters, was gone. Father Behan was going to say a prayer of some kind. But first, Bill Hoyer, whose father owned the funeral home, set huge pillar candles at either end of the blue steel coffin that sat on a raised flag-draped bier. Over the foot was a blanket of white roses and a banner that read, in gilt, *Daddy.* Behind the casket were three massive wreaths of red and white roses in the shape of the Maltese cross, the symbol of firefighters. Bill Hoyer gave each of the adults a taper to light from the big pillar candles, and as the flames began to flicker I could feel my heart seizing up. My younger cousins—Uncle Denny's two boys and Matthew, Uncle John's son— stood with their hands clasped identically behind their backs, snatching glances at me now that they finally had the excuse to really look. Dad's parents stepped up first and held their tapers out to the big pillar candles, and then I was as surprised as anyone else by the gurgling, screeching sound that seemed to come from everywhere at once, and it took a long time, maybe a second—which can be a long time—to realize they were coming from me. For the first time, I witnessed the looks of numb disgust that would become so familiar to me over the years.

"It's those goddamned candles," Aunt Marie finally said. "They must be three feet tall. She's terrified."

And I was. I was so galvanized by panic, I tried to get up and run. I saw my father ambushed again by fire, as he had been ambushed before, and I knew that the fire would take the rest of what it hadn't gotten the first time. I ran and cried until I was literally sick in the washroom, just before Renee and Schmitty hustled me into the car that Grandpa Ernest had driven to the front of the funeral home so I would not have to struggle through the cold.

Afterward, I would never lose control to that degree again. Hysteria has its own majesty. You can no more control it than you can change the direction of the wind through force of will. Anger, at least, was something you did, not something that was done to you. I could turn the volume up or down as I wished. It could not seize and pummel me.

So, although I regularly got angry, it had been twelve years since I had cried. I pointed this out to Kit and asked her, "What do you think about that?"

"That you haven't or that you aren't crying now?"

"Now." I never asked for advice. It felt ridiculous. "Do you think I sensed, like . . . something missing?" I didn't add what I really wondered: Was something missing in the relationship or missing in me?

"I don't know. Maybe."

"But we were happy. As happy as anybody. We never had a fight. Not one fight. That's bull—that's crap," I said. "The thing is, I'm just thinking this because I don't have any basis for comparison. There was Joey my playmate and then Joey my friend and then Joey my boyfriend."

Swinging my legs over the side of the bed, I sat up. Even that small rearrangement of balance dizzied me.

I could not remember a time when I didn't know Joey.

The LaVoys lived on the corner, at the end of the block, in a big yellow bungalow that reminded me of a circus tent. My parents went bowling—who went *bowling*?—with Mr. and Mrs. LaVoy. Joey and Paulie and I and Jimmy Panico and Mary Ellen Dowd played baseball together, in the way every kid on the West Side did—one long game that began after lunch on a summer day and paused when we couldn't see the ball anymore, ending only when we went back to school. We kept score; the scores were in the thousands by the time the summer was over. Four of us smoked cigarettes behind the hedge at Bernard Lobby's house. Paulie LaVoy threw up. Joey beat me by one vote for vice president of the seventh grade. The summer after the fire, someone told me that Joe bloodied Jimmy Panico's nose for calling me "Mummy Girl." We'd been friends all through school. When I was a sophomore, he helped me pass algebra (despite forty absences). In senior year, he climbed into my personal pantheon by asking me to the prom. At the advanced age of eighteen, it was my first date, and also my first kiss—a weird, awkward kiss I carried for three years in my pocket, through all the unanswered yearnings of a new woman, until Joey came back from the service and we met again in college.

Joey.

Strong and cute. Opener of doors, and not just car doors. Holder of coats: not only a gesture of manly courtesy but to shelter me. I wanted Joey back, no matter what, now, ferociously. I could not get up. I could not consider the massive heft of the effort of starting over. I wanted the children we would have and the vacations we would take and the wine club we would join with friends from our neighborhood. If I had never known, I could have been happy. To accept him now would be to betray my dad. Or would it? Everyone has secrets. Not the mortal kind, but everyone has done something no one, not even a husband or wife, can ever know about. Joey was not only beautiful and caring—and good. He was proof. Proof that I had overcome. I didn't question Joey any more than I questioned the noon and six o'clock whistles in Chester—even though hardly anyone broke for lunch at noon anymore and hardly anyone got off work at six. I didn't believe, but there was no life I could imagine without the dry tot of the communion wafer on my tongue. Not everything had to fit or make sense. Joe didn't want much from me, and . . . did I have much to give? If he was marrying me because he owed me a life, was I was marrying him because he was my only chance to have one? And was that wrong?

"I'm going to take a bath," I said. Wobbling, I made my way to the tub. Kit sat on the closed toilet seat as I climbed into the steaming water. She got up and poured shampoo into her hand and rubbed it on my scalp.

"Don't," I said. Hurt and stunned, Kit stepped back.

"I didn't mean it that way. I'm sorry, sweetie. I mean, someone's always doing something for me. I don't even know how to drive."

"Maybe there's a message for you in all this," said Kit. "Maybe this happened for a reason."

When something horrific befalls you, people say that everything happens for a reason. I used to hate it when people said this. It wasn't really to comfort you. It was stupid, cowardly, whistling in the dark. The fear of a fate without pattern. Now I longed to believe it. I understood the motive behind the desire to give structure to something that refused to fill a mold. I was working to grasp a thought, and it was like trying to use chopsticks to raise a grain of rice at the bottom of a pool of water. I thought of my aunt—not Marie but Christina.

There had been a family picnic one summer at my uncle Al's. Kit came up with Marie and me for the weekend. How old were we? Nineteen? Twenty? I'd asked Marie why only one Caruso girl ever got married, knowing full well that Aunt Christina would pipe up and point out that, as a Franciscan nun, she was indeed married—to Jesus.

"I wonder what Jesus is like in bed," Kit said. Grandma Caruso gasped, and Aunt Marie made throat-cutting motions. But Christina hadn't even heard us, since she rarely paid attention to any topic she hadn't raised.

"Definitely aloof," I said. "I'd say a sensitive hottie who makes the woman do all the work." Kit and I cackled.

That night we drove back to Chicago, about a two-hour trip. Marie, ordinarily chatty, funny, and irreverent, said not one word. I tried to spark a conversation, but there might as well have been tape over her mouth. When I finally literally pressed her, poking her in the side, she said curtly that Kit and I behaved like twelve-year-olds and that she was sick of it.

"You want me to act like Sister Mary Augustine? Auntie, why does she come around her family if all she wants to do is commune with Jesus? Why is she a nun anyhow?"

"I don't know, really," Marie said. "She told me that she had a growing understanding that it was only in prayer that she felt free. She said it took her ten years to learn how to pray." Marie shook her head. "Sicily, everybody gives you a break because . . . you know. Not that you deserve it. And, Kit, what about you? Saying that was unkind. You hold nothing sacred."

Kit insisted, "But we do, Marie!"

As she began to list those things—high-heeled Italian boots, sexy guy ballet dancers, Edith Piaf and Wilco, Time Machine and old Springsteen, three-alarm pad Thai and Norman Love chocolates and the Reubens from Myzog's Deli, the Green Mill jazz club and Tufano's restaurant—I felt a green nausea form at the base of my throat. I wanted to say, *No, Kit, don't push this,* I tried to signal her to stop, but Kit wouldn't be stopped. She kept on: We both thought it was a miracle that the light inside the diner in Edward Hopper's *Nighthawks* at the Art Institute surprised you even the twentieth time you saw it. She talked about first snow at her parents' old house in Vermont. She even brought up *sacred* sacred things, like Easter morning at Holy Name Cathedral. "Am I right, Sissy?" Kit concluded. "How can you say we consider nothing sacred?"

"Okay, I see," Marie said. "Things that please you. You just don't care about people's feelings."

That had knocked the wind out of me. How could Marie say that? Everyone on earth except my grandparents—who thought that having a nun daughter was only slightly lower on the ladder of status than having a priest son—agreed that Aunt Christina was a colossal drag, so drearily devout that she complained about having to wear street clothes with her cheesy veil instead of the full floor-length habit that nuns wore in her girlhood, as though she'd been robbed of a job perk like a company car. She was forever telling me to "offer up" my pain, and I was forever telling her that I'd offer it wholesale to anyone who wanted it.

"I care," I said.

"Do you?" Aunt Marie asked. "Then why do you go out of your way to be snotty? Maybe Christina is silly. But there's no meanness in her."

For the first time in my life, there in the tub, sponging water over the pale half cups of my breasts, I thought, *Was* there meanness in me? What else had the fire consumed?

"You can survive this. You survived high school," Kit said. "You survived college and that crap at our reunion. You can survive this."

"Mmmmm," I said. "I don't feel like it. I have to want to. I'm not like me. There's nothing I can say to make this . . . a satire, Kit."

For it had never been anything but difficult—a brisk uphill climb on good days, an assault on a vertical cliff on bad days. I knew that people thought I "got used to" it. But I grieved in reverse. If I had been seven years old, I might have grown up a sprightly little saint. Instead, I had been a newborn woman, who got upset if my hair frizzed up when it rained, who rolled up the waist of my plaid uniform skirt the minute I got off the bus to better reveal my dancer's legs. And then, one night, all those sweet worries were gone. Most people who spoke to me at all spoke to me the way you speak to a pet. Kids from the grammar school who didn't know me proved they were brave by running up to me and touching my book bag. I made myself stand outside the door of the girls' bathroom until I was sure everyone else had gone to class, because I couldn't stand to open the door and hear all the laughter and chatter stutter and then stop, like a music box unwound. And I couldn't have gotten a date by giving blow jobs in a pitch-dark car. In college, the students were so self-consciously hip it was comical. I couldn't count the number of times one of them, startled when I turned around or lowered the hood on my coat, had pretended to sneeze or cough.

What was the one thing I could count on?

My anger.

Why do they make clothing for fat people patterned in gaudy fruit and ruffles and stripes? It's distracting. What did I have to distract people from my face? My sharp tongue. Below the neck, I experienced everything else that other girls my age experienced, but I never got to test-drive my blossoming body. I could have been bulimic or agoraphobic or aerophobic and it wouldn't have mattered, because everyone around me thought the kindest thing to do was to pretend I wasn't there. I became invisible, and I became angrier. If people were going to refuse to see me, they wouldn't be able to refuse to hear me. When Ella Carmichael got her first period in history class, while wearing white pants on dress-down Friday, I was the one who handed her a sweater to tie around her waist so that she could walk out of the room without dying of shame. But I also was the one who called her "Menstru-Ella," and nobody dared to tell me it was a crummy thing to say. Loss hath its privileges. It felt good—in a nasty, guilty way—to be able to say things no one else could. After a time, the guilt went away. Time tempered the nastiness. But I could still draw remarks like a pistol from a hip holster. It got attention that wasn't pity. It propelled me into . . . being part, even if I couldn't partake. Why did I despise my aunt Christina so very much? She meant it kindly, but she wanted me to hide behind the equivalent of a muumuu with palm trees and ukuleles all over it. She kept hoping I'd be a nun, part of a contemplative order that was cloistered. Could she have been *more* obvious? People who pray and wear undershirts made of Brillo inside their clothes are not pious. They're nuts. No matter how many times Christina told me that many a religious found a vocation in disfigurement, I told her that was horse petoot. What disfigured people find in religious life is a place to hide—with the bonus of hiding among people who get extra points for putting up with stuff that gives other people the creeps. There aren't that many beautiful, fresh-faced young maidens who become nuns anymore—unless they're from places like Somalia or Indonesia, where nunning is a great alternative to starving. My opinion was that the rest were running from something. And yet Sister Mary Augustine actually was one of those stern-at-the-time-but-later-valued teachers whom grown students came back to visit when they graduated college.

Who would visit me? Who would be inspired by me? I wasn't one of those admirable disfigured people who walked across America, speaking at churches and preschools on the way, or who created an interactive video game teaching children that sensitivity is for every day, not just awareness days. I wasn't an advocate for anything. I didn't run 5Ks to help find a cure for anything. Maybe I truly was one of those people who was exceptionally considerate—of herself. Maybe I'd so fully embraced being looked after that I'd confused doing minor good at my job with being good in my life.

"Do you think I'm a good person, Kit?"

"I think you're a wonderful person," Kit said.

"I don't mean, like, interesting. I mean good."

"Of course. Why?"

"I don't know. I never . . . had to try to . . . Just, something like this happens to you, and if you don't evaluate your life, you'd have to be really shallow. You have to think about what the hell your life is. I draw bile ducts. I make animated pictures of mitosis and meiosis."

"Don't go too far, Sicily. What Neal and Joey did doesn't have anything to do with you. If you sprain your ankle on the same day you lose your wallet, it doesn't mean you're being punished. Take it easy on yourself. Take one step at a time."

But I had already leapt off the step. There were things I had to know and do if I didn't want to sit in the equivalent of this soaking tub for the rest of my life. People had those idiot refrigerator magnets because they helped you get up and do stuff. Kit was right. It was day one.

I ripped the sheets off my bed and put them into the washer. My sheets stank of flop sweat. I had to hurry. If I did not, I would never be even as good as, much less better than.

Renee Mayerling recognized my voice.

Of course, my voice was pretty distinctive.

"I'm sorry, Sicily," she said. "I'm so sorry."

Neal's inquest was over. That was supposed to have ended something that refused, at least for me, to feel finished.

"Thanks," I said.

"Are you doing okay?"

"Not really."

"Give it time."

"I guess I have no choice, as far as that goes. But, Renee? You could do me a big favor, if you would? I have to ask you some things."

"You bet. Do you want to get together?" she said. I wasn't sure that I did. Only a month had passed since the night of my "engagement party," and that month had passed so slowly that it was evident proof of the theory of relativity. I still vacillated: I loved him. I loved him not. I would take him back. I would spit on him if I ever saw him again. I was still a young woman who was, at some point, going to have to place an ad that read: ARIA MCBRIDE WEDDING DRESS: NEVER WORN. *Push, Sicily. Jump.* We made a date for the following week, to have coffee at the place across from UIC where I once planned to meet Eliza Cappadora. Eliza. I had business later at UIC. But for now my business was with Renee. She had the afternoon free, having come off her shift early that morning.

Renee was the kind of woman who would always look a little like a teenager. Deceptively petite, she could haul heavy hoses up three flights of stairs without panting. Back when I was a teenager, she could chin herself a dozen times, and now, when I asked her, she admitted that she still could. Renee had to be about five-two and weigh about one hundred and ten pounds. Maybe not even. Her curly hair, cut short, looked the way kids' hair does when they tumble out of bed. When I stood up, I felt enormous at five feet six. "I didn't remember you being so much taller than me," she said. "I don't come up to your chin!" We didn't talk about one thing and another. Renee sat down with her black coffee and said, "What do you want to know, Sicily?"

"I want to hear about the fire. The way you saw it."

"Are you sure?"

"I'm sure," I said.

Renee had never described that scene to me. We'd barely spoken of the fire even when she tutored me, even when she drove me to clinic appointments. I think she worried for me. Even good people have a way of hoping you've forgotten the things that redirected your life. You don't remember them, not in the way you did at first. The film stutters and goes blank in places. It stops completely—a still photograph in which the clothing looks dated.

"I remember every moment," she said. "It was the thing in my life. I remember it the way I remember my daughters being born. Maybe even more."

On the three-minute ride to Holy Angels, no one spoke. The silence inside the cab was so charged it seemed to buzz. My father, whom Renee and the others called "Cap," was in the front seat with the driver; Renee and Moory Tillett sat facing Tom McAvoy and Schmitty, who sat sitting backward—all of them trying to relax by breathing out but rigid with knowing that dozens of kids were at the destination and that the engine that would lay the pipe and deliver the water was still minutes away. Renee quietly finished dressing, pulling on her Nomex hood and fastening the clasps on her turnout coat. Cap said nothing. He didn't push the red button on the truck that played the *Superman* theme. He seemed only to thoughtfully regard the blurred glittering of lighted Christmas decorations. Against her better judgment, Renee started to have personal thoughts: This was her first true rescue fire. Working in Chester meant a great many medicals, including the frequent fliers who made lukewarm suicide attempts every Saturday night, or grossly overweight people who fell off the sofa and had to be hoisted back on with the big black rubber sling they all called "the whale tarp." There were some property-damage fires: Renee said Cap made the veterans dummy certificates for the grace under pressure they showed at the Great Dumpster Fire of 2006. "I started thinking about the last time I saw you, pouting because you were nearly twelve and didn't think you needed a babysitter anymore. You'd just gotten your hair cut in that horrible shag thing that looked like old pictures of Joan Jett . . ."

"And you let me drink some of your beer," I said, remembering.

"I would never have done that, Sicily," she said. But she had.

Trying not to get caught up in looking at the building, because it was my father's job to assess it, Renee jumped down carefully from the truck—always carefully, because she would be no good if she rolled an ankle. She followed Jamie at a brisk walk toward the single open door (you never ran; only in movies did they run). They passed a few chil-

dren who were already crying and choking, sitting or lying down on the
snow, some bloodied, a few barefoot—children they ignored, because
the circle driveway in front of the chapel would momentarily be filled
with paramedic vans that would see to them, and because from the
chapel they could hear that screaming, thin and animalistic, familiar to
Renee only from training videos. In person, it curdled her lunch to a
cold bolus at the base of her throat.

"Your dad said into the radio, 'Ladder Nineteen is on scene at the
corner of Winchester and York Boulevard, a single-story stone church
with visible fire and smoke showing.' And the dispatcher acknowledged, and she sounded bored, the way they always do. Jamie said,
'Ladder Nineteen will begin search-and-rescue operations. The first
due engine should begin fire attack. We have people trapped inside.
Children.'" For children, my father always said (although he was never
vulgar), it was balls to the wall. You did things you wouldn't do otherwise. Renee said that my father sent McAvoy and Tillett to do a 360
and told Renee, "Rook, come on." They put on their oxygen tanks.
That gave them twelve minutes. They were the last words she would
hear my father say.

"Then the boys . . ." Renee said.

"Joey. And his brother."

"Yeah. I knew the LaVoys, of course. Just like you. They ran up to
me and said they tried to crawl in through the priest's entrance at the
back but couldn't make it," Renee said. This is one way I've since
learned to tell that people have committed a crime or done something
wrong: They answer questions before you ask them.

"I didn't know the bigger kid. Neal. He ran away down the street,
yelling to everyone who was out on their stoops," Renee said.

Renee had testified at the inquest, and she knew that I knew that
there was a finding of no fault. Whoever sets a fire is responsible for
whatever it burns, by law, even if there is no intent. But Neal was not
quite thirteen years old—and he was truly repentant. The news reports

said only that there had been an inquiry and that a man who had been, at the time, a juvenile had admitted setting the fire. A brief resurgence of magazine stories and retrospectives, local and national, resulted, with speculation about who and how and with what. I'd received a few calls and answered not one.

"Did you think it was a set fire, Renee? Back then?"

"No. Neither did the fire inspector. There was no puddle pattern, no trail that would have been present if there had been gasoline or any accelerant used. As for the candles, Sicily, there were enough candles in that chapel at that time of year to light séances or Halloween pumpkins for the next ten years. And the little votive jars where candles are lit by people making a novena or whatever? They were all over the place. Kids ran into the stand and some of the candles were burned and others weren't," Renee said, and stopped to drink her coffee. She looked up at me, her lips compressed. "It's worse for me knowing it was an arson fire and it didn't have to happen. So it's a hundred times worse for you." She went on to tell me more about the moments before the engine arrived. "We were supposed to make sure that each of the kids was laid down at a distance one and a half times the height of the building, but we didn't. Cap went straight in. I kept dragging kids out. When I finally got inside, I saw the pileup of kids behind that big door." Time for Renee had slowed down from words to whole pages contained in the passage of a second. In the circle of her light, she saw more kids, stuck behind the locked side of the door that she could not kick open. Some of the kids were already PBN. Renee could tell that two of the boys would never top five feet five or grow a beard or kiss a girl, and she thought that two of the girls who would never run down the stairs to tear open their first high-heeled boots or their last Collector Barbies. It was not the first time she'd seen a dead person, but it was the first time she'd seen a dead person she could have saved. She heard a medic's victory cry when a few puffs got one of them breathing. She began to pray silently, then to pray aloud. She had not yet seen me. And then she did. "And for that I was so grateful," she said.

"Tell me the rest."

"Well, Sicily, after the event—after the flashover—they lifted you onto a rolling backboard and I thought, *At least Sicily is in no pain.*" I know that a full-thickness burn was too bad for pain, the nerve endings razed. Someone else made the radio call: *Captain Coyne is down. Firefighter down . . .* Renee talked over it, telling me to look right at her, that it would all be okay.

"But I knew you had seen everything and heard everything. You don't remember it, though, do you?"

Renee was the best, a neighborhood girl, one of my father's special protégées. So I lied.

"Not really," I said.

Ten days passed before my father's visitation. It takes time to arrange the funeral of a ranking firefighter, his last bells, his honor guard, his pipers. My being able to be there with my family was an important concern too, and I could not be released from the burn unit at Loyola, where I was first taken, until there was a solid, reasonable chance I would not contract an infection.

"They always say that at a firefighter's funeral, the only room is standing room, and the only standing room is outside and around the corner. And that was the way it was for Jamie. I was in the honor guard, and I had to jog almost a mile from where I parked my car," Renee said. "I probably haven't met the bravest person I'll ever meet yet. But I think of bravery as being calm in the worst possible situation. And that's how Cap was."

"Do you think that was the death he would have chosen?"

"Sicily, I don't know anybody who wanted to live more than Jamie did."

"I mean, if he knew he had to die," I said.

"That's hard, Sicily. I never thought of it that way. But I guess, if I had to just say one thing, it would be yes. That is the death every firefighter would choose if he wasn't going to get to be old and die in his sleep. He knew you were alive. So, yes, I think he would almost have considered his life in exchange for your life."

With a new decal on her own helmet—*Captain James Coyne, First*

In, Last Out—Renee had the honor of carrying my father's helmet at the head of the honor guard. She was followed by Moory and Schmitty and Tom as well as one of my father's brothers and two of his cousins, who were also firefighters, carrying his casket through a double row of officers from all around the city—and the world, as it turned out. Some firefighters had come all the way from Boston and New York and even from Chester, England, the walled city in Cheshire. They would finally lay his casket on the bed of Chicago Engine 88, Dad's first company, which had requested the privilege of carrying him to Holy Name Cathedral, under an arch of two ladder trucks with an American flag strung between them.

"My grandmother Coyne has that picture in a frame," I told Renee. "It bothers me to see it. But I know it's beautiful. And think it's comforting to her."

"It was on the front page of the *New York Times*," Renee said. "Lots of other papers too. Mrs. Cappadora took it. Vincent's mother. Vincent was a crazy guy when I was in high school, but now he's pretty successful, I guess. He makes . . ."

"Movies," I said.

"Yes. Well, sure. Your grandparents know that family. Of course you would know."

"I still have my dad's helmet," I told Renee.

The eye guards are just wavering shards of plastic, but I recognize it as the one he had when I was a kid. Every firefighter tricks out his helmet. Most of them put a big rubber band made from an inner tube around the circumference of the helmet on the outside, and Dad had all his little tools in there, but they looked as though he'd used a blowtorch on them. He had golf tees and nails stuck in there for picking locks, and his orange Garrity flashlight was secured and Velcro-ed to point forward. They all used a Garrity, because it was cheap and worked even if it melted. They still do. His decals had peeled back in the fire; there was a numeral one with an asterisk (because his was the number-one ass to kiss), and the Chester sticker they all loved: *Chester—A Place to Live and Work,* under which my father had scrawled in permanent marker, *If You Can't Afford Western Springs.* Inside, he had glued a picture of my mom and me sitting on the porch. After he died, someone stuck on a bronze star, the kind the military gives soldiers for meritorious service. "I've never changed the battery in Dad's Garrity flashlight. Sometimes I flick it on for a moment. All these years later, it still works."

"Sicily," Renee said, "I think I know what you're trying to get at. It was a horrible fire. But saving more than half of those kids was . . . It kind of verges on miraculous that he—"

"And you."

"That we could do that in so little time." Renee shrugged. "As for what he would have wanted, he would have wanted to go on fighting fires for ten more years and be part of the department for ten after that. He wasn't a guy to put in his twenty and then buy his own sports bar. I don't know what to tell you. We'll never know all the answers."

"It's okay. I'm glad we got to talk."

Renee kissed me on the top of the head before she left. Her number had come up in Chicago and she now was a captain herself, one of the youngest in the city. She also taught fire science at Merit University. She was married to another firefighter and they had two little girls.

"What are their names?" I asked.

"Mary Katherine, for my mother," she said. "And Elizabeth James, for my sister Elizabeth and, well, your dad."

"That's very sweet."

Renee ruffled my hair again and took off for her car. She had a class to teach in an hour, and it was kind of a haul out to the northwest suburbs.

I stayed. I unfolded the tiny slip of paper I had extracted, just that morning, from the corner of the frame that held my mother's photo. It wasn't the first time I'd picked it up. But it was the most important time.

"This is Eliza. Please leave a message. I'll get back to you right away," said her voice mail.

She did too. I was on my second cup of Mexican chocolate mocha with skim and extra foam when Eliza walked in the door.

CHAPTER FIVE

"Oh, Sicily," Eliza said. "I'm so sorry." This was evidently going to be a theme.

"Well, thank you. I'm sorry too. It's very sad and it turns your whole life upside down. But, Eliza, do you even know? I mean, the part about Joe and me?" Everyone who didn't live in a cave knew about the arson.

"People like to talk." They did indeed. One would not imagine that there are cards that say, essentially, *It Sucks That You Got Dumped Under Really Unsavory Circumstances,* but there are, and I'd received about ten of them. Two weeks before, there had come a letter from Lachele LaVoy, telling me that she was very sad about my loss (it was only *my* loss) but reminding me that Joseph had a life to live and there was no point in "spreading rumors." I wanted to go looking for Mrs. LaVoy with a pool cue, but Marie said to leave her alone, to imagine the shame she must feel. "Joseph" had moved to Phoenix, where he was living with relatives, currently selling cars, and considering entering the priesthood. I tore that letter into as many pieces as human fingers could, but getting it had also started me on a circuit of thought I had traveled night and day since then.

Joey and I were assuredly over.

A single door had closed on my past and my future, transforming both of them from what I'd understood them to be.

And now what? I could go on drawing illustrations for injuries and surgeries and animated presentations of colonoscopies, living with my aunt, my life quieting as hers quieted. Perhaps I would teach at UIC. Perhaps I would meet another man, perhaps a substantially older man who was part of the medical world I lived in. But he would never know me as Joe had. He would never be able even to picture the woman I might have been. There might never be a man. Who gets to lose not one but two lives in twenty-five years? Marie said I had "moxie," a word I loathed because it made me sound like a cartoon character. I did not have sufficient "moxie," however, to put yet another Sicily together. No matter how many different ways she construed her age, my aunt would soon be pushing sixty. She'd done her time. I could move away, to a place where no one had ever heard of the Holy Angels fire, and just start over as a garden-variety freak. I could move to North Carolina and (not) enjoy the sun. I could move to Alaska, where men truly were desperate, and (not) enjoy the cold.

Or I could stand where I was and, for the first time in my life, ask for extraordinary help. I could take a huge risk, in the hope of a huge gain. Other people, years ago, had risked more for less. I could take Eliza Cappadora up on her offer and change my orientation to the world and thus my location within it. After fanning out twice, I could give myself a third at bat.

Kit was shocked when I asked her to have dinner with me at The House, literally a mansion and Chicago's premiere slow-food restaurant—where a meal consisted of seven courses of tiny exquisite edibles that probably added up to about seven hundred total calories. Usually, because her salary was bigger and because her boyfriends most often treated when they went on dates, at least during the early months, Kit bought our dinners out. After we'd been served a single scallop with minced pine nuts and a wasabi mayonnaise on a plate so huge that it could have held a flounder, I told Kit, "I have to ask you a big thing."

"Okay."

"I never told you about it."

"Not okay."

"Things got out of control too fast with Joey, and it just didn't seem to matter—then." I ate my scallop the way people eat oyster shooters, which was the only way that I could. The server didn't sneer, but I saw her lip twitch. "I am thinking of having a face transplant."

"You are," Kit said. "Well, I don't want you to risk your life. And I don't want you to have another surgery." She paused. "And, also, you have to think of my needs. People admire me for having a disabled best friend. It makes them think I'm a serious person."

"That was one of the big factors. Working on the website for a makeup company doesn't give you huge cred as a serious person, Kitty."

"I'm glad you care." The second server appeared (apparently one of the reasons for the cost of this food was the legion of approximately one hundred working staff in tuxedos).

"I have to die someday, and I'm not going to start . . . smoking or mainlining. And every surgery is a risk, although, yes, this is more of one. I could end up looking worse than I do now."

Kit said, "Really?"

I nodded. *How . . . delicate of her,* I thought. *Sheesh.*

"But no one ever has; most of them come out well. They've gotten better every year."

"Then," Kit said, as we received a radish floret inlaid with some kind of sweet butter, on a bed—one leaf—of radicchio, which the server admitted was sort of a "food pun," Kit laid down her fork. "Sissy, I think you should do it."

I was not often dumbfounded. But I'd expected a vigorous argument, even a tantrum. "You're blasé!"

"Marie told me when she got back from London. She wasn't, like, telling me to push for it. But she wanted me to know if you ever brought it up. Just to have the information. She didn't know how to feel about it, except she kept saying that heart patients used to live ten years, now they live thirty."

"She didn't act outraged over the idea."

"It's a toss-up," Kit said. "We knew you when. No one who knew you before wouldn't want you to be like . . . that again. But no one would ever want you to risk your life to be like that again."

"What would you tell me to do if I were your sister?"

"I'm telling you what I'd tell my sister." The two of us finished our meal in as much of a thoughtful silence as Kit and I had ever spent together. Kit made one lame joke about spending a hundred and fifty bucks on a meal that wouldn't provide enough leftovers for lunch the next day. I just sat there, sort of drifting, as though I clung to a pendulum that swung equal distances over two substantial chasms. The pendulum was the only safe place. I could swing forever. If I didn't choose now, with the healing ballast of youth on my side, would I ever choose? If I could have asked my mother, she would have tried to forbid me. If I could have asked my father, he would have told me to measure the risks, the way you do when you assess a fire or an accident scene. Dad considered foolish risks the worst kind of disrespect for life. He considered life without risk undeserving of respect.

How many times had I begun to dial the digits of Eliza's cell-phone number before I did? How many times had I tried to pray, to look for signs like a tracker? How many stacks of medical literature had I read in three straight days at the UIC Medical School library? This would have to be the first decision I made entirely alone (with the consent of about three dozen doctors). So it must have seemed like an impulsive plea instead of a considered pleading I made that day to Eliza at Lotta Latte. It was, however, good practice at convincing people of things they were conditioned not to believe. That would be a skill I would need for things I never imagined sooner than even I would have believed.

I offered Eliza a latte, a tea, or a sandwich. She accepted ice water. She certainly knew what I was going to say. But she couldn't stop her eyes from saucering up (I would learn that her compendium of eye-language symbols rivaled my own) when I told her, "Eliza, I've changed my mind. I do want a face transplant."

Calmly, as though I'd suggested I might want contact lenses, Eliza said, "This is not an unexpected visit. This is a reaction to your grief. Slow down. The clinic is not going anywhere." I could have left then, to convince everyone that I could act normal, to pretend to think over what I'd already considered and reconsidered. Instead, I presented my first argument.

"There's no reason it shouldn't be a reaction to the grief. I considered it when you raised the subject, but I had no need for it. Now I feel I have to make changes in my life. It would make it physically easier too. I do have challenges. I can live with them, but it's very, very demanding."

Eliza said, "That's true for every candidate. And still, everything you said—about your reservations, about the risks and the immunosuppressant drugs—was true. Those things still matter. You need to give this time, maybe months, to think it over."

"You didn't say that last Christmas. You didn't want me to think about it for a year. Am I put on a waiting list? How does that work? Is it patient by patient? Is there a pool of donors? Is there one for me?"

Eliza glanced around her as though she feared being overheard. "Yes," she said. "There may be. . . . Uh, the guardian has to make a choice for the recipient."

"Then I would be that recipient."

"I can't guarantee that, Sicily! I can't guarantee anything! I'm not in charge of any of this."

I was determined. I was scared—who would not have been scared?—but didn't want the traditional wagonload of ifs and buts that always attend a major life transition, especially one that carries a significant risk.

"You've thought about children," Eliza continued. "You would most likely have to adopt your children or store your eggs in advance, although there is a time element. The effects of the drugs on a pregnancy aren't really known. . . ."

"That's fine," I said. For me, having children had never felt urgent, not as it had for Eliza, who'd become a mother at the age of twenty-two. I'd had other things on my mind at that age. "But I was adopted and so were you, even though it wasn't when we were babies."

"Being adopted makes you long for the genetic connection, maybe even more so if you were not a baby when you were adopted and you remember your mother." Why the hell hadn't Eliza become a psychiatrist? I suggested we cross the street together and that she at least give me a packet of forms to fill out and an informational sheet, just as she had wanted to do last December. Then I would take the time that seemed necessary to consider the decision. There would have to be several psychological evaluations in any case. If I was trying to hide behind a new face for pathological reasons, surely somebody would be able to tell. As we walked, I continued my reasoned arguments, in a low, not-hysterical voice. Finding out about the way that Joey betrayed me, even though he had not meant to do that, made me consider my own life more, in terms of what I could do.

I said, "I'm not sure, at my age, that I've done everything I want to do. Personally. Maybe even professionally."

"You like your job."

"I do, but I might want more."

"Your face as it is now doesn't bar you from other professions."

"I was thinking of fashion modeling," I said. "No, I'm serious. I would have a wider circle of friends. That's a support system, not only more dates. I would have a layer removed between me and the world." I realized what I'd just said. "You know what I mean."

Eliza nodded.

"The impulse is a strong one."

Eventually we got to the clinic, where I met Polly Guthrie, who was the coordinating psychologist on the face-transplant team. I wondered why there was a team and was surprised to learn that, at UIC, under Dr. Hollis Grigsby, there was the transplantation of a full or partial face nearly every week; hands and legs and feet from cadaver donors were transplanted more often that that. "It's not common," Polly Guthrie said. "It's not rare either, the way it was ten years ago." Having made an appointment with Polly for my first interview—and after basically swearing on a stack that I *really understood* there were no promises—I asked for the photographic record of the surgery so that I could study it in depth.

"There are individual before-and-after photos of two or three people," Eliza said. "We can show them to you, but you can't take them out of the clinic."

"I mean of the whole process."

"There are line drawings that show a sort of general set of images of the process, like what you do in your work," Eliza said. "Like that series in your binder."

"Yes, but I don't mean drawings that take out all the gore, which is what I do. I want to see the whole thing, with the mess, the musculature in color. I'm talking about the photos of the surgery."

"The surgeons take those only for their own use during the procedure," Eliza said. "They photograph every step so that they're absolutely certain to place and reattach—"

"There's no photographic record?"

"Patient privacy issues," Eliza said. "The face is a very intimate part of the body. Perhaps the most intimate."

"So is the vagina. But you have pictures of babies being delivered."

"It's not possible, Sicily."

But that made no sense. It was possible.

"What if a candidate waived the privacy provision to make a photographic record, as . . . well, as for science and art? So people understood more about the procedure? Isn't there still a sort of *Phantom of the Opera* thing about this?"

"There is," Eliza said. "But people are sensitive to issues about their faces. It's only recently that there have been documentary films of cosmetic procedures, Sicily."

"It shouldn't be a mystery," I said. "It shouldn't be a joke." Eliza nodded patiently when I told her that, during my own preliminary research, I found gimmicky photos of how it would look, for example, if the lower half of a movie star's face was swapped with that of a gorilla. "It's not funny. It's not science fiction. Right? I'm just surprised that no one has asked to have this process preserved." Eliza was watching me attentively, which made me hope I was being convincing despite the fact that I was utterly winging it. This thought had not entered my head until I stepped through the bright celery-colored double doors of the clinic. And yet it wasn't too big a reach. This was not a necessary surgery. I could survive without it. It was not a notion born of narcissism either. If I could invest it with more meaning—more service—I could further my quest for I-wasn't-sure-what. So I said, "If I have this procedure, I would like to have my surgery documented for a public forum."

"That's not possible," Eliza told me promptly. We sat there for another half hour while they tried to explain why I could not violate my own privacy. I raised the subject of the significance and poignancy of the exhibit called *Bodies* that had toured the United States some years before. The bodies were real human bodies. They were Chinese people, preserved—in states of strength and weakness, movement and stillness, sickness and health—with a polymer process. Even children who saw it were not, after the initial surprise, horrified. People were instead rapturous, intrigued, deeply moved to care for their own remarkable bodies in a way that no drawing could have inspired.

"Yes, and some were outraged," Eliza countered. There was considerable controversy about the provenance of those preserved people—questions raised about how they had died. Some of them were young men and women who had been in Chinese prisons or national hospitals. They very likely hadn't given their permission to have their cadavers flayed and displayed to illustrate muscle groups or lung function.

"But I am giving my permission," I said. "It's because I am a medical illustrator that I know that what some people would initially consider frightening can be not only educational but also really beautiful."

"You don't even know if you're going to have the surgery, Sicily. One decision at a time."

I was twenty-five years old, though, and newly un-wed, hungry for substance that seemed to have left my soul a hollow seed. Eliza might as well have told all this to a dog—a dog would have paid more attention. I'd already found out that proceeding on faith could rise up and strike you down. And yet it isn't possible, I understand now, to entirely grasp the scope of the arena you're walking into. Most blessings, it turns out, are mixed.

As we parted, Eliza agreed to speak with the team leader, Dr. Grigsby. Then I asked her whether, if both the surgery and the documentation turned out to be possible, she knew a photographer. This was a trick question. I could read the ambivalence on her face when she said she couldn't think of one offhand who had the training and the equipment and sensitivity.

"What about your mother-in-law?" I asked, using my eyes to hold hers.

"Right," said Eliza. "Well . . . yes, Beth is between jobs right now, but I don't see her doing this."

"I could call her."

"I can't stop you from contacting her. I'm sure she'd be intrigued by it. But she's in a weird kind of . . . mood right now."

Going home on the train at sunset, I wondered if I actually would go through with it, with any of it. I wondered why I had been so insistent. The answer was embodied in the question. My stubbornness was the worst thing and the best thing in my character. But it rankled that, had I been hoping for a kidney transplant, the same ethical issues would not have applied. By the time I got to my stop, I had construed the idea of making my face history a matter of honor, my own and that of the donor. I was young. I didn't know what I didn't know. And I still trust that impulse. I didn't want attention from the larger world for myself. I wanted attention from the larger world for this process—how it would change both the outside of a person and the smaller world of that person, the world within. I intended to break what I saw then as a cycle of self-centeredness. I'm older now, and I look at the price tag before I even try the coat on. Then I decide what is prudent—which is not necessarily better, but always is safer.

CHAPTER SIX

Beth Cappadora might never have met Sicily Coyne were it not for Beth's deeply superstitious belief that her family had been singled out by the cosmos for events that were statistically impossible. The Cappadoras had not been singled out uniquely. But they were a slender slice of a slender slice. If Beth took an angel's-eye view of the households whose predisposition (and she knew it was predisposition) for the unimaginable was comparable to the Cappadoras', if they were clustered before her on a tabletop like Monopoly houses, it would be a bonsai-ed universe that would fill only the palm of one of Beth's hands.

Everything that had happened to these families also was statistically impossible. And yet it had all happened.

More than thirty years ago, Beth's son Ben was kidnapped from a hotel lobby, standing not ten feet from his mother (statistically impossible). Nine years after that, Ben had statistically impossibly turned up, healthy and well adjusted (Beth wasn't certain that Ben was not actually *more* well adjusted than the rest of them), living less than a mile from his parents. He grew up to marry Beth's godchild, Elizabeth (called Eliza), the daughter of Beth's best friend, who also was the police detective who searched for Ben for all those years. When Ben and Eliza's daughter, now a robust first-grader, was just a baby, she had been similarly threatened, also in a hotel and also reclaimed unharmed.

Top that.

Beth could.

She kept a file, and though it was no thicker than one of Beth's slender fingers, it was brimming with similar statistically impossible cases that had happened since: In Utah, Leslie Dorr was forced to live for two years as one of five wives of her abductor, on a farm just outside the town where her parents owned the florist's shop. The truck driver was sick when Leslie's own father delivered a birthday bouquet to the farm. Leslie was outside, taking towels down from the clothesline. And there was the case of Brian Ambeling, stolen after Pee-Wee League baseball practice by his coach, who turned out to be Brian's biological father—something not even Brian's mother knew for sure. Three years later, the mother was waiting in line with her two younger daughters at Disney World when she spotted her son.

None of those things could have happened.

And yet they all had.

No one else in Beth's nuclear or extended family was concerned about this . . . this . . . genetic strain, which Beth considered obvious, like a birthmark, like the certain doom manifest on the face of the young Abraham Lincoln in early photographs. They all acted as though they were like any other family and considered Beth, if not neurotic, then high-strung. But they weren't like any other family. Beth had to pick up the slack for all of them, turning the events of her life over and over in her mind like a snow globe so that she never forgot.

Hence, she lost her job.

Beth was an accomplished photographer, and though she didn't need to work for income—her husband's restaurants were gustatory landmarks in Chicago—she worked for love. In middle age, she was nationally regarded for her black-and-white portraiture and photos of architecture. Her children had burgeoning lives—her oldest, Vincent, making successively bigger films; her beautiful daughter, Kerry, singing progressively bigger roles in bigger operas; and Ben taking a bigger role in the family restaurant business. Because she still liked the challenge of color, and because she loved working with the stylist, one of her regular jobs was shooting long essays and covers for *Sense and Sensibility,* a slick journal that combined the coverage of luxury items for ravishing people with provocative and durable journalism.

She was doing that the day she lost her job.

The dangerously thin and gamine actress Anne Dresden was eating slices of onion, as Beth would have eaten an apple, and struggling to text with her free hand. Every time Dresden twitched, she would knock some beribboned parasol or fold of gown ever so slightly out of place, and Beth, who had set up with her ancient Hasselblad, would have to move her things; then the stylist, the legendary Ginny Culp, would have to study Beth's Polaroids and the blowup of a fragment of Seurat's *Sunday Afternoon on the Island of La Grande Jatte,* which was what this shoot was supposed to simulate. Beth was shooting what she couldn't see—Ginny's digital pointillism—and the children surrounding Anne Dresden were beginning to scratch and sweat in their full muslin getups.

"We're good now," Ginny said. She was famously taciturn, the former editor of *Splendour,* brought low by age, the economy, and the seeming disinclination of her rival at *Vogue* to either grow old or die. Everything was perfect again—the onion coaxed out of Dresden's hand, the children powdered and mollified—when Anne Dresden's phone chimed. Dresden, who would soon star in a film based on a Sondheim musical, although she couldn't sing a note, got up and left. As she passed Beth on her way to privacy, she stepped on the hem of the antique skirt—Beth heard the ancient fabric tear—covered the phone, and confided, "I'm obsessed with him. We can't go ten minutes without talking. And he's in France. Like, buying Old Masters. And I'm doing this. Isn't it ironic? Oh, my God, he just can't stand not being on the same planet with me."

"It's rough," said Ginny Culp.

"But, Anne," Beth pleaded. "We have everything so perfect now, and with the children so restless, it's not going to last. Give me just five minutes. Okay?" Anne Dresden's publicist, whose bronze hair matched her skin, glanced up from her clipboard.

"She prefers you to call her Miss Dresden, not Anne," the woman said.

"I can't do that," Beth said. "I'm old enough to be her mother."

"We need you to," said the publicist.

"I am finished!" Anne Dresden called. "I need to be out of here!"

"It's a chosen name, don't you think?" said Ginny Culp, *sotto voce*. "You couldn't really call yourself Anne Gallipoli, right? Or Anne Hiroshima?"

"Really, it's me," Beth said suddenly, collapsing her aluminum reflector. "Really I'm the one who's out of here. I'm going to be late, and where are we anyhow—Galena? Galesburg?" They were somewhere in rural Illinois (Beth no longer accepted out-of-town assignments, except during school vacations), and Beth knew it would take hours for her to make it to her granddaughter Stella's school on time. Collecting and stowing her things, she set out for the car. Ginny Culp ran after her.

"Beth, this is a cover! She won't really walk. She's twenty-six years old. She's just being shitty. Those costumes are rentals. They cost a bundle. We can't reschedule this. You already shot the background." But Beth knew they could do everything Ginny insisted was impossible. *Sense and Sensibility* could find some hungry youngster tomorrow, probably with a fresher eye, who would kiss Anne Dresden's skinny butt and charge a hundred bucks for the chance to simply make that cover—which was paired with an interior shot of Dresden with Sondheim that took up a single column in a three-hundred-page magazine.

"I really have to go, Ginny. I mean it. I have to get someplace. Right now." Beth kissed Ginny Culp's deeply lined cheek. "I'll see you if they ever hire me again."

"They'll never hire you again."

"Oh, well," Beth said. "Oh, you know. Oh, well."

Stella's other grandmother, Candy Bliss, was the police chief in Parkside. Ben and Eliza lived there with Stella, in a brownstone for which Candy had cleverly given them the down payment as a wedding gift. Because Beth's husband, Pat, was (in Beth's opinion) overly concerned with ostentation—he drove a Cadillac and wore custom-made suits, calling this good sense and good business—Beth lived in some horsey suburb on two acres with a pool only visitors used. In good traffic, she had to drive an hour to see Stella. It was already nearly noon. Candy had reassured Beth that she was one minute from Stella's school, could drive by anytime, and had promised to check on Stella every day when the child got off the bus (it was Stella's first year on the bus and she was enchanted). But Candy behaved a bit too nonchalantly for Beth's tastes, like all the rest of them.

"What if you're in a high-speed chase or something at three in the afternoon?" Beth asked.

"I'll have somebody else check on her. I'll have a squad drive by the house."

"What if you get shot and forget?" Beth asked. "The sitter will be late and Stella will be kidnapped."

Candy laughed—she laughed.

She said, "Beth, I think about stuff like that all the time too. But we have to get . . . past the past."

Ben and Eliza agreed. They would not allow Beth to pick Stella up from school each day and drive her home, delivering her into the plump arms of the sitter. Both of them believed that too much anxiety would frighten Stella rather than reassure her.

Were they insane?

Beth drove as though pursued by Nazi robots in hovercraft and barely made it to Stella's school before the last bell. She had just parked her car when she heard a single muffled *whoop* from the police car that pulled in behind her. Had she been speeding? Since Stella started school in September, Beth had gotten a ticket in Algonquin and two warnings in Harrington, her first traffic violations in twenty years.

But it was only Candy.

"You see that stoplight back there, lady?" Candy said, leaning into Beth's car and placing her elbows on the open window. She wore a cream-colored blazer and long, slim pants, with a scarf at her neck printed in peacock tones, and looked as though she had just stepped out of the shower. Candy didn't chase subjects on foot anymore, but when she had, she would have looked exactly this same way.

"Shit no. I ran a red light?" Beth said.

"You didn't run a red light."

"What then?"

"Bethie, I'm getting these calls about someone hanging around the school every day. . . ."

Beth sat up so abruptly she knocked off her sunglasses on the visor. "So! How do you feel now? Still think I'm crazy for being afraid for Stella?"

Candy pressed one perfect French-manicured squoval against her forehead, between her eyes, a gesture so singular to Candy that Beth could almost hear the sigh that was its invariable companion.

"It's *you* they're complaining about," Candy said. "My guys ran your plates and they were scared to tell me. But parents describe this lady who never gets out of the car. She just watches. People think you're a kidnapper, so to speak."

Beth glanced around her at the other cars sliding into place to gather their children.

"So what are you doing here?"

"I was in the neighborhood. Sort of."

"You mean, the neighborhood as in the Midwest?"

"Sort of." Beth made a face.

"You have to stop this, Bethie. The sitter hasn't been late in five months, not by a minute. And I said, if I can't check it out myself, I will send someone to do that. It's not like I think you're paranoid—"

"I am paranoid."

"Well, so am I. But we have to go on living as though we aren't or we're going to give ourselves strokes, and then Stella will grow up without grandmothers and be weird."

And so Beth was at home when Marie Caruso phoned that February afternoon. Marie was a nice person; she'd started out as one of the hundreds of reporters who interviewed Beth during the days and years after Ben's kidnapping, so long ago, and had become a minor acquaintance. She had grown up in the town where Beth's in-laws, Rose and Angelo, still lived. Pat had known Marie's older sister, Gia, and all of them knew the terrible story of Gia's own family.

Another family peopled with statistical impossibilities!

This niece was the subject of the call. Marie asked if she might come over some weekend morning. Her niece—what was the girl's name, Sylvia? Serena?—had a project to suggest to Beth. Beth had no idea why, but she agreed. Not that she had anything better to do. With only local assignments for newspapers and magazines, and now absent the daily penitential drive to ensure Stella's safety, Beth found herself with long, pensive, surplus days at the dullest time of the year, as Chicago grudgingly gave up winter for spring.

She tried home projects.

Although a nice young man cleaned the whole house each week, Beth told him not to bother with the grout in any of the five bathrooms; she was going to bleach that herself. The grout-bleaching kit became a fixture in the bathroom. Beth and Pat stepped around it. Sometimes, Beth used a sheet of paper toweling to dust it.

"I have an idea," Pat said one morning, when he finished bellowing after he'd stepped on the business end of the grout brush. "Let's just try letting the cleaning guy clean the grout. If he fails, we can fire him and have him kneecapped by my father's friends."

"That's nonsense," Beth said. "I'll clean the grout. I have time."

"That brush and bleach have been there for more than a month."

"I'm going to get to it."

"Why," Pat asked, "would you want to live in a house where the grout hasn't been cleaned since the tile was laid just so you can say you have a project? Why don't you do something? Do you have that disease where people don't like big spaces? What do you call it?"

"Pat, that's a crazy thing to say."

"That's a crazy thing to say? I don't know, Bethie. What are you waiting for?"

Pat was finishing his daily routine of dolling himself up. Their family's trials had nearly killed him. And now Pat was the same chipper-phony guy, dapper and quick with a joke, still able to convince almost anyone that he had truly hoped to run into no one on earth more than that person on that day. Pat had fully inhabited his previous self, a knot of nervous energy masquerading as a fella without a care in the world, bouncing up on the balls of his feet in his four-hundred-dollar shoes as he waited for the restaurant to open its doors—as avidly as he had waited the first time—day after month after year.

Now Beth sat in the nook at the turn of her stairs, pawing through the camera bag she hadn't opened for months, looking for the leather-bound day book—a birthday gift from Pat—in which she might, just might, have written down the time of the planned visit. Dust moozies decorated the strap of the bag like eiderdown. She removed her still-new digital Nikon D3, squat-bodied and powerful, and her profusion of Fuji lenses, then markers and paper, receipts and empty cans of Life Savers singles, and, finally, the book. Now months old and utterly pristine. She had no idea when these people would arrive her house. It was either at ten or two. Beth was dressed in jeans and a sweatshirt from the Atlanta Opera.

If it was two, Beth would run out and buy some chips and dip and wine—wine! It was nine in the morning. Some . . . juice or something. If it was ten, she had forty-five minutes to make coffee and nothing to serve with it except the end of a loaf of bread, hard as horn.

The doorbell rang.

Jesus! No way. It wasn't ten *or* two. It was nine fifteen.

Beth set her cameras down on the stairs.

Through the tall door sidelight, Beth could see Marie, in a winter-white suit and a scarf made of some beautiful, colorless stuff—were these called neutrals? And the girl. She was tall, taller than Candy, maybe five-six or five-seven, with long wavy hair. She gazed the other way, at the DeGroots' horses, which were picturesquely cropping their hay in what would have been, in any other town, the front yard.

As Beth opened the door, the girl flipped her shiny hair and turned toward Beth. For an instant, Beth was afraid that she might cry out. "You must be—" Beth began. Her voice sounded like a fork dragged over tin. She cleared her throat.

"Sicily," the girl said, extending her hand. Beth took it, and then Beth and Marie exchanged a brief shoulder hug.

"Come in," Beth said. "I lost the message about when to expect you, so if you want some stale bread and coffee with nothing, you've come to the right place. Or I can run up and get dressed and we can go to a restaurant . . ." This was stupid. The girl, Sicily, would not want to go into a restaurant, or so Beth thought.

"If you don't mind, Beth, the coffee with nothing sounds good," Marie said. "This is a little private."

"And I was out so late last night my aunt practically had to roll me out of bed," Sicily said, canting her eyes skyward. Okay. So, unless Sicily went jogging in the dark, she evidently didn't avoid public places, despite how painful it was to look at her.

Strangely, by the time they were all seated at the kitchen table, Beth had stopped seeing the lumpen flesh and Sicily's not-real nose. The girls' long-lashed eyes were dazzling, made up as if for the runway. Layer upon layer of subtlety, intended to look like nature's gift but that probably took twenty minutes to apply, had gone into those eyes.

"I'm sorry for staring," Beth finally said. "You have the most beautiful eyes I've ever seen."

"Especially given the rest," said Sicily. The cold had affected her skin, turning the already patchy texture liverish.

"No," Beth said, and then gave a nod. "Okay, yes, especially given the rest. I'm sorry. My father spoke highly of your dad. My father used to be the fire chief in Parkside, and I'm afraid he's started to be a bit of an old fire horse who hangs around all the stations."

"Everyone likes Chief Kerry," Sicily said. "I've met him. And thank you about Dad. It was a long time ago." And then she cut to the chase. "My aunt Marie came here with me for moral support. I'm sure Eliza has told you—"

"Eliza can't tell me anything about patients."

"Of course," Sicily said. "But I know she told you something about my face."

"How do you know that?"

"You said it with your face when you opened the door. I'm a candidate for a full-face transplant. And I would like you to photograph it."

"Eliza didn't tell me that specifically. So. Photograph it—photograph what? Why? And why me?"

"All of it. The before and after. The surgery. Not as a medical record but as a historical document. Because I've seen your portraits and your news pictures. The photo of my mother at my father's funeral. The book of kids all walking away. So I thought I could say something to you that some other people might think is crazy."

"Not just some," Beth said. "I don't know if I could do that, Sicily. I don't know if I have the stomach."

"Well, here's the thing," said Sicily. "I'm a medical illustrator. And people think that is gross. Like, why do I want to paint pictures of the Swiss cheese removal of liver tumors? But the body is so fascinating and resilient that even stuff that's gross to other people . . . Like, do you know that Jacqueline Kennedy, who was the wife of President John F. Kennedy—"

"I'm aware of that," Beth said, smiling honestly.

"When her husband was shot, a portion of his brain—I'm not saying 'rain'—"

"Brain, I understand you."

"It was exposed when the skull was shattered. And Mrs. Kennedy noticed how extraordinarily beautiful that tissue was. Even in her greatest moment of shock," Sicily continued, as Beth went quiet, weighing that detail. "You don't know what you're going to feel. But once you're caught up in it, even if you're afraid, it might be oddly beautiful. Eliza told me that there could be dozens of men and women in Chicago who fit the requirements for having a full-face transplant, but they don't know it. They're too afraid to find out. I want them to see."

"See what?" Beth asked.

"What I've gone through. Not for the hospital, because the surgeons have people photographing every stitch so they don't put my nose on top of my head or something. I want everyone to see that before I had this face, I had an identity. And if I want to make it easier for the world to love me, it's not because I don't love myself. It's because I do."

"I get that," Beth said.

"People who are not disfigured will have to know more than they ever knew about how people like me feel. And they'll have to admit that, beneath this face, I'm exactly like they are." Sicily paused.

"No one thinks that about disfigured people. They feel sad."

"No, they don't. They feel scared," Sicily said. "They think that I am a thing. I was never a thing."

"But how can I . . . ?"

"You can make this art."

Beth said, "Art."

"Yes. Think of a photo you remember."

Beth thought of the John Filo photo of the sobbing teenager kneeling next to the body of a college student shot during a Vietnam War protest at Kent State University.

"We remember pictures of people in pain. They're real. They're beautiful. Like fire is beautiful, and see what it did to me."

"I thought of the photo of Kent State."

"Kent State?"

"A Vietnam War protest that . . . before your time. I'm flattered and intrigued. But I can't. I'm really sort of retired. And this sounds like a substantial time commitment."

"It would be," Sicily said. "That's why, if you're really sort of retired, you have the time."

Beth couldn't help but grin. She had to hand it to this kid.

"I want to do it in a way that means something," Sicily went on. "This surgery changes my whole future. I might become good-looking or just plain. I might get married someday. Someday I might have children. Or maybe not, because of the drugs. You can freeze your eggs, but that takes time, maybe several cycles of stimulation and harvesting the ova. In my case, there's not the luxury of time. The donor they've found for me . . . well, it's a delicate situation. She's been on life support for a long time. That's a horrible thing for her—for her guardian, who wanted to choose a certain kind of recipient. So I can't get pregnant now unless I wait. I have to agree to have a shot at the hospital every month for the first year so I don't get preg—conceive a child. They won't trust you even to take your own birth control. Some of the medicines cause defects, and others they're not sure of. I have to take, like, six of them every day. All my life, I'll have an increased risk of infection. All my life, I'll have to think that I could be more likely to get leukemia and wonder if it was worth it. Some people say a face transplant might take five or ten years off your life, because of all that medication."

"And you're still willing to do it?" Beth watched as Sicily's eyes smiled. "It's a face. Not a heart. You have to have a heart to live. You don't have to have a face to be alive."

"Define alive," Sicily said. "We're talking now. You're not scared of me. But you were. You didn't mean it. No one wants to be heartless."

Beth stood up, put her hands in the back pockets of her ratty jeans, and peered out her kitchen window. The girl had a point. And yet why would Beth want to do this? She wasn't especially squeamish, but the whole idea sounded like a long, exacting, drawn-out bad dream—potentially both boring and disturbing. In her life, Beth had had quite enough of upsetting, drawn out, and disturbing.

"Consider this before you decide: You know how it feels to lose the way you thought your life would go. And then have it again. But not the way it was."

Beth sat back down at the table and placed her hands flat on the surface. "I need to think about it," she said. "I need time."

"There is no time," said Sicily, leaning forward, which had the effect she certainly knew it would, of forcing Beth to sit up straight.

Got me, Beth thought, *you little brat.*

"The tests are done and the doctors are ready and there's a donor. . . ."

"You're determined," Beth said. She glanced at Marie Caruso, with a look that would have said, *Hey, call off your dog here.* But Marie had taken a sudden and concentrated interest in the contents of her coffee mug.

"I would want you to take pictures of the donor too," said Sicily.

"What do you think I am? If they have a donor, she's dead," Beth objected. "She's brain-dead. On life support."

"She's in a coma, what's called PVS, a persistent vegetative state. She does have a breathing tube in her throat rather than a mask on her face because they don't want to damage her face with pressure and they need a way to get to a donor's face, for measurements and so forth. She can't ever wake up because the brain is the one organ that can never be healed. Emma can't ever be healed. And my face is considered healed. Isn't that amazing? I haven't seen Emma, although, well, I'll see her and meet her mother in two weeks. Two weeks from today exactly, actually. But they say she looks like any other cute teenager, like a sleeping angel. I look like a walking nightmare. But she can't get better and I can. That's the mystery. You know? Even if the one to document this isn't you, it would have had to be someone like you . . ."

"Isn't the donor stuff all a secret?"

"Yes, it is," Sicily said. "You see what I mean, though, don't you?" Beth's head thrummed.

"One thing at a time," Beth said. "There are ethical considerations here."

"Of course. They really do matter. Other things matter more right now, though."

Beth felt suspended, as though she floated in some bright liquid among her silvery kitchen appliances, with the huge eyes of these two women turned on her like twin searchlights. Grim images flashed through her mind, none making this project more appealing. Beth glanced down at an imaginary watch and then up at the kitchen clock. Surely they would notice and leave. They noticed and did not leave.

"Listen," Beth said. "I have to get something to eat. I forgot to eat dinner last night. I have to jump in the shower and change."

"I'll go get something. I saw that little place down around the corner," Marie said, and she briskly took orders, while Beth wondered how somebody could convincingly fake a sudden-onset migraine.

When Marie left, Sicily said, "It's for her too. It's for my aunt."

"Sicily, excuse me, but that should have no part in it."

It was Sicily's turn to get up and look out the full-wall windows that ranked across Beth's kitchen. From the back, the girl was exceptionally lovely—her hips high and level, her posture so erect she was nearly retroflexed.

"It's not for Marie, of course," Sicily said. "But she has given me so much. I'd like her to be happy. She's never said anything about being sad about the way I am. But she loves me. Who wouldn't be?"

"Are you a dancer?" Beth asked.

"Since I was four," Sicily said. "I still take class twice a week. Of course, when you're little, you imagine you'll be the next Sylvie Guillem. I was way too heavy and tall for that. But I might have taught it. Choreographed. The way I am is too hard on kids." She said it in a matter-of-fact voice, absent self-pity or melodrama. "I wouldn't want my own kids—if I maybe adopt kids—to be scared. I wouldn't want them to be ashamed."

"They wouldn't be."

"They would be. They would have to get in fights over me. I know that, because I've had a chip on my shoulder since the fire. It helps, but you would rather not have it."

Sicily drew a heart on the weeping glass. Pat, Beth reflected, kept the temperature in the house approximately the same as in a retirement facility for the tubercular. Slowly, as though the window were a mirror, Sicily raised her leg until it extended behind her, the toe pointed in an unnatural and beautiful arch, high above her head, as she gathered her arms gently at the level of her breasts. For five, ten, then fifteen seconds, Sicily was a sculpture, the body at its fine and tested best.

That was the first picture Beth took.

CHAPTER SEVEN

Dr. Hollis Grigsby was sure her patients knew that the cheesy farm picture was actually a two-way mirror.

Why were functional things so blessed ugly and obvious? Why couldn't there be a really lovely screen that would sit lightly in front of a flat-screen TV—instead of some horror that looked like a bad toaster cover in a fishing cabin? Why didn't someone do something about that? It was so unnecessary, as Hollis's mother would have said. Ugliness was just not necessary. Had Mother not believed this so thoroughly, designing and making dresses for rich women to give her daughters the perks of education, propelling each girl to be her most extraordinary self through her own example, Hollis Grigsby would be what she had set out to be, a professor of anatomy, instead of the first doctor to perform a full-face transplant. It was not necessary for people, not all people, to endure a deformity.

In keeping with her new resolve to shim exercise into her every idle moment, Hollis crossed one leg behind the other and began to do calf raises.

"Does your leg hurt?" Eliza Cappadora asked. She had just come into the corridor and was removing the long scarf wound around her neck. It was spring, but Chicago didn't seem to know that.

"I'm building long, lean, sexy calf muscles," Hollis replied. "I'm actually eavesdropping on this young woman."

They stood side by side—Hollis, slender and serene in her immaculate white coat, a full eight inches taller than Eliza—and listened to Polly Guthrie conduct her third interview with Sicily Coyne. In Sicily's case, a decision was more urgent than usual, the reverse of the customary scenario. The face transplant was very important to Mrs. Julia Cassidy, the donor's mother: A year and a half after the young woman's MI, her mother was now ready to remove her from respiratory support. In the past, when they had tried to wean Emma from the ventilator, it had resulted in a code. Every manner of imaging, including 3-D ultrasounds, had been brought to bear to detect that stray spark of brain activity beyond the brain stem. In an elaborate journey by ambulance, the girl was ferried to the University of Illinois Chicago Circle for scan after scan.

Sicily's tissue samples, blood type, and general compatibility with the young donor had long since been determined. They were good—better than good. Because of the Irish part of her heritage, Sicily's skin density and tone were very satisfactory duplicates of the donor's, if not the best Hollis had ever seen. A medical anthropologist had done age progressions of Sicily's eighth-grade portrait and, based on those, had created a spooky life-sized bust. While Sicily mouth-breathed, an anaplastologist made molds of the undamaged musculature of her face, then of her teeth. Cardiologists measured her heartbeat as she ran on a treadmill, and pulmonologists assayed her respiration.

Except for her problems with closing her mouth and the near-constant need for humidity, Sicily radiated health.

But no one wanted a disaster prompted by a hidden mental condition. Not given what Dr. Grigsby had gone through once with that very situation. Was Sicily emotionally out of crisis after the devastation she'd endured in January? Polly Guthrie wanted irrefutable proof.

Sicily raised and flexed her arms, then placed them over her head, as though she was embracing a barrel, her fingers in a delicate splay. They were lovely, lovely arms, tended and strong, without the some-how aesthetically distressing ropy quality some fit girls had. Sicily wore a silver bangle bracelet that Hollis Grigsby had seen before, at their first meeting. Also present at that meeting were Hollis's co-chair, Livingston; the attendings, Alvarado, Lionel, DeAngeli, and Haberlinthe; and the residents, including the chief resident, Sira Barathongon, the senior resident on the cosmetic-surgery service, Melanie Aras, and the most junior among them, Eliza, whose initial, inappropriate, but ultimately forgivable contact with the patient had brought all this to pass. Not long after they sat down, Sicily had removed the bracelet to pass it among them. The inscription was in Italian: *Una cosa da fare and una this that this that.* It meant *Something to do, something to love, and something to look forward to.* Wrought by a silversmith in Siena, it had been a gift from Sicily's aunt following the extinguished engagement.

"So you know what that is called, what the girl is doing with her arms?" Hollis asked Eliza.

"It's a *port de bras,*" Eliza said. "A ballet thing."

"Did you take ballet lessons?"

Eliza grimaced. "You haven't met my mother. I took every lesson. When I came home, I was almost eight. I could barely read Spanish, much less English. It was Bolivian orphan rehab."

Hollis smiled and cut her eyes reprovingly at Eliza. They turned back to the screen.

"I don't mind rep—retelling it," Sicily was saying. "It's just that you can't consider my reaction out of pro—out of bounds."

"I can understand your speech," Polly said.

"It's habit. It's sort of like your mouth being one of those verbal computer writing devices that puts down 'dragon' when you say 'wagon.'"

Polly smiled. "I don't consider your reaction out of proportion, Sicily. Everything you thought was solid ground collapsed. After that, the human mind tends to reach for any possible form of relief. The normal response to that kind of devastation is to grab at straws."

"That's a normal reaction." Sicily sighed. "So I'm normal."

"But you went from absolute certainty that you did not want a face transplant to submitting yourself as a candidate. Dr. Cappadora approached you in December. And it's only April."

"It's my only life," Sicily said.

"That sounds rehearsed."

"It is! This is the third time I've told you."

"On the basis of losing your fiancé, you decided you wanted to have a face transplant?" Polly asked.

Hollis frowned. That made Sicily seem like a girl who was jilted one day and the next day donated all her old furniture and ordered a vanload of new stuff from IKEA.

Sicily thrust her arms up and out again. She regarded the ceiling as if asking for some kind of celestial guidance. "I was on the verge of having a life with Joey. We were a match. I had an unusual kind of good luck that went bad. Now if I want a life, a mate, children, I have to start over."

"Plenty of people—"

"I know. But I want what I had. That doesn't make me nuts, just shallow."

"This surgery is no guarantee of that outcome."

"This face is an almost certain guarantee of the opposite outcome," Sicily explained. "I've not just lost my face or Joey. I lost my family. I've had only hard times. I want an easier time."

"I'd hardly call a twenty-hour procedure and a lifetime of maintenance drugs . . ."

Sicily stood up, crossed the room to the pastoral picture, and wiggled her fingers at it in a covert hello. "You know, I don't have your knowledge of how the mind works. I do know a great deal about medicine. It's my job. I know that the drug regimen for anti-rejection is nowhere near as harsh as it was when the first face transplant took place, what, ten, eleven years ago? I know that this is not an easy operation. But it's founded on basic anatomy. I know that microsurgery is tricky and there is the small chance that the whole face will fail and they'll end up having to plaster on skin from my butt. But that's never happened. So much has happened to me, why should that happen too?"

"Sicily, you know what that's called. It's called—"

"Magical thinking. I know. But there's no reason it should happen now. It's happened with a finger. There have been arms that doctors removed. There's even a guy who had a penis transplant and wanted to have it removed. No one has ever lost a face. The one guy who died—"

"He failed to follow protocols."

Sicily's eyes were eloquent with reproof. "Way more than that. I know peo—some surgeons who were involved. He was basically a suicide. And, Polly, I'm not being a smart-ass trying to show off."

Outside, Hollis Grigsby winced. Sicily was exactly correct.

The first full-face transplant was a stunning triumph. Lily Blackwood-Thorne—a Londoner who pulled her child to safety from a smashed car—was ambushed by flames when she turned back to help her sister. Everything went so well in part because of pure luck—bad luck and good. Lily Blackwood-Thorne's older sister, Adele, sustained mortal internal injuries in the same accident and lingered for months on life support. But a fire brigade had put out the flames. Her face was unmarked. Concussed by grief, Adele's ophthalmologist husband could have opted for a beautiful funeral. Instead, he had asked the golden question: Could anything "be done" to help Lily?

Even on the morning that Hollis Grigsby scrubbed in at one operating room in St. Charles and Kings' Hospital to remove Adele's face—while, in the other room, her hand-chosen team of colleagues prepared Lily's—she didn't feel ready. But then, she doubted that she ever would. She would have gone on studying—perhaps forever—the full square foot of tissue that comprised a human face laid flat and the minute miracles of the trigeminal nerve and its branches that led to expression and sensation. She was overly prone to research, always had been. Hollis's protégé, a crack young maxillofacial surgeon who went by his last name, Livingston (to his dry British chagrin, his given name was, unfortunately, Stanley), had urged her on. Hadn't she set out to do just this? Wasn't this the end result of her lifelong work on the hands of burn patients, since hands approximated faces in their complexity of musculature and neurological amplitude? Donor digits and limbs allografted onto burned stumps could restore their ability to caress a child's face or do a day's work. But when it came to faces, surgery had so far failed them. Pioneering Spanish, French, and Chinese doctors had successfully transplanted a lower face and a dozen upper halves and quadrants of faces, but the results fell short of what Hollis knew was possible. Patients could close their eyes, chew, spit, arch their eyebrows, but better-than-bad was still not good enough. It was not pleasing.

Over the years of the quest, Hollis's obsession with the need and feasibility of such a transplant was not what supported her, but it was what sustained her. Becoming an orthopedic surgeon with a specialty in reconstruction had taken ten years. Her fellowship in microsurgery and the possibilities of transplant tacked on four more. Over the years when she willingly spent hours of her own time and money in the lab, first alone and later with Livingston, she had drawn the suspicion of butchers who wondered at her particular fondness for large batches of pigs' feet—pigskin texture and vascularity being eerily similar to that of human beings. She spent her days at the University of Wisconsin in Madison replacing hips, legs, and knees, reattaching legs and arms separated from their natural locus by everything from the wheels of a train to a vengeful stepfather. At night, she stood at the microsurgical microscope, which was taller even than she, her head pressed against the binocular headpiece, her hands free to use the instruments suturing the veins or arteries of the animal laid out anesthetized before her,

feet working to adjust the focus of the instrument with the unconscious dexterity of a tailor. Her forearms ached. Her lower back
burned.

What was the role of the immune system in determining why some
animals healed without any loss of function and minimal scarring?
Why did one way of making the tiniest stitches produce a better result
than another pattern of sutures? Hollis sewed the skin, photographed,
observed, repeated, and reported. The silent hours fell one onto another with the speed of the pages of flip books she and her sisters had
played with as children. During her fellowship in London, she moved
slowly away from the leg arteries of a dog and a rabbit to the facial skin
of a tender piglet or rhesus monkey, drawn back and back again to the
vivarium and the cadaver lab, from the living animal to the human
being who had disinhabited the body. She had literally worn out cadavers removing and reattaching facial skin—so many reconstructions
that she'd left the poor, thin faces of the gallant Oxford dead ragged.
Feeling like Burke and Hare, Hollis bought her own cadaver. Night
after night she traced the nerves as they wound through the muscles
to the brain. Touch, twitch, wrinkle, sneeze. Enlist the frontalis, lower
the procerus, raise the orbicularus oculi. A wink. Again. Hollis was enraptured by the kind of "muscles of emotion" that made a face human.

"Holly, every face is a face. If you've seen one, you've seen them all,"
said Nathan St. Jerome, Hollis's best friend at the time, who was now
a pricey cosmetic surgeon in Sydney. "You torture that poor woman like
you expect to raise her from the dead."

"How I feel is, I won't really understand the one until I've seen
them all," Hollis said. "If I have to think about it, I don't understand it."

Perhaps all those nights that Hollis came back to the lab after her
sons were asleep informed the relative grace with which her team of
six surgeons and twenty nurses laid that eerie one hundred square
inches of tissue—translucent as wet linen, fragile and yet so resilient
it could withstand a big man's punch without tearing—across the raw
plane of Mrs. Blackwood-Thorne's exposed musculature. With cam-

eras whirring as the surgeons moved from region to region of the face, support staff documented the microsurgical positioning and attachment of every slicked structure, artery to artery and vein to vein, every nerve to nerve, every rod of muscle in Mrs. Blackwood-Thorne's face to every corresponding rod in her sister's face. Because the sisters were so similar, the process was almost like reassembling a human jigsaw puzzle. The moment when the carotid and the jugular that fed and drained the face did their customary job, the vascular "pinking" of the skin, was perhaps the most moving moment of Hollis's professional life.

Eight days later, the bandages were removed. Despite the bruising and swelling, Lily Blackwood-Thorne reached up, touched her own cheeks, and shouted, "Adele!" All their lives, people had commented on the resemblance between Lily and Adele.

Quietly pondering the satisfaction of redeeming at least part of another person's loss, Hollis forgot how huge this moment would be to the world. The press called the first full-face transplant *The Shout Heard 'Round the World.* The news might have consumed Hollis with an endless pileup of interviews. Fortunately, Livingston was more gifted with both the press and the physicians who flocked to study the Grigsby–Livingston procedure.

Eagerly, Hollis received her second candidate, Laurent Girard, an even more heartbreaking saga. Preparing for his family's annual stalking trip in search of roe deer, Girard shot himself in the face while cleaning his gun. A newly accredited kindergarten teacher, Girard admitted that he didn't even like shooting but went along for the companionship with his father and brother. Rushed to St. Charles and Kings', he lay near death for months.

"I just want to go back to the children," Girard told Hollis. "And I'll scare them. They're so little." Girard was himself only twenty-three.

Or so the story went.

A Canadian with French citizenship living in London, Girard, actually thirty, presented more or less the jacket he wanted the team to see.

They did not see his hidden history of severe alcoholism or that the gun "accident" was a suicide attempt, his second in five years. Laurent Girard was quite probably a sociopath who charmed them all: Sociopaths were the dread of every surgical team, since they were nearly impossible to tease out and identify. Depression was the norm for the disfigured, and odd quirks of all sorts were expected. But no one could have spotted Laurent Girard unless he'd worn a neon crown. Or so Hollis told six psychiatric interns, when at least two of them considered a change in specialty after the catastrophe. But why? Hollis asked over and over. What was in it for him? A slow death and the added bonus of leaving earnest people with nightmares for life?

When Girard failed to show for one, then two, and three clinic appointments, word went out to all the contacts he had produced during his family support sessions. Every one was a fake. The kindly mum was a tavernkeeper who thought the poor boy needed a chance. The stalwart older brother, who described his job as a "bit of a minor banker," was in fact a former actor who'd gone down to drugs and lived in a shelter. There was a bank two doors over.

Girard finally turned up at a Vancouver hospital, in liver failure, an emaciated walking corpse who died within days.

Undone, Hollis went back to hands. She refused calls. She turned down the BBC. Hollis was finished with face transplants. Let Livingston do it. If not he, then others.

Six months later, along came the young girl from a patrician family in Spain. She'd been bike riding with friends when a car plowed into three of the kids. The biking stirrups Aurelia wore for safety somehow got hooked to the car's bumper, and she was dragged for two hundred yards. Her helmet stayed put, so her brain was unhurt, but her face was destroyed. She was still razor-bright and knew that in sixty seconds she had gone from being the prettiest girl in school to what she called "a thing," who with bitter sarcasm drove away the friends who rallied around her. Her widowed father left Hollis a dozen messages: "If it is a matter of money, I will pay you anything. Five million pounds. Ten million. Only let my little girl sing and laugh again."

She could not ignore Aurelia.

Nor could she ignore the Irish laborer whose hundred-pound wife had pulled him out of their harvester. "He didn't have a brilliant face, ever. But I was fond of it," the wife said.

So many others could do hands. As Hollis's mother, Evangeline, reminded her, it was a sin to refuse your own gift. At first, Hollis had done just that. At the age of seventeen, Hollis packed four sturdy boxes with things she could not live without—her favorite pillow, her shawls, her collected Shakespeare, her Bible, big plastic jars of her grandmother's specially mixed spices, and all her Beatles and Nina Simone CDs. It was the first time she'd gone farther from her own parish than to Baton Rouge. She'd gotten on her first airplane, New Orleans to Edinburgh, and began her undergraduate study on a Rotary scholarship, courtesy of strings yanked none too subtly by one of her mother's "ladies." Hollis had meant to major in drama, seeing herself swathed in woolens, striding the Scottish streets mouthing classic lines from memory. Anatomy was only a scholarship elective, chosen in the same spirit as Hollis studied small engines in high school—a thirst to know how things worked. When she ended up repeating "The Carpus consists of the Scaphoid, the Lunate, the Triquetal, the Pisiform, the Hamate, the Capitate, the Trapezoid, and the Trapezium" with more passion than "O hateful hands, to tear such loving words!" Hollis realized that, unawares, she'd fallen in love. Grandmother's spices and Nina Simone went back into the boxes and flew with Hollis to Madison, Wisconsin, where she began her graduate studies in research anatomy.

One night during her graduate school years at the University of Wisconsin in Madison, Ralph Mangiotti, the renowned burn surgeon, had come upon Hollis quietly studying his repairs on a young girl whose mother had held first her face then both her hands to the coils of an electric stove. Mangiotti asked what Hollis thought of reconstructive surgery.

"Well, I think that it is the closest thing on earth we know about salvation," Hollis said.

"Why aren't you doing it?" the doctor had asked.

At the advanced age of twenty-seven, Hollis entered medical school. Deep in the rigorous program at Madison, Hollis had scant time for any life, never mind a social life. Prospective surgeons on old nighttime soap operas had more sex in a one-hour episode than Hollis had in a semester. Her most significant relationship at that time wasn't a love affair of the usual kind: It began nearly six years later, when Hollis represented the UW–Madison Burn Center at a conference in London. After Livingston spoke on the dental implications in future of full-face transplant, Hollis waylaid him, voracious for more. Livingston's wife, Gwen, still told the story of calling Livingston once at midnight after the conference banquet would have been hours over, then five times between one and four in the morning, after which she decided there had been a mishap and began calling the various trauma units, starting with Livingston's own. She was shocked to hear that her husband was indeed there, unhurt and deep in conversation over tea with a very pretty American, who was not hurt either. The fellowship post from St. Charles and Kings, Livingston liked to joke, nearly beat Hollis back to Wisconsin. After all the years since, a confirmed and contented expat, and Sidney, her husband, and the boys, when the offer came from Chicago for Hollis to be the one to found the first clinic dedicated entirely to face and limb transplants, she was surprised by the force of her desire to continue to expand the boundaries of this hopeful technology. She was surprised, even more, by the yearning, which ambushed her like an alarm through broken glass, to be home. The boxes made their final trans-Atlantic crossing.

"Look what she is doing," Hollis now said to Eliza.

"These are my facial nerves," Sicily was telling Polly, placing the thumb and finger of one hand on spots on her cheeks, just below the ears. "They say you can't remember feelings, but I dream about my great-uncle letting me hold a duckling once and how its feathers felt on my cheek." She placed both hands over her mouth. "The fifth cranial nerve has upper and lower divisions. Do you have a husband, Polly? Or a boyfriend?"

Polly Guthrie nodded, and Eliza and Hollis could measure, in the slow tempo of the nod, the psychologist's perplexity.

"The fifth facial nerve lets you feel him kiss you. But the seventh facial nerve lets you make that motion with your mouth—what do they say?"

"Puckering up," Polly said.

"That's it. You can kiss him back. I was thirteen when I got burned. I'd never been kissed," Sicily said. "I've got strong heredity. My grandparents on both sides are well into their eighties and they're going strong." Sicily moved her hands down until she cradled the lower portion of the bulbous projection that was her chin. "I want to use the zygomaticus major and risorius muscles, with the help of the buccinator."

Polly Guthrie nodded again.

"I'd give two years of my life to smile."

"She knows what she wants," Hollis said to Eliza. "Let's transplant this young woman."

"There will be no documentation," said the hospital's lawyer, Joel Brodsky. "If it's not medically necessary, it can't happen."

"It can happen," said Sicily. "It just hasn't happened so *far.*"

"Let me tell you why," said the lawyer. "Sicily, it's not personal." The guy explained that the first and most obvious objection—and, Beth thought, escape hatch—was the way in which documenting an entire face transplant, from the location of the donor and the recipient to the aftermath, would violate federal health privacy law. "The Health Insurance Portability and Accountability Act was signed into law in 1996, mostly to protect those with chronic health conditions from being denied health-insurance coverage. But even where that doesn't apply, patient privacy is a primary concern at this institution, not for the protection of our staff but for our patients. This means that Mrs. Cappadora cannot observe the surgery, and there can be no way she could photograph it."

"She agreed," Sicily said.

"It's not a consideration," Joel Brodsky put in. "Mrs. Cappadora—"

"I don't mean Mrs. Cappadora. The donor agreed. She's sixteen. She's a minor. Or she was. Her mother has her health directive," Sicily said. "And she would be eighteen under the law now, and she signed—"

"Dr. Grigsby," Kelli Buoté, the social worker, pleaded.

Dr. Grigsby held up an admonitory finger. The twelve representatives of the University of Illinois Chicago Circle Transplant Clinic regarded Sicily, Beth, Marie, and Julia Cassidy.

"Mrs. Cassidy is Emma's mother," Sicily said. "Emma is my donor. Mrs. Cassidy knows that and I know that. I have visited Emma and spoken with Mrs. Cassidy on several occasions, and so has my aunt, Marie Caruso, who is my adoptive mom, and my friend, Beth Cappadora, who will do the photographs."

"This is an end run," Kelli said.

"And the legal risks are incalculable," Joel Brodsky added, replacing his wire readers as if to announce that the discussion was over.

"What if you were to die, Sicily?" asked Kelli.

"I wouldn't die because Beth was taking pictures. Obviously, if I died during the surgery, it wouldn't be such a good aesthetic and public awareness tool. What if I *were* to die? Write up some form and my aunt will sign it. She has my health directive, just as Mrs. Cassidy has Emma's."

"It would be a disaster," said the attorney.

"As it is a disaster, personal and professional, when any patient dies," said Dr. Grigsby. The tall, slim, dark woman said nothing else but lifted an eyebrow in Eliza's direction.

This is how she gets her way, Beth thought. *She's so used to being the alpha female.*

"Eliza approached Sicily at your bidding," Beth said. Eliza winced.

"My . . . bidding?" Dr. Grigsby said softly.

"If you didn't tell her to do it, then, as her mentor, you made it implicit." Beth took a deep breath. "I didn't want to do this either. But Sicily is determined—"

"I do not doubt that for one moment," said Dr. Grigsby.

"She is committed to . . . to . . . letting people see how this process could change lives. More lives. That's in your interest," Beth said. Dr. Grigsby said nothing—which was a skill Beth Cappadora had never mastered. This woman put Beth on edge: Her face had the kind of serenity that God seemed to offer only to black women, and only some of those. Her hands did not seek each other out to twitch and wrestle, as Beth's did, the tapering tip of each well-tended finger lay motionless on the conference-room table. She wore not even an earring or a wedding band. By comparison, Marie Caruso, although demure in a black silk suit, appeared almost gaudy with her diamond studs and two opal rings.

"You . . . you . . . violated the law even by meeting with Mrs. Cassidy," Kelli spluttered, her knuckles white as the coffee cup, her other hand drumming. "You—and your friend here—were never supposed to meet the donor. This is still new land, Sicily. But there are minefields we know enough to avoid. There's a process. And the legal and emotional ramifications are real." Kelli's eyes filled. "Sicily, you know better than this. You've been around the block. Why? Why?"

"She thinks it is the right thing," Beth answered for Sicily, sensing a wobble in her. Though she'd known Sicily Coyne only a few weeks, already Sicily roused the Irish in Beth. If Beth had lived a life strange in the magnitude of its losses and blessings, then Sicily's was the life of a saint. To her own surprise, Beth realized that she had all her chips in. Even her mother-in-law had encouraged Beth, saying, "Of course I remember that poor child. Elizabeth, there was nobody who didn't have a child or a niece or a friend's child in that fire. It had an effect on people's lives all over the West Side." And Beth remembered how self-absorbed she had been then, twelve years before, with Vincent dropping in and out of college, with fighting Pat, who wanted her to be a lady of leisure, to take her career back. Such petty, petty tempests, seen from her vantage today.

Recovering her nerve, Sicily said, "I'm sorry. But Beth is correct.

Meeting Emma was the right thing. For me and for Mrs. Cassidy. She feels comforted by knowing where Emma's face is going."

Kelli said, "She doesn't know where her daughter's donated heart is going. My apologies, Mrs. Cassidy."

"A heart isn't a face," Sicily said. "Hundreds of heart-transplant recipients have met their donors' families and corresponded and . . . all that."

"We can legally . . ." Joel Brodsky began. "We're talking here about twenty physicians and skilled surgical nurses. Even they have certain rights."

"That's not true," Dr. Grigsby said. "We might object, but we submit our work to colleagues and students every day, and there is no legal prohibition to this. Livingston?"

"Just so," said Dr. Grigsby's co-chair.

"Why are you seeing this as a wrong thing?" Julia Cassidy asked. She pulled a creased sheet of paper from her pocket. "Listen to this. Emma wrote it before she died, right before she went to that party and never woke up afterward." She read: *"What is the meaning of life? I have no idea. Making others happy is the whole tortilla."*

"I don't think the problem here is legal," Dr. Livingston said. "It was a bridge we would cross in due time in any case, since the ideal donor has geographic proximity."

Facial tissue survived, Beth knew from Sicily, for about eight hours. Six hours was better. Four hours was better than six.

Julia caressed the elaborate festoon of her updo. She was a hairstylist, and the "girl" who rented the chair next to hers had come in early to prepare Julia for this meeting. Julia, too, wore a silk suit, in bright lapis, and brown heels, which troubled Beth more than the updo. But she spoke her case convincingly. "It was as though my Emma knew. She signed her donor card just two months before it happened, when she got her first driver's license. It was later than most people, because she kept having to take the class over, sophomore and junior year, so she was almost seventeen; it came harder to Emma for those decisions we have to make all at the same time, like, do I turn now, or do I wait until the next light? Those just weren't instinct for her at first. It was all overwhelming to her, but when she finally got it, she was totally an excellent driver. She never got a ticket. A warning once, but that was at the place that's basically a speed trap, where the sign says forty-five on one side and twenty-five ten feet later. You practically have to slam on the brakes."

"Mrs. Cassidy, no one thinks Emma's heart was anything other than pure," Joel Brodsky said, in the kind of tone that might have induced vegan Buddhists to at least try a hamburger. "If Emma was here now—"

"She is here," Julia said.

"If she was here at this table—" said Joel Brodsky.

"She is here at this table," Julia insisted. "Her spirit is here."

"Well, if she could speak for herself, I'm sure she would say that she'd do whatever she had to, to help, as she wrote. But you and Emma have already done the right thing by consenting. This is an invasion of your family's privacy that you will regret later. Think of your relatives and how they will react to seeing very graphic depictions of Emma's tissue."

"It's her face," Julia said. "Her face and neck. And we have no family. I'm it. No one but Emma and me. Jared's mother is in a nursing home; she has dementia. It was an early thing, and Emma was heartbroken because she adored her Grammy Linda—"

"You have no other family?" Beth said. "Your daughter is your only family?"

Julia said, "I'm a widow. You know that. And I have a brother I don't see. So, yes."

Beth smiled and thought, *Oh, fuck, no. This is impossible.*

"Come on," Sicily said. "Everyone has to do something for the first time, or nothing would ever change. What could go so wrong that it would be worse than the Canadian nutcase?"

Hollis grimaced at Livingston, who could not suppress a smirk.

"And no one even talks about him anymore. Emma is not ashamed of her gift. Mrs. Cassidy is not ashamed of her choice. I am not ashamed to receive her gift. I'm honored." Sicily turned to the hospital's counsel. "Mr. Brodsky, no one is breaking the law. You are advancing it. If you didn't want to handle junk like this, you should have done, like, real estate."

"And right now I wish I had," Brodsky said. "You call it, Dr. Grigsby."

Dr. Grigsby nodded.

CHAPTER EIGHT

They tuck you up in tons of warmed blankets when you're waiting in an operating room, because those places are kept at the temperature of meat lockers.

I guess they are meat lockers.

If you should ever be alive on a really narrow metal bed, looking up at someone, and you want to know why your nose is cold, that person will tell you it's to prevent infection. Which is not true. Even some OR nurses and doctors would be surprised to hear that, because they believe it. The fact is, a person who's hypothermic for a long time gets a weakened immune system, and more people die from hospital infections than from cancer and heart attacks. I'm not showing off. But lots of people die from medical errors too, which is really why operating rooms are cold. It's to keep the doctors and nurses from getting too hot. They have gloves and gowns and hats on over their scrubs, and the lights are merciless, as is the gradual buildup of heat from everyone else who isn't the patient. So you balance the odds of getting an infection with the odds of a doctor having a little slipup and dropping a hemostat into your intestines—or, in my case, my sinuses.

This particular surgery was going to last a long time, like maybe up to twenty hours, and there would be at least twelve people in the room at any given time. Dr. Grigsby—whom I had begun to call "Hollis," because she called me "Sicily"—said that there was every likelihood that doctors and nurses would be replaced by other doctors and nurses so that they didn't become exhausted: There might be four full teams. I didn't know she had four full teams or even that the U of I did.

"You don't mean the second string, right?" I asked her.

"No," Hollis said. "Everyone is the first string."

That's not true either, but it was probably the case that there wouldn't be many first-year interns working on my face. I knew Eliza would be, and that was a source of strength. I had told Eliza I was willing to have a discreet wrinkle or two for the consolation of her and Beth's presence—because Aunt Marie could not be with me. In fact, by the time my surgery was scheduled, in June, I had spent so many evenings and some days with Eliza that Kit Mulroy was saying things to me like, "Is she your new best friend? Do I have anything to worry about here?"

The blankets are a comfort. Those blankets and kind words, no matter how nonsensical, are the only comfort the nurses and doctors can offer a person who's terrified.

And guess what?

I was terrified.

Every other time I'd had surgery, I knew that I would wake up and the doctor would say, *Hey, we really restored some symmetry here but, in fact, not much is going to change.* This time, when I woke up, everything was going to change. I would either look like a cross between myself and Emma or like a raw hamburger. And my whole future would be different.

There was a boy I had met once, in the hospital, a child, who'd had corneal transplants. The first time he opened his eyes, he could *feel* seeing. It was almost physically painful. There was too much to take in, and it was all so clear and brightly colored.

I thought that might be my own experience.

But I was pretty sure that, however I felt, it was going to splatter me all over the place emotionally.

That would be normal. Some of it, Polly and Kelli Buoté had tried to prepare me for—Polly with individual sessions both before and after I was in the hospital, Kelli with a novel's worth of printouts about community resources. There's no Face Transplants Anonymous, but there are body-image groups and post-surgical groups and post-trauma groups that people attend for months or years. Sometimes, friends from these groups are the only ones post-trauma patients have. Sometimes, that's where they meet the special person they marry. The thing was, I'd been to most of them as a kid. As an adult, I'd been the speaker at some of them.

The best thing Kelli had promised to do was put me in phone contact with a guy in Virginia, a fifty-five-year-old grandfather who'd also had a face transplant.

"One guy?" I asked. "Isn't there someone closer? Like in Indiana? Someone I can actually meet face-to-face, so to speak?"

"There are a number of people closer. But he was the one who agreed to talk to you," Kelli said. "And only on the telephone."

"What's wrong with the others?"

"Sicily, most people are very private about this kind of stuff. You're obviously the exception." Kelli still wasn't entirely okay with the fact that Beth had been taking pictures since I'd come to the hospital and was even now receiving her gown and instructions about where she could and could not move or sit during the actual procedure.

"Why are they so . . . guarded?" I was genuinely puzzled.

"They gradually reintroduce themselves to the community."

"You mean, they try to pretend they just had lipo?"

"No, Sicily. Some face transplant recipients have lived their lives in a very protected way, some with only their immediate family seeing them. It's a process, going out into the world, and it's as much about their reactions as other people's reactions to them."

I knew that I would have some bruising and swelling. The team had impressed this upon me, oh, about seven hundred times. I was not to expect that when the bandages were removed after five days I would look in the mirror and see a movie star. Some residual scarring, probably below my neckline, could be permanent, although not cosmetically severe. Someone even gave me a kit of all this therapeutic makeup and demonstrated how to use it to cover the temporary bruises and the permanent scars. I'd already tried stuff like that, which is sort of like corpse makeup and is used to cover birthmarks as well as scars. But it's so gross and heavy, for me anyhow, that I gave it up. For work or going out, I had recently begun to use stage makeup. It worked almost as well and it seemed like it was harder to sweat it off.

It wasn't like I was fooling anyone, after all. My makeup was just meant to take the edge off.

That morning at about 5:00 a.m., a nurse had given me some woozy juice, probably IV Versed, to take the edge off while I was still in my room. When you've had as many surgeries as I have, you have approximately the same drug tolerance as a Clydesdale, no matter what you weigh. I could have recited the periodic table, if they hadn't added all those new, crazy mixed-up elements. I tried reciting the names of the bones of the foot, but I got only to the calcaneus before I fell back to my sad pondering about what Mrs. Cassidy was doing right now. Somewhere on the same floor as I was, she was saying goodbye forever to Emma—or already had.

Because doing the right thing was "the whole tortilla" for Emma, it was better for her to be in the hospital rather than at a facility like Sundial. Once they "harvested" her—my—face, the surgeons would step back and let other transplant physicians take her heart, her healthy lungs, and her beautiful hazy brown eyes. Weather and other delays can really be hell on organs, so it's better that they come from the neighborhood, and I know how that sounds. Mrs. Cassidy would not be there for the horrible bits, but I thought of her agony as something like Mother Mary's. Yes, Emma was gone, but it was also true that Mrs. Cassidy (whom I never called "Julia") had sacrificed Emma, the only thing she loved, so that others might live. And so that I could have the full woman's life Emma never would. And then I realized that this is why you didn't get to know your donor or her family. I cried until I threw up (nothing) in the green plastic basin. The emotions were absolutely torrential. I'd outfoxed myself.

Of course, the way I found out about Emma was by calling Mrs. Viola, the mother of my old school friend Victoria, who had died in the fire. Despite all those months after the fire when she'd become my ghastly, needy stalker, Mrs. Viola had finally remade her life. She found meaning in caring for people who were going to "cross over" soon, to where Victoria was. She'd done this not in an insane way, or so my grandma Caruso, who knew Gail Viola pretty well, told me. I'd called Mrs. Viola one day last winter, after the preliminary testing, because the very few hints of the way Kelli described the place where the young woman was gave me a hunch. Not many places like that were as nice as Sundial and also took welfare, which is what Emma was on. Sundial was not a real hospice, run by the national organization, where some terminally ill people received their last care. It was something between that and a nursing home. In order for Emma to go there when she left the hospital, after there was no more that anyone could do, after it was clear that Emma could never get better, Mrs. Cassidy had reduced her hours, given up her little house, and gone on assistance.

When I called Mrs. Viola, we made some small talk about my grandparents and my aunt. Then I asked her, "Is there a girl at Sundial who's going to be a donor for a face transplant?"

Mrs. Viola didn't even hesitate—no worries about patient privacy there! She said, "Yes, Sicily. There's this beautiful little Irish girl and her sweet mother." And then Mrs. Viola stopped and said, "Sicily? Get out of here! Are you kidding me?"

I didn't have to confirm or deny. I am sure that by the end of her shift, everyone on the West Side who had a phone or could lip-read knew. So I had to hurry up and connect with Beth, which I did. Two weeks later, on a Friday afternoon—Mrs. Viola's day off, but she managed to switch with someone else to be there—we went to see Emma and Mrs. Cassidy at Sundial.

When we walked in, Emma's room looked like the kind of gift shop where grandmothers buy presents. There were things you would never use in real life: elaborate acrylic flower arrangements that looked real, and wooden birdhouses that were actually jewelry boxes with drawers that you knew would never close. Everything was pink or quilted or both. Mrs. Cassidy showed me one of the quilts, made by a close friend of hers, a longtime customer, and each square was a photo of Emma at a different age. All around the walls were framed drawings, some of them very accomplished, from Emma's sketchbook. There was a chair for Beth and one for me, and we sat there as though we were at a wake, just, I suppose, out of respect.

Mrs. Cassidy offered us coffee, which I refused politely and Beth said would be wonderful. Mrs. Viola was there with a mug of coffee in a flash, so we knew she'd been standing outside the door. I didn't mind, because by then Mrs. Viola seemed to have some sort of trunk line to the universe. She acted as though she believed she was living what might have become of Victoria, if she had survived, through me. And wasn't that the least Mrs. Viola deserved? She'd given her whole life to people, most of whom would never get better.

"How often do you come to see Emma?" I asked, because it was obvious that Beth wasn't going to say anything. It looked to me as though Beth was taking her camera entirely apart and putting it back together again.

"Every day after work, and all day Friday and Sunday," Mrs. Cassidy said. "I'm friends with some of the people who work here, like Gail. Sometimes we play cards or do a crossword. I'm pretty good at crosswords. English was my best subject in school, that and science."

At first, Mrs. Cassidy said, all of Emma's friends who had been with her that night at the party came, two or three times a week. ("It wasn't drugs," said Mrs. Cassidy. "She had one beer. No one knows what caused it, and Emma's heart is apparently still very healthy, although she can breathe only with the respirator.") Emma's hospital room was sort of a gathering place. Back then—nearly eighteen months ago—all the friends expected her to wake up, and they competed to be the one who would get her to react. They sang to her and talked about boys Emma had a crush on and called Emma's cell phone. But then Emma's *best* friend came. She fainted right there in the room, because Emma looked exactly like Emma. Her hair was in this little bob, and the roots hadn't started to grow out. After the faint, which gave the best friend a lump on her head, the hospital wouldn't let minors come to see Emma without their parents.

"Do her friends still come? Here? Do they know that Emma isn't going to be kept alive?" I asked Mrs. Cassidy. Beth looked at me like she wanted to crush my esophagus.

"No," Mrs. Cassidy said. "They want to remember her as she was, and they definitely don't want to think about her being a transplant donor. Which is something I understand. It's a highly emotional situation and not an issue that every person understands so well."

For a year, Mrs. Cassidy still acted as though Emma were alive and could see and feel and hear everything around her, which Mrs. Cassidy believed. She'd read all the articles about people who seemed to be in persistent vegetative states but who suddenly woke up and asked for cornflakes; slowly, though, the reality set in. With the kind of equipment that existed, that just didn't happen anymore. But there was a million-in-one chance it could.

Mrs. Cassidy said, "The person who came most often is Eric, who's my business partner. I would ask him, 'Do you think she sees me?' And at first Eric would say, 'Maybe, I think so, Julia.'"

But in her hours alone, at night, Mrs. Cassidy had to admit that even if Emma had some level of awareness, like that of an exceptionally mentally challenged person, her daughter could not bear to live on, to signal her needs with a blink, for all the years left on earth to her, maybe after Mrs. Cassidy died.

Because we were coming, Mrs. Cassidy had washed and trimmed

and styled Emma's hair. As she always did, she tried to uncurl the crab-like clench of Emma's little fingers. They could be pried into a semblance of the attitude of a normal hand. But as soon as her mother let them go, they stubbornly curled again. Emma's brain wanted her fingers—and her small pale feet as well— to point in and down. Cortical contractions would be agony if the person felt them. Mrs. Cassidy had to believe Emma couldn't. But what if she did? For months now, Mrs. Cassidy's only relative, Ryan, a brother who lived in Florida, had said, "Julia, let her go." But her brother had no child, just a stepson he referred to as "The Couch," because the guy was twenty-three and had never had a job. When The Couch was a child, Mrs. Cassidy's brother didn't even know him.

"It's true that Emma was the vainest girl," said Mrs. Cassidy. "She had a will of iron, and if she got five pounds over the magic number on the scale, she could go a week and eat nothing but apples. Apples and water. And vitamin C. And D. Not long ago, I dreamed she came into my bed, like she used to when she was little, like she used to even when she was big when there was some huge windstorm or something—Emma was terrified of windstorms, because of *The Wizard of Oz*—and she said to me, *Mom, let me go to my daddy.* This was just recent, did I say that?"

Jared Cassidy had died very young. He'd fallen off the bleachers, drunk, after a softball game, and broken his neck, the year he and Julia were married. The fall couldn't have been more than six feet. But Mrs. Cassidy was only twenty then, and she still had Emma to live for. Emma grew up lovely and lively and enraptured by words and music, telling her mother that one day, she might write songs.

Then came the accident when Emma was sixteen, at a party. No one knew why. Emma had drunk one beer and felt dizzy, so she lay down on a friend's bed. By the time someone checked on her, she looked like she was napping but her lips were already dark; no one could tell how much she was breathing. "She had a strong young heart and they brought her back right away. But she never woke up," said

Mrs. Cassidy. "We prayed, and all the best brain people, the top ones in the Midwest, came to see her. She opened her eyes, but after a while I couldn't make believe she saw me."

For the longest time, Mrs. Cassidy said, having Emma at all was enough. At least she could care for her the way she had when Emma was a baby, washing between her toes and under the folds of her hard little arms, still hard from all those push-ups Emma had done since she was only, what? Twelve? She could read aloud to Emma and sing to her. She could climb into the bed beside Emma and fall asleep. Mrs. Cassidy could cut and style Emma's hair and whisper in her ear that she loved her little girl more than any mommy ever loved a little girl. And it was true that, even this way, she still did love Emma. She loved everything about Emma.

Beth got up at that point and said she had to wash her hands before she handled her film, but I knew that wasn't true. Beth had had a lot of grief in her life, but she hadn't seen as many heartbreaking and frankly gruesome things as I had, in my work and in my life, and Beth, unlike me, was a mother. I was pretty composed as Mrs. Cassidy went on and on; she needed to tell me these things, I supposed—about the fact that she more or less gave up eating and styling her own hair after Emma "was taken," but Eric had pointed out to her that it could be difficult for a client to have confidence in a stylist who did not seem to bother with her own appearance. "Eric said, 'Julia, you are still a young woman and a pretty woman, and you have to do something. Join a bowling league. Go to a gym.' But I considered it my duty to be at Emma's bedside."

When the muscle contractures had begun, it was the mark of no return. "The neurologist told me that even faith and hope have realistic limits." He said that when Mrs. Cassidy was ready—and that might not be for years—they would discuss options. She knew he meant organ donation, but when they did have that discussion, the neurologist also raised the subject of a face transplant. It was this that made Mrs. Cassidy see the way clear to stop the life support. She understood how it would be if Emma's strong heart and clear eyes and lungs never polluted by smoke would help someone else live and see and breathe. But Emma was beautiful. She was more beautiful than a real doll. "There were pictures of her as a child that my brother, Ryan, took, before he moved. He colored them with paints so they looked like oil paintings. There was one of Emma with her hair marcelled. And anyone who saw that picture said she was just a live doll, she was."

Ryan had come only once to see Emma, early on. It frightened him when Emma's eyes flew open.

"At first I could not sign the consent papers, and the doctor said there was no pressure. Emma was healthy, and this was not the kind of decision a person could make with her mind alone. Then I met a woman who had pulled the plug, right here. Her son was only ten. She said that the family felt that they were keeping a body without a soul. And that is when I made the commitment."

After a while, when there was nothing more to do, Beth set up her equipment and closed the blinds and then opened them again partway, without talking to anyone. I had known her for only two weeks, but I could see that she was furious. She set the little camera up on top and began to take pictures—dozens of pictures, a hundred pictures. When she was finished taking some, she would pass the camera over to Mrs. Cassidy without a word and show her the ones that Beth thought were best. I looked at them too.

"Now, Sicily, I would like a photo of you with Emma," Beth said, and her eyes were gleaming. Beth can be a hard one when she wants.

"I don't think so," I said. "I did, but now I'm scared."

"Before and after," Beth said.

"No one has taken a picture of my face in twelve years," I told her.

"Before and after," Beth said. "This was your idea."

So she took a picture in which you can see all of Emma's face but only a quarter of mine. The rest is covered by my hair. And the way it's shadowed haunts me. My hair is so dark and Emma's is so light that I later said to Beth that I looked like the Angel of Death. She said not to be dramatic.

When Beth said she was finished, Mrs. Cassidy took a deep breath and asked, "Beth, if it's no bother, would you take one of me with Emma?"

Beth nodded.

Mrs. Cassidy leaned down next to Emma, who started to wake up and move and thrash and make hissing noises through the respirator. Coma patients have waking and sleeping cycles. Beth was crying so hard by then that snot was running down over the corners of her lips and I kept giving her tissues. She finally got a picture in which it almost looked as though Emma was gazing up at her mother. Then Beth picked up her tripod, didn't even fold it, and, when she walked past me, said, "Screw this." I had to run to catch her in the parking lot.

Between that day at Sundial and this last morning had fallen away seventy-odd calendar days, each one longer as the hours flexed and stretched toward spring—days and nights of work on projects I needed to finish in order give myself fully to nothing but this, long days of interviews and of medical assays in all their variety, pages of spiked graphs describing my heart and respirations, tubes of my blood and Emma's in ranks like graduates in green and violet caps, images of Emma's gentle cheekbones and my vaulted cheekbones, eerie sculptures of Emma's sweetly pointed chin and my own, small but square and declarative, photos taken by Beth in which the shadows spoke as frankly as the light, stark photos taken by the hospital team in which every shadow was a potential pitfall. There had been six meetings with Mrs. Cassidy since the conference at the hospital, including a meal with my aunts and my grandparents, several afternoons that Beth and I spent at Sundial, and a dinner that Mrs. Cassidy had alone with me, during which she visibly flinched every time a new person came into the restaurant and was stopped in midstride by the sight of my face.

Where was Mrs. Cassidy right now? I knew that she had taken ten days off work, although she would barely be able to pay for Emma's funeral, to be held on Wednesday. This was Monday. "I just know that on the day, and afterwards, I wouldn't be worth anything with a scissors in my hand," she told me the last time we spoke. It had been just two days before, a conference call with the social worker, Kelli, who wanted everyone on the same page, even though these were pages that would have been separated by a whole blank book in a more orthodox scenario. Before she hung up, Mrs. Cassidy told me that her grandmother used to sing an old song to her, a lullaby that went "Sounds of the rude world, heard in the day, lulled by the moonlight have all passed away." She told me she was singing this to Emma for the last time.

"Do you do that every night?" I said.

"Yes," said Mrs. Cassidy.

"What's the name of it?"

"'Beautiful Dreamer.' The song is called 'Beautiful Dreamer,'" Mrs. Cassidy said. Even by pretending I had to cough, I couldn't cover up the sound of Kelli sniffling.

That first photo Beth had taken of Emma and me would not disappear from the easel in my mind. I lay counting the holes in the acoustical tile—as I had three dozen times over the course of a dozen years in a dozen hospital rooms just like this one—trying to calm down. Even I, not at all given to magical thinking, remembered that picture and was tempted to tally as prophecy each improbable element that had fallen into place. Looking through a series of linking crystals, each crystal the defeat of another obstacle to this end, I wanted to see the shimmer of some sort of fate on this enterprise for a magnificent outcome.

What if it were only adequate, only enough to draw off some of the stares and let me daintily siphon up my spaghetti? Would that mean I'd squandered Emma's gift? At last, I got out of bed and began pacing as far as the monitors would allow, two steps in one direction, then two back. A nurse came in, sat me back down, and said, "What's all this?" I couldn't tell her. I couldn't say anything coherent at all. She went off and brought back one of the anesthesiologists, who asked me if I was more than normally frightened.

"I'm not frightened at all," I said. "I'm overwhelmed."

The doctor asked me if I wanted ten milligrams of IV Valium. I said, "*Ten* milligrams? Are you kidding me?"

"Atta girl," said the anesthesiologist. She gave me twenty and I fell asleep.

When I woke, Hollis Grigsby was sitting on the foot of my bed, with her head in a paper cap and that pink quilt with photos of Emma on it across her knees. She looked more contemplative than I'd seen her through all the preparations.

"So, Sicily," she said. "Are you ready?"

"Is that for me?" I asked.

"Mrs. Cassidy wanted you to have it. She brought . . . other things for us to place around Emma."

"How is she?"

"She is remarkable," said Hollis. "Of course, she has her faith, and her faith sustains her."

"Are you religious?" I asked.

"I am," said Hollis. "I'm conventionally religious. I'm a Catholic woman, as you are. But I could not be a doctor if I believed that what happened to you and Emma Cassidy was the will of God."

"My aunt Christina would."

"Have I met her?"

I shook my head. "She'll come today to be with my aunt Marie and my grandparents and Kit. But she's a nun and hates to interrupt her nunning."

"Sicily, you make me smile," Hollis said.

"How do you think of God?"

"As a good parent, I should guess. Who cannot save us from all harm but can comfort us."

"Are you doing the surgery yourself?"

"No. I did the removal with Emma, primarily for her mother's sake."

"What am I, chopped liver?" It was an unfortunate choice of words.

"No, but you have a lifetime of healthy tomorrows ahead of you, and at this moment Julia Cassidy has only her yesterdays." Hollis got up and folded the quilt, laying it gently across my feet. "You have changed the mojo here, miss."

"How?"

"Well, ordinarily we would be exchanging anonymous letters years from now, not in advance of the surgery." She lifted a corner of the quilt and gave me a long, pure gaze. "You are also the youngest person ever to have a face transplant."

"I am?"

"Yes, by several years at least."

"Do you mind that I call you by your first name, Hollis?"

"No," she said. She reached up tall and stretched one side of her spine, then the other. "My grandfather called me Vanny, because I was supposed to be named Evangeline, after my mother. Once she was in delivery, my mother quickly decided that she would never go through labor again—although she did, four more times. She named me Hollis Evangeline, after both her parents. My grandfather didn't approve. He didn't approve of very much about me. Said a girl oughtn't have a boy's name. Said a woman wasn't cut out to be hoisting up dead men's arms and sticking them back on . . ." She began to laugh. "Everyone else in the family was so proud! Little skinny girl grows up to be a doctor! But not Grandfather."

"You loved him, though."

"Why, of course! He taught me some of the most important skills of doctoring I have."

"Like what?"

"Well, tying knots," Hollis said. "He taught me to tie every knot. To fillet a bluegill expertly. To set a bird's broken wing and calm it down at the same time. He never had a grandson, so I was the next best thing. Now, Sicily, we have talked enough. We are at the hour. I'm going to go ahead of you. I'll see you and Mrs. Cappadora in there."

"Thank you for telling me about your grandfather. I'm calm now."

"Good," Hollis said. "He lived to be ninety-nine, and he died on the same land where he was born. That should be true for us all. And he had his faith also. "

"Did he live to see your children?"

"Yes, he did," Hollis told me. "Grandfather died this morning."

On the gurney, I passed under the eyes of Aunt Marie and my grandmother and grandfather. Aunt Marie's face was blurry from crying. "Stop," I said. "It'll be all right."

"You don't have to do this," she said. "I've grown accustomed to your face."

"Everybody is being brave. Come on, Auntie. I have to be brave too. Plus, you can't let your viewing audience down." Hollis's courage and Mrs. Cassidy's were on my heart, as Baptists say, but I decided to see them as a witness to me. Aunt Marie had also taken a leave of absence—for the first time in her career. And on her show the previous Sunday, she had shown a photo of me as a child, a glimpse of footage from the fire, and photos of my father and my mother. She explained why I was doing this. There was no going back now.

Then I was in that cold room, being coddled like a child, swathed in blankets at last. I wanted that part to go on and on. Belatedly, though it didn't matter, I saw that there had been perks to being "special." I'd gotten away with doing and saying pretty much anything I wanted. Not right away, but in years to come, I would be just like everybody else, I hoped. Kit said as much at the family support meetings. She said, "I'm not going to be admired for being your friend anymore."

"I'm going to be better-looking than you too," I said. "Deal with it."

Finally I felt the silvery spurt of anesthetic burst into my veins, but not before Beth made a thumbs-up at me and pursed her lips in a kiss and Eliza smiled at me with her eyes over her mask. Then Dr. Grigsby came into the room with a parade of doctors, and I knew that what was veiled by a moist cloth on the tray that the slender male nurse was pushing so carefully was . . . Emma's face.

When I awakened, it was pitch-dark.

Beth picked up her camera and fiddled with a light and began to shoot right away, and Aunt Marie said, "They knocked you out properly." I lifted my arm and was surprised to see that my hand was not restrained, although I had more IV lines in more places than ever before, even one in my stomach. I asked, "Is it already night?"

"It's night on *Wednesday*," my aunt said. "You talked to us, but it was gibberish about your grandfather being dead. It scared Grandpa. He thought you were seeing heaven or something." She began to reach down to pull up my blankets, as an armada of nurses, ready to measure my levels of pain and awareness, slowly drifted into the enormous room I had to myself.

But Beth said, "Wait. One second." Everyone stopped. As she moved closer and began to shoot steadily, I willed my hand to slowly brush against the bandages on my face. Beneath their dry thicknesses, I could feel geography. I had a mouth. I had a nose.

CHAPTER NINE

Hollis Grigsby came back from her grandfather's funeral in Louisiana for the moment that Beth and Eliza had begun to call "the unveiling." It was five days after the surgery and I was so not okay with it. For one thing, I didn't want to leave the hospital. Six days seemed like an awfully brief stint in the hospital for having your face removed and replaced. The real issue, though, was that it seemed as though my new face, whatever it looked like, would be something I would have to carry in front of me on a tray, as that nurse had in the OR, for the rest of my life. I could not imagine ever picking at a zit or getting hit with a volleyball or, my God, getting a tattoo or something. Or even putting on lipstick. I had never put on lipstick. At the age of thirteen, I hadn't ever had anything except chocolate lip balm. I would defile the face. I would run into something, because I would not be used to it, and break the nose.

My nose.

Not "the" nose.

I had to remind myself that the face was me, a part of me now, not something that I would attach before work. It made me mental.

"This is normal," Polly Guthrie said.

"Is there anything that *isn't* normal?" I asked her, shushing through my bandages. "It's not normal to feel like my face before, which looked like a mask, was real and this face, which is real, is a mask. That's pathology, Polly!"

"No, in your case, that's normal. Sicily, say you had gotten married. You'd have changed your name—"

"Hell, no, I wouldn't have done that!"

"Okay. You don't make anything easy, do you?"

"I'm not normal," I said.

"Touché. So, say you would have, and your name was now Sicily Smith. For months and even years after you got married, you would self-identify as Sicily Coyne. You'd be at work and look down at your wedding band and say, Oh, my gosh, I'm *married*! It would be a new page in your life. It would take getting used to." Polly looked at her watch. It annoyed me that, even at this moment, I was not her top priority. "If you were . . . pathological, you would continue to see your face as a thing. You'd treat it badly."

"I think I'll probably treat it too goodly."

"I can guarantee you that from what I know of you so far, within a year you'll be using, like, washing grains on your face and plucking your eyebrows—"

"Blond," I interrupted.

Polly jumped. She was a blonde and thought I was insulting her.

"Are they blond? My eyebrows?" Emma was a blonde. Had been a blonde. My hair was a dark reddish-brown, like my mom's. I hadn't taken the opportunity to look at the mirror (*in* the mirror! What was the matter with me?) when they changed my dressings, even though everyone made approving noises. Technically I wasn't supposed to, but I hadn't done anything else by the book, so it would have been okay.

"No, she wasn't really blond," Polly said. "Her hair was touched up. Her eyebrows are lighter than your hair, but it's not a big thing."

"Does my skin match?"

"Better than most," Polly said. "It's as if you'd worn SPF seventy-five on your face but not your arms. Like most people." Polly was reassuring, but I could tell she had more to say. It was two days before "the unveiling," and she had to warn me of everything that could be strewn along the road ahead. "The thing is, when you first see your face, it's not going to look the way it will in two months. Or anything like it will in four months. The advantage of your being so young is that you'll heal like a kid. That's not true for people who are forty. That's why those movie stars have plastic surgery and can deny it six weeks later. But there is loose skin under your chin that will have to be trimmed."

"Trimmed?" I knew this, but hearing it was a different matter. Months before, Polly had shown me pictures of Connie Washburn, the fourth or fifth transplant victim—*Patient! Recipient! Sicily, please!* And her face looked like a blimp with these little slits for eyes. Before her husband had done her the courtesy of throwing acid in her face because she'd grown tired of his beating the crap out of her and left him (he did seven years for this; we are such a forgiving society), Connie Washburn had been . . . gorgeous, this fresh-scrubbed tennis-player-looking woman. Afterward, she was ordinary. Plain.

"Yes, you will have to have that skin trimmed, in a minor surgical procedure, a same-day affair."

"Can we just take the bandages off now? And get it over with?"

"Sic-il-y," said Polly. She sounded like my grandma Caruso. "You waited twelve years for this. You can wait until day after tomorrow."

On the day, Beth arrived before the doctors. The sun wasn't even up. "Go away," I told her. "I'm sleeping."

"You remind me of Ben," she said. "He's lucky he works nights. He could sleep around the clock. He once slept eighteen hours. Won't be for long, though."

"Why?"

"Eliza's pregnant," Beth said. "Four months. Stella's going to have a little brother or sister! I'm going to be a grandmother again. Which is probably the only time that will ever happen. Eliza thinks two is the limit, with the way they both work. Vincent will never find a woman who'll put up with him, and Kerry wants to be the only opera singer ever to have a waist."

I was lucky then that the bandages hid my face. This was a sentence I might never hear. It was like a punch in the stomach. I banished the thought. Enough. Aunt Marie had shown me that love didn't necessarily derive from genetics—although, when I thought about it, she was more closely related to me genetically than anyone else on earth. I don't count Christina, who is actually prettier than Marie but who gives me the creeps, still.

Beth said, "Sicily. I hurt your feelings."

"No . . ."

"Yes, I did. Don't deny it. By now you'd have been married."

"No, two months from today, actually."

"Sicily, oh Sicily. This whole thing asks way too much of you. You knew this going in but that's not the same as the reality, is it?"

"It really is okay, Beth."

"You know it's not!"

It wasn't okay. But it was. It was both. So much of me now was both. It sounds odd to say that someone who as a child had lost both her parents and her face could be happy-go-lucky, and I had not been happy-go-lucky. But I had been happy. I'd been happy most of the time with my aunt and with my friends, and I'd been happy especially since Joey and I had fallen in love—or since I had fallen in love and before Joey had revealed himself to be a lying sack of shit. In truth, I still missed Joey. I missed his voice and still listened to it on the cell-phone messages I had kept. I missed his body, his arms holding me against him, the solid male chest. I couldn't hold anyone else's body that way. I missed being someone's, other than my aunt's. For a moment, I missed the baby Joey and I would have had. How can you miss something you never knew? It was as if I had gone forward and backward in life at the same time, as though I had been on an animated ride at Disney World—to which I had never been. Polly would have told me they were "normal" feelings when, in truth, generalizing on the basis of something that had happened at most a few hundred times was not a sampling I trusted.

The Virginia grandfather, whom I had phoned, was quite possibly the least communicative man who wasn't on a respirator. When I tried to dig for answers, he said, "That's probably true" or "I guess so" or "By and large." He was already married before the transplant. He'd already had children, who were now in college—except for the one who'd dropped out and had a child, and she and her baby lived with them. He said he could now breathe much better while he was asleep, and eating was such a pleasure that he'd gained twenty pounds.

Why had I expected people whose faces had been transplanted to be dramatic, singular, and insightful? They were ordinary people who had bad luck and who Dr. Grigsby and her sidekick, Livingston, had transformed into ordinary people again. If I felt this way, antsy and verging on depressed, before I even saw my face, how would I feel afterward?

Beth asked me, "Are you scared?"

"Would you be?"

"I think I'd be puking."

"I have a strong stomach."

There was a rustle in the hall and Kit slipped into the room.

She'd come twice before to the hospital, once on the day of my surgery and once while I was recovering. But we were in a relationship trough, which occurred every time Kit fell in love with another lousy guy. Through each of these hiatuses, I missed her, as I had missed her when she was away at college. For four years, I hadn't seen Kit during fall or winter except when the Hawkeyes were on TV and once when I'd gone to a game with Marie. At the game, the cold punished my face and I had to leave early. Though Kit eagerly wanted me to stay with her at the Kappa Delta house, had I been ready to socialize with girls out-

side my acquaintance, I would not have picked Big Ten cheerleaders
for the test group. With utmost care, Kit chose men who considered
themselves desperadoes of love, were not at all as cool as nerds, and
didn't know how to use computers. Kit worked in computers, creating
the online platform for Fair Made, the big green-cosmetics store. She
would say computer things that even I didn't get, like, "You have to up-
load these on a ASCI DUB bedrock with a coda builder streaming on
a Kibbly Bits Tin Foiler." She found the guys' ignorance of her life en-
dearing. It was an annoying part of being Kit's friend. The glory days
would be spent with her other friends: Mia Zanoni, the twins Merit
and Marta Moore-Grossman, or Francie Bach. The slow, excruciating
defenestration, however, was just for me. We drove past houses, left
notes on cars at bars, and made hang-up calls. When my aunt was a
kid, it was easy to make hang-up calls, or so she says. As difficult as it
was now, Kit always managed. And she always managed to blame herself.

Kit would say, "I'm like a moth to the flame," which sounded like
the limp lyrics her boyfriends wrote. I would tell her, "You're more like
a horse to strychnine." But Kit had excuses: The guy was "so obviously
a Pisces." Or she'd just noticed that she had a mirror instead of a water
jug in the relationship corner of her feng shui setup. And she believed
in all that stuff.

"If it were true," I'd tell her, "everyone would believe it." Kit would
point out that there *was* a horoscope section in the newspaper. I loved
Kit. And I didn't want to lose her. But I needed more friends, maybe
some who didn't start each day with the tarot.

Mutants can't be choosers, though.

I wasn't surprised that she came to the hospital. But I was stunned
that she'd brought Marc-Until-Labor-Day. While we were having a
fifteen-minute fight about my willingness to push her out the ninth-
story window rather than let him into this room, Hollis showed up
with Livingston and what seemed to be about twenty other doctors,
some of them not even part of the practice of reconstructive surgery.
They were just . . . interested. Why wouldn't they have been?

Hollis said, "Are you ready, Sicily?"

"I'd like everyone to leave, please," I replied. Nobody left. "I don't mean you and Beth and Eliza and Kit, I mean the other professional people. And I don't mean forever, but for a few moments? I just want to have a private moment to . . . uh, meet myself."

So Hollis banished everyone, except we six women, with a gentle shooshing motion. "Now," she said, "let's get to the good part." She began to unfurl the bandages. Although I had medication to dull the pain, I don't think there would have been much. It takes time for the nerves to activate after being reconnected. Even the muscles would need weeks to really motivate, although basic things, such as being able to open and close the mouth, would be pretty established. Hollis sat down with a big mirror on her lap. "You hold it," she said. "When you are ready, go ahead."

I went ahead.

It was like the boy with the corneas, like looking into the sun. Although the face was swollen, it was not so swollen as I'd expected it to be. It looked like the face of a girl who'd been in a skiing accident. I say that I looked like a girl, not like a woman seven years older, which, even in the moment, seemed to be a bonus. I felt as though I was looking at a TV. Then I saw my own eyes and I made them answer me. I saw my own . . . expression, my nature, under the face. Both my mother and father had strong, sharp noses. Now I had a pert Irish nose with a little tip-tilt at the end of it. My chin was still square, but my Irish bonbon of a mouth was replaced with a brick-pink pout. I touched the lower lip, felt its contours, plump and firm, almost too exaggerated for prettiness. It was a really good mouth, almost cosmetic.

"Sicily," Hollis said. "Beautiful."

"Not Sicily. Not really Sicily. But it's wonderful," I told her. And the general exhalation in the room would have made my hair blow back if it hadn't already been contained by a white cotton headband. Beth had been snapping away the whole time, but she stopped then.

Hollis said, "Sicily, it's early yet, but can you try to move your face?

Don't do anything that feels unnatural. Just try to do something. This isn't a test, my dear."

I expected it to feel like trying to use a robot arm to grasp one of those toys in a vending machine. It did feel slow and a little stiff. But I smiled.

Eliza burst into tears.

Kit said, "My God, Sissy. It looks like your smile. It looks like your own teeth."

"They are my own teeth," I told her. But I was caught on the prongs between joy and distress myself. I said, "Propose. Pompous. Propaganda. Primate. Profligate. Priest. Popular. Bubbles. Bunches. Benefits. Booster . . . Baby."

Aunt Marie said, "This is a miracle. Oh, Sicily. Oh, my Sicily. Oh, Dr. Grigsby, thank you. Thank you. If her mother could see this."

I smiled then, again. I had a dimple. It was as though I was cherishing something newborn but also familiar, back after a long while. I smiled and my throat closed and, though I did not cry, I felt as though something frozen was melting.

I suppose something was.

CHAPTER TEN

Now began the loneliest period of my life.

Something was missing. I assumed it was that singular purpose for which I had strived and had expected would descend upon me, like some raiment from heaven, conferring a sense of achievement. But I had achieved nothing. Hollis had. Mrs. Cassidy had. Even lost Emma had, in her way, if I believed in a consciousness after death, by endowing a community of mortals with her generous spirit.

But I?

I should have hit my knees, morning and night, and thanked God for my reclamation. But to what purpose was the reconstituted Sicily? What was I meant to do beyond the completion of my facial surgery? I had no larger ambitions than any other twenty-five-year-old with an adequate job. I did have an insufficiency of guts and enterprise to search out what more I could do. I'd spent my life building a tough, supple body that I daily put behind a desk in front of a computer. Had all that sweat equity been to foster vanity and defeat depression? Should I actually try choreography now? Should I train as a volunteer paramedic and literally put my strong back and my medical knowledge out on the street? I certainly had the spare time. Hollis told me that my ordinary life was exemplary and that if there was to be something further required of me, it would become apparent. She added, furthermore, that life was not a horse race. I met with Polly Guthrie weekly—which I would do, apparently, until one of us died.

"I like you, Polly," I said. "But what am I supposed to be confiding?"

"Whatever you like," she said.

"I keep waiting to figure out when all this is going to be ordinary to me."

"That's going to take a long time, Sicily. You have to be patient with yourself and heal slowly, physically and psychologically."

"I've done slowly forever! Tell me how I can catch up to everyone else."

"Next week let's talk about feeling left behind."

"Next week? For how long?"

"It's the law, Sicily," Polly said.

"The law?"

Polly had rarely shown any discernible sense of humor. But now she said, "The law that guarantees full employment for psychologists."

As for the photographic documentary, Beth was doing the heavy lifting on what we had named "Fate-to-Face: A Physical Hymn." She came often to my house and sometimes went with me through my days, photographing me at the computer, at the ballet barre—once even capturing my shadow on the wall while I tried to execute a *grand jeté* in a small space. Beth photographed me in silhouette against my windows and peering into my bathroom mirror, my hands framing my still-swollen face. One that I still love is of me holding in my hand what appears at first to be an unusual little piece of primitive pottery—in fact, my prosthetic nose. Of all the pictures from that early time, my favorite is of my smile the first time since I was a kid that I fully tasted and felt the texture of a cannoli. The whole photo is one of my eyes and a quarter of my turned-up smile, displaying the mascarpone and powdered sugar on my upper lip. I look like a little kid on Christmas morning. In fact, as I experimented with the joy of eating normally, I no longer could content myself with my supereasy supermodel diet— scrambled eggs for the protein, spinach and nuts for the fiber, apples and peanut butter so I could tell Marie I'd eaten dinner. In six weeks, I gained ten pounds. I started eating crap, like taco chips and dough-nuts, stuff my mother never allowed me and for which I had no use as an adult. I got takeout and gleefully devoured quart cartons of lo mein and big, gloppy, dripping-with-everything cheeseburgers, which I could finally, literally, sink my teeth into. Beth brought me a pound of lobster fra diavolo from their restaurant, The Old Neighborhood, which I ate in one sitting. I chugged green tea lattes and mocha lattes and pump-kin lattes. I sampled wine and cheese and more wine. Although I com-pensated with extra miles on the treadmill, all I could do was walk, at least for another month—no running. There were no weights, no strenuous dance. For the first time in my life, I had trouble zipping my jeans.

I learned why food is a substitute for pretty much everything else.

Living the mainstream life to the degree I'd managed seemed to most people more than a sufficient achievement: The common herd would have admired me even for being able to put one foot in front of the other. My face had restored me to the crowd but also upped the stakes—the way April reproaches someone who's spent the winter hid-ing her butt under a big sweater. I had done my reading. There's a hol-low feeling some people experience when they think cosmetic surgery is going to change their whole lives totally. They think they'll get good men and six-figure jobs. They think they'll dress up and be proud. They're heartbroken when they end up the same not-terribly-dynamic people but with bigger boobs or smaller noses or tauter chins. I was pretty sure I'd gone ahead with this for something bigger, and yet noth-ing had changed.

I loved my face, especially as it slowly emerged from the surgical trauma. Every day there were fewer and lighter bruises. I could begin to see the chin and cheekbones I would have in a few more weeks. Marie accused me of falling in love with my reflection. I had. I could have *climbed into* a mirror. I looked at the poignant pictures of me in Beth's house the day I met her, which would not be part of the magazine piece planned for *Sense and Sensibility* (all was forgiven after they saw Beth's portrait of Emma, Mrs. Cassidy, and me). I wondered how I had lived so long. When you move out of a house you have sheltered in, you notice that the carpets are worn and the walls scuffed, that your pictures have left holes in the walls and vivid rectangles of the color the paint was before time and sunlight did their work. You once snuggled up and watched old black-and-white movies on the couch you'll leave at the curb, but outside in the sunlight it looks shabby and disreputable. How did you keep it so long? My face had been dreadful. I had thoughts that made me ashamed, that somehow, down the road—when the first year ended and Beth found the right gallery for an exhibit—I would want to hide the pictures that before had seemed so raw and moving. I would want to leave them at the curb and disown them.

Having a life and having my life, it turned out, were two different things. Polly the psychologist was right. I had trouble reentering the world. For the people in groups who stayed home, mostly alone and out of sight, I'd felt pity. I'd also felt—and this was disturbing—scorn. I'd been quite the adventurer, in a circle so tight and small that, not counting clients, everyone could have gathered at a table for ten. At thirteen, I hadn't even been old enough to ride the train downtown with my girlfriends. My young woman's life had been my boyfriend, my job, my few girlfriends, and my family. I had never traveled. That was a big one. Every summer, my parents and I went for a week to Uncle Al's house on Lake Madrigal. Every winter, my mother and I rode in a sleeper car on the Empire Builder to Grand Central Station for a weekend with Aunt Marie in New York—on Marie's dime. I'd gone skiing with Kit's family at her parents' place in Vermont. Her dad drove. I had never been in an airplane or on a boat or a Ferris wheel or dived off a diving board. I had never obtained a passport or a driver's license, just a student ID. I'd never seen an ocean.

Here I was, having lived an epic life. I'd lost my family and my face but had never been in a book club. While I could speak Italian, I couldn't cook it. I could draw you a snazzy sketch of the gastrointestinal system but not knit a potholder. Now that my life didn't need to be compact, I had no idea how to expand it. For every disfigured or disabled person who hid away, there turned out to be ten others on a carousel of causes and confraternities. Polly and Kelli encouraged me to reach out to kids on burn wards—to offer hope to them by my example. They suggested I join support or even social groups. Kit proposed I create a romantic personal ad on an Internet service, or, as Aunt Marie said in acid tones, make a date with my very own murderer online. Polly said she would suggest weekly group therapy, along with my weekly one-on-ones, but my emotions were "normal." Kelli thought it would be good for me just to talk those emotions out with people in different parts of the city, even online. Two months after my surgery, through Polly, I met a guy online four or five years older who'd had a face transplant *and* a hand transplant—the result of a bad farming accident. (There are no good ones: Everything on a farm, from a cow to a combine, can mess you up completely.) He was very nice and funny. He said he used to imagine his profile for a dating service: FORMERLY FACELESS FARMER SEEKS FRIENDLY FRAU.

Together, we made up mine: I HAVE: A NEW FACE, A NEW LIFE, NEW ROSES, AND SEVERAL AWARDS FOR DRAWING TUMORS. YOU HAVE: LOW STANDARDS AND A PULSE.

I thought we might be friends, but when it came to posting a picture for me to see him, he would not do it. What he told me was that he would have been glad to meet me on the street—if I hadn't known about his surgery—and he would have told me about it later. My knowing in advance made him not confident but self-conscious. I had taken a picture with my computer cam and sent it to him, so I felt cheated, awkward.

We lost touch.

All through the long, cicada nights of that long summer, I kept waiting for . . . something.

Of course, I worked. In advance I'd planned a few months of working from home. Until the worst of the swelling subsided—and I got
that facial "trim"—there would be no disconcerting meetings with
clients, no annoying double takes.

It wasn't as though I hid under the bed. There was a big dinner for
the main doctors and nurses and my family. There was Beth. There
was Eliza, who turned out to have exactly the personality she would
need for the work she wanted to do. She was caring and noticing. On
what would have been my wedding day, she made a point of asking me
in advance to have dinner at her house. She made Ethiopian food, the
hottest stuff I'd ever eaten, so hot it made me sweat while I ate. Stella
had Rice Krispies, and, afterward, Eliza let her watch *The Little Mer-
maid* until she fell asleep in a big recliner. That night, Ben came home
early—for him—at about ten o'clock. I'd met Ben only once, but he
was a person you already seemed to know before you met him. I asked
about the rest of the family.

"I had two brothers in Bolivia," Eliza said. "Older. Alejandro and
Cruz. They were good boys. I loved them. The memory of them goes
away more every year. I can remember Cruz swinging me up over
something, like a well, and pretending he was going to drop me. And
when I went to the orphanage, Alejandro cried and gave me blue
shoes."

"Do they write to you? Or call you?"

"No," Eliza said. "Ben and I have talked about trying to find them. I
don't want to yet. They knew me as Maria Agata. For a long time, I was
surprised to hear 'Eliza,' and then 'Maria Agata' began to sound odd to
me, like it would if you said, 'Spoon, spoon, spoon,' over and over until
it lost its meaning."

"The real reason is Candy," said Ben. "Her mom."

"Your mom doesn't want you to contact your brothers? Or your
mother? Your real mother?"

Eliza said gently, "Candy is my real mother, Sicily. And I'm not trying to be sentimental or politically correct. I just can't imagine I would love anyone more than my mother. And she would be fine with my seeing Cruz and Alejandro. It's me. I don't want her to feel she failed me."

"I know," I said. "I know and I don't know. I wasn't as young when my mother died, but when I think of my mother, I think of Marie first and then of my mother, the way she was when I was little."

"I didn't know my mother after I was four," Eliza said. "She died. I lived with my brothers and my aunt. And, you know, they were good boys, relatively. But they worked for . . . the drug trade. And my aunt was a prostitute, as my mother had been." She said it so matter-of-factly.

"Is that why she died?" I asked. "Did she die of AIDS?"

"No," Eliza said. "A man beat her to death." I gasped, then tried to hide it with a cough. "It's okay, Sicily. I didn't see her death. I don't remember her really at all. The nuns were pretty cute and terrific, and I had clean clothes for the first time and TV and . . ."

"And food," Ben said. "Regular meals. She doesn't talk about it, but there were plenty of days when it was a little rice and that was it. The orphanage was her Four Seasons."

Eliza, not Ben, drove me home. She said she liked to drive downtown at night. She had gone to undergrad school at Northwestern and sometimes wished that she still lived in the city. "It never closes," she said. "You watch the people and it's like a performance." There was still so little I could say to her, and I was not a person customarily at a loss for words. Eliza's life had been brutal. Mine had been brutal but also sheltered. I could not imagine wanting for food. Before I got out, Eliza kissed me on both cheeks. "I hope you don't get sick from my cooking."

When I lay down that night, I realized that I had not thought of where I would have been since I'd awakened that morning. Kit was right. I had gotten over Joe.

In those first eight weeks, Kit also insisted I go out, pointing to the obvious irony. "Out," she said. "Not to someone's house. Out. We'll start slowly. With the deli."

So we went to Myzog's, where the wreck I had been before was as familiar to patrons as the henna on the waitresses' shellacked updos.

People stared at me more than they had when I was the girl who had no face. My face *now* made people uneasy in a different way. With my swollen cheeks and the big dewlap of skin under my chin, which was not removed until July, I looked like I had neurofibromatosis—and, yes, I know how that sounds. Once, back in college, for a life-drawing class (we did have to be able to render perfectly from life, despite the fact that the sixth of seven generations of Illustrator and Photoshop were up and running), I used charcoal to draw a woman who had neurofibromatosis, which is commonly known as Elephant Man Disease. Her tumors were like tentacles, burrowed and bursting under the skin of her face and neck and back. She insisted that she would not risk neurological damage by having them removed. It was better for her to have a face that looked like a kind of root vegetable than a mouth that wouldn't close. She brought her grandson, and I heard other students—right in front of me—marvel that somebody had married her. The boy was about three. After he laid waste to all the pens and sketch pads we weren't fast enough to grab, my professor put him on the floor with some old Cray-Pas and a sheet of paper as big as he was. Professor Arneson told him if he could fill the whole thing with different-colored squiggles, there would be a giant Kit Kat at the end. (Arneson weighed about eighty pounds and ate supersize Kit Kats all day, washing them down with cold black coffee. I'm sure she threw it up or had some disease like pica that made her eat strange things because her body needed trace minerals.) The little kid was diligent. He took forty minutes to cover that page with snakes and lightning strikes, but he did it. The drawing of his grandmother, with her strange fairy-tale-creature face, looking down at him is one of the only pictures of my own I've ever framed.

Until the surgeons removed the flap of skin that was left over under my chin, I wouldn't go shopping with Kit—or almost anywhere in daylight. Which was nuts. I'd gone shopping at the freaking Mall of America when I looked like a baseball that had been whacked once too often. Now, however, I wanted to be . . . not transitional. When I went out into the sun, I wanted to be finished.

Loyally, Kit took me to the Green Mill and listened to Nicky Hixon sing Ella in the darkness that smelled of salt and vodka. We did not go to Slicker Sam's or Jimmy O's. I had unreasonable fears that I'd run into Paul LaVoy—or even worse, Neal. What would I do? Scream? Slap them? The one open-range outing Kit and I took, to a street fair near my hometown, was just terrific. We did encounter several high-school friends. They could not have reacted with more dignity or enthusiasm. *Sissy!* they cried. *We heard your voice and knew it was you! Or, This is so amazing . . . You look like . . . yourself! You're beautiful, Sicily!*

They were right. In some eerie way, the more time passed, the more the swelling subsided, the more I looked like I would have looked. When the excess skin under my jaw was removed, it was a cursory procedure by an ordinary cosmetic surgeon that left a tiny line of a scar. The swelling subsided within what seemed days, revealing my strong, firm jawline. And I was pretty, as pretty as I would have been, as pretty as sweet lost Emma deserved to grow up to be.

My art-major professor at UIC had been Gary Gottfried, which is like saying I was taught to be a medical illustrator by Walt Disney. Dr. Gottfried was a real artist, whose medical paintings hung in museums and public buildings—the one tracing the history of ophthalmologic surgery took up a whole wall at the Eye Institute in Philadelphia. The program at the University of Illinois Chicago Circle accepted only twelve candidates a year. Some of Professor Gottfried's best had gone on to be movie animators, biomedical engineers, and fine artists, although none, I think, ended up doing what I finally ended up doing.

In the second week in September, he asked me to visit his senior class for a small seminar.

"When Sicily began her studies here, I knew she was one of the few who would actually be a medical illustrator," Dr. Gottfried said. "Because of her history, she had a passion for helping to show the how and why of the mysteries of the body, in sickness and in health, the macro and the micro, the beautiful and the fearsome. She was the illustrator's illustrator, with an eye for precision and beauty and a knack for speed."

I was blushing. Blushing was one of the new weird sensations that accompanied this perfect skin, along with no visible pores.

"But I never knew that my personal destiny would intersect with Sicily Coyne's in the way it has." It was Dr. Gottfried, back in the 1980s, who had created the software for age progression, which was originally used to help the FBI find missing children, based on how they would have looked years after they were abducted. At UIC, the transplant team used that software to design the way that my face, last seen at thirteen, would look at twenty-five. In fact, it was also used with Ben Cappadora, when he turned up, nine years after he was kidnapped, with the husband of the nut-job woman who'd taken him—a nice guy who never knew that the little boy he adopted as his own was stolen from someone else.

Identity is a weird thing.

Now in the mirror I began to see Sicily—but it was a Sicily I had never seen. Sicily a woman. Sicily with Emma's turned-up little Irish nose.

When I had coffee with Mrs. Cassidy after Dr. Gottfried's class, she asked if she could touch my skin. She started to cry, and I held her while she did. She said, "Emma . . . Emma." That very night—I could have predicted this—I woke up screaming, so loudly that my aunt came pounding on the connecting door between our apartments. I dreamed I opened my eyes and Emma was standing there in her long lace nightgown, and she had no . . . well, you can imagine. She said, "Bitch, give me back my face."

That week, Polly finally had to do her job as it was construed. Something was finally not a normal reaction. I was certifiably depressed, more than I had been after my parents' deaths. I didn't get excited when I woke up. Music didn't set me in motion. Polly said that if it lasted too long, she would refer me to a psychiatrist who could prescribe something. *Why,* I asked Polly? *Why now?* I had been sad. I had been frightened. I had been fiercely angry. But never, ever, until I looked like a pretty girl with a barely visible necklace of scar in the curve of her neck, had I been depressed.

"I'm not a directive kind of psychologist," Polly said. "But I would guess you feel guilty."

Well, there you have it. I had outlived everyone, and I looked good too.

Emma was innocent. She died and I survived and then I thrived. Her mother had nothing but this bittersweet satisfaction for the sacrifice of Emma's body to the whole tortilla. My father had died and he could not see me restored. His last glimpse of his only little girl was alive but who knew how damaged? My poor mother would never see me except as the human equivalent of a boiled potato.

I began sleeping too much. As in, noon was early.

Whenever I hauled myself out of bed, I worked on this project for Frank Bom, the TV doc who had the show *The BOM!* about *health topics that concern you.* I was making an animated presentation of the way flu antibodies captured and fought off the H2N, what everyone called the Zoo Flu, to be projected on a green screen that Dr. Bom could move around with his hands. It was a cool-looking project, if I do say so, because, of course, nobody knows what color a virus is—and so we can imagine they're anything we want. We can make them yellow and purple and neon-blue, like spined sea creatures, and set them moving in the artistic version of an acid trip—although that was another thing I hadn't done. I was still a recreational-drug virgin.

It was when Beth saw my preliminaries for that up on my screen that she invited me to come along with her to California.

"How would that move?" she said. I showed her.

"Get out of here!" she said. "That's amazing!"

"It's not that difficult," I told her. "Medical illustrators believe that God's middle name is Mac."

"That's like digital photography. Sometimes I use my medium-format camera just to prove to myself that I'm still human. If you can erase your mistakes, you start believing you never made them."

"But the results look different," I said.

"Nowadays, with that," Beth gestured to the computer, "you can make anything look like a painting. But, yes, really, you can't replace the large-format-camera or a medium-format-camera look. When you look at a picture by Richard Avedon or Alfred Stieglitz, that painterly thing that's going on . . . For our thing, I want to mix it up, black and white and color, snapshots and set-up portraits. But tell me about this computer-drawing thing. Aren't there people who are better than others? Software can't make an artist out of a dud."

"No, but it can make a working graphics designer from somebody who just knows what she likes."

"Vincent should see this," she told me. "Vincent is my son who's the filmmaker?"

"Beth, I still had eyes and ears. And my aunt is a TV news anchor."

Beth shrugged and made a pistol out of her hand, which she fired at me.

"Vincent is making an animated film now. It's about this guy who shrinks to the size of a cell or something to go after this bacteria that a terrorist has voluntarily put into his own body, and he's spreading it all over the Midwest, at county fairs and zoos . . ."

"How original," I said.

"Isn't it?" Beth said. "It's so cool!"

Obviously, Beth had not seen *The Fantastic Voyage,* the corny old classic about the ultra-miniaturized submarine *Proteus,* which carried two surgeons through the bloodstream to do microcosmic surgery on a brilliant scientist, who had a secret that could save the world but was unavoidably detained by a coma. Back in the day when that movie was made, Beth would have been a kid. But all movie culties knew about it. I didn't have the heart to tell Beth that somebody had more or less had the same idea as Vincent, and back when his mom was eating crayons. I liked Beth. Sort of in the aunt-ly way I didn't feel about my own aunt. I didn't want the little goldy lights in her green eyes to go dull. *The Fantastic Voyage* was based on a famous Isaac Asimov story. Remakes happen all the time. Probably, Vincent's twist (in our terrorism-obsessed country) would be a big hit anyhow. People who remembered *The Fantastic Voyage* and *The Abyss* and those other wacky sci-fi medico things would take their grandchildren to see it. The computer animation would be over the top now.

I thought about it for a moment.

"If they know who the guy is well enough to send this molecular inner space guy after him, why don't they just take a gun and shoot him?" I asked Beth.

"There's a reason," she said. "I think that it's either two guys or that he'd blow up and infect everyone for fifty square miles if they did that. In fact, yeah, I think he's like a human time bomb, going around infecting, and then he's going to blow up in Times Square. Or something."

"It's always Times Square. Terrorists are just drawn to it."

"Filmmakers are just drawn to it. Times Square is always there," Beth said. "Anyhow, why don't you come with me to California? I'm going out there because the Ossum Tate Gallery wants the photos for a show, after the magazine piece runs in *Sense and Sensibility*. I'm demanding a main gallery, and they agreed. They're going to have to do it up big, a whole reception thing and the right press."

"I don't go places, Beth. The thought of getting on an airplane makes me want to throw up on your shoes. I would have to be sedated."

"Don't," said Beth. "I like these shoes. But come on! Vincent lives in Venice Beach. It's this cute town haunted by old Hollywood types, gorgeous lioness faces on these withered-up bodies. He has a cute little house. He used to live in a house—I'm not kidding—that was a guy's garage." She stopped and got out her camera and began to circle me, shooting close in. "He sold that garage for about two hundred grand. Life out there is nutso. It's Halloween every day. Maybe he would want you to work with the computer animators as an adviser."

"He's probably got plenty of advisers."

"Not advisers who are real medical illustrators, I bet."

"He could probably find one."

"You'd probably be cheaper than anyone who'd ever worked in the movies." Beth stopped shooting. "What? What's wrong? I didn't ask *you* to blow yourself up in Times Square. You could stay at a bed-and-breakfast if you feel funny staying with him and me. It would be interesting—your first trip as a person who looks just like any other person. Are you afraid to visit my family?"

"No, I visit your family all the time. I like your family."

At least half a dozen other times since that first dinner, Eliza and I had gotten together. We'd taken Stella to the Brookfield Zoo. But now, her pregnancy advancing, Eliza was literally dragging, with barely enough energy for her patients. Kit wasn't so attentive anymore either, although I expected her back momentarily. Fall had come, and Kit's romance with Marc-Until-Labor-Day had inevitably entered decline. Soon she would be by my side, as I rode shotgun and tried to see if there was more than one black Toyota Camry in a dark parking lot behind wretched Marc's ex-wife's apartment building.

I thought about Beth's offer. I wanted to see California, the ocean, and Vincent. I'd never met a filmmaker. It might even lift my general misery, for which I now honestly considered needing medication.

"I can't get on an airplane," I told Polly Guthrie. "It's out of the question."

"Well, easy does it," Polly said. "At least you're identifying your fears. You'll do what you need to do, in your own time." My sigh of relief was genuine. I had Polly's official permission not to go to California. I had a medical stamp that permitted me to be . . . something I had never imagined myself being. A coward.

"I want to go, though," I said.

"Like I said, Sicily, slow and easy."

"I want to go now. I want to knock down one of the fears."

"Well, what would make it easier?"

"I'm all for drugs," I said.

"I'm all for going for it," Polly said. She said she'd ask Dr. Grigsby to give me a prescription for six tablets of diazepam, five milligrams.

"Please, Polly," I said. "I may not be the size of a wrestler, but this body is a one-woman drug cartel."

She agreed to ten mils, fifteen of them. Within days, Kelli Buoté, the social worker, had arranged for me to have a new UIC student ID and to have my Depo-Provera birth-control shot a week early. Its effects waned at the end of the three-month period in any case, Polly said.

"I so don't even need it," I told her.

"It helps control acne," said Polly, who was becoming quite the jokester.

Finally, I called Beth. "Remember California?"

"Yes."

"If you still want me to come with you, I'm . . . I'm game," I said. "I'm not really game. But I would love to go. I am terrified of the airplane, of anything that has to do with fire."

Beth said calmly, "I felt weird and awful for nine years once. People think you can't help it, but in the end you're the only one who can. You can help it. You don't just face your fears. You have to put your face right up against your fears. What's the worst that could happen that hasn't already happened?"

"You've used the word 'face' twice in ten seconds."

"Face the music," said Beth. "That's three."

On the day we left, I took two (okay, three) ten-milligram Valiums right after I'd explored the immediate area around me on the plane, just so I would be able to recall having been on it. Then I slept all the way. Beth had to wake me up five minutes before we landed. Since the Ossum Tate Gallery had paid for first-class, I got to wipe my face off with a hot lemony towel and put some gloss on my lips, which were dry as pavement. Then I followed Beth down the labyrinthine mall that was LAX. It was a cool day for early October in Southern California, maybe in the middle sixties. I slipped my black sweater out of my bag and over my shoulders.

Down in the luggage area, I saw this guy right away: In a whole airport filled with people who were six feet tall, of indeterminate gender, and who'd never met a piece of blue leather or a tattoo they didn't like, he looked larger than life, although he was not even large. He was slight and thin, not much taller than I was, and wore jeans and this soft blue shirt with long sleeves rolled up. He had longish straw-colored hair and a way of standing that wasn't cocky but seemed to say that nothing ever made him panic.

I thought, *That must be an actor.* I also thought, *That is a sexy guy.* Already, I had cheered up. I had noticed a guy.

But when that same guy saw Beth, he looked as though someone had just given him a shopping cart and five minutes to run through the Vatican and grab whatever he wanted to take home. She walked up and put the heel of her hand on his forehead and shoved it back and then laid her head on his shoulder. He covered the back of her head with one hand. He looked nothing like Ben. He looked everything like Beth.

A moment later, the guy put his hand out to me. Close up, I could see he was older than he looked at a distance, with little lines arrayed at the corners of his eyes—eyes that were really gray, the same color as mine. He said, "Welcome to the land of smog and Botox. I'm Vincent. You must be Sicily."

I was sure that I was. But I couldn't say anything at all.

CHAPTER ELEVEN

Initially, I slept.

I was shocked by how exhausted I was, much more than could be explained by jet lag or the discharge of tension following my first and uncommonly long plane flight. Maybe away from the pressure to answer the telephone and smile for my aunt and Polly and Dr. Bom and act so much more normal than I felt, I just deflated like a balloon in hot weather. Hearing Beth and Vincent chatting downstairs, the door opening and closing and the soft ebb and swell of radio music and voices, the smells of mustard and salt and exhaust that drifted in like ribbons from the boardwalk . . . and, farther away, the susurrant regular breathing of waves—all this was experienced by me as the events of a dream.

When Beth finally shook me, I held up my hand to block the bright yellow square of sunlight.

"I was checking your pulse," Beth said. "You've been asleep for sixteen hours."

"No way."

"You have. Are you sick?"

I sat up and gulped my immunosuppressant pills from the little ten-pack Eliza had given me, drowning them in the most exquisite swallow of iced tea I've ever had to this day.

"I could eat a cow," I said. "But I'm so humiliated that I slept a whole day in the house of someone I don't even know that I want to leave by the back door."

"If you mean you're embarrassed because of Vincent, forget it. He's been gone most of the time. He had a dinner meeting and then he stayed at Emily's. He's going to be home in a little while and apologizes to you for being rude."

"Who's Emily?"

"His girlfriend, Emily Sydney. She's a film editor. She worked on the documentary with him. They've been dating on and off for about a hundred years. I don't know what's up with that. Maybe Vincent has commitment issues. Maybe Emily does. She's Canadian." How did that signify? I wondered. A citizenship issue? Allegiance to different hockey teams? "Anyhow, they're in the dreaded talking stage. I always hated the talking-it-over stage," Beth said. "I don't think Vincent slept over there for reasons of, uh, passion. When they're on the phone, he sounds like a mute. I hear him say, Yes. Kind of. I guess. No. Not really."

"Did you really ever go out with anybody except Pat?"

"Sure. Three or four guys. But I take great pride in the fact that I never said those words to anybody. You know: 'We really need to talk.'"

"Me either."

"Yeah," Beth said. "Well. The towels are in the bathroom, and there is a big bunch of French toast and bacon on the table. And the beach is across the street."

"I'm going to take a run quick."

"It's high noon in California, Sicily."

"I'll wear SPF seventy-five and a baseball cap. I have to move around. I've been in, like, the fetal position for the past day." I pulled on running shorts and a modest sports halter. Beth knew what she was talking about as far as high noon in California. After a mile, I turned around, spent and cooked, and tried to pour it on and sprint most of the way back. Although I'd only recently been freed to work out hard again, I'd been running like a madwoman and I ached, real liniment-quality ache-age. Still, it had been worth it. I felt like the rightful owner of my own body. To be safe and not lose my way, I'd run in a square, from Vincent's corner, down Shore, up LaFlore, over to Cabrillo, and back toward Vincent's small blue clapboard house on the corner. There were so many joggers that the sidewalks should have had fast and slow lanes, but everyone was cheerful. I hit the porch, sweating from every pore and smelly as onion soup, just as Vincent pulled up in his car. He got out. I took off my ball cap and looped my hair into a knot at the nape of my neck.

"Hello!" he said, and bit his lip to avoid the obvious scan of my body. With a kind of mental pop, I realized that Vincent was looking at me not the way men did once—because my body *didn't* match my disquieting blob of a face—but because it *did* match the face I had now. "You like it here?"

"It's obviously and completely beautiful. Runningwise, a big improvement over Chicago. Everybody here is, like, *Hi, nice day,* and everybody there is, like, *Fuck off, passing on your right.* Oh, God, excuse me. Nice first impression."

"Don't worry," he said. "I grew up there too." He opened the door and let me step in in front of him. I pulled off my shoes, and sand dribbled all over his lava-colored carpet. "Don't worry about that either. This lady I know collects sand. I let her have mine without paying me for it."

I nodded. He must have thought I was retarded.

"I mean, the housekeeper will vacuum it up. It was a joke."

"Oh, sure," I said. "Sure. I'm going to, uh, shower and . . . uh, then . . ."

"Don't go back to sleep," he said.

"Sorry about that. I'm a very good sleeper."

"Do you like Japanese?" Vincent asked suddenly. I told him I'd never had it. "Let's go later, then. There's a great joint just down a couple of blocks." I was halfway up the stairs when he said, "It's amazing that you can't tell." I knew right away what he meant. The high neck on my sports halter covered the larger of my scars.

Lightly, I said, "That's the idea!"

But I walked back down, every atom of my cerebrum shouting obscenities in protest. *Face it. Just face it, Sicily.* I lowered the strap of my halter. "Right there, my skin is a slightly different color. And if I raise my neck, there's still a scar."

"But even that—it looks like a sunburn. I've seen some of my mother's pictures. I think they're some of the best stuff she's ever done. When you were . . . scarred, did it hurt you all the time?"

"Not after the first five or six years," I said. "I've really got to clean up." Five minutes into our first conversation, I'd sworn like a Teamster and shown Vincent my ouchies. I had planned to impress him, maybe even snag a consulting gig on his germ flick. And that was before I saw him.

I didn't bother to dress up for lunch. I did dress carefully, choosing cream linen drawstring pants with a lemon-yellow sleeveless crop top. I heard Vincent downstairs trying to cajole Beth into coming along, which somehow made me feel not tender toward him but vexed. What Italian guy doesn't love his mother, I thought, as I downplayed my eye makeup? And yet, why couldn't she want to stay home with a cup of tea and sort her negatives.

She didn't. The three of us took off about seven p.m.

When we went outside, I saw that apparently no one (no one) in Venice Beach had heard the news about skin cancer. I'm not fair-skinned by any means, but the strip of my exposed belly, compared to the general populace, looked like the gesso I used on my canvases in college. We walked to this little sushi place where it seemed that everyone expected him to show up every day at more or less the same time. I had tempura shrimp and summer rolls, which I ate so fast that Beth asked if I wanted some of her cucumber sushi. And I ate all of that too.

The perfect lady.

Later that night, Beth made me show Vincent my virus-chomping antibody project and he was appropriately impressed, particularly by the color field. We watched a rough cut of the new movie that Gwyneth Paltrow had directed, then Beth had this desire for ice cream. The two of them walked across the street to a little stand with sweet, cheesy old-fashioned Christmas lights strung across the roof. I watched them from the window, the rising moon copper like a veiled coin between their heads as they stopped to take off their shoes.

I had seen Beth with Ben and they were easy together, teasing and comfy. On Labor Day, Marie and I had gone to a picnic with all of the Cappadoras at Beth's, and it was the first time I met Ben's grandparents and one of his aunts, Teresa—called "Tree." Pat was grilling burgers—you would never have known that he owned a restaurant, because he looked like he was trying to figure out how to operate a particle accelerator. We ate in stages, first the potato salad, then the corn, and finally the burgers. When Ben had a third cheeseburger, Beth lightly patted his tiny bit of a gut. "Cut it out, Ma!" he said. "I never get to eat ethnic food!"

She was different with Vincent.

Perhaps because she saw him seldom, Beth watched Vincent with something that verged on infatuation. She did not miss an opportunity to touch him, to pat his arm or mess up his hair. Eliza had once made a passing reference to a time when things between Beth and Vincent were worse than strained, when they were splintered and raw. Beth's joy in whatever healing had happened was clearly still unstained. It made me happy to see her so proudly courted by her successful son.

When they came back, Beth said, "Do you want to go with me tomorrow for the first meeting at the gallery?" It was too soon for me to remember that people could now read my expressions, and I felt silly when she started to laugh. "Don't look like you're going to throw up, Sicily. You don't have to go."

"I want to go," I said. "That's not it."

"Then what?" Beth said.

"I majored in studio art and biology. I can tell you what's in half the galleries at the Art Institute and in what order. That's all. It was one of the only places on earth where people looked at something besides me."

"What would you like to do?" Vincent asked. "I don't have anything to do tomorrow. I can show you around. Do you want to go to a studio? Or shopping in Beverly Hills or something?"

I said, "I would like to go to Disneyland."

They both laughed.

You have to understand that, in some very basic ways, I had never grown up, and so I was more interested in the teacup ride and the haunted house than I was in the food, the parades, or especially the performances. We went through the haunted house only twice, but I believe I still hold the outdoor record for consecutive spins on the teacups. All the baby rides, especially the Peter Pan ride over a cheesy, charming scene of Olde London Towne, drove me wild. I grabbed Vincent's arm and practically shouted, "Look at the mermaids in the pirate lagoon!" He nodded, pressing his lips together, maybe to stop himself from saying something insulting or else something loud that would let other guests know that he would have to take his mentally challenged sister back to her independent living complex this evening. I would look back on this later and realize that I probably was more oafish than girlishly charming, but at the time Vincent seemed to be the perfect companion. He knew his way around places I didn't, and also I would never see him again. Beth, not her son, was my friend.

After four or so hours, Vincent began to pale visibly. I would have

stayed all night. He said, "Would you mind terribly if we went somewhere quiet for a while? Where there aren't several thousand kids all
screaming?"

"Don't you like kids?" I asked him.

"I do. I like Stella. But this reminds me of some gladiator scene
from an old movie. It's been a long time since I've been here."

"How long?"

"My whole life. I've never been here." We began to walk quietly
toward the exit, shoulder-to-shoulder with ranks of fat parents in college T-shirts dragging footsore, outraged, sticky children. "A lot of animators work for the Rat," Vincent said. "It's a great job environment, if
you can stand it. Emily worked here when she was a kid."

"Your girlfriend?"

"My ex. I guess. We're like a puzzle that doesn't ever quite fit. I
really care about Emily. But some of her stuff . . . Life is hard." He
shrugged. "Let's go to the Cub Bar at the Peninsula and look at movie
stars, okay? It's a long drive but, I promise, I'm a very bad driver. It'll be
like a thrill ride."

I was ready to leave. Belatedly, I'd noticed that the Grumpys and
Dopeys looked the way I had post-surgery, with my stretched and
swollen mask face. Suddenly it seemed that everyone was staring.

Vincent noticed my silence and said, "What's the matter? Are you
disappointed?"

"Just . . . they can tell, I think."

"They can't tell."

"Maybe they saw it on the news. I think my aunt did a syndicated
photo-essay thing."

"There's a lot more on the news than you."

"I didn't mean that, Vincent," I said. "You can drop me on the way
to the star bar."

"Don't be touchy," Vincent said. "They're looking at you because
you're a pretty girl who has hair down to your elbows. I have some experience with hostile stares. The women just wish they could go back

twenty years and thirty pounds. Get used to it, Sicily. That's what you came for, right?"

We drove through the Technicolor twilight to Beverly Hills, a place as bone-deep unreal as Disneyland, where everyone looked dressed for the kind of event I'd never been to. As we walked from the parking lot, several of the people who acknowledged Vincent, some with a kiss, were people I'd seen on movie screens with foreheads twenty feet wide. I expected the bar to be vast and gleaming, but it was tiny, unremarkable, although outside the azaleas were the size of the teacups on the Disney ride. When Vincent asked me what I wanted, I told him, "A martini. Absolutely. A dirty martini." Kit drank martinis. I'd never had anything stronger than champagne. Of course, with the day of unaccustomed sun and nearly continuous spinning, two fast martinis knocked me on my ass.

When we left, I'm afraid that I wanted to swing dance in the parking lot and insisted that I was very good at it. Instead, we drove to a sui generic California drive-in, where I restored my equilibrium with something called a Cyclone burger, large fries, and half of Vincent's modest BLT.

"Are you a wrestler or something? Women don't eat like you," he said. "I always thought they ate like Scarlett O'Hara—a loaf of bread at home, so they can come out and pick at a thirty-dollar steak."

"Well," I said, "I couldn't really eat in public for a long time. And eating was a nuisance. A good dancer is never over a hundred and ten pounds. I weigh, well, more. And the guys are tiny. I have to work out more now, because I eat so much. But I'm a dancer—I don't mean in parking lots. I've danced all my life. Ballet. I got too tall to be really good at it but . . . I'm devout. You get strong."

"Why couldn't you eat in public?" Vincent asked me. I was on the way to sobering up by then but not all the way there: We were not far from his house. *In vino veritas.*

"The food fell out of my mouth unless I tossed it back like a shot of booze. Which I have never had, by the way. Or a martini. I have to believe your mom showed you the pictures of me before." Vincent gazed straight ahead, betraying himself only by minutely adjusting his hands to the very correct ten-and-two position on the steering wheel. "What you can't see in pictures is that my mouth didn't close all the way."

"That's rough," he said.

I didn't answer.

"I have to do something in the morning, but do you like to go swimming? I could take you guys later. My buddy Rob has this little house on a quiet part of the beach, where's there's almost no current in the afternoon and you can snorkel. It's cold—you'll need a wet suit. But Rob has twenty in girl sizes."

My first reaction was terror for the face. But Hollis had said I should use my face just the way everyone else did. I murmured something about not having brought a swimsuit—to California. Vincent said his mom probably had ten swimsuits at his house and—since men think all women can wear anything from a size four to a fourteen—one would probably fit me. I'd gone to Phil's Beach in a high-necked tank suit in front of Joey and worn the same thing in therapy pools at the hospital, but never in front of . . . a regular person. Then again, although I was having a really great time with Vincent, as I did with all the Cappadoras I knew, I would very likely never see him again, so he was virtually disposable.

"If it's a two-piece, it probably would. Beth's skinnier than I am, but she's shorter too."

Right after that, we got stuck in traffic and I fell asleep, my cheek against the soft leather of the headrest, my legs curled under me. I woke up in my bed, and the thought of Vincent having carried or helped me up was unsettling. Except not in a bad way. I wished I could remember him touching me. I also wondered how he got up a flight of stairs carrying someone who weighed a hundred and twenty pounds.

In the morning, I breakfasted on toast, aspirin, coffee, and anti-rejection drugs. Beth was going to drive and we would meet Vincent at Rob's house. But the bathing suits she offered me were way too Bolivian. I got the strong feeling that they had not ever really belonged to Beth, whose was a well-made black Speedo.

So we drove up to the little shopping mall and I ended up buying two of them, my first bikinis: one red, with a halter top that nicely hid the still-red scar that sat just below my collarbone like the border between the United States and Mexico, and another that was a delicate spring-leaf color and hid practically nothing. I had to remind myself again that there was every chance I would not use either of them, that Vincent would get tied up in meetings and forget he'd ever undertaken the obligation of squiring his mom and her project around town.

He did show up, however, and big, bluff Rob Brent, Vincent's business partner, opened the house to us. It was very tidy, with miles of white leather couch and one gigantic black-and-white photo Beth had taken of a Banksy wall. There seemed to be computers on every flat surface. I sat down and starting fooling with one of them, and Rob and I ended up spending an hour goofing with the virus hunter, like two guitarists in an impromptu jam. Then Rob took off, reminding Vincent to punch in the code that locked the door, and we got ready to swim. Standing in Rob Brent's bathroom, I tried the red swimsuit on and then the green swimsuit and then put the red one back on again. Then I went back to the green suit, which was just so pretty and, what the hell, so was my body.

I would never see Vincent after this week, I told myself. I *reminded* myself.

Of course, he looked right at the scar. It pissed me off, and I made a point to stare right at the bulge in his faded surfer-dude trunks. For a good ten seconds. Vincent laughed, low-pitched and ticklish, ending, like Beth's laugh, in a goofy snort. "Gotcha," he said.

Then I struggled into my wet suit. It took me no time to get the hang of the snorkel and mask. Then I wanted to never come out. Hours passed. Every common coral and angelfish was a magic messenger. Farther out, in the murk, I saw a turtle loft itself toward the surface like a winged drum. As I turned to swim back, Beth tapped me to say that she needed to get inside: She was worn out and the sun was making her skin prickle in an ominous way, despite the thorough slathering we'd given each other. Reluctantly, after a few more minutes, I followed Beth and Vincent through the strip of sand to the rear of Rob's little house. There was an outside shower and we all rinsed off. I liked the way the salt water made my hair feel, so I didn't wash it, just slipped on the drawstring pants and a light linen shirt I'd brought.

I'd assumed we'd go to dinner, but Beth said she wanted a nap and a tuna-salad sandwich. Vincent asked me, "Do you want to go someplace fancy?" I shook my head. "Do you want to have a picnic on the beach? I have a permit I never use."

So we drove to Santa Monica and parked near the pier. Then we carried shopping bags of wine and apples and cheese down the beach for about five miles, until Vincent got to just the place he wanted. At that point, I was ready to fall asleep. I wasn't used to being outdoors all day. He spread the blankets near this small rock circle, then went over to a lifeguard sign and started hauling back the tarp loaded with driftwood and thick branches. I slipped my sweater over my head.

"You'll warm up when I make a fire," he said.

I leapt to my feet. "A fire? I thought that stuff was just to block the wind. I'd rather put my hand in a fan than sit next to a fire."

"Oh, Jesus. Sicily. I'm really sorry. All I had to do was think instead of running my mouth . . ."

But, by that time, I was thinking too.

Face the music. Face your fears. Put your face against it.

"Go ahead," I told Vincent. "Go ahead. I'm scared of it, but nothing will happen. It's a proper fire pit with sand all around. I have to live. We're at a beach at night. Make a fire."

He hesitated.

"I don't want to be the one to give you a brand-new trauma," he said.

"No. If I feel like I'm going to flip out, you can douse it, right?"

Vincent studied me, as if gauging how serious I was. Eventually, slowly, he laid the fire and then, even more slowly, lit it.

I yoga-breathed and watched the spurting column of orange and blue flames, carefully locating myself outside the radius where sparks could fly. We ate our apples and cheese and I drank a single glass of wine. Then we sat cross-legged on the blankets, just listening to the water. The night was egregiously gentle and extravagant with stars. I couldn't help but see them as "cels," the old-fashioned form of animation, when artists painted on cellophane and occasionally increased the illusion of depth by laying one cel over another. That was what the stars were like, layer upon layer, some close enough to touch, some distant as underwater pearls. I lay back and felt that the world had reversed and I could dive into the stars. I asked Vincent if the nights were always this beautiful. "You must want to do this every night."

"No," he said. "There's way too much smog most of the time. But this is pretty great. If you live here, you think it'll always be here. Like the running path out by . . . what, Marina Towers? How often do you run along the lake?"

"Maybe twice a week."

"Well, mainly what I do is drive an hour to see somebody for ten minutes."

"Why isn't anyone else out here?" I asked.

"Well, it's a Tuesday night. Kids are in school. People who aren't in the business have real jobs." Vincent lay back on his elbows, slowly folding down the cuffs of his shirt. "Generally I hate California, but this is all right."

"Why live here?"

"It's easier to work. My partner lives here. This neighborhood, it's not so bad. People have families here."

"Thanks for going to the trouble to take me around," I told him. "I was so afraid to fly. I never swam in the ocean. I was afraid to sit by a fire. I should have had the sense to be afraid of the martinis. But, wow—I may just keep on going, new thing to new thing, from now on."

I thought that Vincent was leaning forward to point out a feature of the light-lacy skyline. Instead, he kissed me. It was a gentle kiss, not preliminary to anything. But I got engrossed in it, not just the sour-and-sweet taste of wine and apples but the pressure of his lips, the warmth and softness, the way he fit his mouth to mine. When he drew back, after a thick strand of my hair blew between us, I said, "Okay, one more. That also is my first kiss."

"Uh-uh!"

"I was thirteen when the fire happened."

"But you were going to marry some guy."

"I didn't say it was my first anything, forever and ever, amen. Just my first kiss, with a mouth."

Vincent shook his head.

"With me having a mouth." Instantly, I regretted having mentioned it: For some people, the notion of kissing the mouth of a girl who'd died would be obscene. For me, I wondered briefly if I could have had it all wrong about immortality and if Emma was smiling.

Vincent said, "Sicily, that's such a crazy thought, it's hard to process it. I didn't know it was an occasion. Did I do okay?"

"Very well. I would do it again." We lay down facing each other and kissed like starving people. Gently then, Vincent raised my sweater and, after asking me if it was okay, put his lips against my belly, my breasts, and then my scars. It was the most sensual and considerate thing any human being had ever done to me. My core rang like the final tones from a tuning fork, spreading outward, every nerve pitched high.

"It's hard for me to imagine, a beautiful kid like you, living all that time that way. . . ." he said.

"I'm not a kid," I told Vincent. "And I'm not beautiful. I sure wasn't then."

"How old are you, Sicily?"

"I'm twenty-five," I said. "How old are you?"

"Real old. But this is probably the only place on earth that a girl like you would be over the hill."

"Do you mean . . . like, something's wrong with me? You don't want me?"

"I said I was old. I'm not crazy or dead, Sicily. Of course I want you. Although I feel my mother's hands tightening around my throat. And there's a technical issue: I didn't come . . . prepared."

I placed my hands on the warm back of his head and held his face to mine, and, light as leaves, our clothes opened and fell around us.

Vincent cupped my breasts and then traced my spine with his hands. He said, "Sweetie. Wait. I mean I really didn't come prepared to do this. I didn't plan on making love to you. We should go back to my house. Or wait. Until tomorrow."

Wait?

"I'm impregnable," I said. "They make you take supershots because of the anti-rejection drugs."

"It's not that. . . ."

"You don't have a disease. You're Beth's son. I don't have a disease. It would have turned up on one of my one thousand blood tests. And I'm one guy away from a virgin," I said. "Please. Do it."

"Sicily, I'm not a jerk. But I feel like you're brand-new. I don't want to give you the wrong idea."

"Like, you took off all my clothes so we could have an ethical discussion? Do you think I'm going to fall in love with you and hide under the porch when Beth leaves?"

"No."

"Are you afraid I won't like it as much as I liked the teacup ride?"

"No. I'm afraid you will."

"You have to face your fears," I said.

The moon came out, and both of us, naked, were silvery as the fish in the cove. I guided Vincent's hands into the shadows of me, throwing off the nuisance quilt, pressing myself small to lie beneath him. I was telling big lies through my pretty white teeth. I was already ten times drunker on him than on the dirty martinis. But I said to myself, *Sicily, this is ordinary adult recreation.* Vincent moved so slowly and so

gently. I tried, I really tried, to do the same thing, to be as shy and dif-
fident as I had been every other time in my life that this had happened.
But my body was disinclined to be gentle or shy, and the ache in my
belly grew more insistent, until finally a . . . it was like . . . it was like a
flashover, consuming and dangerous and filled with awe. I thought,
during it, that this was the only time I'd ever really felt that thing you're
supposed to feel, your customary self vacated, like the planet could
blow up next to you and you would attend to it later. I wanted to have
it happen again, a hundred times all at once.

I wanted to hold the outdoor record.

When I was ready for thirds, though, Vincent made a noise that was
halfway between a laugh and a sigh and pointed out that while I was
twenty-five, he was not. He mentioned also that it was by now 4:00
a.m. and fifty degrees, not to mention that the tide was about ten feet
from us. We got up and carried the damp remnants of our innocent
picnic back to the car. Oh, the Sicily who had been so sleepy when she
arrived, I was not she. Now I was certain I would never waste an hour
of my life on sleep again.

Everything I wanted was in the front seat of Vincent's car. He looked
at me as he started the car and said, "Don't smile like that."

"How come?"

"You . . . you're so cute. Cute and eager."

"Is it about Emily?"

"No. It's about me. I mean, I live in California, and that implies
bad behavior, but I met you only the day before yesterday, not to mention . . . this is crazy."

Lights that even Vincent admitted he had never realized he had in
his house announced themselves like fanfare behind every window
when he pulled into the driveway. As soon as he cut the engine, Beth
pulled open the door and said, "Excuse me. But, Vincent? What the
fuck?"

I had never heard Beth talk that way. I had never seen her this way. She seemed literally larger.

Vincent defended himself. I defended him. He defended me. At last, he said, "Ma. We're both adults. I semi-understand why you're awake. I even semi-understand why you're out here. But I'm not going to be okay if you say anything else."

We stepped into the foyer, where I stood with my hands in the pockets of my pants. As I turned and started to scamper up the stairs to my room, up past all those lights blaring against the dawn, Vincent said, "Sicily. My room is at the end of the hall. I'm not as much of a neat freak as Rob is, but I do make the bed." I thought Beth was going to sock him in the face right then. She began to huff in a way I would have found funny if I hadn't been scared of her. If I went into Vincent's room, I would feel oddly disloyal to Beth, but if I did not, it would telegraph the message that the night had been no more than an inebriated impulse.

I went into Vincent's room, brushed my teeth with a wet washcloth, pulled off my clothes, and lay down and willed myself to sleep for just ten minutes. After a long while, I did slip into a doze, but for the next hour I heard Beth turning off lights and slamming cabinet doors and rearranging stuff in drawers and talking to Vincent in words I couldn't discern but that sounded like someone throwing handfuls of stone against a metal shed. All this I experienced gradually, as a dream, that tumbled into the dream of Vincent's body in the hot firelight and then in the cold moonlight and then in the morning light, when he was there and real, beside me and then on top of me.

I had come here through the air and gone under the water and faced the fire. I didn't forget that if you set a fire, you were responsible for whatever it burned. I knew that. But in just three days I'd become a woman with wings spread for the first time, with the knowledge that they had the force to take me where I wanted to go.

Every night, Beth and Vincent and I ate a brittle dinner and did something else that passed the time before Beth gave us a laser look and headed upstairs with her book. Then, before he and I lay down and did it again, Vincent said to forgive him, he knew he was nuts. Every time we made love, he was careful, using extra protection, which I appreciated, although I also didn't give a damn.

After that first night, there were only six more days left for me to ride that spinning cup. I did.

CHAPTER TWELVE

"You don't mess with this," Marie said. "We should call Dr. Grigsby. You probably caught something on that plane. Nothing but a can of germs in the air. You didn't wear a mask, did you?"

"No," Sicily said. "Everyone else on the plane did, though."

That Sicily still had the vigor for sarcasm was comforting. But the way Sicily looked contradicted her bravado. Deep hollows under her eyes looked artificial, as though meant to be seen from the balcony in a heavy-handed production of *La Bohème*. She complained that her head ached as though someone were using a fork to pry her skull off her spine. She had no energy for ballet—and ballet was Sicily's church—and barely touched the computer that she ordinarily checked every hour like a pioneer bride tending her hearth.

Only ten days before, Sicily had returned from California, frothing like champagne cooled too long in the freezer. She sang and drew and danced, the thump of her music against Marie's adjoining wall reassuring now instead of irritating. Every report of Sicily's adventures seemed to begin with, *Vincent took me to . . .* and, *Vincent said he'd never seen that depth of color in . . .* and, *Vincent showed Beth and me scenes from the animated . . .*

Vincent.

Marie was many unfortunate things, she thought, but she was no fool. Initially grateful to Beth for the change of scene that had restored Sicily's spirits, Marie now wanted to slap every Cappadora except Eliza. *You arrogant jerk with your Oscar. You with your so-fabulous black-and-white portraits. You with your license-to-print-money spaghetti joint. You with your . . .* Marie couldn't think of anything bad to say about hearty, sweet-spoken Ben.

Vincent. Was he too dumb to know a permeable heart when he saw one, or could he simply not be bothered to care?

Two more days passed, then four, then six. Sicily's ebullient chatter slowed, stuttered, and stopped altogether.

"Have you heard from Beth's son? The one whose house you visited?" Marie asked lightly. "What's his name? Victor?"

"Vincent. And no," Sicily said. "Let me sleep." Sicily's long naps were punctuated by brief visits to the bathroom to shower and brush her teeth, after which she slipped into one of the pairs of blue surgical scrubs she'd collected during her many hospital stays. And then Sicily slipped back into bed.

"You have to eat," Marie said. "How about a spinach salad?"

Obligingly, Sicily got up and pushed the dark-green leaves around on her plate, speared a cherry tomato, and gazed at it as though it were some kind of rare shell.

"Sicily, what is wrong with you?" Marie said, teetering along a line .that wavered between sympathy and a slow burn. "Do you think this is an episode of rejection?"

Sicily laid her fork down on the yellow place mat. The cherry tomato rolled off the edge of the table.

"Kind of," Sicily admitted softly.

"*Kind* of? We need to be at the emergency room, then, Sicily."

"It's not that kind of rejection."

"Okay, then, let's hear it."

"Just let me sleep. Haven't you ever heard of sleeping it off?" Sicily laid her sleep mask over her eyes and resumed a pose that would have been just right for a sarcophagus.

Resigned, Marie retrieved her briefcase and sat down in Sicily's slim leather recliner. Grabbing the remote, Marie sat, eyes glazed, through three reruns of some old show about a minister raising six daughters on his own. On TV shows, everyone killed mothers off. Single fathers were adorable. Single mothers were pathetic. After switching off the lights and the television, Marie was about to make a quiet exit, when Sicily sat up, wide awake and clearly alarmed.

"You don't have to leave," Sicily said.

"Do you feel worse?"

"Not when you're here."

"I don't need to leave."

"Auntie, remember the day we found out about the fire, the day of my engagement party? When you told me that you fell for my father after just five dates? Can a person really fall in love at first sight? Isn't it possible? Why else would people have written all the poems and songs?"

"I think it's something people like to believe," Marie said evenly, and thought, *Oh, give me strength.* And yet, wasn't this bound to happen? If Sicily learned to fly, she was going to hit the ground hard, and not just one time. There would be men who would consider her . . . well, just a pretty face, an interesting case, her transformation a beguiling twist on the common run of girls. But why did the first have to be some himbo who lived three thousand miles away, surrounded by the human equivalent of gazelles in short shorts? "And, as for Jamie, oh, for heaven's sake, that was just silly girl talk about a thirty-five-year-old error of judgment. Your dad and your mom—my sister—were a match made . . ."

"You can say a match made in heaven. People say it all the time to me. You don't have to treat me like I'm made of glass."

"What this proves," Marie said finally, "is that you can feel all those things again. That's good news. The bad news is, it's so tough to experience a high like that and then come back to the everyday world. And so soon after it was over between Joe and you."

"Do we have any aspirin?" Sicily asked. "My head is going to split up the back like a gourd."

"You're not supposed to take aspirin if you might have flu."

"Do we have any heroin, then?" Trailing her comforter, Sicily padded into the bathroom and returned with a bottle of Tylenol. "Auntie! I've missed everything! Why didn't you tell me what I was missing?"

"How many times did I ask you to go with me to California? Paris, London, Sydney? Dallas?"

From the habit of years, Sicily had placed the tablets on the back of her tongue and tilted her head back before sipping water through a straw to swallow them. Then she quickly turned to Marie and said reprovingly, "Dallas? Who wants to go to Dallas?"

"All I meant was, the first time *Beth* asked you—"

"Was also the first time anyone asked me to do anything after the face transplant." Sicily lay back down. "Dallas! Marie, you know I didn't mean restaurants and historical sites. You know I didn't mean I'd missed out on the hot spots of Dallas. Or even El Paso."

"I hoped you meant that. I gave it a good try." Marie smiled. "I know you weren't referring to sightseeing."

"I mean I didn't know. I didn't know what love was. Why didn't you tell me?"

First, Marie thought, *because you were missing out on it and then because I thought that what you had would be all you ever needed. And now, Sicily, I can't say, Get up and stop sulking. Just chalk this one up like the compressed equivalent of a summer romance. You're on the rebound. You're on the mend. You're confusing lust with trust and a moment's enchantment with a life's commitment. I can't say that, because you can't hear that when you're twenty-five, especially if you're really eighteen going on twenty-five going on eighty-seven, the newest and oldest woman in the world.*

So Marie talked tough in another way. "I have to say, Sicily, that I had some zingers in my time when it came to one-night stands, and after they were over, I didn't take to my bed."

"It was a seven-night stand."

"And I have to wonder how Beth could . . ."

"Allow this? She was not at all pleased," Sicily said. "But it wasn't any of her business. It's actually none of *your* business, except you're my mother and who else can I act like an idiot with? I think about him every five minutes, other than when I'm asleep, and when I wake up I start thinking of him all over again, playing it back like you play the good parts of the movie. The beach. The sky. The birds outside the window waking me up. How do you stop doing that? You've had a hundred lovers."

"Maybe not a hundred . . ."

"How do you get over them?"

In fact, Marie thought, with a few exceptions her own relationships had been cheerful, robust affairs, and it was more often than not she who got engrossed in a story or in Sicily's latest issue and woke up one morning to realize that she had forgotten until Thursday the call she'd promised to make the previous Saturday. Sicily had lost her outer layer of skin in more ways than one. She was like the Visible Woman, that old toy that Gia had, the plastic model of the human body with all the veins and organ systems plain to see. Like the statue in the block of stone.

"Did you make plans to see each other again?" Marie asked.

"It was sort of presumed that we would, when he gets out here again, maybe when Eliza's baby is born, if not before then. But maybe not before then. He's in the middle of making a film. But he hasn't called me. I called him and left a message. Well, I didn't leave a message. He would have seen my number and known it was Chicago."

"His whole family lives in Chicago. You could have been anyone."

"That's true. But, really, it was me. I was the one who started hoping. He kept saying that it was a crazy thing to do."

"Didn't stop him, though." *The little rat's ass.*

"I'm not sorry. I thought that what I felt for Joey was as big as it got. But I felt more in seven days about Vincent than I felt about Joe in three years. Vincent's funny and smart. He saw things sort of twisted, the way I do. He's solid. I know that sounds impossible. But he cared too. He couldn't have faked all of it. He made me feel protected and safe."

"I'm so sorry, Sissy."

"Well, I'm not sorry I felt that way. I just wish I could stop it, now that it's over." Sicily's eyes closed. Within two minutes, she was breathing slow and deep, her lips slightly parting as she murmured something from a dream.

The next morning, when the temperature outside climbed into the fifties, Sicily sat shivering in a hooded sweatshirt from the Tower of London, with a robe over that, and sipping hot tea. Marie made a mental inventory of the signs she'd been warned to look for that signaled rejection—fever, chills, muscle aches, redness, itching. Check. Check. Not check. Not check. Not check.

"Would you tell me if you thought you had rejection sickness?" Marie asked.

Sicily almost smiled. "It's not like radiation sickness, Auntie. My hair isn't going to fall out."

No, thought Marie, *your face will fall off*.

Unable to get Sicily to return her calls, Kit Mulroy came unannounced, bringing a bag of croissants, the most innocuous food she could think of, and a swag from Fair Made. Kit wanted the details, and Marie sighed as Sicily haltingly provided the edited version.

"I have lived through more than my share of bad breakups," Kit said. Kit's hair, naturally light brown, now was the color of a ripe bing cherry. "It's a process. Just accept that you're going to feel like warm cat shit for a while."

"The hair is very peppy," Marie said.

"I like it," Sicily put in.

"It's my new thing," Kit said. She stood up and stretched, one arm arched over her head, then the other. "Every time I ditch the latest Mister Wrong, I'm going to change something. I'm going to rewrite a page of myself."

You'll end up transgendered, Marie thought. But she was happy that Kit had come, happy for the CD of torch songs that brought Marie to tears ("Once Upon a Time," "Come Rain or Come Shine") and Kit's own brand of clumsy condolence. The three of them sat on Sicily's terrace like See-, Hear-, and Speak-No-Evil. Then Marie heard the buzzer sound from within and walked over to depress the button, expecting a package.

Instead, Beth Cappadora said, "Marie, can I come up?"

"It's a free—of course, Beth," Marie said. "Please come."

The two older women met at Sicily's door.

"I feel like a complete idiot," Beth said. "Vincent has called me. He talks about her all the time. He says he can't stop thinking about her. She's too young for him. She's like a child. I know he really liked Sicily. But what I think is, he won't admit it but he's back with Emily again, this Canadian girl he was dating before."

"He could call and tell Sicily that much," Marie said. "That at least."

"I said so," Beth went on. "Maybe he's like every guy. He thinks it's kinder to just let her hate him than to admit he acted like an ass. I used to think, If you don't have the guts, just lie. Say you're dying. Say you're gay."

Marie considered this. Possibly Vincent was right. Eventually Sicily's molten heart would harden against a man who had made soap bubbles of her dreams and popped them. What could Vincent tell Sicily that would make her believe anything except that she'd fallen short in his eyes, in his arms? Distance could be overcome. Age could be reduced to a comic issue. Even men, Marie knew, weren't immune to the ambush of love. What they meant when they said they cared too much to call was that they couldn't be bothered.

Those very words were probably written in charcoal on the walls of caves.

Sicily came in from the terrace.

"Beth," Sicily said. "I thought you'd given up on me."

"No, just . . . Eliza's been feeling really lousy at night, but she won't stop working no matter what anyone says." Beth shifted her gigantic purse to her other shoulder and crossed her arms. "Actually, Sicily, I kept waiting for you and Vincent to talk before I starting working with you again. I feel like a silly ass. I don't know what to say."

Kit thoughtfully freighted the food inside and, expertly accustomed to Sicily's cabinets, measured out coffee.

"There isn't anything to say," Sicily told Beth. "It's not your fault." She sank down into her absurdly cushy sofa. "It is what it is."

In a gesture Marie recalled from Sicily's childhood—and, in truth, her niece looked reduced, no more than twelve—Sicily rubbed the backs of her hands against her forehead. Gia had preached to Sicily that the surest way to get pimples was to put your hands all over your face and, instinctively, Sicily still tried to finesse that.

"If I don't feel better soon, honest to God, Marie, I will let you take me to the doctor. I'm totally dizzy. And cold. And I could throw up from the smell of the coffee." Springing to her feet, Sicily *did* barely make it to the sink, where she delicately heaved up her bite of croissant and teaspoon of tea. She grabbed for a dish towel and said, "Oh, this is totally humiliating."

"That's it," Marie said. Now Sicily was exhibiting three of the five or six symptoms of rejection. Furious, she stood up and rang for Angel to bring her car to the front from the garage.

"No, not now," Sicily protested weakly. "We don't even have an appointment. It's Sunday."

"Sicily, you need to go. Call me later," Beth said. "If you have flu or something on top of all this, I may kill Vincent."

Kit insisted on riding along. It was a measure of how punk Sicily felt that she'd worn no makeup and hadn't even changed out of her scrubs and an ancient knee-length sweater that Marie thought had once belonged to Jamie. Sicily usually dressed more thoughtfully to sleep alone than she had today.

At the clinic, Hollis Grigsby's lieutenant, the young Brit they all called Livingston, breezed out of the sprightly lavender hall at UIC's Urgent Care.

"Sicily Coyne," Livingston said. "How pleasant of you to pop over!"

"I'm hardly popping," Sicily said.

"Ladies, why don't you come back here and wait in one of the offices and we'll do an inventory. I have to say, Sicily, you look a bit done in. Too much party?"

Sicily shook her head.

"Well, if I had to guess, I'd say maybe a bit of anemia. We'll get you stuck with a few dozen needles and do you right up."

Sicily disappeared with Livingston and a nurse Marie vaguely recognized. Left alone, Kit and Marie made a few rapid-fire stabs at small talk: How was work? Crazy. Christmas shopping started? Not one bit. They then seemed to mutually agree to occupy themselves with seeing how fast they could flip through magazines that promised they could take ten years off their look with one fashion trick and walk forty pounds off for the New Year. There were more than a dozen magazines in the office. By the time the nurse returned, absent Sicily or Dr. Livingston, Marie and Kit were down to trying to find the hidden comb and the kite in the *Highlights* drawings. Marie glanced at the clock. Sicily had been with the doctor for ninety minutes. Sweet Christ! Some of that blood work must have shown an alarmingly high—or was it low?—white-cell count. Something was terribly wrong.

"Dr. Livingston will be out in a moment to speak to you," the nurse said. "Sicily's just resting."

"Resting?" Marie said.

"Dr. Livingston?" Kit said. "That's his name? Like, Dr. Livingston, I presume?"

"Bingo," the nurse said wearily. "You're the only one who's ever said that." She smiled. "Someday there'll be a whole generation of people who've never heard that line and Stan will be happy."

From every deathwatch of the famous she'd covered, from the night her sister Gia died, from every receptor in her palette of senses tuned up to the highest frequency, Marie knew that good news in a hospital travels fast. Indeed, when Livingston approached, he seemed almost to stroll, noticing the scenery, as though deliberately placing each step on some invisible path.

Kit stood up.

Marie stood up.

"Mrs. Caruso," the doctor said. "Sicily is not in rejection. Her vitals are great and we don't think there's any kind of disease process going on from what we can determine. We are going to run a few more tests, and for that, we'd like to admit her overnight. So, in a moment, I'll take you back to see her and then you and . . ."

"Kit. Katherine Mulroy."

"You and Miss Mulroy can go and get her some trashy mags and the things she might want from home."

"Dr. Livingston, what are you worried about?" Marie said.

Livingston examined his immaculate hands. "This is potentially an extremely sad situation. Let's hope not. At best, it's an unfortunate inconvenience. Sicily's life is not in danger."

"What is?" Kit said.

"Doctor. This is my kid. There's a very heavy shoe that hasn't dropped in this room," Marie said.

"Yes. There's that. It seems that our Sicily is pregnant."

CHAPTER THIRTEEN

How many nights had I lain gazing up at acoustical-tile ceilings of hospital rooms and wondering if acoustical tiles were simply cheaper or were intended to muffle the cries? I didn't even look at Dr. Livingston when he asked me if I wanted my aunt to stay with me while Kit went back and got me an overnight bag. I did not want my aunt to come in just then. Aunt Marie would pretend that she was angry, when she actually was heartsick, but beneath her concern she would be thinking that I was a half-wit and the female version of Jonah, her own personal bad-luck charm.

I was my own bad-luck charm.

Pregnant? I thought.

Pregnant?

Of all the things I had been fearfully yet grimly prepared to hear Dr. Livingston say, this had not been on the list, or even in the vicinity of the mental paper on which I'd written the list. When Vincent and I made love, the condoms weren't linked in my mind to any real possibility of . . . pregnancy. They were like a courtesy, like a hook-and-eye latch on a screen door, truly preventing nothing, a barrier that even a little . . . a little kid could defeat.

A little kid.

I couldn't be pregnant. I could not be. But they'd taken enough blood from me, it seemed, to transfuse every trauma patient admitted that night to the hospital. They'd run that test over and over. The results were conclusive. And so was my fear, a kid's fear. I'd only felt this way one other time, the first time Eliza and I talked transplants—a thousand years ago—disoriented, like Alice through the looking glass. There must have been a terrible accident. There had been. The accident was within me, the size of the head of a pencil.

I wanted it out.

Out now. Even when Joe and I were first thinking about marriage, Joe was talking kids long, long before I was ready to consider them in anything except—please excuse the expression—a conceptual way. In hindsight, I knew that the kids were Joe LaVoy's beard, not just his mother's obsession: If he had pretty kids, it would blunt the impact of being shackled forever to the girl who had no face. It would give him something to show off, the way guys showed off their wives. As I lay there, curled on top of the covers, I wondered if I ever would be meant to be a mother.

And I decided I would.

But not now.

Then I thought about Vincent and was surprised by the awful wave of hunger that barreled through me when I considered that this . . . this accident was a product of my one week as someone's beloved.

Well, as someone's pretend beloved.

As someone's roomie with benefits.

As for the abortion itself, I wasn't at all frightened. I wished I could have it tonight. I wondered how it was possible at this stage that there was not some medical remedy, like a long-acting morning-after pill. All I could think was, *Hold on. You have been through so much worse, this isn't even a blip on the screen. Tomorrow this will be all over. All over.*

Dr. Livingston returned, and the nurse everyone called Derry— although her given name was Adair—helped me get as comfortable as you can get in a hospital bed. "I see you won't need to change for surgery," Dr. Livingston said. "You can just scrub in."

I didn't answer.

He let out a gusty breath and said, "Sicily, I apologize. That sounded wrong. I didn't mean that. Frankly, I don't know what to say. This is a bit unprecedented and all too tough for you. I suppose that the best-laid plans . . ."

"That's one way of putting it."

"Alas. I've got both feet in my mouth now. You did use a second form of birth control."

"Yes."

"And so both a condom and the shot failed."

"Well, there was a second form except once."

"Which is, as they say, all it takes. And you know, Sicily, this is a bit of a non-starter." He drew himself up. "It's more than that. I know you have read all about the fellow you refer to as the Canadian crazy. Well, he died a horrible death." I began to speak and Dr. Livingston held up a stop-sign palm. "He died a horrible death because of being off his medication. At any point, perhaps he could have been saved, but he still might have died from sepsis as his transplanted skin became necrotic. A slow death. As Americans say, we aren't messing about here, Sicily."

"What they say is, we're not messing *around,* Dr. Livingston."

"Just so. I know that this must be very sad for you—"

"It's not. I wasn't planning to have a baby."

"But for all women, having an abortion is sad."

"How do you know all women? Aren't you thinking only of your wife or your sister? And what if your life was at stake? Or theirs was?"

Dr. Livingston placed his immaculate hands on his knees and studied them. "Well, Gwen and I are only now trying to adopt a child. We couldn't conceive," he said. "And perhaps I should not have used the term 'very sad.' What I meant, really, was . . . unpleasant. Unavoidable unpleasantness. I'm grateful and happy that you're being so reasonable in a situation that might shatter another girl. You really must be careful."

"Dr. Livingston, this was a mistake, not a plan to defeat my transplant. I'm not nuts and I'm not a schizo and I'm not suicidal. Don't you dare suggest that I sabotaged myself," I said. "I won't put myself in danger. I won't put my face in jeopardy. This is my fault. But you don't have to rub it in."

Livingston said, "I'm sure there's not a person in the world who would say this is your fault. You have been a model patient. If anything, the fault is utterly our own for not considering the factors that could pertain to a woman so young and, if I may say, so very pretty as you are now." He narrowed his eyes. "Disneyland apart, I would not, uh, have explicitly prescribed a theme park."

"And yet that's not where I got in trouble. Gosh, that's what they used to call it. Back in the day."

Livingston stood up. He said he'd paged Hollis, who would be along presently. *Oh, great,* I thought, *great.* Another disapproving mother-age figure who, as an added bonus, never said anything argumentative, so you couldn't disagree with her. Hollis bent you to her will simply by being aloof, withholding the approval you somehow wanted from her so badly. Eliza had told me as much, that the interns and residents fell all over themselves like performing seals, trying to win a brief nod and a "just so" from Dr. Grigsby.

Dr. Livingston left. I crossed to the bed and lay down.

To my utter disbelief and breathless rage, I realized that I was . . . sad.

I wanted to call Dr. Livingston back and tell him off.

And then I recognized that this had everything to do with the truth that the body, as I had told myself so often, has a head.

Oh, Vincent, I thought, *I did it with you, with all the feelings you're supposed to have when you do that for the purpose it's intended.* Maybe one of those feelings somehow got into the slipstream of reproductive destiny, and biology decided that I was the woman from the neck down who I can't ever be from the neck up. Does everyone have regrets, the way Dr. Livingston suggested? Even in California? What if all the chips were not stacked on the side of my face? Would I tell you right now? It would have sounded like the antediluvian ploy for snagging the guy. Surely I had more chops than that. But I didn't need to have chops. In this fix, I didn't need to be pro-choice; I was already no-choice. And if there had been a choice? If we were just two mokes who experienced a technical failure? Why would I tell you and make you suffer too? And what if you didn't care? What if you thought of this like . . . having your hard drive blow up? Did I really want to know that either?

I glanced at the giant schoolhouse clock and, as I had become adept at doing, immediately corrected for the time it was in California. Five in the evening. A sunny Sunday at the little blue clapboard house across the sandy street from the beach that stretched away to the end of reckoning, so that the mind had to conjure what the eye could not observe.

The silly-assed music began to swell: There we were, Vincent and me, dragging the picnic basket between us, a chunky little kid running ahead, too close to the tickle of the tide . . . No.

I didn't want a child. I wanted . . . maybe a new job. Maybe to be a professor. To go skiing in Utah. Maybe—someday—that kid.

Damn it!

Why in the hell did they give me a whole night to lie here without a good sedative and think morbidly mopey thoughts about a guy?

I sat down on that beach. It was late October. Even the surfers, too dumb and stoned to feel the cold, had gone off to Mexico or

Hawaii. The little stand that sold ice cream was boarded up for the winter.

There wasn't a single person on that strand except one woman, her shoulders lost in a big old stretched-out sweater, her arms wrapped around her drawn-up knees, her long hair snarled by the rising wind.

She sat looking out to sea. You couldn't see her face.

CHAPTER FOURTEEN

"Vincent," Beth said. "Are you awake?"

"Now I am," he said. "What time is it?"

"It's eight o'clock on Monday morning."

"Wait," Vincent said.

Beth listened, not patiently. Something metallic clanged and something heavy, like a thick book, thumped on Vincent's end.

The sounds made Beth want to scream. She was not a terrifically neat person herself. Still, it drove her over the edge when people on TV knocked the phone off the nightstand and mumbled, "Yuh," even when it was the detective calling to say the woman buried alive had only one hour of oxygen left. What was that about? Were people who slept heavily supposed to be more virile and serious, unlike Beth, who could be awake and cogent in one second? Were these shows written by the same people who thought it was sexy if women ate meat?

"Vincent, are you there now?"

"Yes, I am. I am. You do know it's six o'clock here—in the morning."

"Well, I'm not calling to ask about the weather."

"Ma, is something wrong? Is Eliza okay? Is the baby okay?"

Beth thought, *Is this possible?* Of course not. Why would this be the first thing to spring to Vincent's mind? Now what could she say? She could say that she dialed the number by accident when she knocked the phone and the lamp off the nightstand. She could say she was lost in South Dakota.

"It's about Sicily Coyne," she said.

"What?"

"Is Emily there?"

"No."

Beth tried to gather and sort her thoughts, but they were fragmentary. She could not even match up the emotions with the various slices of fact: One thought was about the baby, but not Ben and Eliza's baby. Another was the fact that Sicily was pregnant but, by tomorrow, she would not be. Sicily did not want Vincent to know. Beth was refusing to honor Sicily's privacy (guilt). Vincent was a gutless, self-centered egoist whose behavior with Sicily made Beth ashamed, despite the fact that she fully intended to defend him to Marie Caruso at lunch just a few hours from now (ambivalence), and his brevity at this moment was indicative of some strain of Vincent's personality that Beth had known well, twenty years ago, and wanted to believe had improved with time.

"So," Vincent said. "If this is about what happened between Sicily and me, I've told you, Ma, I feel terrible about it. But it would have never worked. She's so young—"

"Gee," Beth said. "How could a girl whose father burned to death in front of her and whose mother died in a car wreck and who lived with a horrible injury for more than ten years be such a ninny? I can see why that was stressful."

"What's going on? I can tell you're mad. Like, irrational."

"Sicily is pregnant."

"Wow."

Wow? Beth thought. "Despite whatever form of birth control was used, nothing is foolproof, and, yes, Sicily is pregnant."

"You're saying she's . . . I'm the father?"

"Are you stupid?"

"Well, how long has it been?"

Beth realized she had been married too long. She had become her mother-in-law. "Vincent, do you think there is any reason on earth I would be calling to tell you this, especially at six in the morning, if you were not the father?" Beth said, and immediately repented. She did not want to say "the father," because that implied there would be a child, and there would not be a child.

The previous night, Marie, crying so hard that she was incoherent, had pulled her car off the road because she couldn't see to drive. When she finally calmed down enough, she called to tell Beth that the impossible had happened. Was this why Beth had stayed up all night, in a fury, when Sicily and Vincent were on the beach? Of course! The sweet little fling would have statistically impossible consequences, and Beth . . . had had a premonition. Or was she just crazy? Beth never mistrusted her intuition. Had she ever counted the times it had been wrong versus right? She was almost always right, she was sure of it.

Here was proof! Stick two people from families with the statisti-cally impossible gene together and what did you get?

Then Vincent confirmed exactly what Beth had been thinking.

"This is hard to take in," Vincent said. "I knew it, though. I just knew it. I knew something was going to happen with this, Ma, but I didn't know what. She was so into it."

"Why did you . . . why were you so . . . foolish, then?"

"I've asked myself that a dozen times."

Beth's distress and pity flipped over again, and she was indignant. A dozen times? A full dozen? Since she'd learned about Sicily, Beth had been able to think of little else. Perhaps it would be impossible for Vincent to grasp, as a man—as a human being—how Sicily, given all she had endured, might consider the need for this abortion nothing more than an obstacle, an unfortunate patch of rough ground. Maybe Sicily did think exactly that. Maybe girls didn't agonize over such things as they had in Beth's youth.

"Are you there, Ma?"

"Yes. Just thinking. So, I'm sorry. I shouldn't have said you were foolish."

"I was, though. Sicily got the impression that there was way more between us than there was."

Again going from contrition to disbelief, Beth could barely speak.

"The thing was, I had something she needed."

"Are you really saying something that's going to make me want to kill you, like that she needed a good—"

"No. Ma, if you think I'm that big a jerk, why did you call me? I've been thinking about it, and why we did what we did, and I think that what she needed was to feel as beautiful as any other girl. And she is beautiful. She has things that aren't, you know, Hollywood perfect. But you know how people can lose a bunch of weight and look in the mirror and they still see a fat person? She was like that."

"You're saying it was mercy."

"What's wrong with mercy?"

"Nothing. But how do you think it would make her feel if she knew that?" There was more rattling and rustling, familiar sounds, of Vincent opening and closing his front door, something he did, as did Pat, every morning—for no reason anyone could ever discern—and measuring coffee into the maker.

"She is a proud person and I guess she would feel bad. But there were other reasons. Obvious reasons I don't want to have a conversation about with my mother. But I have feelings for Sicily."

"Why didn't you call her after? Ever?"

"Ma, I didn't call Sicily *because* I have feelings for Sicily! Uncomfortable feelings. And that would have made it worse. I live here. She lives there. . . ."

"People move."

The next pause was so long that Beth believed Vincent had hung up on her. But at last he exhaled, a long breath. "Don't you wonder why I'm not married?"

Beth thought, *Vincent's gay. He's a good dresser and always wears cologne.* "No," she admitted. "I just figured you weren't ready."

"I'll never be ready. That's it. My life is . . . People talk about having baggage? My life is a wagon train. Everybody has a way of being in life, and mine is, I'm better off . . . Well, the other person is too. So basically, for the same reasons Ben got married almost as soon as he could drive, I didn't."

"Why didn't you tell me this? Ever?"

"Because you would think it was your fault." Vincent paused and said then, "You called because you think I should do something. What should I do?"

"You would think that two people like you and Sicily would have more in common."

"Like alcoholics?"

"Okay. Well. Sicily can't have children, Vincent. The drugs she has to take . . . If she ever does, she'll have to adopt them. Probably. She didn't have time to go through freezing her eggs—"

"Tell me what you want me to do."

"I think you should call her."

"She's having an abortion? When?"

"As soon as possible. Today or tomorrow," Beth said, and gave Vincent the number that Marie had given to her.

When she put down the phone, Beth realized that the abortion was probably not only today but at this moment and that for Vincent to call Sicily now would seem forced and artificial. But even a faint gesture was better than nothing. For all her children's adult lives, Beth had told them that nothing, no matter how grim or humiliating, was made worse by talking about it. She hoped she was right.

———

Marie stood up as Beth staggered into Le Giraffe, shoved by the wind that leapt up the avenue, leaving her breathless. Even Beth, who knew almost nothing about clothes, could recognize the unmistakable lines of vintage Chanel, wool as supple as silk. She guessed maybe . . . 1958. Maybe 1950. Definitely five grand.

"Hello, Beth. Do you want me to order you some tea?" Marie said.

"I'd like a drink," Beth said. Marie waved politely to the server, who made a promissory gesture. "I want a vodka and cranberry juice thing . . ."

"That's a cosmopolitan," Marie said to the waiter.

"No, the one with orange juice too."

"That's a madras."

"Huh," said Beth. "I didn't know that a little juice changed the name."

"It raises the price too. Restaurants get you coming and going," Marie said. Beth ignored the jab. "Here's to better times. And, Beth, here's the thing. Sicily thinks she's in love with Vincent."

Beth thought of the way Sicily, in California, looked at Vincent, her eyes infatuation in animation, emitting little holograms of goopy pastel butterflies. And when Vincent looked at Sicily, it was with a bemused and bittersweet indulgence, something almost big-brotherly, except when Sicily bounced down to breakfast in running shorts and one of Vincent's shirts—and nothing else.

"The operation was scheduled for this morning at nine," said Marie. "I called and asked you to meet me because Sicily decided to postpone it. Now it is scheduled for tomorrow. The doctors want this done immediately, and not only for their own reasons. For Sicily's well-being. Vincent has to call Sicily and tell her to go ahead. Sicily is a very, very bullheaded young woman. *Testarda*." Marie tapped her forehead. "But if she were to have some idea about keeping this baby, withdrawing from those drugs would not just take her back where she was before. She could get a massive infection and die."

Beth tried to cleanse her mind of horrific pictures. "I told him the same thing," she said. "This morning."

"So we agree."

"He's a grown man," Beth said.

"She's a grown woman," Marie said, and began to cry openly, making no effort to sponge away the tears with her thick serviette. "She is all I have. And she has been through so much. I love her so much."

Beth said, "So do I, Marie. Not like you do. But I've spent at least three days a week with her, for nearly seven months. She's very dear to me."

They lined the glasses up, like little chess pieces. After three Mahatmas—or whatever Marie had called them—Beth knew she couldn't drive home. At Marie's invitation, she rode back in a cab with her to her apartment for a nap, to be followed by some strong coffee. Beth left a message for Pat that she would be home late, then wondered why she had: Pat never got home before one in the morning. She then called Ben's cell phone to check on Eliza but she got his voice mail.

Eliza had strained her back the previous night, helping to move a girl whose leg and hand and lip had been reattached after a neighbor's four young dalmatians attacked her. Eliza had taken the morning off, and Beth didn't want to risk calling the house in case her daughter-in-law had slept in. The baby wasn't due for at least a month, although Eliza was so big that the other residents teased Dr. Cappadora for getting her dates mixed up.

Marie directed Beth to Sicily's newly made bed. On Sicily's bedside table were photos of her father, her mother, and her much-younger self. There was also an enlargement of a photo Beth had taken: Sicily and Vincent were sitting on his porch swing, arguing elaborately with Beth over something—probably to not take the picture. Sicily's hands were palms-forward in protest; Vincent had buried his face in her neck. Sicily had seen that photo on the digital camera and asked Beth for a print. Beth lay down on the bed and studied the picture: She had disapproved so strongly of the friendship initially. Throughout the early days, she made no secret of that. On a few occasions, she'd been downright chilly. But by the end of the week, they were just so damned charming together. Seeing Sicily so fully happy . . . for perhaps the first time since she was a child; seeing Vincent so natural, so unguarded, perhaps for the first time since *he* was a child . . . The mother in her could no more resist that private little snapshot than the photographer could.

Beth closed her eyes and, instantly, she dozed. When her cell phone, in the pocket of her coat, nudged her ribs, Beth took it out and tucked a pillow in its place.

Sometime later, she woke to a loud chime in a room that was dark except for the lights from the concrete cliffs outside. Breaking the surface of her hard sleep like a swimmer, Beth narrowed her eyes to read the bright little screen. It was from Ben: GRANDMA: WHERE R U? CHARLES VINCENT CAPPADORA. BABY FINE. MAMA 2!

Eliza's back pains hadn't been work-related at all! Nearly giggling into the darkness with excitement, Beth texted back that she was already downtown and would be there within the hour. She also wrote: WHY DID U WAIT SO LONG? DAD THERE? A grandson. She and Pat had a grandson! Stella had a baby brother! As she sat up and fumbled for Sicily's bedside lamp, about to call out to Marie, Beth again caught sight of the photo on Sicily's bedside shelf.

Sicily and Eliza were in the same hospital.

What, Beth thought, *have I done?*

Reluctantly, Hollis Grigsby entered the staff meeting in one of the hospital's largest and most comfortable conference rooms. The sky outside the floor-to-ceiling windows, gravid with what could only be snow, and so early, was by then fully dark. Hollis opened the door to the sharp, unmistakable smell of Chinese takeout. Evidently, everyone knew that this would not be one of those nights when people got home in time for the seven o'clock Pilates class at the community center. She sat down and said, "I hope some of that has meat, even if it's mystery meat. There are a few of us left who haven't gone over to veg and are taking our chances."

The joke hit the ground like a manhole cover.

Kelli Buoté pushed a carton down past several others toward Hollis, who was spooning up some sticky rice. As she made a big business of exclaiming over the joy of pork, Hollis inventoried the faces around the table—not every member of the team but every discipline, from surgeons to social services, was represented. The only urgent face missing was that of Dr. Cappadora, who had just given birth to a healthy baby boy, providing this doleful day its one sweet note. No one sneaked in a surreptitious glance at a watch—well, these days, it was often a phone. So this was not only obligatory, it was interesting. It should be, Hollis thought, since it was unprecedented.

At least in Hollis's opinion, Sicily's dilemma should not continue to be unprecedented. Restricting face transplants to women who already had their families or were past the age of childbearing was expedient but unfair, particularly as those standards did not apply to men. It had been her hope that someone would work up a study that would definitively establish the counter-indications of the anti-rejection drugs on the developing fetus and what alternative medicines might be substituted, at least in the short run of a pregnancy, when the majority of teratogenic events expressed themselves. Most laypeople said that birth defects "occurred" during the first trimester, and it was true that the developing neurological system was most vulnerable to damaging agents during that time. Yet most birth defects were present at the moment of conception, and many of those—which altogether were a small number—were correctible. With other organ-transplant protocols—kidneys being the most common example—the anti-rejection drugs were rarely suspended. Although Hollis considered her knowledge of gynecology and high-risk obstetrics about on the level with that of a good paramedic, she knew that the likeliest complication was an early delivery, forced by a threatened rejection. Kidneys, however, often came from perfect-match donors—some unrelated; many near relatives—so the theoretical likelihood of rejection was smaller in any case. But the sampling for limb and face transplants was still so small, and the black box so large, they nearly overlapped. Although face transplants had accelerated after the first tentative decade, they were still as exotic as heart transplants were in 1978. To Hollis's shock, she still met people who believed that a transplanted heart would last "a lifetime" in the chest of a forty-year-old man—not perhaps ten years, maybe a few more. Nothing medical science had yet contrived could make a solid-organ transplant last the way a soft-tissue transplant would. Perhaps it just wasn't possible.

"If there was something definitive we could tell her, it would be so much easier," said Sira Barathongon, the chief resident, as if reading Hollis's mind.

"We have told her, over and over, that we believe there is quite possibly substantial risk to the fetus, of birth defect or early spontaneous abortion, from the protocol we have created for her," Livingston answered. "I'm betting she will go ahead. She was upset, understandably. The procedure is scheduled. Sicily wanted some time to adjust. But we talked last night after the pregnancy test. She's invested in her face. She's come too far. She understands what is at stake. She further knows that she can perhaps harvest ova, for later, when she is in a relationship. We're not dealing with some peasant girl here. Sicily knows her medicine."

"But listen to the words you just used," Polly Guthrie put in. "'Possibly substantial risk.' You don't even know what kind. From what I see here . . ." Polly made an open-accordion gesture that encompassed the stacks in front of each of them, which were the materials given to every potential full- or partial-face-transplant candidate and donor family. "The phrase 'not proven' is used more than anything else!"

Hollis said, "But I do believe that the way that Imuran can disrupt the synthesis of DNA and RNA and cell division makes an adverse outcome more than a slight possibility."

"The British study has been considered invalid for years—"

"Only because there cannot be any sort of definitive data without a sampling, and the population is just too small," Hollis said.

"And what if Sicily should contract an infection during the pregnancy?" asked Tony Coles, a neurological surgeon in his forties. "We have her medical records that show she had her MMRs as a child, but those aren't foolproof, any more than our foolproof birth control."

"With any pregnant woman, we proceed as though she's immune to rubella," said Dr. Sara Glass. "But that Sicily is not. Of course, there'd be a nuchal translucency inventory at the first opportunity."

"Why," Hollis asked, "are we talking about the potential health of the fetus only? Say that the chance she carries on with this pregnancy is small. Fine. But what if she actually does? Isn't that why we're here, to discuss the elephant in the room, the pregnancy that might really go forth? Should it, the equal or greater concern is Sicily's transplant. A full rejection would destroy her emotionally. And, although I think we could fight off a deadly infection, it could kill her."

There was a long interval during which everyone tore open their chopsticks and applied themselves to their meals. Their agitated cogitation was nearly audible: None of them had ever seen a full-blown rejection.

Hollis had seen only two. Who was the man with the hand? Arthur . . . Arthur Wilkie. That was it. The dusky red line of blood poisoning, the high, foul smell. There could be no question of taking off only the hand: They'd had to section the arm above the elbow. "It's better," Wilkie had said the next day. "It never felt like me. It never felt like it belonged there." And Hollis was reminded again how the body indubitably had such a mysterious head.

Finally, Livingston said, "Hollis, you're right. This is a harrowing possibility. Sicily has done so well. Not a sign of an episode. Nothing. No hand tremors. Headaches, but that was stress. No blood-pressure elevation. No increased hair growth. Nothing. We virtually expect— well, at least the beginnings of—a rejection by this point. I can think only of one other time—"

"Marilla Santiago."

"With so smooth a course," Livingston finished, nodding. "That's what I can't bear. She might be thinking that since she's doing so well, why couldn't she have a child? The irony of her own good luck. It might influence her."

"Yes, but the very fact of her doing so well, I have to say, makes me bold enough to wonder if we actually have some latitude," said Hollis.

All of them turned toward the two doctors who represented the medical side of the team, Dr. Elizabeth Ahrens and Dr. Andrea Park. Hollis had never noticed how twinlike these two Asian women were— or was she being racist? Each of them had shoulder-length hair cut in a bob, identical black-rimmed plastic glasses, and immaculate complexions.

On the legal pad between them, they had sketched out possible alternative dosages, which Dr. Park now described. Then Dr. Ahrens told Hollis, "I'm not entirely satisfied here. I'm going to mess with this and get back to you. There's also something else, some research I need to follow up on, and the guy is in Germany. We need a baseline flight plan if she should choose to go through with this and were to have a serious episode in the fifth or sixth month."

"And that's where we're open to legal exposure," said Joel Brodsky.

Hollis delicately plucked up a few mouthfuls of what she now assumed was lo mein with chicken and thought before she said anything. Technically, the hospital was not liable for anything Sicily Coyne chose or anything that befell her as a result of the transplant— emotionally or physically. Stacks of forms released the University of Illinois, the University of Illinois Chicago Circle Campus, the University of Illinois Chicago Circle Campus Hospital and Clinics, the University of Illinois Chicago Circle Campus Transplant Clinic, the University of Illinois Chicago Circle Campus Department of Psychology, Dr. Hollis Grigsby . . . her heirs, their heirs and their assigns, the city of Chicago, the known universe . . . and, at the end of the day, all of those came to nothing in a situation for which there could have been no planning for this foreseen consequence.

"Here," Brodsky continued, "it points out that should Sicily Coyne willingly or unwillingly fail to present herself on the assigned day each month for her injection . . . and should a pregnancy result from that failure . . ."

"She didn't, though," Hollis said. "It was the medicine that failed, not Miss Coyne."

"But she absolves us of any responsibility for any resulting—" Joel went on.

"I think in fact she does absolve us for any result," said Hollis. "Not in legal terms but in real terms. As Livingston said, Sicily knows her medicine."

"So our course here is . . ." Polly Guthrie said. "To counsel when asked? To advise, as Livingston did initially?"

Hollis shook her head. "Our course is to wait," she said.

CHAPTER FIFTEEN

When Vincent called, I didn't recognize the number. It was a Chicago exchange. So I picked up without preparing myself and said crisply, "This is Miss Coyne, Coyne Illustration and Design. Please leave a message. I'll call back sooner rather than later." I didn't try to beep.

"Sicily, it's Vincent," he said, as I put my hand over the microphone opening. "I'm glad that you didn't answer, because I need to get this all out before we talk any more, and that might be hard, especially since we haven't talked for a while. Which is my fault. What I want to say is how sorry I am. It sucks that you had to find this out alone and make this decision alone. It sucks that something so sweet turned out so painful. Maybe I don't know how you feel, but I think I might know a version of it. Like, thinking you won something you never imagined you would and then finding out you could lose more than you ever imagined you could lose. I'm here in town. You know Eliza had the baby. You might be too sad to see me—"

"I'm not that sad," I said.

"What? Who's there?"

"I said, I'm not that sad. There's nothing to be sad about yet. I suppose I will be soon, but not yet."

"You sat there and listened to me the whole time?"

"You were speaking into a telephone, Vincent, to me. It wasn't like I was eavesdropping."

"It feels that way! I completely had my guard down."

"So, if I said anything, you'd have put your guard up?"

"I didn't mean that."

I hadn't meant what I'd said either. My big mouth, which still seemed to have a life of its own, after all it has done to me, jumped out like some crazy warrior waving a shield, eager to demonstrate that I would defend the chance to hurt my own feelings before anyone else could. Beyond my unfortunate inability to pass up any opportunity to be flippant in unfortunate circumstances, it was also true that everything about Vincent's speech, so carefully mournful, pissed me off. So after my first riposte, I held my tongue.

Finally, Vincent said, "But, Sicily, what could possibly be the upside of this?" As though that wasn't obvious.

The first thing that popped into my head was "It's a normal experience. It's what might have happened to me in the ordinary way of things. It's interesting."

"It wasn't supposed to happen, Sicily."

"Neither was any of the other stuff."

Vincent sighed. Suddenly he seemed so much older than I. He asked if he could come over, today or later in the week, or if I would meet him someplace.

Of that, I wasn't sure. It seemed abrupt. I did want to see him. Of *course* I wanted to see him. There was no reason that I shouldn't have wanted to see Vincent, except that he hadn't managed to intuit by ESP that I was pregnant—when that thought hadn't even crossed my own mind. I'd known about it for two weeks now. He hadn't called me or shot me a text or spent a couple of bucks on a greeting card since I'd left California. (Although what would it have said? *The story's always true . . . a screw is just a screw . . .*) Why avoid Vincent, now that he'd shown up in Chicago for some *other* reason entirely than seeking me? Why, except that we'd done it like rabbits for six days and then he seemingly forgot we'd ever met?

So I gathered my courage to refuse. But my courage was rinsed away by what I could only call the unreason of desire. Softly, I said, "I'll drive down to see you. I'll pick you up . . . You'll be my pickup." I was paraphrasing a line from an old movie, one that I loved, and I should have known that Vincent wouldn't miss something like that. It was maybe one of the saddest movies of all time.

"That was a great film about very poor impulse control," Vincent said. "And its adverse consequences. . . . So, are you going to come with Marie?"

But I just said a quick goodbye and ended the call.

He didn't know I had a car.

I'd had it for only six days. I bought the car before I had a driver's license. I paid cash. All that money I'd saved for my wedding and fancy kitchen appliances.

I GPS'ed Beth and Pat's town and was surprised to see how far away it was from the city. But that was okay. Driving was a novelty for me. It did not at all intimidate me that my previous trips were precisely two—one to the mall, where I sat in the parking lot and said to myself, *You have just accomplished the same thing as most sixteen-year-old people do,* and one to the clinic. I would now be traveling, if I counted traffic, a good ninety minutes, straight, up to Harrington, and I did not even really know where that was—just one of those pretend towns somewhere south of Wisconsin. I'd been there only once, with my aunt, and I remembered nothing except the look on Beth's face as she opened her bright-blue front door. A bright-blue door in a swanky subdivision. That would narrow it down. I could call back and get the exact address, but I would have rather swallowed a handful of straight pins. Luckily, I found Beth and Pat Cappadora in the online white pages. I was actually looking forward to what now seemed as though it would be a sort of journey, a road trip.

My driving lessons had been remarkable for their succinct and precise nature, eight hours on two consecutive weekends requiring nothing more than twin Styrofoam cups of black coffee, my aunt's nerves of steel, her stalwart Toyota Camry, and the huge parking lot at T. J. Hintzey. I'd passed my test first try. What amazed me more than the car was my driver's license picture. How could I stop staring at it? I rearranged it in different places in my wallet as though I was a sixteen-year-old kid, which was exactly what I was in this regard, developmentally delayed by nearly ten years. My driver's license picture was my first ordinary photo, just a picture like anyone else's picture. When the woman who took it made me pose a second time, I almost started to hyperventilate—had she noticed something odd about me? But it was only because I wasn't close enough to the white line and the top of my head would have been sliced out. *Smile nice,* the woman said. She couldn't tell and she didn't care, and her indifference was one of the epic moments of my life to that point. There were plenty of photos Beth had taken after the transplant—photos from California, sumptuous portraits, and even one of Vincent and me together. I kept it next to my bed, near my father's fire helmet. Before I fell asleep at night, I would sometimes look at it and think, *This is how I would feel if I were any other woman looking at the picture.* It was color, in that kind of color that's juiced up, that reminds you of a carnival. On these glacially still and solitary nights, as the dark closed in—light draining from my big windows earlier and earlier each day—I imagined myself a woman looking at a picture of herself and her boyfriend.

Who loved her.

Who lived far away.

Who was . . . in a war or . . . law school.

Or was in the Peace Corps.

Or was an archaeologist.

A boyfriend who wanted terribly to reach her by any means and touch her as soon as distance would permit, who took out her letters and got a rush just from looking at her handwriting.

Then I would put the photo away.

Before I left, I dressed three or four times, finally settling on black jeans with gray knee-high boots and gray suede gloves. I don't remember the colors of the sweaters I wore, just that there were a bunch of them, and scarves twisted together to warm my neck. My hair had begun to grow quickly and was trimmed into a long, thick bob with bangs, which made me look like something that wouldn't be out of place in a documentary about Julius Caesar. So I braided it and rolled it up and stuck one of my pairs of silver-plated chopsticks through the knot. My car was a powder-blue Chevy Cachet, a four-door demo from the previous year that I bought from a guy in our building who worked for a dealership. The car I had planned to buy whenever I got around to learning to drive—which seemed like part of an indefinite future a year before—would have been a Toyota like my aunt's, only a bit sportier. But I was already making an offer on the Cachet before I asked myself why. I didn't have to ask myself why.

I was buying it in case.

Just as it seemed that everyone on earth was now driving a four-door powder-blue Chevy Cachet, it also now seemed that every restaurant and gym, every coffee store, every lobby, library, local park, and deli was stuffed with pregnant women. There were ranks of them, waddling in step, so many there was barely room for them at a given venue. Some were cute wifeys, athletic and slim-hipped, their planned pregnancies invisible from the view of their tidy rumps. Some seemed to have been caught unawares and now sported a baffling new rim of peripheral flesh around their customary silhouettes, as though a second layer of arm or chin had been drawn around the outline of the original and then colored in. A few had the childlike arms and legs of supermodels with great protuberant melons of bellies sticking out, like the bottoms of hammocks under their long sweaters. Some were alone, holding the wrists of recalcitrant toddlers. Some were proprietary, holding the biceps of big, vaguely bewildered-looking guys.

Where had these women been before? When had they come outside? I studied them with an almost indecent interest; but they did not exchange a complicit glance with me. It would have been impossible for anyone to tell that I was one of them. My stomach was still concave and my belly below it taut as a fitted sheet.

Once I found Beth and Pat's place, I was surprised to see how ordinary their house looked. Beth didn't care much about appearances, unlike me, but she was still pretty at her age and had a distinct low-key. flair for dressing up anything she wore.

The house looked like what a kid would draw if you said, *What does a rich person's house look like?* It was all wheat-colored brick, with loads of windows and height, on a base structure that was not quite colonial and not quite anything else. The big wraparound porch had gray rocking chairs arrayed along its length behind a gracious sweep of railing. There were rows of arched windows along the front. A ribbon of maroon stonework lapped it like a waistband. The only touch of Beth's peculiar humor was the bronze fountain in the little side yard at the front, which was in the shape of a crash-test dummy. The house did have a bright-blue door, as I remembered from the first day, literally a lifetime ago.

I got out of the car and sat on the hood. It was so warm from the drive—which had taken not ninety minutes but more than two hours, forty minutes idling in traffic—that it gave my butt a little start, despite my layers of cashmere and the cold temperature. I sat there for a couple of minutes, finally pulling the chopsticks out and shaking my hair loose so that I could put on the hat I had in one of my pockets. As I pulled it down over my ears, I saw Vincent.

He was sitting on one of those rockers almost hidden by a porch pillar. His hair was longer and he looked thinner, hunched, his body swimming in a beat-up leather jacket that must have been as old as he was. He was like a savannah creature out of his habitat, tawny and restless, stretching, chafing his hands, shrugging. He also wasn't so goddamned great as he was when he starred in my fantasies. Just a too-skinny guy with a big nose and a hippie haircut and the only eyes I'd ever seen that exactly matched mine. What was going on with me? Why was I expecting so much of this . . . hookup? For that was what it had been. A hookup. Fun, intense, voluptuously backlit by the landscape that had launched a million unplanned pregnancies.

And still, just a fling.

But did he remember what kind of fling it had been?

We had lived together for a week, almost . . . as husband and wife. He cleared a drawer for me. Our showers weren't necessarily taken together. He had invited me to his production meetings and I'd attended, and not just to gaze at Vincent and be gazed upon by his associates. I'd used his razor and he'd complained. He'd walked into the master bath while I was using the toilet and I'd screamed. (I still don't do those things in front of anyone over the age of six.) When the paper came, we divided it among us, Beth claiming the arts section, Vincent the entertainment pages, and me the news. He'd prepared his one dish—which we called Vincent's Wrong Assumption Pasta, because he could not have cooked his way out of a Honduran prison. We'd created a world that was the façade of a suburban town with a concrete box behind it.

And then I left. The set was struck. Mutually, without the need to say so, we'd faced facts. At least, he had. If I'd faced facts also, I had no right to be so angry with him. Why was I so angry? Why did I feel every right to be so angry? That time together was, in the moment, so much more than, and afterward was so much less than. I still feel that it was probably something that happens to everyone once in a lifetime, but it certainly hadn't happened to me. Had there been a single plan exchanged, a commitment to meet again? Had there been any terms to our endearments? There had not. And, still, I was left with the awkward and painful need to regard what read like the opening of a story as a sentence that began and ended in parentheses.

Vincent had been perfectly appropriate.

Vincent had been nice, in a callous, guy sort of way.

It seemed then that he couldn't have participated in the same moments that I had and behaved with such pragmatism. But that was the appropriate response. It didn't come easily to him; he was working at it. You're either calibrated to do a one-night stand or you aren't. He was probably calibrated for a one-night stand, but not with me.

At the time, I had a whole litany of hypotheses about why Vincent and I became the soundtrack of my life thereafter, for quite a long time thereafter: It was hormones. It was my quasi-filial attachment to Beth. It was transference—the wish to replace my imploded presumptive future life with something handy and easy-to-install.

Only years later could I admit what it was: Love. Of a kind. Not every love is meant to last forever.

As I sat there on my car hood, watching Vincent on his porch and wishing feverishly to run into his arms and have him carry me upstairs, I realized that he thought I was someone else: He didn't recognize me as the pilot of a car. I have no idea of what Vincent's image of me was at that time, but I would venture he thought of me as fragile-but-plucky. I stood up.

Vincent did the same. "For Christ sake! Sicily!"

"It's my car," I said.

"You're skinny," Vincent said.

"Not really. I was going to say the same thing to you."

"Just busy. I forget to eat." Not *busy and preoccupied thinking about you, Sicily, and wondering what the next chapter of your story will be. Busy. Busy with my work and my friends and the bar at the Peninsula and Emily, probably.*

"Me too," I told him. "Too much work! I have, like, fifty unfinished projects. And for me it's a holdover from the days when I couldn't taste food. At first it was like the world festival of eating, and now . . . half the time I get sick, anyway."

"Yeah," Vincent said, and tried but couldn't stop himself from glancing down at my midsection, his eyes coins to a magnet. "Do you want to come in? One of my aunts that you haven't met is here."

Maybe not so much, I thought. What would he say to introduce me? Miss Sicily Coyne, the girl who previously had no face? You've seen her in a bunch of Mom's photos? She's the one who came out to California, the one I hardly know who's a little pregnant with my baby? That sounded not so convivial.

"Another time," I said. "Let's go someplace."

We couldn't decide where to go.

Vincent had just finished a massive brunch, and I didn't want to be one of those couples at the chain-store coffee place, unable to look each other in the face but staring into soup-bowl-size coffee cups as if they were oracles. People went to have coffee to break up. How could Vincent and I break up? We'd never been a couple.

After driving and driving, we finally landed at the Milton Arboretum near his grandparents' house, near where I grew up. There was an evergreen garden there. The firs and spruces and pines looked overbright, spray-painted against the metallic sky. There was a place where an old bridge spanned a skating pond. My father used to take me when I was little. I learned to skate on chunks of wood that he tied to my snow boots—the way, my father said, he learned to skate. The pond wasn't yet frozen, but Vincent soon was. I kept tromping along the avenue between the evergreens, and he kept shuffling along behind me. Neither of us said a word. I handed one of my scarves back to him and was surprised when he accepted it, turning up the collar of the coat and winding it around, California style.

"Spartan-wannabe woman," he said. "Sicily, are you craving exercise?"

"I hike to forget," I said. Vincent sighed again and I asked him, "So what do you think about everything? How's it going in your mind? I wouldn't know, because you've never spoken to me about it, or, come to think of it, about anything. You never called. You never wrote. I sound like an Italian grandmother."

Vincent sat down on a wooden bench that seemed to have been put there for the purpose. "I wanted to," he said.

"Please don't say that. It's not the biggest load of bullshit—that would be my aunt, Sister Mary Augustine, who you haven't met, telling me that God saved me from the fire for a purpose that I, being only human, wasn't meant to understand—but it's close. No one who wants to call you doesn't call you. If somebody actually wants to call you, he'll climb eight thousand feet to the top of a mountain to get good reception. Say you thought about it in passing. Don't say you wanted to."

"Didn't my mother tell you why I didn't?"

"Your mother is a classy woman, Vincent. She hasn't said a word to me about you or your motives for anything you did or didn't do."

"I'm really cold," he said. That was evident. He was huddled up on that bench like a wet cat. "I don't mean in the emotional way."

"We could go to my house, I guess. You've never seen it. The view is pretty."

"Is that a good idea?"

"You're bigger than I am, Vincent, although not by much. I'm not going to rape you, if that's what you think."

"It's not you I'm worried about."

"Charming touch of wistful lust. Very good."

"Why are you being sarcastic? You aren't making this easier, Sicily!"

"It's not supposed to be easy," I said, tromping past him on the way to the car. I grabbed my scarf from Vincent's neck as I passed him, intending only to put it back on—the sun was setting, and it genuinely was getting colder. But I ended up pulling him off the bench. "I'm sorry. I'm really sorry. I didn't mean to hurt you."

"I didn't mean to hurt you," Vincent said, and put his arms around me, holding my head against his chest as though I were a child, making wings of his leather jacket to enclose both of us. He placed his hand under my sweater and said, "Your skin is hot." One touch of his hand and my whole body snapped to attention.

"It's physiobiology," I said. "That's how you . . . are. Hotter to the touch."

"I've never touched a pregnant girl."

"Yes, you have. At least once."

Vincent kissed me and kissed me, and when he moved his face to kiss me more thoroughly, I kissed his throat, and he slid his hands into my hair and pulled my face up closer to his and kissed me again. At first he barely opened his lips, and then he was almost rough, as though he could engulf me and swallow all that fear and wonderment through the gateway of my mouth. It worked. Maybe it was my lack of experience of the world, but I thought then, and I still think, that nobody else could ever reach in and wring my core the way Vincent did.

As it turned out, the backseat of my car was just as the previous owner had described it—excellently roomy. I was on the brink of yet another first (car sex) when the shed layers of coats and scarves on the seat began to make me feel that we were trying to connect on the floor of a coat closet in some teenager's room—or my closet, for that matter. "I'm pretty flexible, as people go," I said. "But this is going to be kind of awkward."

"Did I hurt you?" Vincent asked. "Or the . . . your stomach?"

"I didn't know you cared."

"Sicily, shut the hell up. You did know I cared. This has nothing to do with my not caring. It has everything to do with trying to face life in a practical way."

"Like screwing in a car in a public park when you're both homeowners."

"Okay, let's go to your place. I'll drive," Vincent said. "I'm a bad driver, but you're worse. You drive like you do everything else. Like it was a rodeo and you were the only rider." So he drove and put on music that was sort of like blues, the kind of music you hear on a summer night from someone else's open window. I fell asleep. In what seemed like a moment, Vincent was shaking me and asking what the address was.

"I'm hungry," I said, sitting up. "I'm starving! Could we go out to eat first?"

Vincent said, "No."

When we finally got around to looking at the view from the graceful span of glass that made up the eastern wall of my bedroom, it was close to midnight. Why do people do things like that?

———

We didn't eat takeout in bed with my silver chopsticks.

I'd like to think I'm not that fully a cliché.

We ate takeout pizza in bed with a beach towel spread across our knees.

"Is your aunt home?" Vincent asked, elaborately casual. I smiled at him and shook my head. If she had been home, she wouldn't have heard the sounds I made, like the sounds of wounded birds, sounds I'd never heard myself make—even one Tuesday night at the beach. If she had heard them and considered the source, Aunt Marie would have tried to pretend she was having a nightmare.

I began, "It must be true what they say about hormones, because nothing I ever did—"

"You are just so . . . sweet," Vincent said. "For what that is worth. But it's not worth much. What we did in California was nuts, and now it's nuts-er. It's nuttier, I mean. It actually must be true what they say about hormones. But we should talk now, Sicily."

I would rather have continued to talk about the various gradations of orgasmic experience. He did have a point, if not the genuine right to ask.

"I want to hear your answer. What are you going to do?"

"I know it's high time I answered. It's high time I answered everybody. But I don't know. Something's keeping me back, and it's not Eliza having Charley. It's about me. I've scheduled the abortion for next Monday . . ."

"I'll stay," he said. "I'll stay to be with you."

"You don't have to. It would not be the worst medical thing I ever went through, at least not physically, not by a long shot. But, anyhow, I'm not sure I'm going to have it."

"Have what?"

I realized from the look on his face that Vincent thought I was saying that I didn't know if I was having the baby. I glared at him.

He said then, "You mean, have the . . . procedure."

"It's an abortion. A 'procedure' is getting Botox or porcelain veneers. I hate when people use euphemisms like that."

Vincent got up and pulled his jeans on over his naked rear end. He didn't even bother looking for his underwear. Since the "nonstarter" had taken hold of me in earnest, I'd felt as though my body was trilling with sexual longing about ninety percent of the day, waking or sleeping, and though I knew simply from his stance, from the hardening of the muscles in his back, that we were about to transition from love-making to love-unmaking, I still felt almost nauseated with lust. Or maybe just nauseated, as I learned two minutes later when I had to run in to the bathroom and toss my green-pepper-mushroom-and-onion. In the bathroom, I also brushed my teeth and hair and pulled on a clean white leotard and a white dance skirt that I found on the floor. I couldn't walk back out there with a towel around me. Instinctively it was clear to me that being nude when someone else is dressed is sexy only if you're both burning up, before you do it, or entwined afterward, and we weren't any one of those. As I pulled back my hair and made a knot of it, I noticed that the leotard top was pretty see-through, but the light in the bathroom was superior and there was only one light turned on in my room, with a pale-blue scarf over the shade.

When I came back, Vincent was sitting on the end of the bed, still wearing only his jeans, his hands palm-flat against each other between his knees, his head inclined. "It is some view," he said, nodding toward the expanse of my windows. "Sicily. There are about fifty reasons you can't have a baby now. For reasons of your own health, obviously. I do know that much from the Internet. And what it could do to a baby. So why do you keep putting it off? It's just making it harder."

"You were there too, as I recall. I didn't assault you."

"You did say you were impregnable. Do you think I would have done that if I'd thought we were conceiving a baby?"

"That's how an unplanned pregnancy generally happens, unless someone is tricking someone else, and you know that I wasn't." I felt far less cocky than I sounded. There was something tightly set in Vincent's jaw, a bully's scowl. I could tell it was not the first time he'd ever worn such an expression. I wondered if what I was seeing was the Vincent from long ago, the one Renee had alluded to, the crazy, selfish kid.

You can change your behavior, and if people are smart, mostly they do. But *people* don't really change as they get older; and when they really get old, they just get more like their original selves, like the distilled essence of who they were to begin with. Everyone has a mean streak. Vincent's was more like a fault line.

"What?" I said. "If you think I'm going to decide this based on what you . . ."

"On what I think? Isn't it partly my choice too?"

"If it was, why didn't you find out about it sooner?"

"How, Sicily? The guy doesn't get morning sickness!"

"You could have asked how I was. You could have wondered if I was doing great or if I was doing lousy. Or if I was alive."

"I didn't know it was going on! I thought you were this cute innocent kid about ten years younger emotionally than she was physically and about ten years too young for me, physically and every other way. You've got to know how . . . just, I mean . . . appealing you are to men, Sicily. They don't see that you have a scar on your neck. You're very sexy. I don't want to be responsible for something happening to that face, because of something I did. You look just the way you should look. You have to put this behind you and think of the future. You have to think of the future you're going to have."

He didn't say, *The future you're going to have—not with me.* But he might as well have.

"How would I know that? How appealing I am? Does the fact that I like doing it make me sexy? I didn't even know until the last couple of months that I really liked doing it. How would I know that, Vincent? On the basis of twice? I still don't trust this face, Vincent. All I ever knew was that I was pretty from the boobs down, maybe."

"Don't be an ass. Your face is great. You can see the little scars at your hairline, and that only makes you not perfect in a way that's . . . I don't know, Sicily. I'm not a freaking songwriter."

"And still, six months ago, you—you in particular, Mr. Hollywood, who could date actresses—would have crossed the street not to have to look at me. Who would have called me even average? My ex-boyfriend, the arson accomplice? My hundreds of other lovers before him?"

We were fighting, and the dampness of our lovemaking was still inside me, the scent of bleach on my hands, along with some lavender stuff or cologne Vincent used.

"You don't see how you look. You only see how you don't look. You're trying to have something you can't have right now, the way you think you want it!" He grabbed his sweater, neglecting his T-shirt. "So maybe it's just the effect you had on me. Maybe I'm drawn to birds with broken wings—"

"Beaks," I said.

"I'm not listening to you. You always get the last word. Not this time. Maybe you didn't know the effect you had on me. Here I am with this girl who likes everything I say and do, and I lay one finger on her and she goes through the ceiling. Wouldn't any guy want to make a woman feel like that? That would make you even more . . . I don't know what . . . sweet, like I said. But that doesn't mean we should ride off into the sunset."

"Now tell me, *It's not you, Sicily, it's me. Don't blame yourself.*" I pulled on my sweater and looked at him. "That's the final part, right?"

"It is about me. You had an awful unfair childhood. And I had a scary unfair—let's not get into all that. But this is the truth. Life isn't a song. I would fuck this up like I've fucked up everything I've ever done, except the one thing I don't fuck up, which is making believe."

"Oh, please. That's about as bullshit as *I wanted to call you, but the tides of life held me back.* This isn't a made-for-TV movie about ditching someone, it's really ditching someone. Tell me you don't want to stand in the way of my future happiness."

"You're good at that verbal crap. Hats off, Sicily. I really don't want to stand in the way of your happiness. You have this thing I don't know how you got that makes you able to be happy, or at least you think you can be happy. But here's the thing. I'm not a bad person, but I'm not a nice person. Ask my own mother. Ben is a nice person. My sister, Kerry, is a nice person. I'm adequate." Vincent stepped into his shoes.

I thought, *No, wait, this isn't going at all the way it should. Don't leave. Don't leave me. Wait. Slow down.*

"Someday you're going to have everything you want. Better and more."

"You don't get to be the judge of that," I said. "Don't I get to choose at all?" I was swamped by a sudden tide of sympathy for him. Vincent really believed he was just adequate. He had a past in which he'd needed to choose to fight almost every day.

He reminded me of me.

"But who are you to judge men? Especially men a generation older than you? You have your father the hero and your ex-boyfriend the shit-head loser, so I would look pretty good."

Let's rewind, I thought. *I want a chance to tell you things.* But I said, "Why is this so freaking different from anybody else? People have to figure this out all the time in their lives, and sometimes they don't even know each other. And usually that's a disaster. If you think I'm asking you to have a baby with me, Vincent, I'm not." Certainly, at least in that moment, that was a big fat lie. I was asking just that and he knew it.

I sat down hard on the bed and deliberately pulled my hair over my face. Vincent cupped the back of my neck in one of his hands. I felt myself merge into his touch. Just biology. It was cold in the room except at the intersection of Vincent's hand and the nape of my neck. I bit my lip hard, and it hurt; I realized that I'd never bitten my lip. Effectively, it stanched the tears that would have come crowding into my eyes if I let myself think that I would never forget the precise way that his hand felt there. So I pushed out the words: "I'm not saying I want you to be my partner. I'm saying I don't know if I want to end this pregnancy, because . . ."

"Because why?"

"Because I might want to share my life with someone I love."

"That's what I said, Sicily. How could we know, either of us? The reason I didn't call you was because it was easier to let you hate me and think I was a jerk from California who used you to get over my girlfriend. After you left, I got back with Emily. Did you know that? Then I broke up with Emily again. I couldn't stand being around her. This was after we were together for, like, five years. And I don't think of Emily anymore. If I ever loved anyone, it was Emily Sydney, and I don't think of her anymore. How could you love anyone like that?"

"Do you think of me?"

"What I love is my work. I love my grandfather and my sister and my mother and my brother and my dad. That's family to me."

"Do you? Do you think of me? I don't care about Emily Sydney."

"Why does it matter so much? If I say yes, does that mean you're going to have the baby? Sicily, why are you prolonging this? It's . . . perverse. You could be hurting yourself right now and you don't even know it. Don't do that."

"I'm just talking, Vincent. I have to . . . have the abortion. I think I have to. But do you blame me for wanting a little of what other women can have if they want?"

He stood up, and I realized with alarm that I was about to puke. This certainly would not have happened in the TV version. I ran into the bathroom and held my hair back, paralyzed with shame, then pulled myself up onto the sink, brushed my teeth with my finger, and sluiced my face with cold water. Vincent came into the bathroom with a wet washcloth and pressed it to the back of my neck.

"Settle down, Sicily," he said. "Come on now. Settle down. That's a girl. That's my girl." The sudden crimp in the lines around his eyes and the way the color in them deepened, got too bright, the way Beth's did—it gave him away. He meant what he'd just said. And he also didn't mean it. The melody in the minor key was lovely, until the flat note. "Sicily, I thought of you all the time. I thought of you when I got in bed with Emily and said I was tired and pretended I had to go to sleep right away. Are you happy now? Because I'm not. I will not ever be a father. I don't know how I could. The kid would never see me." Vincent took my hand and led me back into the bedroom, where we sat in the darkness, side by side on the couch. "That's not true. It's not because I'm busy. It's because I don't know how to do things . . . Ben knows how to do them naturally."

And at that moment, I realized that I had been playing a kid's game myself. I had no idea how to be a mother. I'd been raised by two good mothers, but they had never called upon me to take care of any living thing. I had no idea how to raise myself. Now I believed at last that Vincent wasn't trying to do a slow and easy fade. He meant it. He meant that he couldn't love me.

I said softly, "You're doing this whole riff, Vincent, about how this is all about you, and you didn't hear what I said."

"What?"

"What I said about sharing my life with someone I love, I didn't mean sharing my life with you."

Vincent blinked.

"I meant with . . . the child. Someone I would love. That's what I wanted. I'm selfish. And I am confused."

"That's what pregnant teenagers think—a live doll of their own."

"I didn't say I wanted to have the baby so he or she would love me. I'm not a pregnant teenager. My life is behind me. . . ." I recognized the truth in what I was saying as it unfurled word by word from my lips. All the life I knew was behind me, a literally burned bridge. There was no direct connection between the Sicily I was then and the Sicily I was now, except perhaps this maybe-baby, which was the child of my inmost being, my substantial self. The raw substance of this caught me in mid-sentence, forcing me up against a metaphysical mirror.

Was I considering this baby a human bridge back to normal, to a previous self? How dare I do that? But was it wrong if I wanted to build the bridge, not just walk on it? Did it have anything at all to do with Vincent? If it didn't, which one of us was not such a really terrific person? Did I want to feel that I'd wound the clock for someone, just to prove I could? Even with the best of intentions, what kind of selfish person would use her own . . . well, flesh and blood to try to prove her life was entire? I had never felt so absolutely alone.

It seemed plain then. I could see past the thick walls. I needed to be alone to make this decision. Vincent couldn't hold my arm, nor could Beth or Marie. For nearly twenty-six years I had been a child, cared for, shielded, disabled in the realest sense. Vincent said he wasn't sure he knew how to love someone who needed him. I was sure that I didn't. I knew how to be loved. I wanted my own way. Children want their own way. It was possible that I wasn't woman enough to admit that, just once, having my own way was not only wrong but wrongheaded. I could burn my future down as surely as my past had fallen away, consumed.

"I'm sorry," I said. "I am being foolish. We played house in California. I guess some small part of me thought we were meant to play Mommy and Daddy. I'm sorry for putting you through this. I guess I made a wish and there you were. At the luggage carousel. The perfect imaginary boyfriend."

"So you're not . . . you don't think you're in love with me."

"No. Really, how could I be? It would be almost easier to say goodbye if I thought I was. I've always had good luck with being angry. I'm not angry. I want to be your friend. And I mean that. I guess what it comes down to is that I was scared to be on my own. But that's just one more fear to face. Being this woman I keep claiming to be."

Vincent got up fast. "Where is my coat?"

"I'll drive you," I said. "What's wrong?"

"I'll take a cab," he said. "I'm rich. I'm in show business. Right? Didn't you say that? Mr. Hollywood? Your, in quotes, friend? Your buddy? Plus, in that little confession there, you just treated me like . . . there was no one else here but you." There were two spots of dark red on his cheeks, the rest of his face an absence of color, even of pallor, like one of my aunt Marie's "neutral" outfits.

"You don't have to leave either. Stay here, Vincent. Please, Vincent. It's late, and who knows how long it will be before we see each other again? I don't want to forget that—"

"Take care, Sicily." He kissed my forehead.

"Don't go like this."

"What other way is there for me to go? I was . . . It was tearing me up to have to say I didn't want a kid. Then you say, hey, no offense, but it's not going on with you. I need to get to know myself. You're the one who should live in California."

"I'm sorry. I don't know why you're angry."

"I don't either. I'm not angry. I'm . . . just . . . I got what I came for. And I don't mean in the bed."

I should have told Vincent then that, had I been with fifty men, it wouldn't have erased the strong intuition I'd had about him, the first time I saw him, standing there at the airport. There would be no way to prove that, ever. But I had no doubt of it back then. In fact, I still don't. Everything was happening too fast, as though timed by a stopwatch. It was possible that Vincent was playing a role too, because he was used to it, because he'd never seen himself any other way, and trying to do that felt like a dangerous swerve from the known path.

"Here's my card," he said, thrusting it at me. "A machine will pick up. But I check my messages."

"Your card? You're giving me your business card?" I flicked it through the air at his chest. It drifted to the floor between us. "I didn't do one thing to deserve that. Why don't you leave a fifty on the pillow?"

"Let me know what happens, huh? Or tell my mother, so she can send me a text if it's door number one? Or a sonogram, if it's door number two? Or some goddamned thing?"

"That's what they are called. Sonograms," I said. "Ultrasound pictures."

"Sicily, I know that. I do have friends who have children."

"You do have friends, then. Despite not being a nice person. Come on, Vincent. Please. Stay here with me. It's cold and I don't want you to go. I really don't want you to go."

"I'm halfway out the door. Don't say anything else," Vincent told me.

"I had one—my second ultrasound. For them to make sure how to proceed."

"And?"

"Nothing. Only a dot. You couldn't tell anything. It's too soon." It had not been too soon. I had seen a strong, fast fetal pulse and the faint tracing of a spine. Just what you would expect, if you were expecting. It looked alarmingly like something I would draw for a textbook on gestation. The pulse was the worst. It was such evident proof of potential life. The nonstarter had a forming heart. I had to wrestle down the impulses of my own heart.

"Well, that's good. Isn't it? Everything that should be bad news is good news. Take care, Sicily."

"You too."

After Vincent left, there was nothing I wanted to do more than to go downstairs and start my car and lie in the backseat. The upholstery was soft cushy pale-tan leather and reminded me of my father's old Crown Vic. My father had been near-psychotic about safety, but somehow neither he nor my mother ever thought I was in danger lying down on the backseat of the car, with or without a belt, as they drove home through the purple summer night. And I had never felt safer anywhere as a kid, every muscle languid, in that delicious interval between consciousness and sleep, my father's scanner chattering away on the dashboard. I knew I couldn't do that, though. Talk about nuttier than nuts. If my aunt had come home from this glitzy restaurant opening she was at, parked her car next to mine, and found me in the backseat of my car, she would have thought I was trying to commit suicide, even though I could have let my car run for two weeks in the three-story cathedral that was our parking garage and have absorbed so little carbon monoxide that I'd still enjoy perfect health.

The last thing I wanted was to worry anyone.

Anyone else.

Instead, I slid out of my clothes and into the stupid T-shirt Vincent had left on my bedroom floor when he did his reverse strip. I put on my scanner and took out the framed photo of Vincent and me. *When that photo was taken, I already was pregnant,* I thought. Already, the only going back was strewn with broken glass. Exhausted from too much sex and emotion, I fell asleep with a pillow held tight against me.

I don't know when I pulled the picture off the shelf. I woke up and it was beneath me. I rolled over and somehow, although I lunged to grab it, the glass smashed against the corner of my bookshelf. Carefully, I picked up the pieces and then inspected the photo. The glass had cut a crease right through Vincent, so that his face was no longer pressed against my neck but scratched half away.

Holy symbolism, Batman.

Gently, I tried to smooth the image and massage that silly, sidelong gesture of confidence back into place. In my playhouse of life, it was a family picture of all of us, maybe the only one there would ever be, because Vincent and I would not last, and the baby would not last. I would last.

I would ask Beth to make another copy for me, but I decided I would not set it up again, framed among my relics. It had been too big anyway, bigger than the others, putting out of balance the family that had been real—a mother, a father, and a child. Missing was a picture of Marie and me. One did not exist, because through all those years with Marie I had been faceless. Beth might take one for me, and there it would go, one more among the others, with plenty of room left for time to bring what it genuinely could.

I kissed Vincent's messed-up forehead and put it under my dad's helmet, tucking all the corners in carefully so nothing showed. I got up and stripped the bed and put on clean sheets and resolved to be like Kit, starting my twenty-one-day diet of losing Vincent.

I decided to forget that picture was there.

And I did.

CHAPTER SIXTEEN

Those who think that callous women can have abortions on demand have never demanded one. I was a special case. Not only was I a transplant recipient, for whom urgency was key, I also would be in a real operating room, medicated with IV Versed so that I remembered nothing. Still, it took two weeks to get an appointment. Perhaps it was the Christmas rush, the time college freshmen bite the bullet before they go home for break. Perhaps it was the fact that I'd made and canceled four appointments, including the one I'd scheduled for just after Vincent left Chicago. That was juvenile and rude to the staff. And masochistic to me. Still, I waited. There were whole parts of days I willfully shunted the decision out of my conscious mind. Weeks passed like playing cards flicked into a hat by a restless child.

At last, I couldn't ignore my body changing. That was too much to bear. I scheduled the termination.

When the appointed day arrived, 1 drove myself to UIC. Marie had a story to work on. I would call her when it was over so that she could come by taxi and drive me home in my car. When she objected, I was firm: There was no need to further alarm or involve her. I was sad—that was expected—but also relieved by the relative peace conferred by the new ability to do private things on my own.

In the parking lot, I sat for a moment in the car.

The classical station that was one of my seven settings played "Claire de Lune," which had been one of my favorites since I was a child. As I listened, I admitted that I should have done this sooner, before the noticeable small changes in my body. The pregnancy was a pregnancy. I'd wanted to experience an annunciation. What a selfish fool I was to let the inevitable conclusion drag out week after week. When Dr. Ahrens explained the possible alternative protocol for anti-rejection drugs to me should I proceed, I'd allowed a sliver of my rational mind to hope. Dr. Ahrens had also, and firmly, made sure I understood that it was experimental, a last resort with no guarantees, and that if it failed to protect me from rejection, I might have to have a late-term abortion that would require a court order. All the days and nights of considering and reconsidering pointed me toward this inevitable conclusion. I needed to arrange what was incontrovertibly—to me at least, despite everything I knew about viability—a death. I could still have an abortion legally in Illinois and I would be able to for nearly two more months. Now the doctor's time was booked and the room reserved yet again. I had to choose life, as all those cruel billboards proclaimed. I had to choose my life.

As I clipped my keys inside my purse, I saw that it had begun to snow. I'd worn what the physician, a Dr. Thorpe, had suggested, loose and comfortable clothing and flat shoes. As I hurried, the wind plucked at my thin wool coat and forced my hair across my face like a veil. I had waited too long. The anguish I now felt was only what I deserved.

I didn't notice the car that came peeling around the corner into the circle at the revolving door. In the front seat, an elderly woman was strapped, slumped forward, listless and agape. I later learned that she'd had a stroke at her great-granddaughter's fourth birthday party, and, because the family lived just five blocks from the hospital, her son had decided to drive her to the emergency room himself. He had, however, missed the ER entrance, half a block behind him, the way he had come.

All he saw was a hospital with a door and he made for it, one hand on his dear mother's shoulder.

I probably hadn't needed to leap quite so athletically as I did. At the last millisecond, I sprang away from the nose of the old car aimed at my rear end. But I, along with the old lady (who did recover), ended up in the ER. My butt was unscathed, but I hit my head on the patient-loading sign and went sprawling on one side, my cheek scraped, my knee bloodied, and a bump that would swell to the size of a tennis ball on the back of my head. I was never unconscious, but I was dazed.

The contrite driver, Kobena, who had moved to Chicago the year before from Ghana, not only kept poking his head around my curtain to apologize ever more earnestly but came to see me the next day, to assure himself that "God was watching."

When I fully came around, a resident was leaning over me, asking the usual questions: *Are you taking any medication, Mrs. Coyne; do you know what day it is; are you here by yourself; could you be pregnant?* All of my answers were true, but they were also enough to prompt the resident to hotfoot it for his attending. A nurse quickly put an IV in my hand and started a drip; I held an ice pack on my head while I waited for a doctor to whom I could quietly explain why I was at the hospital that day. Then a nurse came back with a portable ultrasound machine, that zippy kind that fits right inside the vagina, and before I could stop her she said, "Let's just quickly have a look-see and make sure everything's copacetic here."

The solar system inside me resolved into a clear picture after a few little nudges. And then I saw the sole of a foot. It was a perfect, actual human foot, with a high arch, and as I watched, it poised and launched itself through space like a swimmer off the blocks.

The attending leaned in and said, "Don't worry, Mrs. Coyne. The baby's fine and active and you're going to have a headache the size of the Hancock Center tonight. I, uh, pulled up your chart? And, given everything, you might want to consider letting us admit you overnight to be on the safe side."

And that was all she wrote. I couldn't turn my back on someone who was swimming that hard for the shore.

I was asleep, at around two in the afternoon, when Hollis arrived in my room.

"You are just full of surprises, aren't you?"

"I didn't intend this."

"But evidently your pal in there did," she said. She sat down in my bedside chair and told me that, before she and her husband were wed, she became pregnant with their first child, unplanned, and she had called her mother in Louisiana to ask how to know if it was the right time. Hollis's mother had said that the only time a woman could be sure if it was the right time to have a baby was when she knew for sure that she was too old to have one.

"And so?" I said.

"One day at a time, Sicily."

That was how each of us lived. We never stopped long enough to completely consider the possible alpha and omega of all our choices. In my situation, I had to. From that day on, each day was a page.

When Marie arrived for a fleeting visit before hurrying back to the station for the news, I told her, "I thought you'd be offended to be a grandma so young, Auntie. But I got stuck in traffic."

" 'Tain't funny, McGee," she said. "There is still time."

"I don't feel I should."

"Do you think you're the only person who's ever had to do this?"

"No."

"You're not. I wasn't the only person either. I was three months' pregnant before I knew I was pregnant. And the guy said he would marry me."

"Then you didn't want children."

"Oh, yes, I did. I even wanted the guy, at least at the time."

"Why then, Auntie?"

"Well, his wife wanted him too. She wasn't with him when he was working in the London bureau, where I was for two months. He was going to wait for me back in New York. He sent me a letter instead."

"Couldn't you have raised the baby yourself?"

"Maybe if I'd stayed in Europe, bought a wedding ring in a pawnshop. Not here. Not with my parents. Not in my world then. Not broke and starting out and twenty-four years old."

"I'm not broke."

"You're not rich," my aunt said, standing up and deftly looping her scarf around her neck. "I've been careful with the money your parents left you. I've been careful with my own money. But have a sick child who won't get better?" She snapped her fingers. "That's gone, Sicily. You'll knock the cap off your insurance like that. I can't raise a child. I'm too old. What if something happens to you?"

I'd expected Marie to be worried. I hadn't expected her to jump down my throat.

"I'd . . . have a guardian."

"Do you know how the world treats disabled children whose parents die?"

"Yes. I was one."

"Where are your brothers and sisters, Sicily? Who'll raise this child? One of your cousins on Jamie's side? Don't count on it. No one ever loved her kid more than I love you. But it was no picnic." Marie kissed my eyes and turned to leave. "I have to get to work. Think this over. Hard."

She left then. I made handles of the parts of the sheet I could gather up—every hospital bed I've ever been in is short-sheeted, like a cruel camp joke—and tried to hold on. I had not considered a handicapped adult, a grown person who was still a child. A good foot didn't guarantee a functioning brain.

One of the nurses brought me a phone. "There's a call for you, Mrs. Coyne."

"It's Miss Coyne," I told her. The call was from Marie.

"Sissy, I'm sorry. What I said when I left was just plain cruel. This pregnancy might end up being your kid. But you are *my* kid. When you're terrified for your kid, it can make you say things that seem cruel. I did want you to end this, here and now. You'd be safer. But if you won't, I will love your child more than anything on earth, except for how much I love you. We'll get through this together. On the way to work, I got desperate and called Christina. My sister now has the whole convent, the whole school, the whole order, and several very well-placed contemplative nuns praying twenty-four-seven. I know how you feel about God. But let's say, for shorthand, it's in God's hands now."

Before I went home the next day, I had my first thorough obstetrical workup with Dr. Glass, the high-risk obstetrician. She attributed a slightly high blood pressure to entirely understandable and unremarkable anxiety. The new, lush growth of my hair was down to ordinary hormonal activity, not to rejection. What my medical bills were by now would probably have paid every citizen in the Commonwealth of Massachusetts a Christmas bonus of a thousand bucks, but not once in my life did I receive a medical bill from UIC. I never had litigious intentions, but each time I asked, Hollis simply shrugged eloquently. Marie's opinion was that UIC knew how thin the ice was legally, and my experimental protocol was adding to the literature.

At my second appointment, just a week later, we were joined by Dr. Andrea Park, who was making me into a research study of one for the experimental anti-rejection protocol. I got my prescriptions, which now included prenatal vitamins. I made a point of asking Dr. Park, "Is this okay?"

"You mean these drugs or all of it?" she said, her face utterly impassive.

"I don't know," I told her. "I don't know anything."

"Me either," she said, and shrugged. "It's better than it was in 2005. It's better than in 2011. It's better than last year. But, Sicily, I'm making phone calls all the time when I think about what's okay or not. I call Germany and Japan. I get up at night and call Poland. In the day, these old-time rock singers used to shoot up and snort when they were pregnant. In the literature and popular press of that time, well, it was believed that heroin use should be deemed child abuse. Of course, it's still child abuse. But it ended up that the whole coke-baby thing wasn't founded on science. It seemed like it should be. But it turned out that mothers who had a couple of glasses of good wine every week were more likely to have damaged babies."

"Is that what we might be talking about here? Like fetal alcohol syndrome?"

"No."

"Down syndrome?"

"I don't think so. No. Dr. Grigsby, as you know, is concerned about chromosomal issues. That was with the original protocol of medicines."

"There has to be some syndrome we're worrying about."

"I'm sure there is, but I'm not going there," she said, and it was final.

Dr. Park said, "Here's what's going to replace all those bottles, Sicily. It's a single pill, once a day."

"What is it?"

"There was all this hype a few years ago, from Strauss–McManus, the big pharmaceutical company, about an experimental immunosuppressant that would have way fewer side effects such as increasing the patient's risk for lymphoma and so forth. I'm liking that because what's good for the outside's got to be good for the inside," Dr. Park said.

"When do I start it?"

"Right now, unofficially. Officially, when I scope out how far I dare go with the limited work that's been done with human subjects. Which is not a lot. And the studies have been with other soft tissue. Hands and noses. With faces? Only you."

"I'd be a guinea pig."

"Guinea pig. What a phrase. So . . . twentieth century."

Dr. Ahrens knocked, came into the room, and smiled at me. I looked closely at Dr. Park and Dr. Ahrens. I could never tell how old either of them was. Dr. Park was young. Ish. Older than I was, but how much? She walked like a runner but used expressions that weren't used by people under forty. Her hair had not a strand of gray or that flat weird look that's common with even the best coloring, and she seemed to defer to Hollis in a way that internists didn't usually defer to "orthopods" of any kind. But then, Hollis was famous and not classically a reconstructive surgeon but instead a microsurgeon, despite having started out—I love this—with hands and knees. The joke is that orthopedic surgeons all used to be hockey players and are like the finish carpenters of surgery, while internists are the big thinkers who just palpate your gut and say, *Hmmmmmmm, interesting.*

"Are you a resident?" I asked Dr. Park.

She said, "Hello! No. I'm old enough to be your . . . older cousin." Both of us laughed. "I am young to be an attending. That's because Chinese people are smarter, as you know."

I said, "Do you have kids?"

And she said, "I have a daughter who is ten. I am not married. My mother has disowned me. Fortunately, she has not disowned my daughter, so it's all good. Chinese mothers are mean, but Chinese grandmothers are doting."

Andrea Park was smart. She also was nice.

The high-risk OB–GYN . . . yeah. Not so much.

The next ultrasound I had was not long before Christmas. It showed a big-headed bean with alarmingly evident and distinct finger buds, lying on its back. Dr. Glass stood with her arms folded.

"Is that great?" I asked her. "It's great, right?"

"It's better than a sharp stick in the eye," she said. "We'll know more at twenty weeks. What we need is an amnio, but I want to wait a month or so. Although by the time we get the results for one, you'll be ready for the other. It's up to you, Florence."

The ultrasound tech gasped.

I cracked up.

"What is it?" asked Dr. Glass.

"It's Sicily. My name isn't Florence. It's Sicily."

The doctor colored up lightly, and I continued, "If it's a girl, I'm going to name her Pompeia or . . . Madrid. Do you like those?"

What a wretched stick up the ass she was. And I have a prejudice for women. As for this doctor, I needed her to be on my side or I needed another doctor. I wanted to say, *Do you say crap like this to every expectant mother? Or do you say, wow, Mommy, that kid's waving at you, or some happy horseshit? I know for a fact you don't act like what's in there is a nasty tumor that doesn't seem any bigger.*

But even Dr. Livingston, although he was a tremendous person, had never really stopped thinking of this pregnancy as the "nonstarter." I felt him watching me rather than looking at me these days, waiting for a clue.

Nobody asked if my morning sickness was settling down. Nobody asked if I hoped for a boy or a girl. All of them, even my family, seemed to hold their breath collectively, except for one person: my aunt. This was not my aunt Marie. Marie was scrupulously cheery but not cozy, after the first day, about my accident-related nondecision to have a nontermination. It was a given how much she would love a child of mine, how much she would love to be a grandmother, in fact if not by designation.

The person who was nearly swoony with happiness was my aunt Christina, Sister Mary Augustine Caruso. She displayed pure, un-smirched joy at what seemed to be one Catholic's refusal to have an abortion against both her own and the child's best interests—steering toward disaster on purpose being the best sort of faith-based decision, I guess.

One Saturday we had brunch with my Caruso grandparents. If not for me and my delicate condition, Grandma and Grandpa Caruso, as well as Grandma and Grandpa Coyne, would have been getting ready to leave after New Year's for their condos in Florida. But these days,

Florida seemed like . . . well, Florence. No one was going anywhere, for which I felt guilty. Anyhow, after everyone watched me eat enough quiche and salad for three large people and then retire to throw half of it up, Aunt Christina said, "Sicily, darling. Would it be okay if I explained the Catholic perspective on this to your doctor? Would you mind if I met with her?"

"Met with my doctor," I repeated.

"Yes," said Christina.

"No, of course you can't, Aunt Christina."

"Sicily, it's important that she understand that this is a situation in which you aren't to be pressured toward a most grievous—"

"She knows that," Marie said. "The doctor knows that."

"In this case, I'm not sure where the most harm would be, Aunt Christina," I said.

"What you've done here is noble, Sicily," said Aunt Christina. "If you should lose this . . . well, this facial beautification for the sake of the unborn child growing in your womb, it is virtually a martyrdom."

"You're not getting this. I've made this decision almost against my own will, Aunt Christina. I'm scared to death. Every day. This could be an actual martyrdom. It could maybe kill me if I lose my face," I said. "Let's talk about the Cubs."

"But you would choose that, for the baby to survive," said my aunt.

"Which, if I did die, would do both of us a lot of good," I said. "What if I had the baby and gave it up for adoption? Do you know I actually considered that? Wouldn't that be more pure and awful and painful and really holy?"

My grandmother, who had been busily making sure that everyone had way too much food, said quietly, "Sicily." I turned away from Christina and looked down the surface of the shining mahogany table at which I'd sat all my life—every Easter and every Christmas and every other Sunday, in a high chair, on a pillow over telephone books, as a bored twelve-year-old trying to hide the earbuds of my iPod under my hair, and as an isolated, fearful teenager wishing I could conjure a mist to obscure me from my family's eyes. In all those years, I had never seen my bustling, fit, domestically stereotypical Italian grandmother as an old woman. Old women didn't jog from the yard to the oven to the neighbor's house, cooking and crocheting and chatting, going on long bus trips to Broadway shows with her girlfriends. Until recently, very recently, I'd rarely seen Grandma Caruso interrupt her bustle even to sit down at her own table long enough to eat. My father used to call her a stand-up lady.

She looked old now, solemn and doleful, her cheeks motionless and grooved as a line drawing.

Grandma said, "I haven't said the things I think. As a Catholic, I think the only situation in which abortion is not a mortal sin is to save the life of the mother, and old Catholics believe that even in that case we must choose the life of the child. But I lost my child, Sicily, my firstborn baby girl. I saw your father, who was like my son, die. I'm an old woman. I pray to the Sacred Heart because I don't think I could bear to lose my only grandchild, who I almost lost already, for the sake of a baby, any baby. No matter how precious this baby's life is, to God or to our family." Grandma raised her hands to her temples, drawing the skin at the corners of her eyes back in an elegy of distress that was horrible to me. "Sicily. I would say, have an abortion, Sicily. I think you should have an abortion. I know this is a sin on my own soul. I don't care. One day, when you are really in love with a man who is good, you can adopt a waiting child together—"

"Mother!" said Aunt Christina.

"Christina, I know your belief. Don't talk anymore."

"Mother . . . what you're encouraging Sicily—"

"I said, don't talk anymore! Am I a fool? Don't you think I know what I'm saying at my own table?" said Grandma Caruso. "This baby's life is nothing next to Sicily's life. It's nothing! This family has suffered enough. Sicily has suffered like a hundred martyrs. No. I think she should stop this now." My grandmother covered her face with one of her delicate tatted table napkins. "I want Sicily to live. I want Sicily to keep the face God gave her to replace her beautiful face. I want Sicily to live her life, which is my Gia's life too. Even if I go to hell. I don't care if I go to hell. This is hell."

Shame washed over me like nausea. I got up and went into the bathroom, but not to be sick. I splashed my wrists and my face and tried to think. What was I doing? How could I torture them and gamble so ruthlessly with my face and my future because I somehow thought the love of a guy had burrowed into my belly and made an accidental pregnancy somehow sacred? My heart skittered, faster and faster. I didn't want to be a . . . an ICU case, an urgent giant oozing wound, a pitiable crash rescue, hoping for a face that at best would look like a battered melon? Was I bringing this on myself, like the nutty Canadian guy? Had these years of privation and longing tied off a section of my brain?

When I sat down again, I said, "Grandma, I'm sorry. I'm so sorry for what I'm putting you through. I didn't think of how scared you must be. I'm even sorry that I disrespected Christina, thinking this is for religious reasons. If I thought I was really in danger . . ." But didn't I? Was I? How the hell did I know? And I wasn't telling the whole truth either, to the people who had loved and raised me, which was the least that they deserved. "I know I'm emotional. Even if this baby was conceived in sin, to you, it was also conceived in love, to me. If I didn't think this baby's life was important, I wouldn't even consider this. I wouldn't trade my life for her life. I just can't take it lightly. I can't. I tried."

But that wasn't all of it either. What was missing from this sentence? I'd weighed the odds, and I believed they could favor me. The sentence was missing an entire, other independent clause. Would I be clinging to this pregnancy if there had been bliss but not Vincent? Was this all some . . . offering to Vincent?

No, it was not!

"I promise. I'm going to think it over more. I'm going to talk it over more with the psychologist. Maybe this fear is a warning. The doctors know what they're doing, but maybe I'm asking too much of them."

No one said a word. We could hear the whipping of the tiniest bare branches of Grandma's big old pin oak, rapping the window the way a conductor raps a podium. It sounded like mindless rain, fingernails tapping thoughtlessly, nervously, awaiting a decision.

Finally, Grandpa said, "All your aunt is doing is praising your faith. All your grandmother is doing is loving you. You are a loved young woman. You are a Catholic young woman."

I nearly yipped when I felt a blow to my shin. Even wearing a soft ballet flat, Marie could make herself felt.

"Of course," I said. "I'm not discounting that."

Christina jumped right back in. "So I thought, if I spoke to your doctor, it might make her feel more at ease."

As for me, I felt increasingly not so well. I was chilly, although my grandparents skipped around in short sleeves and kept the temperature of their house about the same as late afternoon in Death Valley. Wasn't it time for Aunt Christina to go to vespers or matins or some prayer break at this point? I wished that I could have a drink—even though I couldn't have had a drink even if anyone had been drinking.

"She's a Catholic too," said Aunt Marie. "Sicily's doctor, Dr. Grigsby, the surgeon: She is a Catholic too."

"I thought she was from Louisiana," said my other aunt.

"They don't call the counties in New Orleans parishes for nothing, Aunt Christina," I said. "Hollis, my surgeon, is a southern black woman with a British accent who is a cradle Catholic."

"You know what I want? I want to have a look at that new ride, Sissy. Let's see your car," my grandfather said, and the entire table, except Aunt Christina, rose as one.

That night at home, Kit and I had our little Christmas. Kit gave me this beautiful antique album with a picture of a girl in a swing on it. The journal was filled with postcards from a girl called Emma Rose Gunnally, all sent to her mother from her honeymoon trip "by motor car," down the eastern coast of the United States. The album was fashioned so that the backs of the postcards were visible. *This morning in New*

Hampshire, I'm afraid that Thomas became very impatient when the car would start steaming as we waited for the most cunning flock of lambs to cross the country lane.

"Do you like it?" Kit asked.

"It's just exquisite. When did this happen? In 1912? Kitty, that was the time of the *Titanic,* more than a hundred years ago. Can you believe it?"

Kit put her hand on her chest and let out a deep sigh. "I got worried you would hate it."

"Why?"

"Well, I got it for you a while ago and just realized that the girl is named Emma and it's a honeymoon."

Now I felt my breath snag in my chest. The shivers came back and I pulled the mohair throw from the back of my couch around my shoulders. When was the last time I'd spoken to Mrs. Cassidy? Of course, she didn't know anything about this . . . issue. It wasn't as though it had gotten around the West Side. She deserved to know. But what would I say to her? Here was my Kit, woebegone, looking as though someone had eaten all her Norman Loves and then rewrapped the box.

"A lot of people are named Emma. It's like Rebecca. It's an old-timey name. It's even better, Kit. I think of Emma all the time." *Except not,* I admitted to myself. "And, wow, a wedding is the last thing on my mind." I faked a good smile and said, "Now you open yours."

I'd given Kit an Italian martini set, a blown-glass shaker, and two glasses in her favorite colors (I know, God help me), black and pink.

Afterward, she cooked dinner for both of us—her specialty, chicken divan, which we'd called "chicken dive-in" when we were kids and her mom made it—and I listened to Kit's litany of complaints about her job. These mostly centered on how Jon Archer, her boss, kept taking credit for all of Kit's color schemes and ideas for the home page. Kit would quit tomorrow—if it weren't for the six figures and the trips to London and Milan and the corner office on Michigan Avenue and the mandatory exercise hour and the indoor pool and massage room and all the free makeup and body butter and other extraordinary loot, a load of which she now hauled out to give to me in a satin Santa bag—samples of all the "super-eco" brands. It all sounded just absolutely, hideously unbearable and dreadful, really, sort of like getting dressed up every day to go to a spa and play princess on the computer until dinnertime. I'd majored in art. Why couldn't I be Kit? Eye-shadow palettes versus the bombardment of rectal tumors with angiogenesis inhibitors. Like Kit's job, mine was also a six-figure project, if you counted the two zeroes after the decimal point that made up eight thousand bucks. Being a medical illustrator was useful and, for me, it was pretty easy. But it was often—as in, oh, 80 percent of the time—about as interesting to me as if I'd owned a lawn-care business. When it had suited my neat and very medical little world, my job felt like a perfect fit. Now it felt cramped.

Soon, I thought, I might need a real job with real benefits. I didn't have a mortgage, thanks to my beloved mom-auntie. But after next year I wouldn't be covered under Marie's policy. One more thing to gnaw on. After we ate coffee ice cream with marshmallow whip, Kit and I watched *The Bells of St. Mary's,* as we did every Christmas. Unlike every Christmas, Kit smoked a joint, which I picked up and took a hit from. "Jesus!" Kit shrieked, as though I'd pulled out a big jug of Apple Valley and taken a long swig while tamping down a pack of Marlboros.

"It's okay," I said. "One puff of dope isn't going to make any difference here in the valley of the pills."

"Am I the godmother?" Kit said.

"Sure," I told her. It was the first time I'd thought about the not-abortion as a someday-child with ceremonies and clothing. She brought out a last present, one she'd been hiding in her bag—a CD of old-fashioned lullabies sung by young jazz artists. I couldn't say anything except "My God."

"It's three months now," Kit said. "I'm guessing we're going to have a birthday this summer, huh?"

It might have been the dope, Bing Crosby, or how much better a

nun Ingrid Bergman made than my aunt, but pretty soon I felt all oozy
and sentimental. I said, "Kit, I don't say stuff like this. But tell me it's
going to be okay."

Kit put her arms around me, patting my back in the make-it-all-
better way good people do. I was on my own in the world with this,
though. I had a good family. But there are no two ways of thinking
about being a single mother: No one will ever love the kid the way you
do, and if my kid turned out to have problems, no one would love the
kid at all after I died. The idea of five years shaved off my life by a face
transplant abruptly seemed like a very huge deal indeed. What would
I do with my for-certain handicapped child? I was stoned and paranoid. I would . . . raise him with . . . with understanding and love and
valor and respect for his abilities, as Marie had raised me. But what if
he were really disabled and I got really, really unlucky?

"Would you raise him if I died?" I asked Kit.

She hesitated, just long enough. She had recently become involved
with Anthony—and Anthony-Since-Halloween had been the most
durable of all Kit's ridiculous romances. Anthony wasn't even married.
He had his own house. Although he played an instrument, it was a
church organ. He was studying to be a Presbyterian minister. After a
whole season of lovey-dovey, Kit was starting to wonder if pearl gray
was too old-lady for bridesmaids' dresses or if the old standard of a
black-and-white wedding was still the classiest route.

"Of course I would," Kit said.

And, also of course, I knew the moment she said it that I didn't
want Kit to raise my child if I died. She was a doll but a ditz in the best
of circumstances and was just one of those people you could tell would
always have it going on more about her husband than her kid—who
would have kids because her husband wanted them. She would not
take a bullet for my kid.

My dad had.

Who would be my child's guardian?

Who would be my child's guardian angel?

The only person I could think of whom I would trust even remotely was Eliza Cappadora. And I didn't even know her. I barely knew any of these people who suddenly loomed so large in my now double life. Perhaps I should talk to Vincent. Would I name Vincent as the father? Would I expect child support? What if I said the father was unknown? On the line for mother's name I could just write SLUT. "Kit, you couldn't take care of a cat," I said.

She told me, "Anthony has four cats."

It figured.

The one puff of dope (I didn't indulge and had tried this exactly twice since I'd had my face) was making me ravenous, dizzy, and cross-eyed. I grabbed a handful of chips and then jumped up to find something to slather on them. The only thing I could find in my fridge was Thousand Island dressing. It would do. My forehead itched and my joints were achy. "What the hell is in that joint?" I asked Kit. "Pet tranquilizers?"

"I don't know. I got it from Anthony."

"Presbyterian seminarian marijuana?" We both laughed until I thought I would pee the couch. Kit got up carefully and made omelets for both of us, heavy on the cheese and peppers, swimming in butter, which we carefully ate with about a whole loaf of toast. It had been only three hours since we'd had dinner. My stomach was bulbous by then, but not from the obvious. Kit said she was too stoned to drive, so we went into my bedroom and I tossed her a nightshirt as I slipped into mine.

"You can sure tell," she said.

"How?"

"Your boobs are the size of water balloons."

"They feel like they're going to explode too," I told her. "I think my days of tank tops without shelf bras are over."

Then we slept together in my bed, huddled like little girls at Scout camp. Through the thick and damp veil of my sleep, I heard my phone go off several times. Who would call me at this time of night? This time of night? What time of night was it?

I opened my eyes, feeling surprisingly refreshed, although my chin and forehead still itched as though the active ingredient in my face cream was poison ivy. The sun was full bright, high over the hem of the lake. It was ten in the morning.

The messages were all from Beth, inviting me to their house for Christmas Eve.

The first message said, "Sicily, I know this is very, uh, strange. And I'm not trying to make it not be strange. We have a small open house every year. That's a contradiction, huh? An open house that's mostly closed? But we'd like you and Marie to come. It's just family. Close friends. It seems like you're one or the other, huh?" When she called back a second time, Beth repeated the message and apologized for being so last minute and said she would understand if I declined. Then she called back to say she hadn't meant that she wanted me to decline.

I decided that I would go. But would Vincent?

I made coffee and brought Kit a cup—otherwise she would have slept through until Tuesday—and told her about Beth's invitation.

"Just go there and tough it out, Sissy," Kit said. "You don't have to be ashamed of anything. And they're rich and your baby is an heir."

"They're not rich like that, Kit."

"Rich is rich."

"All I want to do is sleep."

"Well, it's not Christmas Eve today, Sicily." I heard the shush as Angel wedged my big weekend newspaper against the door. Carrying my coffee, I picked it up.

There I was.

Under the fold on the front page, there was a little-bit-bigger-than-usual story about where-are-they-now, my unveiling picture after the surgery (I looked like a giant pink sponge with button eyes), and a recent picture of me, smiling up at Beth from what looked like a pool of green-and-pink play foam. It was in fact a pile of old ballet costumes I was sorting to donate to my dance teacher's studio. The reporter hadn't interviewed me but, instead, Mrs. Viola, who remained close to Mrs. Cassidy. "Julia knows that Sicily has to start a new life," said Mrs. Viola. "She knows they'll get together soon." There was some more

fiddle-faddle about me and the face transplant and then a quick up-
date on the families of other survivors and a teeny bit about the
planned art exhibit.

It was the anniversary of the fire, and no one, not I and not even my
adoring auntie, had remembered that, more than a week ago, I had
turned twenty-six years old.

CHAPTER SEVENTEEN

"Are those people alive?" I asked my aunt.

"Of course they're alive. They're carolers," she whispered, barely moving her lips. "They're . . . caroling. But I don't think they come from the neighborhood."

The men wore stocking caps or rusty stovepipe hats, the women ankle-length dresses and short jackets buttoned to the neck. A young teenage boy held a carriage lantern aloft. We stepped around them and proceeded up the flagstone walk to Beth and Pat Cappadora's front door. Beth opened it before we could knock. Although she was dressed in a long velvet dress and boots, the look on Beth's face was like that of a kid trying to hide a bad report card.

"Listen," she said. "I'm not an idiot. I had my tree decorated by a decorator because I have so much to think about this year that I would probably have blown out the electricity in the neighborhood. But the ornaments are my ornaments. Well, they are except for those . . . dumb Styrofoam balls covered with tablecloth material and gold pins. I am not responsible for that. Or for those people out on the front walk."

"Merry Christmas, Beth," I said.

"Oh, God, Sicily, Marie, I'm sorry. Merry Christmas. I'm just so embarrassed. Those people are actors. They were hired to do this by a friend of my husband's, as a gift, so we couldn't turn it down—and now we can't turn *them* down. They get louder with every song. . . ." The carolers in their artfully draped rags piped up, reminding everyone to let nothing us dismay. "Anyhow, you're the last ones to arrive except Vincent, and so at least I don't have to explain this again. The carolers should leave in twenty-five minutes, unless someone tips them again, which . . ." Beth beckoned us in, closed the door behind her, and spoke to the room in general. "Nobody better give them another tip!"

"I think they sound nice, Ma," Ben said, getting up to take our coats. "I was just about to go out there and give them a fifty or something."

But all I heard was *Vincent. Vincent. Vincent.* All the voices, even the singing, seemed very far away.

"They have families," Beth said. "Actors live miserable lives, away from their families on holidays. Or else they have other neighborhoods to torment. It was very nice of Johnny to give us this little . . . show. Which I'll be hearing about from the DeGroots and the Haverlins for two years. But it's over now."

We walked into the center of a room that was rimmed by an endless sofa, a Nile-length sofa of wheat-colored suede, with deep-seated caramel leather chairs stuck in along its length and blue and red pillows as nervy as signal flags. All this furniture was new. Beth apologized again.

"*Lasciala andare,* Beth!" said a small old man, who stood up from a corner of that immense sofa, his posture erect as a rifle. He held out his hand. "Hello, darling. I am Angelo Cappadora, and this is Rose, my wife. We are Patrick's parents."

In her three-inch heels, Rose Cappadora was the same height as her husband and conferred the same sense of wry, affable knowing, along with a formidable power. She wore a green silk suit with a cameo on a satin ribbon around her neck—a neck I could tell was unlined by dint of genetic kismet rather than cosmetic intervention. Not once, Beth said, had she seen Rose lose her temper—although Rose did the standard amount of Italian-lady yelling around.

"Hello, Mrs. Cappadora," I said.

"Rosie," she said. "I wouldn't know how to answer anyone who didn't call me Rosie. I think you must be Sicily." I nodded.

Angelo smiled—he twinkled—at my aunt. "And you, Marie Caruso. Every night you are in my bedroom!" My aunt was now the sole anchor of the nightly news at ten.

"Why, you're the one!" Aunt Marie said, rolling her eyes.

"Angelo, our guests need some food, don't you think?" Vincent's grandmother said. "Don't pay any attention to him. If you do, he'll think he's smart and charming."

"Well, he is," Aunt Marie answered, and everybody laughed. "He's smart enough not to say it again." Aunt Marie waved to everyone. Thank heavens, in Chicago, Auntie was a bona fide celebrity, so no one had to notice me. Much.

People sat at little makeshift tables draped with long swaths of white fabric bowed in silver and green and set about with silver bar stools (I sensed the decorator at work again), or they clustered on the endless sofa with their plates and cups. A server in a long skirt and a tuxedo vest passed through the group, collecting dishes. At the back of the room, near the doors to the patio and pool, a bartender was uncorking bottles of wine, squeezing limes, and skewering stuffed mushrooms with the ease of a priest preparing the sacraments.

Maybe Kit was right: Maybe the Cappadoras weren't rich-rich, but rich enough.

Beth returned and led us from group to group, repeating our names. After just one sofa section's worth of introductions, I was worn out. I held a plate of tiny crackerish pizzas. I'd also accepted some crab puffs and cream horns, although I doubted I would be able to eat any of them. My stomach felt like a balloon filled with seltzer. Aunt Marie stayed by my side as I searched for a place to cordially hide out. The pregnancy had apparently been coming on strong, because lately I felt as though my daily goal for wellness was to rise to average. Perhaps I wasn't up to Beth's "small" open house, which apparently included about thirty-five people: I had shaken hands with sisters-in-law and brothers' daughters and brothers-in-law's fiancées and the wives of cousins and remembered not one of them. The room was hot and whirly and bewildering. Inserting myself into a leather chair nearly behind the tree, which must have been twenty feet tall, I felt as though a bit of my face was not just reflected but literally inside the circle of every silver tendril that twitched and wound on the branches. I searched for the ones Beth had referred to, the Styrofoam balls covered in layers of tablecloth, but instead I caught sight of a primitive ornament laboriously cut from tin in the shape of a star with some kind of punch holes worked through all the limbs. In the middle of the star was Vincent's face, maybe six years old. I leaned over to set my plate down and everything slid off.

"Hello," someone said close to my ear, in a voice that sounded alarmingly familiar. I glanced to my right and there was this older guy nimbly hunkered down next to me, with Vincent's thick lion-colored hair but painted at the crown and temples with dark gray. "I'm Pat, Beth's husband. Vincent's dad. I know everyone wants to see you. Eliza can't wait to see you. And if I wasn't such a moke, I'd probably just say hello and Merry Christmas. But I have to say this. I'm not sure about Vincent's way of handling it so far. But if this works out, honey, this is our child too. *Mio cuore.* My heart. Just like Ben's over there. No different. And that goes for whatever Vincent does. *D'accordo?*"

"Sure," I said. "*D'accordo. Grazie. Buon Natale. Solo cose buone. Lei e molto gentile.*"

"*Parli Italiano?*" said Pat.

"*Assolutamente.*"

He hugged me. "What a girl," he said.

I wanted to bawl. He could have been my daddy. He was probably about the age my dad would have been and had that same old-time everybody's-pal manner my father had. I loved him instantly. I wanted to throw myself on Pat's shoulder and cry until he led me upstairs and tucked me and my fatherless fetus into some big bed and took care of both of us. Behind him, slightly out of focus, I could see Eliza sitting in one of those big caramel leather chairs. Perched on the arm of the chair was Eliza's tall, slender blond mother, Mrs. Bliss—*Chief* Bliss. She was brushing back little Stella's waist-length hair and trying to se-cure it with an elastic band, while Stella, red-faced and sweating, un-dulated like an eel, clearly about to have the kind of meltdown every child had on Christmas Eve. Although Chief Bliss looked delicate in her black wide-legged pants and white blouse, it was obvious that Stella wasn't going anywhere. The older woman put no pressure on the little girl's wrist, but Stella clearly was a prisoner, and she finally qui-eted, rolling her eyes like the teenager she would become.

"Anyhow," Pat went on, "you're very brave to come here with all of us. And I already knew, from Bethie, that you were brave. I knew your dad a little, and he was a brave man too."

I really thought I would burst like a dam then. Blinking hard, I looked up at the ceiling.

Then Eliza came toward me, leaning in over Pat's shoulder. "I missed you so much, Sicily. Marie, it's so good to see you. Merry Christmas." Pat stood up quickly, and Eliza hugged Aunt Marie and then me. "I want to bring Charley over, but I had to wait until I knew it would be okay. Do you want to meet him now? You'll have plenty of time to get to know him."

It was pretty delicate of Eliza to consider this. Many times before this night, I'd given serious thought to how I would react to Charley. I'd never seen the new baby. I'd barely seen Beth since Thanksgiving. I ex-pected to have mixed and convoluted feelings. He was as closely re-lated to my own unborn child as anyone alive. My mind repeated those words—*unborn child*—as Polly Guthrie had long ago explained how new brides inwardly exclaim *I'm married* every time they glance down at their gleaming wedding bands. Charley and Stella were among the closest blood relatives that Patient X would have. Eliza's life and mine had intersected first outside, then inside the operating room. Then we had become friends and, for an instant, mothers-to-be, when I was about twenty minutes into my pregnancy and she in the stretch run. My gratitude for Eliza's quiet beacon was immense. Eliza was an experienced mother. Her baby's future was already assured (Of course, I know that no one's future is ever assured). Charley and my child would grow up virtually as age mates, separated by less than a year. But despite what Pat said, could an unplanned and . . . perhaps even unwanted child be accorded a slice of the pie of family inclusion? What would happen at future Christmastimes, when Vincent brought his current starlet?

Eliza placed sleeping Charley in my arms, a fat baby seal with huge hands, peachy drooping cheeks, and a pelt of black hair. Someday, would my own little son be running around, breathless and whiny, spilling orange soda on a fifty-dollar outfit and asking if there were presents under the tree when Santa hadn't even come yet? They were Italians. They liked bad kids. I felt the gazes of people on me but didn't care. I sort of fell into Charley as though he were a pool of chocolate. If you had asked me about the number of babies I'd held and played with in my life to that point, I'd have said that the number hovered around zero. Kit's younger sister, Alison, wasn't young enough to have been a novelty when we were children, only a pest. By the time I would have taken that sort of little-mommy interest in kids, I had a ravaged face and my parents were dead. Neighborhood babysitting didn't exactly fit in to the routine of a mutant. Charley was extraordinarily beautiful, his lips working on an absent nipple, his fat hands folded prayerfully under his abundance of chins.

"I like him," I told Eliza. "That sounds dumb. I mean, I haven't spent much time with babies, but he's just so yummy." Eliza smiled and almost preened. I held Charley against my cheek and inhaled that inexplicable narcotic smell of unalloyed newness.

At that moment, the front door burst open and a general roar rose. I looked up at Vincent and he looked at me, and at the baby, the sight shoving him to a stop in the doorway with that same slack-jawed incredulity he'd had when he first saw me with my car. He stood there so long that someone behind him pushed past, a beautiful light-haired girl with a body like the arch of a harp. She said, "Honey! What are you doing? Making an entrance?"

Vincent had brought a girl.

I decided I would hate Vincent forever and might as well start doing the exercises.

A few minutes later I'd splashed enough cold water on my face to restore the pace of my breathing but rinse off most of my makeup. Using a hand towel, I blotted the rest away. Unable to leave an expensive Christmas hand towel covered with streaks of mineral glow, I flattened it out and stuck it inside the back of my underpants. Pale didn't begin to describe my face. I looked like a chess piece and cursed the polite impulse that had prompted me to agree to come to this dumb shindig. I straightened the ruched black top I wore, meant to draw attention away from my enormous boobs and to my still-indented waistline.

Die young, Vincent, I thought.

As though that was still possible.

Why couldn't he have installed his "honey" at a hotel long enough to wish the woman who was pregnant with his maybe-handicapped kid a happy holiday? How had this woman gone from unknown to meet-the-family status in . . . what . . . six weeks?

"Let heaven and nature sing," roared the fake carolers, outside the window.

Let heaven and nature sing.

I was going home to make a voodoo doll.

Pulling open the pocket door of the powder room, I nearly fell into her lap, the woman with the bright hair. Vincent stood just behind her.

"I'm sorry," I said. "I hope you haven't been waiting too long. I'm Sicily. I'm not from Sicily, that is my name. . . ."

The pretty woman, perhaps the same age as I, maybe a few years older, displayed a row of slightly overlarge teeth.

"I know who you are. Nice to meet you. Vincent is a pig for not introducing us. But he's a pig all the time."

Vincent punched the woman in the back, hard enough that she stumbled.

She whirled and pummeled his arm. "You want a piece of me? Huh?"

Before I could react, Vincent pulled me into a slightly bashful hug.

"You asshole," I said to Vincent. I was sure he didn't hear me. But he did.

"Hey, Sicily, great to see you too. How are you? Are you okay? Did you get my emails?"

I hadn't opened my emails for weeks. I was trying out a new life strategy: People who really needed you would call. Or show up.

"Hello, Vincent. No, I didn't."

"From Upstart Productions?"

"I didn't associate that with you. Sorry. I forgot the name of your company. I've been busy. But now I'd love to meet your friend."

"She's not my friend."

"Your girlfriend, then," I said, and thought of how Vincent would look with a shovel sticking out of his head.

"This is Kerry, my baby sister, the famous opera diva and knuckle puncher."

"Oh, dear. Oh. I'm sorry. Kerry." I put out my hand. His sister. I knew he had a sister! Kerry was his sister, and they must have met up at the airport. Had I made some kind of odd grimace, accidentally or with deliberate vengeance, out there in the living room? My already sweltry face seemed to dial up a notch. Was I sweating? "It's just, you know, it's so warm in here. How good to meet you. You mean you show-biz folks don't get to come home for Christmas until halfway into it?"

"If then," Kerry sighed. "My understudy practically wanted me to promise her my firstborn child to go on for me tomorrow and the next day . . . and . . . I—oh, boy. I'm sorry. The opera is *Madama Butterfly* and I could use a nice *seppuku* dagger right now. I can't believe I said that. I'm so sorry. The first thing I say to you, after all Vincent told me, all the way from Denver, and I blow it sky high. And you're right, he is an asshole."

"Don't be silly," I told her. What had Vincent told his sister? All the way from Denver? Vincent knew that I knew that he knew that I hadn't gone ahead with the abortion. I had never spoken to him, but my aunt made a point of telling me that she'd called Beth to inform the Cappadoras that it was game-on. How had he described me? Half-wit nymphomaniac? Stone around his neck, rapidly increasing in diameter and heft? Medical curiosity and gold digger? A poisoned apple? The love of his life? The sorta-like of the previous fall? "Really, don't be silly. It's just an ordinary phrase."

"I didn't mean anything about your baby—my little nephew or niecie who's in there. I'm going to be the old maid here and wear my bird-watching shoes to take all the kids to the zoo. . . . I'm sorry about that too," Kerry said. Both she and Vincent were blushing. "Vincent, why don't you say something? If you think she's so terrific and unusual—"

"Stop it, Ker," Vincent said, low and toneless.

"Why should I stop it?"

I said, "It's okay, really. Please . . . um, it's fine. Vincent and I haven't had a chance to talk about anything. I didn't even answer his emails!"

"Why don't you say something? Like, try not being an asshole?" Kerry asked, her stance belligerent as a cat in a downpour. "Try a little. Then try harder. You know?"

"Don't you have to go to the bathroom, Kerry? Or out in the fucking snow? Nice introduction," he said. "Let Sicily know there's definitely insanity in the family."

Kerry stepped into the bathroom. Vincent said, "Come into the kitchen."

I did.

"Is this a hard time of pregnancy? You look tired." This is code for *You look like shit.*

"I don't know. It is for me. I think I should feel pretty great, but . . . I'm sort of a lump. It's good to see you, Vincent. I hope that—"

He took both my hands and kissed me. I drew back, breathless, and when he kissed me again, I put my arms up around his neck and leaned into him. This time, it was he who stepped back.

"I can feel it," he said, and laughed, as though he'd invented this. "You have a little belly. It's real." He kissed me again, and I was helpless, a sexual imbecile, my hips slipping under his of their own accord. The thing about the way a person smells, that you can't want that person unless his smell—even if it's not pretty—lights up your receptors? It's all true. Five minutes before, I'd pictured Vincent wearing something in a nice . . . avalanche. Now he could have turned off the lights, opened the door of the cupboard, and nailed me to the wall right then and there.

Eliza came in. She wasn't one of those kinds of people who say, *Oh, sorry, I didn't mean to interrupt.* She grinned and said, "Now, that's how I like to see people I love say hello. I have to sit in the dining room and nurse the baby. But this house has five bedrooms. Go upstairs and talk." She smiled again, as Charley's yips erupted into a grouchy whine.

"Hi, pal!" Vincent said. "Hi, you big fat little boy baby! I want you to meet my—"

"Sicily," Eliza said. "Do you feel okay?"

"I didn't, but I'm improving," I told her, blushing.

"I don't mean with him. I mean, let me look at you in the light."

I sat in a kitchen chair as Eliza unceremoniously handed Charley off to Vincent. The whine dialed up to a full wail. "Eliza, I don't have the equipment for this," Vincent said, trying to bounce Charley.

"Get Ben," she said. "There's a bottle in my bag." In the living room, someone was playing the white baby grand and Kerry was singing "O Holy Night," her voice a river of silver. "I'm just being careful. Your face is looking . . . Does your face have any odd things?" Eliza asked.

Alarmed by her slip out of the American vernacular, I nodded. "It's hot. But not really."

Eliza laid her hand against my cheek. "Do you feel funny anywhere else? Itchy or trembling?"

"For days," I said. "My neck itches like crazy, and my hands itch . . ."

Before I could finish, Eliza was on the phone, giving the address of the house to someone. "I'm a physician," she said. "I am with her now. . . . Are you sure? Ten minutes, no more than that?" Eliza put the phone back on the receiver. "Sit down, Sicily. *Madre de dios.*"

"I know that much Spanish." Vincent had returned with Ben and knelt beside me, taking both my hands in his. Ben was feeding the baby, his face knotted with concern. It was as though there were two stages in the house, each featuring a different play.

"Don't be afraid. Dr. Glass and Dr. Ahrens will meet you at the hospital, and now I'm paging . . ." Eliza punched numbers into her cell phone. "I'm paging Dr. Grigsby. I know that she is in Louisiana, but I'm sure that Livingston is here. So it will be fine. Everything is going fine."

I didn't notice that Ben had left until my aunt and Beth arrived, virtually sliding into second base. Marie was a bit loopy, smiling. Evidently, no one had thought to assign her part in this other play to her. Marie tried to kneel but was unsteady. Beth crouched with her knees bent like a street child tending a grill.

"What's wrong, is she bleeding?" Beth asked Vincent.

"No, she's hot and itchy," Vincent said, as though we were a couple. "Eliza called the ambulance."

Marie grabbed the edge of granite countertop. "Really, an ambulance? Eliza, do you think it's serious?"

Eliza said, "Marie, everything is serious for Sicily. Whatever it is, they will see to it. But Sicily needs to go to the hospital."

"Did you eat something?" my aunt asked.

"I feel bad. I think I must have a cold. . . ."

"Are you having a miscarriage?" said Beth.

"Are you having a miscarriage?" Marie repeated.

"It's her face," said Vincent. "It's not the baby." I gripped his hand tighter.

"Can I have some water?" I asked, and got up.

"I'll get it," Eliza said. "Sit down, Sicily."

I'd had one sip when the swoop of a Mars light along the bank of windows announced the arrival of the ambulance. On either side, Vincent and Eliza walked me into the front hall. By then, everyone looked very small and distinct. Angelo stood in the hall, with Kerry clutching his arm. My aunt grabbed our coats from Beth's hands. Two medics came into the hall, spoke briefly with Eliza, and asked me to sit down on the stairs while one of them took a quick blood pressure and rolled a thermometer over my forehead. While one stayed beside me, the other wheeled the cot in from the porch. As they helped me onto the bed, the paramedic radioed the ER. "This young woman has a BP of one-forty over ninety and a fever of one hundred one. The MD here is a resident at University of Illinois Chicago Circle and says the young woman is in the early stages of tissue rejection. . . . Yes, a transplant patient. It is a face transplant." She paused. "Miss, could you be pregnant?"

Eliza said, "Yes, she is three months' pregnant."

Very softly, my aunt said, "Rejection?"

"Is one of you riding with her?" the paramedic asked.

"I am," Vincent said. "I'm her . . . It's my baby."

"Right," said Marie. "She is *my* baby. I'm her mother."

"Come on then, ma'am," said the medic, who began tucking blankets around my feet. To me, she said, "Little ride. I'll be right next to you."

"I want to go with her," said Vincent. "Marie, I'll ride with her. Let my mother or father . . . Ben . . . you drive Marie, okay?"

"Don't be stupid," Marie said.

"I'm sorry?" Vincent said. "This is not time for any—"

"I want him to come," I said. "I want Vincent to come with me."

"Give it up, Sicily," my aunt said. "This is serious, and the boy wonder here hasn't been . . ."

The room began to revolve slowly; it was almost comical, reminding me of the teacup ride at Disneyland, the room's occupants at first curious, white, extravagantly dark-eyed, ovoid, their half-raised champagne flutes blinking gold and blue like stained glass, Beth, tears streaming sooty trails through her makeup, picking her camera up from a side table and beginning to shoot, then the people's jaws thickening, stretching, spreading, connecting like a border of faces—AngeloPatRosieBenChiefBlissElizaBenAngelo . . .

"Are you dizzy?" the paramedic asked, and before I could answer, she said, "We need to go."

"I'm ready," Aunt Marie said.

"She wants me," Vincent put in. "She's not a child."

"Nonsense," said Eliza. "Ben, I will go with her in the ambulance. You two can stay here and fight like fools."

My aunt grabbed a swag of garland draped over the long curved banister and jerked it, setting the lights bouncing. "He's here by . . . accident!"

"Accident, accident! Life is all an accident," Eliza said loudly. "My mother is my mother because the little girl she saw in the picture died of influenza, and when she came to bring home her child, they give her Maria Agata and say it is Maria. We are all Maria. Vincent has a right here too. Now we'll go, Sicily. You come when you aren't drunk."

And there we went, past the neighbors, who were all outside, red-faced with drink and shivering in their finery. The carolers stood next to them, the teenager holding the carriage lamp overhead to light the progress of the cot down the walk and out into the street.

Ambulances speed along with such authority and dispatch that you'd think it would be comfortable in one, but it isn't. It's like being a package in the back of an ice-cream truck. The drivers are hot dogs, and if there weren't rails on the beds, you'd be on the floor. As we shrieked along, through the quiet neighborhoods and onto the expressway, I felt as though I had the vantage of St. Nicholas, high above clusters of identical houses, all four walls frosted in racing lights and rugged blinking lights and ethereal LED lights, ice-blue and green and silver lights in the shape of icicles and oversize tree ornaments and chili peppers, and it was impossible for me to put away from my mind the story Renee Mayerling told me all those months ago, about the silent ride through the dark afternoon bravely illumined by outdoor mangers and gables festooned with candy canes—from Engine Company 3 to the chapel at Holy Angels.

When we arrived, the doors were open in the bay and the doctors and nurses surged out. I knew from years of hospital habitation that they'd had time to do what they called their preps, from throwing down a sour cup of coffee to washing their faces to a stolen thirty seconds of yoga breathing. And then they were all around me and I was, for better or worse, home again.

Dr. Park and the senior resident, whose name I could never remember, did not ask me to pause at the desk to register. Up to the ninth floor we went, where my new obstetrician, Dr. Helen Setnes— who'd replaced Dr. Gloomy Glass—came hurrying down the hall, pulling on her lab coat over a red velvet Christmas dress. At the huge triangular central station, nurses were gathered, singing . . . what child is this? Around the corner of the desk came Dr. Livingston, as the medics lifted me onto the bed. In the hall. "What is this with our Sicily?" he said, and I felt my blood pressure swoop right, left, and settle to center.

"I'm sick," I said. "I don't know what's wrong with me."

"The vascularity and the beginnings of a pattern of tracery beneath the skin of her upper left cheek . . ." Eliza said.

"That's just right," Dr. Livingston said. "Spot-on. You've never seen an episode of rejection." Eliza got an A-plus. What did I get?

"Will my face slough off tonight?" I asked. "Will it start with layers? Bits? Like sunburn?"

"Sicily, no, of course not. Now, you know that we can bring this under control." I was in a room by then, the transplant nurses helping me out of my black silk and into sprigged blue cotton and the pair of bottoms to a set of surgical scrubs I'd asked for. "Everything will be fine."

"Hey, Sicily," said Dr. Setnes. "I didn't expect to see you until next month." A sonogram tech was wheeling in a portable machine. "Let's have a look and see what's going on in there before I give you over to the supersleuths here." The tech, a sweet-faced blond young woman wearing an elf hat, rolled down the band of the scrubs and gelled my belly. And I didn't notice that my aunt and Vincent were at the foot of the bed until the little alien appeared on the screen, displaying the palm of one perfectly formed miniature hand. My aunt gasped and Vincent swore softly, but when I looked up at him, his face was thrilled and agonized, his eyes squeezed nearly shut, his lips compressed.

"I didn't expect it to look so real now," Vincent said. "Yet, I mean."

"Well, this is a very early pregnancy," said Dr. Setnes. "These are features that—"

"It's my baby," said Vincent. "That is my baby." Vincent reached down and touched all there was of me within his field, one of my stockinged feet.

As I stared at the slip of printout that Dr. Setnes had first handed me, Dr. Ahrens explained that what was happening to me was understandable, an undesirable blip, but not necessarily a failure of the new protocol. "We might expect a period of adjustment as the body . . . well . . ."

"Is she going to be okay?" Vincent asked.

"The baby?" said Dr. Setnes.

"Sicily," he said. "Is Sicily going to be okay?"

Dr. Setnes shrugged. "I wish I knew, let's hope." To me, she said, "What we have to decide now, Sicily, are two huge things. And deciding right now is critical. One, there is still plenty of time to reconsider your decision to terminate the pregnancy in light of this event. The other issue is the alternative protocol. Do you want to continue? The human-subject group for this protocol, with a face transplant, is one."

Dr. Ahrens said, "Human hands aren't human faces, although there are striking similarities. And the face-transplant animal studies are extraordinarily promising, but they are animal studies. Essentially, if we go ahead, you know that this would be a drug trial with a single subject, for which the hospital ethics committee has given its approval, considering the nature of the circumstances. But you didn't start this drug protocol right away. We don't know what the earlier protocol did to this fetus, and we don't know what this one will do."

"You don't know if it will work."

"I think it will work. But, no, I can't be sure," said Dr. Ahrens.

"And if I have the pregnancy terminated?" I looked up at Dr. Ahrens instead of at the shape of the tiny hand.

"Well, we'll put you back on standard levels of the commonplace immunosuppressive drugs we've always used for the first year after transplant, and you'll be out of here in a couple of days."

"That would straighten you out immediately," Dr. Setnes said.

I breathed in and held it. Could I let this baby soul go, this inconvenient child, and lasso it again someday later, in a child I adopted, in a child another woman gave birth to using some likely donor's sperm mixed with my egg? This baby now seemed to slip away from me. This had all seemed possible for me to do—sustaining the pregnancy, being a single mother—but now I saw the full gruesomeness of a face that would not even be patched on carefully, as my previous topographical mash had been over months and years, but slapped on to keep life in and infection out. There would be hanks of cultivated skin and strips torn in haste off my back and my buttocks, which would leave not the tiny snail-trail scars that lurked under this discreet fold and that but raw, red, raised, welted ridges. My beautiful body. My one vanity, transformed by urgency into a hell of stinging striped scrawls, a bombed field seen from the air—and for all of this nothing saved but my life, a changed and solitary life, my apartment a place to crawl back into. I wouldn't come out again. I wouldn't. Swathed and long-sleeved, I would receive my newspapers and work correspondence from Angel, my takeout from a series of acne-stippled boys. Or perhaps I would no longer work. There would be no more brave interviews with new clients. No one would want to hire the grotesquerie I would be—the girl who lost her face, twice. I might subsist on disability. My apartment was paid for and was my own.

And my child would live with me, in that dimly lit world. If he turned out to be a mutant like me, we might be boon companions. If he was a normal child, I wouldn't be able to go to baseball games, kindergarten graduation, parent–teacher conferences, to the zoo, and . . . to ride on the teacups at Disneyland. He would love me, as the grandchild of the woman I'd drawn in my art class loved her. And as soon as he could, he would flee, to college, to the world, where torment meant losing a job or a girl. There would be no pictures of me in his dorm room, no pictures of me holding him triumphantly in the birthing room, at the baptismal font, helping him put together his wooden train under the Cappadoras' lavish Christmas tree.

I might live for thirty years, for fifty years, for sixty years, long after Aunt Marie was dead and my grandparents were dead.

Long after Vincent was married and a father.

That was if I lived at all.

The baby and I might die together—him with quick and blessed unawareness. I would go slowly and in pain, as the hospital staff pulled out all the stops to save me. . . . To save me for what?

Or maybe, if everyone on this crack team I'd so abused acted quickly, my face would be just fine and, after counseling—lots of it— I would no longer feel as though my heart was a gourd filled with sand.

Beth would not photograph this, my loss of face. The project was over. What combination of ego and altruism, stubbornness and arrogance, had moved me? Why the exhibit? Why, oh, my God, why the pregnancy? What a fool I was—a hateful, irresponsible, self-centered, grasping, greedy, impractical, dreamy-eyed fool.

Why had I ever met Beth? Or, worse, Vincent?

"I need to see my aunt and Vincent alone for a moment," I said to Dr. Ahrens. "I'll have the pregnancy terminated as soon as it's possible. You do believe you can save me? Right?"

"I really do believe we caught this very early, Sicily, and that you will be fine."

"How soon can I have the termination? Do I need to be conscious for it?"

"Not tomorrow," she said. "That would just be too sad. The next day. And, no, you can be thoroughly sedated."

"Will it hurt the . . . fetus?"

"Sicily, there's a huge amount of controversy about things like that. Nothing will hurt for very long."

"If it can be tomorrow, then I want tomorrow," I told her.

My aunt rushed to the side of the bed, reaching down and holding me to her with a fragile strength. "Tell Beth not to open our gifts," I said to Aunt Marie. "It's important."

"I gave her a first edition of an Alfred Stieglitz book from both of us," Marie said. "Why?"

"Mine is like this," I said, thrusting the ultrasound picture at my aunt. "From last week. I put it in a little silver frame."

"There's nothing wrong with that," Marie said.

Over my aunt's head, I studied Vincent, his pelt of thick light hair disarranged, his perfect California-guy shawl of cotton sweater hanging askew. Our baby would have gray eyes, like Vincent's and mine, eyes as gray as the clouds reflected in a pond.

Or in a ditch.

"Did you want this?" I asked him. "Is any part of you in pain over ending it?"

"Sicily, I promised in the emails I sent to you. I would have wanted to help you support a child of mine and even know it."

"You want to know it."

"I mean that I want to be a father in any way I can."

"In any way you can without being a father, really," I said, and inhaled deeply.

"Sicily, wait. Tonight when I saw you . . ." He looked at Marie. "This really is private." My aunt whirled and left the room. "I wrote to you that I wanted to try to help and support you in having this child, my child. Our child. But tonight I saw you. And when I touched you, it was different."

"What happened? You got aroused? I did too."

"I thought what I thought the last time. What I never got to say.

Maybe we can get to know each other. Over these few months. I have a bunch of work to do with the movie coming out. But I can make time. I'll visit. We'll talk about what we do and what's important."

"What's important this minute?"

"This emergency."

"And you? And the baby? And me?"

"I want to be a part of this."

"Vincent, this is a terrible question to ask anyone but one you have to consider right now. If I were to have this baby and lose the face I have, if I had to have a face that was mainly scar tissue, like my face before, would you still want to get to know me? Would you still want to know the baby?"

"I can't think of that. I can't. No one could."

"If I died, would you want to raise our child?"

He stood still for a long while, head down, gripping his elbows with his arms folded across his chest.

"No," he said. "I would want Ben and Eliza to raise the baby." Vincent took a deep breath and shook his head. "It's not worth the risk to you. I know you. I don't know some unknown, unformed child."

"It's too great a risk to me, Vincent. I have to have an abortion."

His eyes widened. "I'm so sorry. It's so horrible. We've seen him, and he's alive and real. You're doing this and we just saw our child, alive and real, with hands and a little face."

"But I'm alive and real," I said. "And I have a face. And I need this face to face the world. I do want children someday, some way, and someone to love me, Vincent. And if I kept this baby but I lost my face, you wouldn't be able to stomach me. I don't blame you for that."

Vincent pulled his beat-up leather jacket off the hook and stuck his arms into it. "You don't know that for sure. I don't know that for sure." For a moment, Vincent pulled up a metal chair and sat down beside me. He took my hand, careful not to dislodge my IV. Then he said, "I do know it would scare the hell out of me, and I couldn't be sure if what I was feeling was love or pity. And you know what, Sicily? It would scare you too. I know you had a face before that was hard to look at. But you were used to it. Now you're not used to it. You're used to being pretty. You don't even know who you'd be after something like that. Or how you'd act. If I could be sure you'd be that girl I met that day at the airport . . . but you can't be sure. And I can't make that decision with a gun to my head. If I was wrong, that would be the worst thing of all." He called to my aunt. "Do you need a ride, Marie?"

She came back into the room. "I'll stay here with Sicily."

Without another word, he left. I heard the *ping* as the elevator arrived: There was almost no wait for an elevator at a hospital on Christmas Eve—when everyone well enough to be pushed, pulled, or dragged goes home, at least for the night, even if it's to die. I heard the whoosh of the doors. And Vincent was gone.

My aunt held me and tried to pretend that she wasn't crying, but her tears soaked the front of my dainty gown. The nurses had candles now and were walking slowly from door to door, stopping at each one—where someone had received a kidney, or was in isolation waiting for marrow, a heart, a liver. *A face to face the world.* I had to remember the girl I was once, who would have closed her eyes to shut out the sight of the candles.

Dr. Ahrens brought me a cup loaded with my discs and cylinders of drugs and I gulped them down. In a soft voice, she told my aunt that she had arranged for sedation for me at six in the morning before the procedure. I asked Dr. Ahrens for something that would make me sleep, sleep deeply, so I would not think of that little hand, swimming unawares within me through the dark water, toward the shore, toward me. Dr. Ahrens brought another paper cup, tasting of dry wood, and a glass of water that did nothing to quench my immense thirst. But she'd given good drug, she had.

As I began to sink, I confused the voices of the nurses with angels. I saw their scrubs with polka dots and polo necks and smiley-faces as gowns of white, and they sang of hope and joy and of the baby in the barn. And I rushed into the dark until it closed over my head.

CHAPTER EIGHTEEN

I woke with my nose chilled, the familiar cocoon of warm blankets and the clang of bright lights the telltale signals of the operating room. I had awakened before, and someone had generously put me to sleep again, treating me like an animal that might become anxious if it sensed its fate. Slowly, the darkness of morning returned to me: the nip of the IV—which I noticed of late, because needles and IVs were no longer customary for me—the balm of the Valium, a good dose, a Sicily dose, straight to starlight.

"It would be unkind to wish you a Merry Christmas, so I won't," said Hollis.

"Why are you in this dream?"

"You're not dreaming, Sicily, though I can't say that it wouldn't be easier for it to be a dream," she said. "I came back last night as soon as I heard about this."

"I'm sorry."

"It's not yours to be sorry. I should be sorry. I am sorry. I should have been more of a doctor. I needed to be here," she said. Hollis had taken my hand, the one without the IV. I was drowsy. The anesthesiologist murmured through his mask about IV Versed.

"I'm doing the right thing," I said.

"Well, probably best, honey," said Hollis. "But I sympathize. This is a loss now, and I hate that you have to bear it. But you'll wake up just as you did when the bandages came off. And, as for the rest, time will come again." Rustlings and adjustments were going on around and under me: *Can-you-lift-your-hips-just-a-little-Miss-Coyne, that's-great-thank-you, now-let's-put-one-foot-here, warm-enough-now-good.* Through a gauze, I saw Hollis recede, and in her place came a burly man, whose face and ginger fringe of hair I didn't recognize. He leaned close to study my eyes.

"Can you hear me, Miss Coyne?"

"Of course."

"Maybe she can have a little more?"

"Nope," said the anesthesiologist. "Already got the Mike Tyson amount."

"Where is Dr. Setnes?" I asked.

"She's not here," said the red-haired doctor. "She's not needed for this morning."

His voice was mellow, if terse. I had taken this man's Christmas morning for a grim purpose, so that my psychological suffering would be eased. But it would never be eased. I would always have scars on my soul. The doctor was gowned and masked and gloved. I wondered if doctors scrubbed in so rigorously for routine abortions. I was a special case, though. An infection could thrust me farther into the shadows. But wasn't abortion a bit of an ordinary process, performed each day on dozens of sobbing teenagers and tight-lipped forty-year-olds, in office settings? A suck and a scoop?

"Dr. Setnes is an obstetrician, Miss Coyne," the doctor said, and I felt the cold tongue of the speculum. "I'm a gynecological surgeon.

And I'm going to take the best care of you. My name is Doug Sherry. This isn't going to take very long, and you won't feel a thing. Please relax."

I began to breathe slowly, deeply, in and out, willing my shoulders down into the table. Soon it would be over. Soon I would have the chance to begin again, to take up where I had stopped so abruptly. I saw those vulnerable drooping cheeks on the grainy TV screen of the sonogram. The furled tiny hand. I saw myself naked in the night, Vincent's body golden and red in the firelight, our arms so supple in light and shadow, so tightly against each other that we were like estuaries of a single river that met in a hollow of sand. Wide-spaced eyes. Babies not meant to be. Vincent's eyes, his shock and awe. Annunciation. Swimming little foot. All unawares. I heard myself speak to the doctor and he murmured in return, adjusting the drape over my knees—so kind, even the drape had been warmed. I tried again. Could they hear me? I tried to sit but my legs were cumbersome and thick. The anesthesiologist spoke up.

"Dr. Sherry, she said no."

"I don't think so. She's not aware."

"I did," I told the room wearily. "I said no. Stop it. Stop everything."

"Sicily, do you need more time?" the red-haired man asked.

"I don't need more time," I said. "I need to go back to my room, and I am not going to schedule another procedure. Ever. *I am half sick of shadows.*" I had memorized only one poem ever, Tennyson's "The Lady of Shalott," and then only under duress. But I had gone to Catholic school, and I remembered it well. *God, in his mercy, lend her grace.* As the Versed ebbed like something uncovering my lucid mind, I saw the rest of my body ringed by a dozen faces, all peering at me with various degrees of astonishment, annoyance, amusement, anger. The red-haired gynecological surgeon pulled off his mask.

"Did I have an abortion?" I asked.

"No," said the surgeon. "No. You refused it."

"I refused it. I was not saying, no, this can't be happening to me. I was saying no, this will not happen."

"I'm glad Dr. Haryana heard you. You don't need me now. If I leave right away, my kids won't be up yet." He turned to leave and then looked back. "Don't worry. Good luck, Miss Coyne. Good luck, and I mean that."

"I will need it," I said.

"Happy Christmas. I got a good feeling," said Dr. Sherry.

I did too. This guy had grown up on the West Side. I heard it in his voice and saw it in his big-veined nose, which had seen more than a few cups of kindness in its time.

"Good luck from me too, Sicily," said the anesthesiologist, whose liquid East Indian eyes and lilt I now recognized.

"I won't be seeing you again, I promise," I told him.

"You never know. Maybe six months from now, you could have a stubborn baby who doesn't want to come out. Apparently he is a stubborn baby already. Determined to stay put. I think he has got a right to his chance in this bad world. Maybe not always bad."

Of course, Hollis was waiting outside the doors of the OR. Although there was nothing for me to be ashamed of, I wanted to look away. As the nurses at the head and foot of the rolling bed wheeled me toward the elevators, she walked beside me, whistling softly, "O Come, O Come, Emmanuel," which she could not on earth have known was the song we were singing when the Christmas trees exploded on the altar. Even I had forgotten. She said, "What's your favorite Christmas carol?"

"'Silent Night,'" I said. "I'm very big on sentimental nonsense. As you have just seen demonstrated."

"Like some kinds of religion."

"Hollis, this had nothing to do with religion."

"I didn't mean the Catholic religion," she said. "I meant the religion of love." Hollis thumbed the button while the nurses slipped the cot into the elevator: It barely fit. They always had to jockey it around and slam it against the walls. Why was that? Why didn't somebody suggest changing either the size of the bed or the size of the elevator? Didn't they have different sizes of elevators, some for an urban hospital, some for a French restaurant, some for the W Hotel or Lincoln Center? Hollis waved and told me she'd be back later, after getting on her computer to chat with her family in Louisiana.

Dr. Ahrens was waiting in my room on the ninth floor. She was not tapping her foot, but I could tell that her restraint was forced.

"Hi," I said. "What are you doing?"

"Oh, roasting chestnuts on an open fire, which I'd like to put certain people in," she said. "I was halfway to Brook Park."

"You don't have to mess with me today."

She did have to mess with me that day.

The brief bubble of satisfaction I'd felt as the anesthetic cleared abandoned me with a declarative pop—as Dr. Ahrens explained the next not-few days of my life.

Just down the hall, equally irritated nurses were preparing a double room for negative isolation, which meant sterilizing all the surfaces and covering the ones closest to the door with replaceable sterile film. They would use police meters to test the room for various obvious contaminants and install a heavy clear-plastic door (not unfamiliar on a transplant floor).

What would go into that room was me.

Period.

I could have my computers, if they could be wiped down with antiseptic cloths and covered with the computer equivalent of full-body condoms. I could have a TV with movie channels and a new iPod and an e-reader that would also have a condom. I could have my aunt, if she wore, like, a level-four biohazard suit, and no other visitors except for mime-guests through the plastic—as though I were doing twenty-five-to-life at the Supermax in southern Illinois.

"After the medication does its thing, how long until I can go home?"

"If there are no complications with the baby . . . well, you'll have to ask Dr. Setnes about that," said Dr. Ahrens.

"So, after the nuchal translucency screening—"

"Sicily, I mean after the baby is *born*. If we get your rejection under control, there is no way you are leaving this hospital until you get wheeled out to a four-door with an approved car seat in the back."

"You're not serious."

"I am absolutely serious. And, yeah, yeah, you can bring up MERSA and staph infections and anything else you want to, but the fact is, this staff is going to bend over backward to be triple-careful and keep that baby where it is and that . . . pretty face right where it is, and you're just not going home. So get someone to water your plants. Get lots of great novels. Long ones. Get life insurance and hire a nanny. Learn Japanese."

"I'll go nuts," I said.

Dr. Ahrens smiled and said, "You're already nuts."

"This is like a punishment for trying to be responsible!"

Dr. Ahrens paused to consider that. "Yes, it's kind of like that." She left, presumably to mix up a batch of the Strauss-McManus drug, the alternative protocol, called only SM965,900, and a nurse in a sterile gown and gloves brought me a turkey sandwich. I wondered if the turkey was at least kosher. I also wondered how long it would be—how long a seemly interval—before I could call Beth's house and speak to Vincent. Not that I wanted to call Beth's house and speak to Vincent. As complete idiots go, I was the gold standard that early Christmas morning and knew it. I could easily visualize the sweet gathering under Beth's designer Christmas tree being interrupted by a phone call pointing out that she should forget I'd shown up at her house the previous evening *enceinte* and decided to become unexpecting by the next morning. The dopey ironies of the season were just too cringy, and visualizing Vincent's stricken face after having seen the baby's face and hearing my announcement made me want a mask and headgear like the nurses wore when they came back to take away my untouched turkey.

"You have to eat now, Sicily, okay?" one said. "Not this minute, but now and regularly."

"I will."

"Would you like some soup?"

"Yes, please."

It was cream of celery, which would have been just below cream of raw gizzard on the list of soups I absolutely hated—which was almost none at all. I liked soup. How could they pick the only one that savored of icky church suppers, and not special Catholic suppers, like St. Joseph's Table but supper with Jell-O at nondenominational churches? I ate it anyway, gagging at the pasty texture and the sticky cool temperature. Then I chased it with two cups of cranberry juice and brushed my teeth with my finger in the washroom, which also was draped like some sort of place of execution. Bloody execution. By then it was . . . 10:00 a.m. Ten? Four hours since I woke up? That was it? I knew that my aunt couldn't bear to be there for the abortion and would show up very soon, figuring it was all over but the sobbing. It cheered me slightly to think that she would be pleased—at least someday, if in a bittersweet way. Where was she, anyway? Where was my aunt and mother?

Why wasn't she right here, to be with me when I woke up? Why had she left at all? I pulled the hospital phone cord to its fullest length, because my cell phone would never work in here and, in any case, had not yet been sterilized. The telephone had a full, clear-coated skin on it, the hole in the receiver barely pierced. I decided to call her.

"Merry Christmas, Auntie."

"Sweetheart. Is it over?"

"Yes, it's all over. Auntie, I have to tell you something. Wait, where are you?"

"I'm at home."

"You're at home? You went home? Why did you leave me?"

"I needed a change of clothes, and I didn't want to sit in the waiting room crying and listening to the nurses singing Christmas carols."

"Aren't you even going to go see Grandma and Grandpa?"

"I'll see them later. Sicily, nobody had the heart—or the stomach—

for presents and turkey and bracciole today. As far as they knew, Ernest and Annette were on the verge of losing their only granddaughter and their only great-grandchild, all at once."

"Well, Auntie, I didn't have it."

"Didn't have the abortion? Hmmm." Uh, *hmmm?* What was *hmmm?*

"I decided against it. For sure now. Forever."

My aunt didn't say a thing. I thought she must be crying quietly. Shock and grief. Hope and forgiveness. *Let nothing you dismay, Auntie,* I thought.

"Well, that's great, Sicily. You've put your life in real danger now. Thank you for that. You've stuck pins in hearts all over town."

What the hell? I thought.

"I will love your baby, and I'm sure that I'll get over wanting to pinch you 'til your arms bleed. Sicily, I hope I live a long time, because you have to be the most immature, flighty person, and your child is going to need some stability."

"That's so not fair! The stakes are pretty high here!"

"They're damned high. They're the highest stakes in your life and, I might add, my own. And you're trusting in things that no one knows will work. Not for sure."

I sighed. "The best things can go wrong. Nothing is for sure, Auntie. That's why I didn't do it. Not one thing is for sure. You're always telling me to stop busting Christina's chops for believing things that I'm actually pretty sure are not real. I'm not taking a damned-fool risk. I'm doing what a firefighter would do. Like my dad said. I'm taking a measured risk. If no one ever took a measured risk, no one would ever start a fire, even to cook. No one would ever go near a fire to put out one out."

A nurse came into the room, garbed as an astronaut, one giant step for womankind. She didn't bother to knock—although knocking on a plastic sheet might have presented its own challenges. Earlier, someone had told me I would soon get a buzzer, a loud bell that would announce a visitor so I could go sit on the other side of the door and they could view me. Things had not yet progressed to that point. Just considering myself sealed in a blue-walled, two-windowed Tupperware container for six months made me want to keen with self-pity and anguish. And here my aunt was, cussing me out for the very thing she'd wept in mourning over the night before! A promenade of deprivations paraded before my weary mind's eye. A barre. Live music. Fresh air. Air of any kind, even exhaust! Spring. The smell of spring. Cologne. Rain . . . when was this baby going to be born, anyhow? June? Makeup. Deli. Coffee from Lotta Latte. Hello? This was incubation hell.

"Auntie! Do you realize that I have to be stuck in here for . . . until the baby is born? I can't even go outside for a walk? Don't you think that made the decision even harder for me?" (I hadn't known about the isolation at the time, but I was definitely not getting my propers here.)

"You're not on bed rest," Aunt Marie said. "You can prance around. You can try reading, for the first time in your life. Maybe it will cross over the placenta and the baby will be literate—"

"Stop it!"

"Sicily, don't overdo it. I spoke to Dr. Grigsby this morning. I already knew you had decided to have the baby. That was probably a violation of your rights, since you aren't a minor, but she wanted to tell me that I didn't have to hurry to get to the hospital. I will hurry, though. I had to sort something out here. And I'm happy, but it's difficult to be entirely happy. I feel the way Grandma does. Your life is the important life, for all of us. It's also no fun to be on the sidelines of this emotional tug of war, although I know—"

I hung up on her.

It was noon and I had the rest of my Christmas to spend alone, me and my fetus, with some more nice cream of celery soup. (What kind of mind would ram cream of celery soup down the throats of sick people on Christmas? People who hated their lives because they had to spend the day at work in an institutional kitchen, no doubt.)

I sat up suddenly. It was gone. My morning sickness was gone. I felt . . . spectacular, the itching in my palms already subsiding, my woozy febrile state clearing like morning mist under the imperative gaze of the sun. How long had it been since I'd thrown up? People had told me that my nausea would get better after the first trimester, but I hadn't expected it would quit as though nature were holding an hourglass. If my aunt was going to come to see me, couldn't she possibly bring a nice antiseptic Reuben with sweet potato fries from Myzog's? Mr. Herzog (Mr. Myzog had been dead these seven years) would be working on Christmas. Didn't I deserve at least that, not having been able to keep down a mouthful of anything redolent of garlic for months? I picked up the (encased) hospital phone to call Aunt Marie back. No texting for . . . six months? I would email! I would email! Forgive me, St. Jude, my patron. I would email every day. My dance clothing and pajamas, my ballet shoes, my pencils—all things that would have to be laundered here for me with something like lye.

But I was too proud to call Marie back.

I was too sad to call Vincent.

That lasted for an hour.

Just before two, I called Beth's house. Probably because she didn't recognize the number, she answered.

"How are you, Sicily?" she asked evenly. Disturbingly evenly.

"I'm fine. Do you know . . . ?"

"Vincent told us last night. We are all very sad. I'm as sad as I've been in . . . a very long time. For you and for us. But we're happy for you too. This is the right thing. You come first. But Vincent is . . . I don't know how to explain it."

"Beth, I have to tell you—"

"It was the right choice, Sicily. I think we all just held out hope. Which was foolish. I think Vincent did."

"May I please speak to him?"

"He's gone, Sicily. He left a few hours ago for the airport. He didn't have his heart in it."

Super. This was getting better by the moment.

"There was . . . His grandfather Angelo is put out about Vincent's views about the baby. Or at least his actions toward you throughout this. Pat is too. . . ."

There was no way I could abort myself—not the baby but my adult self—although the thought crossed my mind.

"I didn't have the abortion."

"What?"

"Oh, Beth. I feel awful. I mean, I feel physically much better. But awful. I decided at the last minute that I couldn't go through with it."

Long, pregnant—if you will—silence.

"I decided that I wanted my baby even though it means that I can't leave the hospital at all until the baby is born. I have to stay in isolation."

Nothing. No sudden geyser of contrition and sympathy. Her son had taken it on the chops, on one of the few days of the year all of them were together, for not wanting to marry a girl he'd seen three times in his life. It must have sounded like soap-opera extortion. Beth was following her son down the sterile, echoing glassed skywalks of O'Hare, where none but the world's restless lingered today.

Finally, I drew my last card. "Did you open my gift?"

"I did. I opened it before Marie called to tell us not to. I kept looking at it all night. I couldn't sleep."

"Beth, I'm sorry." And she could bite the tailpipe too! What in the hell was I apologizing for? Did I decide to get my face burned off and have my parents go down like milk bottles at a carnival in a pitiless one-two punch and find out that my fiancé went into a chapel conveniently filled with votive candles and watched his best friend move one to the worst place his small evil brain could imagine . . . and then, all that behind me, have the most beautiful moment of my life end in a colossal awkwardness, after having the person responsible offer me the personal equivalent of his business card? Joke her.

Beth could send this grandkid postcards. I was moving to Australia.

"Don't you dare be sorry, Sicily. Don't you dare!"

I hesitated. This could be taken two ways.

"None of this is your fault at all. I love Vincent and . . . I think you do too, you poor kid. I'm very happy that you're having the baby, and the baby will be fine. And you will be fine. I know it. I know you will.

And optimism isn't my strongest trait. This is the best gift you could have given us." She covered the phone and I could hear the sounds of people exclaiming. "And I'll come to see you every single day."

"You don't have to do that, Beth."

"I want to do that, Sicily," she said. "Can I ask you normal questions now?"

"I guess," I said. What did I expect from Beth? So far as she knew, really, they'd given me some cough syrup and I would be all better in a few days. She didn't understand even as much as Marie did—and Marie didn't entirely understand—that I was still walking a tightrope on a blustery day.

"Do you hope it's a boy or a girl?"

I had never even allowed myself to consider that. "I hope it's not a mutant. I hope I don't turn out to be one too. Or worse. I hope we both make it with ears and noses and functional brains. That's all I hope."

"How is your face?" Beth asked the question as though she'd asked, *How is your rash?*

"They gave me a massive . . ." I paused as Hollis pushed her way through the plastic door. My surgeon sat down in the steel rocker and patiently regarded the ceiling, as if counting the holes in the acoustical tile. "Beth, someone is here and I have to go. Do you mind telling Vincent? I feel very awkward." She said she would try to reach Vincent before he boarded the flight—that maybe she could even turn him around and get him to come back. He was to have stayed four days at home. My heart folded on itself. If he was to come back . . . I put down the phone and faced Hollis.

"You didn't open my presents," she said. "Now you can only see them. These are sterile. You cannot touch them." They were encased in individual envelopes of clear soft plastic. There was a yellow sleeper with a bright crescent moon on the minuscule breast pocket; the embroidery beneath it read, *Once in a Blue Moon*. The leather-bound journal was the kind I liked that I could lay open flat, to draw and write in with ease. "They'll bake it or something so that you can have it in here," Hollis told me. In sturdy block print, the deep red cover was embossed with *What I Wondered, As I Waited.*

"They're so sweet, and so appropriate. Thank you."

"I guess I knew the way this would go," Hollis said. "I knew on some level you'd end up in isolation too."

"The journal is such a clever idea. Though most people are so busy, it's almost like it was made for someone in a situation like me, with nothing but time." There was no reason to believe I had anything except oceans and valleys and highways of empty, empty time.

"It was made expressly for you and engraved expressly for you. For only you."

"I thought it was an artisan idea. It means even more now."

Hollis stood and, as was her custom, stretched one and then the other arm overhead. "I believe that I will go home now and make myself some hot chocolate with a generous, generous amount of Kahlúa in it and read a few novels. How does that sound? No one to bug me or get in my face. No teenage James working so hard to ignore me that he has to stand right in front of me to do it." I smiled at her. "You enjoy your day. Get some sleep if you can."

After she left, I planned what I would write after they autoclaved the journal. I would write, *Christmas Day. The first day of me and you. I'll explain later.*

I would explain.

Once I knew what to say.

I would leave space, in the journal, in my given life, for the man I . . . once loved. I used my teeth to rip away a shred of sacred lip and tasted the penny tang of my blood. If I had not been pregnant with Vincent's maybe-not-that-great baby, he would still have been the man I loved. Eventually, because of Beth's photo exhibit, I might have met him in any case. By then he would have been engaged to a German actor who had formerly been a model and tennis pro, six feet tall, with a sexy mauve mouth, jonquil hair cut long over her eyes.

And I would have had her whacked.

In the hall there arose such a clatter, well, I sprang from my bed to see what was the matter. (How dare my aunt call me illiterate just because my idea of fun wasn't reading four books a day, like hers was?) While Hollis occupied me, my Caruso relatives had set up one of those long metal tables in the hall, covered it with a cloth, and laid out the Christmas china, the china my mother Gia had painted—which, if we used it more than once a year, would probably kill us all with the lead content. The nurses had brought chairs. The turkey sat in the center, and beside it were a steaming casserole of my grandmother's gnocchi, braided bread, and melons with lime and prosciutto. Kit and Minister Anthony were there. Everyone lifted their wineglasses at the same time and my Grandpa Ernest said, "To Sicily and our bambino . . ."

"Come on," I said. "Come on. This is too sappy even for me."

On the other side of the plastic from the feast, from plates prepared for people in isolation, I ate three helpings and drank apple juice. (I didn't know if you could irradiate food and decided not to think about it.) All the nurses took their turns at the table as well. My aunt unwrapped my presents, including a leather bag tooled in Italy with inlaid patterns of gold and green; it was the size and shape of Utah. I could literally feel its silky heft on my shoulder.

That night, after the last person had left, I noticed my lower belly was protruding over the waistband of my scrubs.

I'd eaten far too much. But it was still that way the next day.

It would never be flat again.

CHAPTER NINETEEN

My life was *en pointe* at the end of the diving board.

Finishing my projects, which numbered precisely four, took up all of three weeks. It was astonishing how much you can accomplish if you don't have a life. I watched so much TV that my aunt pointed out that I was speaking in phrases that sounded like commercials. "Put your trust on wheels," I caught myself telling Marie, quoting a tire commercial, one night when she had to hurry to the TV station during a snowstorm. (I would have given my molars to feel and breathe a snowstorm.) Dr. Setnes came daily, and I got to know her better. She was as mellow and given to random positive statements as Dr. Glass had been to flat, dour disclaimers. A hippie in her late forties who'd been a doula before she was a doctor, she said that the way she figured it, there would be plenty of time to feel bad about things. There was no use doing it in advance.

"Here's what I know," she said, one day not too long after Christmas. "Nature is always contriving, the way Thornton Wilder said." Great. A quoter. "Most babies are born healthy. Most babies are born healthy even if they don't get prenatal care. Most babies are born healthy even if the mothers don't take care of themselves. Most birth defects are correctible. I'm betting on Dr. Sherry. He said this baby wanted to get here."

"That was Dr. Haryana," I told her.

"Everyone says it."

"Is there a betting pool?"

"You want the truth? Or the classy, professional answer? If there was a pool—and I'm not saying there is—well, the bettor who says the baby won't make it would get a lot of money and the people on the other side would each get two dollars. If there was a pool about your face transplant, the odds would be about three to one on you too."

"AT UIC, every delivery is a special delivery," I told Dr. Setnes. She burst out laughing, asking if I'd been watching the hospital's closed-circuit channel. I not only had been watching it, I knew exactly what I'd do if I ever needed a knee replacement, treatment for diabetes, surgery for a detached retina, or pediatric immunology (for that, I'd go to Seattle).

The room quickly filled with nothing.

I had to beg for the few sticks I got, things that were my equivalent of an oxygen tank—my computer, my iPod, my drawing pencils.

My ballet barre.

After a portable barre had been baked, I began to stretch and do light ballet drills. From behind the plastic sheeting, Beth photographed me, the ballerina who ate the softball. Then the soccer ball. "How much are you exercising?" she asked as we sat down on opposite sides of the curtain and I turned on my little intercom. It was like prison, except you didn't have to touch a phone that someone might have spit tobacco juice on. Or some smeary substance a lot worse.

"One hour. Sometimes two hours. It helps me to sleep."

"I think that's too much," she said.

But I'd seen the commercial. I reminded her that working out was making love to your heart, according to the National Heart Association. In Hollis's opinion, anything that didn't make me feel a cramp was okay. Dr. Setnes agreed. My heart was indeed healthy, although still as a sleeping bird. The protocol with oral SM965,900 was effective and my pregnancy uneventful. Everything was uneventful.

When Eliza stopped by, I asked her about Stella and Charley. I asked her how it was to be back at work. Finally, she made a face and said, "Don't you want to know about Vincent?"

"I was afraid I'd never ask." Beth hadn't caught Vincent at the airport that Christmas Day. By the time she reached him, it was days later and he seemed to have overcome his distress at his altercation with his father and grandfather. Of course, the Cappadoras, with the exception of Eliza, who had been at the hospital during the argument, didn't realize that the risk to my face was a risk to my life. Their understanding was the understanding of most people. Beth tried to get a word in, but even she didn't truly grasp the gravity of the situation until later. Apparently, the argument had been much worse than Beth let on, and Vincent had walked out in a rage. Beth kept telling me that Vincent told her he would be in touch with me, but Eliza was dubious.

"You have to understand that he feels dumped," she said.

"*He* feels dumped?"

"He came at Christmas thinking he would try to ask you that day not to marry him but to consider a future. He put himself out there."

"How do you know?"

"I think he told Ben."

"You think he told Ben? Why aren't you sure? Does Ben keep that stuff a secret?"

"No. That's what Ben thinks Vincent said the last time he talked to him before Christmas."

How could someone not be quite certain what another person, especially his own brother, had said? "Do men communicate with clicks and grunts?" I asked.

"Yes, they do," Eliza said. "But that's not why. Vincent doesn't tell things straight out."

"Who knows Vincent best?"

"Beth thinks she does. My mother knows him pretty well, more than Beth does. My mother is like Angelo—she's crazy about Vincent. But Ben knows him most." Eliza paused. "But the truth is? Nobody really knows Vincent. He keeps his cards under his shirt."

"You mean close to the vest."

"Yes."

"That's the expression. So other people won't see your cards."

"Of course," Eliza said. Her pager sounded and she consulted it. "It's a hysterical person with a grafted finger. I don't have to run right now. I think it might be good for you to get in touch with Vincent."

"Okay."

"Send him an email and . . . let it kind of grow, Sicily. Things grow better with a lot of space."

"You're a philosopher, huh?"

"No. But I like this idea of you and Vincent. I saw you that night in the kitchen."

"That was just biology, Eliza."

"Don't knock biology." She went to visit her hysterical grafted finger. That night, I wrote to Vincent.

If I was a serious kind of person, I would say I'm sorry for being such a ditzy woman. That would reveal that I'm a ditzy woman instead of a serious person. But I never wanted to lose the baby, Vincent. I never wanted to hurt you. You have to understand the confusion I felt. Imagine choosing between a baby you didn't know and a face you would have your whole life if you were lucky. Imagine a much worse choice, your baby or your life. I've never had a child. I don't know what it's like to have a child. I assume parents would give up their lives for their children. But it's not a child yet. My face is something I saw only in dreams or old pictures. Except for right after the fire, I never wanted to die, even when my face was disfigured. People say all the time, I'd rather die than be blind; I'd rather die than be in a wheelchair. But it's not true. If you're a sane person, you always want to live. Inside that face, I always was that woman you met at the airport. I just got to find myself finally. Somebody said once, it was like pizza. If you didn't have anything else in your life, sometimes it was enough to have a good piece of pizza. I guess you can't imagine that. Things here seem to be going well. I hope you're fine. Don't worry about me. Call me anytime. I'm always here.

I signed it, *Gestationally yours, Sicily.* I tried to joke.

Even in my trash and my junk pile, there was no return mail from Upstart Productions. From my aunt and from Beth, I learned that *Germinators* (please) opened to a huge audience and was a big box-office draw. On the third Tuesday of January, before it officially opened, Vincent had flown all the family out there for the premiere, which was one of those slinky, sultry California affairs that I imagined Vincent attended all time, although Eliza swore that Vincent said he avoided them like prostate exams. That cracked me up. What she said next didn't.

"I did write to him," I told her.

"I don't think he's with anyone," Eliza said. She let her stethoscope swing like a pendulum on an old clock.

"But he brought someone to that party."

"He had to. That's what he told Grandma Rosie. He had to so that people wouldn't think he likes boys."

"Tell me about the girl."

"No, Sicily."

"Okay," I said. I reached over and switched off my side of the transmitter, which I did when I wanted to sleep without hearing nurses discussing novels and divorces and patients gabbing with their relatives. After about thirty seconds, Eliza mimed for me to turn it back on. I made a motion that said, *Come on, give it up.* She nodded.

"She was like this dumb B-movie girl you see in vampire movies,"

Eliza said. "About sixteen years old and about ninety pounds. She had blond hair that she kept brushing away so she could see you, and she was—"

"Really tall."

"Yes."

"Hmmmmm." I was already loving this. It was as funny as canned farts.

"But it got bad." For me, it had already been bad. "She was hanging all over Vincent all night, and Grandma Rosie marched up there and said, 'Vincent, you never told me: What did you buy your baby for Christmas?' His date was upset. She sort of went over to the bar. Vincent told his grandmother that he knew what she was up to, but couldn't they have just one happy night without discussing the issue."

I knew what he'd given his baby for Christmas. It had arrived last week. Ten shares of Disney stock, which I considered extremely thoughtful. "But Rosie said, 'The issue? That's what it is? An issue? You would pick this . . . hat pin with rubber lips over the girl who's risking her life to have your child?'"

"What did Vincent say?"

Eliza hesitated again, checking her pager, although I knew it had not sounded.

"Come on."

"He said, 'She's not doing that for me, Grandma.'"

Oh. Well. Technically, Vincent was right. And still, I could imagine his discomfort and defensiveness on what was supposed to be his night, not to mention the embarrassment of his date, from whom I hoped that Vincent had contracted a slight and curable STD.

"Then Rosie called Vincent *sciocco,* which means—"

"I know. I took Italian in college. It means fool."

Rosie had left then, and Vincent got drunk, which he never did, and everyone was sort of pretending to be happy. There were lots of movie stars.

Eliza offered to bring me her pictures the next time she visited. I said that would be nice.

After that conversation, I did start to read. I read right through Dickens. I read right through Hemingway. That brought me to February 5. I lost my appetite. Polly Guthrie visited and made a ritual plea for the baby's health. "It's got to be lousy being stuck in there."

"I'm not good company for myself," I said. "Here's the problem. I have a case of unrequited love. First I loved him and he thought I was fun. Then I got over him and he loved me a little. Then he got over me."

Polly sighed. "Sounds like the story of my life," she said. Big help. "Time changes everything, Sicily. You have a strong will, but you can't will someone else's emotions."

One picture that Beth took around that time shows me with my hands outstretched, pressed against the transparent door, as though I were trying to break out of one of those cryogenic machines I'd described to my aunt. Everything is flat except my nose and my belly.

Life settled into a dull routine—soap operas on TV and the windows in my room my only conduit to the real world. I loved the soap operas because they provided a daily drip of misery, the dramatic portrayal of the worst that could happen, even worse than my life. Plus, on soap operas, people had children in every conceivable fashion, literally, even while they were amnesiacs and trapped on desert islands. (My isolation suite at UIC was sort of a desert island, although it lacked a ruthless and handsome criminal and palm trees.) I'd watched *The Young and the Restless* in college and was astonished to see that the adults hadn't aged a day, while the dreary-eyed toddler actors, who never seemed to really get why they were there, were already dating. I'd been out of school for only four years! Aunt Marie teased me about shopping the soaps for names for the baby. She wondered if I'd be so utterly saturated with TV by the time of the birth that I'd end up with a daughter named Destiny or a son called Ransom.

At night, like somebody's reclusive aunt, I listened to my scanner, that deadpan tragicomic patter that still was my urban lullaby. "Two two-six responding to the box at Twelfth and Washington . . . Ladder Thirty-eight, we have repeated reports of a structural fire with a child trapped inside, address one three seven Freeland, cross street Twenty-ninth . . . Ladder Thirty-eight to base, we are en route . . . Ladder Thirty-eight on scene, rescue operations commencing . . . We have the child, Medic Sixty-one is in radio contact with Methodist Hospital . . . continuing resuscitation efforts . . . Thank you, Medic Sixty-one, let's make this a happy ending. . . ."

The apricot moon rose and swelled and waned in the upper right corner of my bedside window. I slept and woke and checked on Cricket, Rafe, Sabrina, and Lucas. I read six books about Henry VIII's six wives. I ate pretty much all the time. When I stepped onto a scale, I weighed 141 pounds. I could have sat on Vincent and crushed him without trying. Dr. Setnes's assurances that most of this was fluid could not stop me from thinking of those waif girls with their short black dresses and biceps the size of tamales.

The baby and I liked tamales.

We liked brownie sundaes and bracciole and hot bagels fresh from Hardenny's. The pernicious combination of my belated discovery of recreational eating, pregnancy, and boredom would leave me with two hundred crunches a day in my future. At least I would be able to look after the baby for a few months without a frightening pressure to hit the bricks looking for clients. Aunt Marie's zest for work guaranteed that. The only thing she liked more than a juicy story was the sight of me, a little rounder every day. Her love for me probably surpassed anything I could ever have expected from two parents. She was my everyday heaven and earth.

Beth also spent days with me—not every day as she'd promised, but many, a few hours a few days each week. Given that she was the baby's grandmother, the doctors had conferred and made an exception for Beth. I had no idea what they did with Marie and Beth before they came in, in their white gowns and hats and little surgi-booties and face hoods like semi-space garb. Did they put them on tanning beds? Run them through a shower that had six nozzles, all spouting bleach?

When she was allowed in, Beth brought her camera in a box thing meant for scuba divers, and after we talked or ate together, she would

gently raise her camera and begin to shoot. By then I was so used to
Beth taking pictures of me that I would have drawn the line only at the
toilet. She photographed the lonely Madonna, in my leotard, twirling a
strand of my hair, sitting in a hump up on top of the nonfunctional ra-
diator. My favorite from that time is of me pulling up my T-shirt and
giggling at my reflection in the mirror of the closet. (Beth sent Vincent
an image to his computer. Vincent emailed me, *Is this what is called
showing?*) He was on the road, everywhere. Sometimes he dropped me
a line:

Opening in London. No queen.
Weekend in Las Vegas.
Opening in San Francisco. Queen did attend.

I wrote back:

Ninth-floor isolation. Chicago.

In the journal Hollis had given me, I wrote, *I miss you. I don't even
know you. I'm sure that you'll take after Vincent and me, which means
you'll be the sort of distilled essence of difficult people. That's okay. I need
to keep busy. My job is a little dull. My life right now is a little dull. I've
been reading aloud to you, but from Virginia Woolf. Don't get bad ideas.
I'm going to have Grandma Auntie bake me a book of children's poems
next week, and then I'll read to you about the moon that is a griffin's egg.
Love, Mommy.*
Mommy.
I covered a whole page with names. *Bonnie. Anne. Claire. Natasha.
Kelsey. Sylvie. Daniel. Gray. Owen. Martin. Francis.* And *James,* of
course.
Then I covered the rest of the page with *Mommy, Mommy, Mommy,
Daddy, Daddy, Daddy.* I drew a memory portrait of Charley Cappadora,
asleep in Eliza's arms. I drew things I liked: butter-colored horses, day
lilies, Montrose Beach.

Kit was loyal and called daily. The advent of a phone call was like getting flowers. It was coarse of me, but her calls were absorbing because she had become very twitchy and curt, as the thing with Anthony, which had passed the Kit equivalent of a silver anniversary, was now on the wane. She told me they'd had sex only six times in the past two weeks. I replied that was better than one time in the past five months. I got real flowers, which I could not keep because of the rules of isolation (nurses showed them to me and then trundled them away to other wards), by the wheelbarrow after my aunt did one of the little essays with which she sometimes closed her show, called "The Last Minute."

Sitting in a plain chair and leaning forward with her elbows on her knees, in a way she never did (in her publicity pictures, Marie's head was always tilted curiously, thrown back in amusement, or resting studiously on one hand), Marie had concluded, "In her lifetime, my niece, Sicily Coyne—whom I adopted as my daughter after both her parents died, her father while saving the lives of children, fighting the Holy Angels fire—has endured every kind of loss. Except two. She has never lost a child. And she has never lost hope. I love Sicily, and tonight, as my old friend Gale Sayers once wrote, I want you to ask God to love her too."

The next morning, along with letters, checks, music boxes, telegrams, baby clothing, stuffed animals, and—yes—a bright-green baby-sized Harley-Davidson from the company itself, I got a call from Renee Mayerling.

Her first words were, "Vincent Cappadora?"

As though we'd never said goodbye, I let the laughter bubble up.

"The grapevine is that good?"

"It's a short vine," Renee said.

I told her, "He was the only one there."

We talked for two hours. Renee was now the lieutenant at the legendary Engine Company 78 in Wrigleyville, the Waveland Avenue Miracle. She had received three commendations for bravery. What she said next stopped my breath: Renee had been burned. She was knocked down by the explosion of a water heater in a manufactured home and pinned for critical seconds before one of her rookies hauled her free, knocking aside the superheated oversize tin can on her back with a single adrenaline kick of his work boot. She'd been burned so badly on the back of her neck and lower scalp that she was furloughed for three months with full pay and had undergone skin grafts. They were thirteen years better than my first grafts and thankfully didn't show under her curly brown hair, which Renee now wore long. "I never dreamed what you went through, Sissy," she said. "I guess I didn't really want to know. Maybe that's why it happened."

"That's magical thinking, Renee. I've been told that a hundred times in the past year. You're not supposed to know how a victim feels. You're a victor. You gave me a hell of a hand once upon a winter's day."

"Sicily, you're the sweetest kid. My gosh, you're not a kid anymore, are you? I can come and see you, right? Even though you're the bubble girl?"

"Sure," I said. "Sometimes much is asked of those to whom not much is given," I said.

"Awwww, Sissy," Renee said.

I told her, "It's okay."

"So, you and Vincent. It's great. Who would have thought that it would be you and the scourge of the neighborhood? He was the legendary delinquent when I was in high school. Then the movie and the Oscar and all that? Does he have an Italian car like all those people? And what is the commuter thing like?"

Imagine how that was. Imagine. You know how badly I wanted to tell my old babysitter, my tutor—my savior—that it was all Cristal and yellow-diamond engagement rings and daily devotional telephone calls, videos on MyShare with Hollywood stars all wishing me Godspeed and fair winds? More than you know. More than I know.

"We don't talk," I said.

"What do you mean? You mean because you're in the isolation tank?"

"No. That's not why. We're not together, Renee. You know, this happened as a result of a brief thing in California. He didn't want any part of the pregnancy. Then he did, but I didn't want him to have any part of the pregnancy anymore. Then I wanted him to. Then he did. Then he didn't."

"Are you in love with him?" Renee asked.

"Yep," I said.

"Oh, Sicily. Come on. Really?"

"In some sick, self-loathing, denial-of-my-own-rights way."

"That's true for everybody."

"Not you."

"I outrank my husband. I have to spend my whole life being apologetic and faking how sexed up I feel and making pies and chili from scratch at home when I *don't* have to cook at the station."

Renee was good. On Valentine's Day, she came to the hospital, bringing me what she promised were sterile 82 percent cocoa chocolate bars, a set of new DVDs of horrific on-scene training videos, a fire-science textbook she used, and all twelve volumes of Anthony Powell's *A Dance to the Music of Time,* said to be the longest single narrative ever written.

"That should keep you busy," she said.

"Until Monday," I said.

"And all this will keep your mind off Vincent Cappadora. He was cute, I'll say that. Good genes."

"Like Henry the Eighth. He was a looker too."

"But Good Queen Bess, right?"

"We can hope."

"Sissy," Renee said. "Let's crack open one of those fire-scene DVDs. They'll make you feel lucky. In fact, you're going to be lucky, I can tell. You've got a long streak of good luck owed to you."

On Valentine's Day, both Beth and Aunt Marie came to see "the big ultrasound." I lay on my bed and the tech slicked my undeniably topographic belly. She used the teeny handheld ultrasound machine, simply because it had fewer places on it that could freight infection into my room. The smaller machines were touchy, she said, and it might take a moment to find the little one, but instantly . . .

Wow, I thought. *Hey, that's my baby.* Big eyes. A *big* nose. Fairy fingers. The tech displayed our window on Baby Coyne's world to each of us. For the first time, I had the equally weird and epically sweet sensation of sharing my body with another actual person. What had popped up on the screen, as though playing a game, no longer looked like a vaguely humanoid bean, bent over by the stresses of growing milk teeth and a liver. It looked like a baby, a very active baby, with pudgy cheeks and a definite pout, rolling around. My throat tightened when the baby reached up and, seemingly intentionally, rubbed its eye with that quintessential gesture of unself-conscious innocence. As I reached out toward the image on the screen—as though the baby lived in there, instead of inside me, the way the world now seemed to live in the television—Dr. Setnes came bustling into the room. "I'm sorry," she said. "Emergency. Had to get all cleaned up before I came in here."

"No problem," my aunt said. "The more we get to peek."

"Let me have a look at those measurements," Dr. Setnes said. One of the risks of SM965,900 was that a fetus might not grow as well, or at least not grow in size, before term. While having all its essential parts, the baby could just be smaller. At the time, this meant approximately nothing to me—small baby, easier to push out. If it's essential, you can put aside everything you know better than to believe.

A moment later, in her own gear, Dr. Ahrens joined Dr. Setnes.

We resembled those old films of people inside spacecraft, trying to eat ice cream through a straw. After a moment, someone delivered a strip of images sent wirelessly to a printer down the hall, which somehow—like my food—didn't have to be put through an autoclave before it was passed through the door. The doctors stepped away from the doting grandmas standing around me and the sonographer.

Dr. Ahrens said, "Hmmm."

Hmmm.

I could have paid for the college education of every kid in the hospital if I had a dollar for every time someone in a medical setting took a look in my direction and said, *Hmmm.*

"Nothing's wrong," said Dr. Setnes before I could ask. "But this is a small person for its gestational age."

Dr. Ahrens said, "Maybe this has nothing to do with the medicines. Sicily, the usual reason for this is that you aren't completely sure of the date of conception. Are you positive that conception took place—"

"Not to the minute," I said. "But within a four-hour span."

Dr. Ahrens said, "Hmmm."

But Dr. Setnes was her matronly and assuring self. She said, "If this is a small baby, he or she might require some extra attention, Sicily, that's all. From what I can eyeball, the developmental markers seem on target. I can't eyeball everything. The drugs you need to take can have this result in animals, but most babies that are small at birth for no reason other than a mother's size or medical condition do as well as bigger babies and much better than babies that grow overly large as a result of factors such as gestational diabetes. Let's not go looking for zebras." Oddly, although the medical expression—when you hear hoofbeats, it's usually horses, not zebras, so don't seek exotic solutions until you run out of ordinary ones—was so old it had moss on it, at that moment, from Dr. Setnes's mouth, it was supremely comforting to me.

"Now let's talk about something important," she said. "Do you want to know the gender?"

"You bet," I said. Turning to my aunt and Beth, I said, "I have to know whether it should be named Taggert or Ambrosia." My aunt, who was valiantly trying to carve a compact but serviceable nursery from a hedonistic single-girl digs in the approximately eight hours a week she got to spend at home, was enthusiastic. Beth, on the other hand, said she loved surprises, the good kind, and might put her hands over her ears.

But they couldn't get that rascally baby to turn around enough to assure what they were seeing at the cleft of its bowed legs. The tech kept trying. Finally, I told her that I should probably just wait. I was starting to feel sort of lousy and drowsy and sick of the prodding. After each grandma got a picture, Beth went home and my aunt left to do an on-site interview. I pasted the eye-rubbing image in the journal Hollis had given me. *So here you are,* I wrote. *You're literally the size of a little turtle without a shell, all scrawny and vulnerable. I have to think you'll be brave. You were brave to break through in the first place. As for what you'll have to handle in your life, it will probably all seem ordinary to you, because you'll never know anything else. I'll help you. We'll help each other. I have no idea how, but I'm going to be the fixed point in the universe for you . . .*

I heard a *ping* and pulled my table toward me. There was a Valentine from Upstart Productions. It was an e-card that read, *Love is like trick or treat/At its best, fine whiskey neat/At its worst, prickly heat/For me, a ringside seat . . . Vincent Cappadora.*

I guess he signed it that way so I didn't confuse him with Vincent van Gogh.

Slightly encouraged that he'd written at all, I started to finish my now-nightly note to my fetus, but I got tired and laid down my pen. It was odd to feel too worn out even to write, when I'd spent the whole day doing nothing. I was sapped, tired in body, and thought that if I didn't sleep I'd melt.

In the night I woke and asked for a glass of ice, which a nurse slipped through the Velcro'ed window in my door. I glanced in the mirror. In the half dark, my face was pallid as bone. I depressed the call button as though I was throttling a joystick. Dr. Ahrens must have come through a pneumatic tube, she got there so quickly.

She confirmed that I was in rejection.

CHAPTER TWENTY

"This is not as bad as it seems," Dr. Ahrens told my aunt.

"This is as bad as it seems," my aunt insisted. "This is her second episode."

"Most people have three and some have five. The first year is dicey," said Dr. Ahrens. Dr. Park had turned up by then, as had Hollis, who was soon to scrub in for a surgery, along with Wayne Neville, a critical-care perinatologist.

He was cut from the Dr. Glass mold, as warm and fuzzy as cut glass. "As far as the fetus, whatever has been done to it with that stuff has already been done, frankly."

Frankly.

And here we all thought he'd been wearing kid gloves. Dr. Neville had a case and promised to return later to do an ultrasound. I thought,

The baby will emerge looking like something from an old Warner Bros.
cartoon, like Sylvester the Cat sticking his finger in an electrical socket,
hair standing out straight as stickpins.

"Should she go back on the old protocol if what he said is true?" my
aunt asked.

"I'm not thinking so," said Dr. Ahrens. "Let me go tinker."

She went to tinker with SM965,900.

The new dosage began that morning.

By the following night, the normal skin color of a human being
crept slowly back onto the disturbing pearly surface of my face. The
heavy lassitude began to subside. Although I still didn't feel entirely up
to par and my blood pressure wasn't its usual steady low fraction, I was
up, if not exactly around, within a week.

One thing was very worrisome.

A bit of skin just under my jaw had become discolored, obviously
dead tissue. Hollis was reluctant to cover it and so treated it with an-
tibiotic gel and cautioned me (not that I needed the caution) not to put
my hands anywhere near it. Daily, she measured that spot and photographed it, sometimes as Beth photographed her. I began to have terrible trouble sleeping. Studying the spot, which was half an inch
square, I imagined my whole face simply crisping up to a brown frill of
burned egg and sloughing off. When I dreamed of that, I woke up
screaming in my cell. One night, after I dreamed twice of washing my
face and seeing my nose and eyebrows come off when I splashed on
water, Aunt Marie sat next to me and held my hand for hours. In the
morning, my face was noticeably better, my blood pressure down.
With a local anesthetic, Hollis excised the bit of skin from under my
chin. "You won't notice that scar," she said.

"Especially if there are even bigger ones, like one hundred and
twenty square inches of them," I said.

"Don't, Sicily. A couple of episodes of rejection are not uncommon at all. You've done beautifully. This is a special circumstance, isn't it?" Hollis said, patting my tummy. People cannot resist doing that, even if your face is coming off.

"If she's in rejection, why are you still using the new experimental thing?" Aunt Marie asked. "What if it's not going to work?"

"I still think it's going to work," Dr. Ahrens said.

"I don't even know why it works," Marie said. "The other stuff was pretty straightforward. You suppress the part of the immune system that has to do with the T cells—which is why she's at a greater risk for cancer, at least possibly—and she can still fight off infection with her natural immune system."

"Exactly, Marie. But things that were pretty crude when the first face transplant took place have come a long way."

"So with that, she might not have experienced any rejection?"

"She might well have. And if she had, in the early months, that would be no indicator of how well she would do after the transplant really took. It depends on so many factors. We immunologists started out just studying infectious diseases, so that's what we knew how to prevent."

"I thought you were an internist," my aunt said.

"Both," said Dr. Ahrens.

"So what you suppressed at first . . ."

"Was the kind of immunity that depends on T cells—in the very simplest terms, the cells that basically yell, *Hey, look, kill this!* But when we suppressed them, there was no real backup, no real surveillance system, so it makes sense that certain kinds of viruses, like Epstein-Barr—which is linked to an increased risk of lymphoma and maybe leukemia—have an easier time sneaking into the house."

"But this is different."

"Auntie," I said, "it's like homeopathy. You give a bit of the bad stuff so that the body learns to protect itself from the bad stuff, except it's not really bad stuff. It's just, for my body, unfamiliar stuff."

"Homeopathy is quackery," Marie said.

Dr. Ahrens said, "Sicily is putting it a little too simply. What we're giving her now is what we would have given her *before* the transplant if she had been on this new protocol. Which isn't approved for us to do. We're giving her donor-specific class-two MHC peptides—"

"No—please, I work in *television* news," Marie said.

"We're giving her medicines that contain protective protein materials like the ones that were in *Emma's* body, so Sicily's body doesn't scream, *Kill that!* And since it's more like Emma's body, there's just less . . . mismatch strangeness and . . ." ,

"Fewer burglars sneaking into the house."

"Exactly."

"Why didn't someone think of this before now?" Marie asked.

"People have been thinking about it for nearly fifty years," said Dr. Ahrens. "But the big research bucks for transplant technologies weren't really there, because this isn't what kills sixty-year-old bankers. It's only in the last ten years, when people like Dr. Grigsby proved that a hand transplant or a face transplant could be a life-enabling issue and not just a quality of life issue for some people, that the work started to look really, really good." She paused and instructed the space-suited phlebotomist to draw two more purple tubes of blood, then said, "This is going to be okay. Sicily is the first cathedral built with this therapy, but we already had three-D blueprints for the design. We're just tinkering with success here. I know it. I know."

"Okay. Should I know?" I asked.

"Yes, It will help if you know. Your father was a fireman, right? Every day he had to exercise a little denial, right? It'll be good."

And so it seemed. The numbness and itching disappeared quickly, as did the overall flulike aches, but part of that might have been inactivity. Exercise is making love to your heart—and your joints—after all. Before any of this ever started, if I didn't get my workout, I got a pain in my neck and became a pain in the neck to everyone else. I'd done my best, but this situation was in every sense the true meaning of "confinement."

Dr. Neville decided it was time—"It was high time," he said (frankly)—for an amnio. And so, using an ultrasound machine, with my bladder engorged with water, Dr. Neville searched for a place to withdraw a syringe of amniotic fluid. Every time he thought he had a bull's-eye, the baby moved. When that happened, Dr. Neville turned and stared at me.

"I'm not making the baby move around," I said.

"I realize that," he answered. He set forth again. Just as he was going in with his needle, the baby did a full roll, and I heard Dr. Neville's muffled curse.

After forty minutes of near sticks, Dr. Setnes said, "We have the nuchal fold—"

"That's not really as significant as what we could have here, Doctor."

"But you don't want to take the risk of doing harm to the fetus," I said. Dr. Neville must have been mute in his childhood. His transparent blue eyes were eloquent with sour scorn. "From my point of view, we've had enough tries. This is not going to happen."

"Well, I will not do this procedure, then," Dr. Neville said, "although I am concerned and think it would give us necessary information about what needs to be done if this baby should be born in distress."

"We'll monitor it very closely," said Dr. Setnes as Dr. Neville, syringe aloft, made his exit.

When he was gone, Dr. Setnes, far from handing me a folder of readings about parenting the challenged child, endeared herself to me for life by saying, "I have always had difficulty taking anyone seriously whose first name is Wayne." I started to laugh and she continued, "It's like naming a baby girl Lula or Nettie. It's asking for trouble."

On the following Monday morning, my buzzer sounded. I'd requested and been given blackout shades in my room, so I could sleep in the cocoon of darkness I needed. It felt like it was freaking four in the morning. My sleep since the second episode had not been the best. I got up, looking like a Japanese drawing of a girl demon—all ratty hair and nasty breath—and pulled open the inner door.

There was Julia Cassidy. It was only the second time I'd seen

Emma's mother since the transplant. I hadn't heard from her since Hollis laid the pink quilt with the screened photos of Emma across the foot of my bed.

"Sicily," she said. I didn't hold out much hope for a great chat. The look on her face was grim. She was rightfully pissed at me for not getting in touch, for her having had to read about the pregnancy in the paper and hear it *on TV* from my aunt instead of in person and from us.

"Mrs. Cassidy." By habit, I placed my hand palm out on the plastic, my prison way of greeting people I couldn't truly touch. Mrs. Cassidy didn't respond. She looked different, in a good way, dressed in a short skirt and a little jacket, her hair in a thick layered bob with tiny stipples of blond through the brown. She stood formally, one of her hands looped around her wrist. I said, "You look wonderful."

"I'm married," she said. "Eric and I are moving to Myrtle Beach. This week."

"Congratulations," I said. "I'm very happy for you. A new life. It's good." I had thought that Eric, Mrs. Cassidy's stylist partner, was gayer than Christmas. Maybe he'd had a conversion experience. Maybe they were fabulous business partners. Maybe—I had personal experience of this—loneliness was the most potent aphrodisiac. In any case, whatever Eric did with Mrs. Cassidy had revived her. She appeared ten years younger—buoyant but also quieter somehow, as though she were a haunted house that had surrendered its ghost, cleansed in light when it departed. Maybe she had let Emma go, I thought. It's difficult to understand how I could have thought that, how raw and shallow I was even then. I smiled at Mrs. Cassidy and said, "I'm sorry for how I look. I hadn't gotten up to dress. I thought it was earlier. I tend to sleep a lot in here."

"How could you do this?" Nothing on my face betrayed the shock I felt. Annoyance, I'd expected. Some part of me waited for her to go on. I thought I knew what she meant, and I did—but not to the degree she meant it. "How could you take Emma's sacrifice so lightly?"

"I never did, Mrs. Cassidy."

"You could lose your face! You could lose the face Emma gave you!"

"I could die, actually, Mrs. Cassidy. But I'm betting against that and so are my doctors. I think the odds are on my side this time."

"You accepted Emma's beautiful face and then went and got yourself pregnant."

This is one of the most troubling turns of phrase in the English language, and I'm sure people say it to women in German, Urdu, Amharic, and Portuguese. I've never known exactly how to counter it effectively, not that I'd ever had to. Careful was the way to go. Careful and thoughtful and acknowledging and respectful both of her loss and her renewal.

"I'm sorry you're upset," I said. "And I'm sorry for the way this seems to have happened. But it didn't happen that way, Mrs. Cassidy."

"There's only one way it can happen, Sicily."

Careful. Respectful.

"Yes. Of course that was unwise of me. But you and your husband were young and in love, and if you had been expecting Emma before you were married, you would still have wanted her, right?"

"We were expecting Emma before we were married."

"It wasn't a planned pregnancy?"

"No. But I wasn't a woman who'd made the choice to give that up."

"Give up . . . I didn't give up wanting to be . . . to have . . . I had the face transplant in part because I wanted a normal life as a woman."

"I thought it was so you could function," Mrs. Cassidy said bluntly.

"It really helped with fully closing my mouth and eating," I said. "And breathing normally. I could do those things before, but I had difficulties."

"I didn't think it was to get men."

Whoa. Wow. I was caught hard and breathless by that. Dozens of retorts popped up and were flipped away or crushed, like bad attempts at a love letter. It was, in fact, Mrs. Cassidy's sacrifice that had given me my face. Emma was past the point of being able to make that decision. I had to remember that and remember that a basic bluntness was part of Julia Cassidy's personality. She didn't mean to make me sound like some cheap slut for whom Emma had given the whole tortilla.

I finally said, "Mrs. Cassidy, you care more about your appearance now. You look wonderful. That's part of being alive, isn't it?"

"I think a transplant should be for a higher purpose."

And I did too. For weeks and months, I had agonized over Emma's loss measured against my gain, wondering if I was worth it. And now I realized that this baby might be the purpose. I had prayed to change my life but not specified how that change must be manifest. I had wanted to feel passion—to feel, altogether—but those feelings didn't come with guarantees on parts and labor, like toaster ovens. I had gotten my heart's desire, albeit in a way that was different from anyone else's way. It might be that my way—my parts, my eventual labor—would always be different from anyone else's way. Standing there in silence, separated by my barrier from Mrs. Cassidy, I began to see that I was only beginning to use Emma's face, now my own, for a purpose beyond my own happiness. Even my way of making my living had been nearly reclusive, tailored to my disability; it did not take full advantage of all that I could do or be or care about. My life with my child, I decided at that moment, would be lived on roads I had never risked. There was no other choice, so I might as well seize the one in front of me.

"You're right, I think," I told Mrs. Cassidy. "You're absolutely right to remind me of that. And I can't ever be grateful enough to you. All this, even my child, is part of what my parents would have wanted for me, and you made that possible. Please don't be angry. If I risked Emma's face for this reason, well, that's what Emma would have wanted. It's part of the whole tortilla, isn't it?"

Seemingly baffled, Mrs. Cassidy paused for several excruciating minutes, during which I knew it would be disastrous to say anything more. Then she quietly told me goodbye. At the last, just before she disappeared out of sight on her way to the elevators, she also wished me good luck.

Five more weeks (and ten long novels) crept past.

In my journal I wrote, *Now it's really spring. Outside, there are children in a playground I can almost see. If I could open the window, I would hear them being mean to one another and forgetting it an hour later. Someday that's going to be you. Hang in there. Love, Mommy.*

The aches and pains I experienced now were from inactivity. I was getting too big to really move, much less do a plié. I wanted my joints to stay nimble, so I did my stretches lying down. Each day I waited for an email from Upstart Productions. When one came, I waited until I had written ten letters of comfort to other fire victims, or studied the book Renee brought me, or eaten as much raw fruit as I could without become the monster of flatulence (there were benefits to living in a sealed room). The notes were innocuous.

You must be going buggy inside. Vincent

and

It's so hot here I envy you in Chicago. V.

and

My mom sent me a picture of you in your leotard. That must be why they created stretch material. She says it will all pop back into place. Vincent

and

Busy. Will write more later.

I wrote to him to congratulate him on the success of the film, which no number of lukewarm reviews could stop from making a wad of money. My aunt asked Beth for a pirated copy of the movie. The animation was crude but the actors were pretty believable, especially the head terrorist. He was truly frightening—a fanatic of the first order. That night, I dreamed of him trying to take my baby. Sleep was uneasy. The twingey things—the hardenings of my belly that were called Braxton Hicks—came and went, but that night, because I was restless, they clenched closer than they had before.

In the morning, when Beth arrived, she was surprised to see how much care I'd taken with my appearance. I had showered and braided my hair and dressed carefully—well, as carefully as I could given that I had no real clothes except leggings and men's shirts, which comprised my entire maternity wardrobe.

Renee Mayerling had sent me a book about the great circus fire in New Haven, which arrived at almost the same time that Beth did. As Beth and I chatted, I opened it and tried to sit cross-legged on my bed to read it. The comforts of sitting with my legs folded under me were about as available to me then as they would have been to a sweet potato. I felt more cramps and one pain that was decidedly unpleasant. "Wow," I said to Beth. "I better not try for contortions. Is it okay if I look at this stuff for a minute? And then we can talk."

"It's fine," Beth said. She was checking out a drama about two gay men who could not manage to impregnate their affable next-door neighbor, who'd offered to be their surrogate.

"I just have to lie back to read, because it's too uncomfortable." I lay down and tucked the white shirt like a little diaper between my legs. There's no way around the fact that growing a person and gaining thirty pounds in seven months tires you out. It's also true that you tend to invest moments that turn out retrospectively to be huge in your life with contextual meaning—as though the stars lined up to inform what was in fact a just-daily moment. It's unbearable to think that our destinies are random. I knew—I would always know—it was only chance that Mrs. Cassidy had come to see me and that her visit had prompted my certainty that my child truly was part of a beginning life, not a mistake I was trying to live with because I couldn't correct it. I knew that, and yet I would never be able to extricate her visit and that determination from what came next.

Beth said, "Hey, Sicily. Where's the buzzer to call the nurse?"

Reading, I said, "Wrapped around up there. It gets in my way."

Beth pressed it.

"Yes, Sicily?"

"This is Beth Cappadora. We need a doctor here right now. Right. Now."

"Beth, what's wrong?" I said, struggling to sit up. Beth held my shoulders, easing me back against the pillows, but not so much that I could not see the blood, the big delta of staining on the shirttails.

CHAPTER TWENTY-ONE

So long, so far. It was not far enough. I knew of dozens of times that people had lost babies late in pregnancy, beautifully formed babies, tender and downy as peaches, still as effigies. Among Italian women, the peculiarities and perils of gestation were the equivalent of a sports channel. But I had never known of any baby coming so far, against such a tide, against such Himalayan odds of happening in the first place, only to leak away on an uneventful Monday morning not long after March blew through town.

"Beth," I said. "The baby's going to die, right?" My voice was so small, it didn't even sound like me. It was the voice of a child, at the top of a staircase too dark to be safe even to run for the mellow haven of the light.

"No, no. It's going to be okay. If only I hadn't been here . . ."

"What do you mean?"

"It's because I'm here and I'm related to the baby. Something that just can't happen has to happen. It'll be all right. Don't move."

I was alone and bleeding in an isolation room with a crazy person.

Within minutes there was another crowd in my room, all in haphazard versions of their space suits. A sonogram tech wheeled in a familiar machine with its blind TV eye. I sought out Dr. Setnes's wide brown eyes. "Can't you sew the cervix closed?"

"Too late now," she said, and told a nurse, "Please start an IV, stat. Sicily, take some deep breaths and let me see what's going on in there." Gently, with a tiny gloved finger, she examined me and sighed. "Well, honey, you are in labor. But we are going to stop it."

I raised my chin and keened. I howled in rage and entreaty at those thousands of holes in the acoustical tiles.

"Sicily, hush now," said Dr. Setnes. "It's too soon for this kiddo to have a fighting chance in the world. Your baby needs to stay put, so we're going to stop the labor. You just do everything I say, okay? Let's see what the monitors say and the sonogram shows us."

While there was no mistaking the cold ultrasound conductor on the round-topped timpani of my belly, I could not bring myself to open my eyes. I didn't want to see any anything sweet, furled, and immobile.

"There you go," said Dr. Neville, whom I had forgiven for being named Wayne. "The baby is very active."

"I put this at a two," said Dr. Setnes.

What's a two? "What's a two?" I called out.

"It's a stage-two placental abruption. The placenta is beginning to detach from the uterine wall," Dr. Setnes said soothingly. "My heavens, with the number of ultrasounds we've done, this should have been obvious. This is why the baby is small-sized."

"Not necessarily," said Dr. Neville. "I didn't observe this. It could have just begun."

"What's going to happen?" I said.

"Well, short-term, you're not going to move," said Dr. Setnes. "The contractions have slowed down already. Long-term, you're not going to move. We're going to have you waited on hand and foot."

"So I can't walk around or exercise? Just go to the bathroom and shower?"

"You can't go to the bathroom and shower," Dr. Setnes said. "The nurses will take care of that." She whipped a calculator out of her pocket. "You're at twenty-six and a half weeks. Term is forty weeks. That means that your job is to stay still and keep that baby in there for about—"

"I can add," I said in wonderment. "More than . . . two months?"

Giving my shoulder a light tap, Dr. Neville put in his two cents. "The baby is in no distress and the heart rate looks good. Actually, it all looks good. Hang in there, Sicily." He glanced at the screen. "Hang in there, kiddo." Then Dr. Neville left, promising to return after he attended to a baby "in more trouble than this."

"Sicily, I've had patients on complete bed rest for eight *months*," said Dr. Setnes. "They got bed sores. They got rashes. They hated my guts. They wanted to cut their husbands up into pieces. But they had healthy babies and they got up and the rashes went away, and I'm not going to say that they forgot, but it was time well spent. It was time well spent." She smiled. "The good news is that there's a placenta delivering oxygen and nourishment to your baby. And the bad news is that it's starting to pull away from the uterine wall."

"That sounds like the bad news and the bad news," I said.

"Not if it doesn't pull away any more. We're not going to know if this is a little critter by nature or because of the drug protocol or because . . ."

"If the baby is not receiving oxygen, he is going to be retarded or die in utero," I said.

"But the baby is receiving oxygen. Look. You can't do cartwheels if you can't breathe." Obligingly, the baby did a forward roll. "Do you want to know the gender? It's plain as the nose on your face."

"No," I said. "I've come this far. Is he breathing?"

"Yes. And you're fine. You keep breathing. We'll get a yoga coach up here."

"Tonight," said a nurse.

"And teach you some breathing exercises. Now you sit tight. I'm going to step out and I'll be back in a couple of hours. That monitor is connected to the nursing station. If there's a problem, you won't have to call us, we'll call you."

Beth crept to my side as the doctors dispersed, leaving behind nurses who moved as silently and efficiently as . . . well, as nuns and monks in a cloister. "What do you feel right now?"

"I'm terrified. And I've never been terrified in my life for anyone else more than for me. As much as for me, yes. But not more. I would die gladly."

"You won't have to do that. It's going to be fine, honey. It's like having the baby here since they put that screen up. Kind of like a virtual cradle. I didn't call Marie; I'm going to go and get her myself. I don't want her to drive, and it's early in the day. I'll bring her back. What you want to do is try to sleep."

"Be real, Beth," I said.

She pulled the blackout shades, extinguishing the sun. When I asked her to, she pushed my bed closer to the door, so I could reach up to turn on the faucet and brush my teeth. Spitting in a basin and letting it sit there would be too nasty. The swishes and beeps of the monitors were like those sounds far away, a dog barking, a child calling to another, bike to bike, a bird settling down to sleep . . .

When my door buzzer sounded, the shades were up and the room was dark.

My aunt was not there and neither was Beth. I was still so steeped in sleep that it seemed that Vincent, standing there in a black T-shirt from the Hong Kong Film Festival, was just part of a drawn-out dream in which everything was connected, strung out like a rosary I didn't yet know how to repeat.

Through the transparent wall between us, Vincent said, *Sicily, I've come to my senses. You are the love of my life. I knew it the moment I saw you. You and the baby belong with me. I've purchased a small compound*

in Northern California. Marie can live in the coach house after she re-
tires. I hope you can forgive me. . . .

Even as hallucinations go, it was cheesy.

The truth was, I hadn't even turned on the intercom thing. I
couldn't reach it. How I felt was as though I were in an "environment,"
the way higher-order mammals are at a zoo, a place that had all the ac-
coutrements of a home—a swing and a bed, plenty of food and
water—but no simple affectionate touch, no freedom, no privacy, no
will. I always imagined that this was the reason orangutans looked so
sad. I pointed at the simple system and at the nursing station, trying to
get Vincent to summon someone to turn the damned thing on. I was
afraid to stretch to depress the button. So I smiled at him, at his cotton sweater tied around his shoulders in a way that would have looked
femme at best on any other guy and at his sad-amused gaze, like a song
I used to know. He put two fingers to his lips and laid them on the
Vestex in the vicinity of my distant lips and then again in the neighborhood of the mound of my belly.

Because there was no way he could hear me, I shook my head and
said, "Vincent, I love you. I have such a crush on you. Maybe I'm a
jerk, but I can't lie. I know I'm going to lose you. But loving you was
worth the price of admission."

At the time, Vincent probably thought I was talking about needing
a brush for the dust. Maybe that I was saying I couldn't get the thing
to work and didn't know why. He probably read my lips and believed I
was telling him that what I could use was a good electrician.

Finally, he got the message. A nurse came and flipped the little
switch.

"Houston," I said. "We have contact."

"What are you in for?" Vincent said.

"Two more months and then some hard labor."

"Well, I was in the neighborhood . . ."

"Really! Shooting viruses in Chicago?"

"No, Sicily. I got here as soon as I could. As soon as my mother
called. Actually, I got here sooner than I could."

"How?"

"I chartered a plane."

Now, I was still only twenty-six years old, a kid from Chicago who'd been on an airplane once and had come back with a hostage. "Get out," I said. "You chartered a plane for just yourself?"

"It's okay. I wanted to get here and I didn't want to wait in line and be scanned and get stalled on the tarmac. It's the way to go. Rob and I have flown private a couple of times, and if I had real money, I'd buy a plane and find somebody to share a pilot with. You just get right off and into a cab. It's like you're a diplomat."

"What did your mother tell you?"

"She said you were in labor and that you might lose the baby."

"But that settled down. It's still not so great, but here I am. And there he is." I couldn't move, so I made eyes at him, my old gift. "You were going to come here even if I lost the baby?"

"Sicily. Especially then. I let you go through hell alone before. I won't do that again. But I don't think this will end that way. I think that's a pretty cool little girl in there."

"It's a boy," I said, deadpan. I was testing him, to see if he looked too delighted.

"It is? For sure? That's great. But I would have loved a girl."

"The truth is, I don't know at all what it is. Stick around. They're bound to do an ultrasound in twenty minutes tops, maybe before lunch. Lunch is around three-thirty on this floor, dinner at five." I turned in bed slightly.

"Don't. Do you want something?"

"Just some water. I can get it. When I talk through the curtain, I feel like I'm yelling. Earlier, I was yelling. I was pretty tense."

"My mother was having a nutty. She was convinced it was the Cappadora curse."

"So she said."

Vincent approached the nurses' station, and in no time, a brigade of more nurses than it would have taken to treat the injured in an eight-car pileup wheeled me even closer to the Vestex panel, positioning me so my mouth was near the intercom. Someone brought Vincent a chair. Everyone had figured out by now that this was *the* Vincent Cappadora, of germ-warfare pop-movie fame and sensitive Oscar-winning documentary fame. He was humble and charming and cute, and they were fluttery and deferent, and the whole thing made me very proud and also made me feel like it would be fun to push him off an overpass.

"I saw *The Germinator*," said the nurse named Derry. "I took my boys. They're nine and twelve. Lance and Porter."

"Wasn't it profound?" Vincent said, with a straight face.

"I thought it was more . . . fun," Derry said. Good for her.

"I saw it last night for the first time. It caused preterm labor," I chimed in.

"Are you serious?" Vincent said. Derry shook her finger at me as she walked away.

"No, I'm not serious. I did have a nightmare about that first terrorist."

"Serge. He's the sweetest guy on earth."

"There you go," I said. "Appearances are deceiving. Take you, for instance." He laughed. "You look like you wouldn't hurt a fly. Much less break a lady's heart."

He made a mobster face. "I don' see no lady here." Then he said, "Sicily, I never meant to even bruise your heart, much less break it."

"I know that, Vincent. And when you left at Christmas, I was a complete idiot. I knew I wanted this, but I was so scared."

"I was the idiot. Your life and what you went through, Sicily—you had every right to end this the second you found out. It was the sane thing to do. I got all . . . *Look at me. I'm a father!* And I got carried away. I'm sorry."

"And so am I."

"So what comes next?"

What came next was an unexpected ceremony.

An ultrasound technician turned up, trundling her machine down the hall. "Dr. Neville requested some images earlier, but you were asleep, Sicily. We didn't want to wake you. If this is a bad time, we can come back," the woman said.

"See?" I said to Vincent. "Right on schedule."

Actually, I couldn't have been happier, despite the intrusion. It was the techno-biological equivalent of a greeting card. I thought, not unreasonably, that it would be wonderful for Vincent to "see" the baby.

"No, let's do it, but is there a way that you can sort of squeeze in here where I am?"

"I thought we'd push back so you could have some privacy," the tech said. "Is your brother going to wait?"

"He's . . . not my brother." Jesus Christ. "He's a friend." Now I sounded like I had the roundest heels in Chicago. "He's my . . . whatever. He's the baby's father."

"I'm her whatever," Vincent said.

"So you want to share this with him?" the tech said.

Oh, kind of! More than I want about anything else! This was precisely the fourth time that Vincent and I had seen each other, and we were about to observe something usually vouchsafed for people who were smart enough or dumb enough to be charmed by it. We were both.

"Would you like to see it?" I asked. Suddenly, I was unaccountably shy. Vincent nodded. *Okay*, I thought. *This Moment, Brought to You by Fate.*

"At least let him come in," I said. "Let him come in for the ultrasound. Please. Privacy. Like you said. He's the baby's father."

"Let's ask somebody," the tech said. "I'm just the lowly hardware lady."

The senior nurse paged the resident. After the fifteen minutes it takes in a hospital to reach you if you're spouting arterial blood, the resident came ambling around the corner of the desk.

"Miss Coyne would like another person to come in. This is the baby's father. He's come from out of town," the nurse said. Her admiration noticeably wobbled. He was famous. But perhaps also a dickhead. The resident paged Hollis. For the first time in the history of me, Hollis wasn't around.

"Page Dr. Cappadora," I said. "Eliza Cappadora."

"I'm a third-year resident," said the third-year resident. "She can't make this call and neither can I." The resident was adamant: He couldn't do a thing without the permission of an attending.

"My aunt and his mom come in all the time. My aunt interviews criminals and drug addicts. How could his germs be worse? He flew here on a plane with only him in it."

In any case, the young doctor continued, I was used to Beth and Marie. At least, my body was. Vincent's germs might be even more of a threat because they were new and imported, and who could tell if Vincent was sick and simply not showing any symptoms yet?

"But on any given day, who could tell that about my aunt or Beth? They might just have come from volunteering in a typhus ward. They don't live in sealed capsules," I argued.

"No, they don't. But I still can't make this call, not in a situation like this. That Vestex panel is in place for a good reason. You're in isolation on an ultraclean floor and you are in a compromised situation. I have a hunch it would be fine. But I can't proceed on a hunch. I am sorry, though."

The resident asked if he was needed anymore. I told him that he certainly was not, ever.

Despite my pout, a draped nurse and the sonographer did crank my bed higher. Then they tucked a paper drape around me and the monitor in a way that made me feel absurdly self-conscious. Then the tech began the baby-baby-where's-the-baby search with the transducer, and suddenly there it—he? she?—was.

In silence, Vincent took another live-action look at the little creature, which now resembled a slightly miniaturized version of the real thing. "Wow," he said. "Wow. What's the gender?"

"I decided that—" I began.

"It's a girl," said the sonographer. Damn. Vincent was right.

"It's a girl? It's really a girl?" Vincent stood up, raked his hair, walked around his chair like a child in a game, and sat down again. "It's a little girl."

All I wanted was to touch him. Stupid skin hunger and rude biology once again overcame my having the intellect of an avocado.

"So what do you think, huh?" I asked evenly.

"It's my daughter. It's our daughter. A little girl," Vincent said softly. "Oh, Sicily. What do you know? We made a little girl. Wow! I feel like a million bucks. And you. I wish I could be in there with you, all the time. Until she comes."

The sonogram was running off images, taking measurements, snapping pictures for Vincent, Marie, his mother, the *Tribune*.

"Why didn't my aunt come back?" I asked. "Or your mom?"

"So we could be alone for this."

The sonographer said she was going to slip the machine out and that she'd bring a durable picture for Vincent to keep, from the printer down the hall.

"Sicily, I'm so proud of you."

I didn't want him to be proud of me. I wanted him to love me.

"You're such a tough kid."

Say anything, Vincent, I thought. *But don't treat me like I'm on your little brother's softball team.*

"And I meant what I said at Christmas. I'm not abandoning this baby. I know that she's my responsibility. If you want that in writing, I'm ready to give you that. And if you need support during the early months, I can help with that too. It's the least I can do."

"It certainly is," I said.

"I'm glad you agree." He looked a little taken aback, as though he'd expected brave talk and demurrals.

"Wait a minute, though," I said. "Don't you think we should talk about this?"

Vincent answered with a wry twist of his mouth that could barely be called a smile. "About what we do afterward?"

"Well, I will feed her and help her sleep and teach her to walk, and you—what will you do?"

Vincent, I thought, *for shit's sake, now is the time for you to say, I'll come here. You come there. We'll have two residences. Or I'll commute. Or you will.*

Vincent said, "I mean, we should just talk."

I went on. "We don't know each other. And we're going to be, like, related. Your chromosomes married my chromosomes. And the parents of those chromosomes are virtual strangers." I thought, *This is how people end up, fifteen years later, on cable reality shows.*

Vincent sighed and leaned forward in his chair. "Sicily, my mother is waiting downstairs. Marie is there. She has the night off. I have to go back. I have about twenty meetings tomorrow."

"That's more than two an hour. You'll set some kind of indoor record." The last time I'd said anything like that had been in California, in Vincent's bed—my body discovering its new vocation in its fusion with Vincent's body. Now, I felt old and cold and absurd. Out in the land of tangerine and violet clothes, not to mention sunsets, the meetings that masqueraded as kiss-kiss hug-hug but were actually $100-million-serious, things had to go forward. The people needed movies about special ops and spy girls. Who cared about the occasional too-early-to-be-born baby? Who cared about the woman with the scar under her chin, the one that Vincent had thankfully not noticed, at least so far?

How calculating. How cowardly. How unworthy of me, either way.

Vincent said, "Sicily, you look good. Funny. Cute. So different in such a short time."

"And yet you haven't changed. Ain't that a kick?"

"How far along in the pregnancy are you now?"

"What time is it?" I asked.

Vincent consulted his phone. "Nearly eight o'clock."

"That would make me twenty-five weeks, five days, and about eleven hours pregnant."

"Always the comedian."

"That's me. Every day's a party."

"What happened under your chin?" Vincent asked. So much for the tiny scar no one would ever notice.

"I had an episode of rejection."

"Another one? Will this keep happening?"

Every one of my neurons itched for me to say, *Uh-uh, no way, all over, never again. . . . You'll never wake up to a faceless, swollen . . . monster. I promise.* But I said, "I hope not. The first year is almost over."

"So, Sicily."

"So, Vincent."

"I love that I got to see . . . her."

"Yep. Alive and—" Then, just where I imagined my appendix to be, there was a distinct tap. Then another tap. I dropped my hand. I had no experience of what "quickening" felt like. I'd felt a lot of flutterings and a few rolling waves, but they stopped before I could say for sure what they were. Some people said it felt like bubbles. Some people said it felt like indigestion. Some people said it hurt. This didn't hurt at all. It was a distinct tap at the door of my womb, a human summons.

"It moved. She moved," I said. "The baby. I know she moves all the time, but I was never completely certain that it was the real thing before."

"Are you sure?"

I nodded.

Vincent beamed. "I got to be here? This is unreal!"

It was so awful, like your-life-coming-soon-on-DVD, a parody of Taggert and Alisandra on some soap opera—or anyone else anywhere on earth at that very moment. He had to leave. She would say goodbye. Isn't this just the way it would be? I wanted to give every ounce of attention to this everyday holiness. I wanted every second with Vincent. I also wanted this moment alone with my daughter.

"I'm staggered. I came to try to comfort you, fearing the worst, and I got . . . this new dimension. It was real before, but now it's really real." Vincent paused. "I can't believe I just said really real. I've lived in California too long."

"Well, I've been here the whole time. It's real to me. So, when will you be back? In the neighborhood? Don't you think . . . that we . . . ?"

I wanted Vincent to put his hand up on the plastic so I could feel the heat of his skin. And as though I had willed it, he did. We let our hands linger together.

"This is so sad. Maybe this is more than I think it is. I . . ." He touched his shirt in the region of his heart. "I really want to say that right now, but it would be stupid. We'll know more later, right?"

"Right. Sure. It would be stupid now. We'll know more later."

"The timing is so bad, Sicily. I'm not in a position to make films in Chicago, New York, whatever. My life is just getting started out there. I'm finally becoming known. So maybe this wouldn't be the right time for me, even if everything else was worked out."

"Now for me was exactly the right time," I said. "It was downright convenient for me to spend months on my left side in bed."

"I didn't mean that. I meant, right now I have to live in Los Angeles. My partner is there. My career is getting off the ground. We've said all this before."

"An Oscar for your first movie . . ."

"It's the kiss of death," Vincent said. "No joke."

"Absolutely," I said.

"So even if I did let myself believe that I was halfway in . . ."

"In?"

"In love. It would have to be a long-distance thing. Now. At this point. And I've tried that. They never work. Never."

"And I'm not portable."

"Don't make this harder, Sicily. The truth is, on this thing, you've always been way, way . . ."

"What?"

Vincent turned his face half away from me, and something in me that had flooded out toward him at the moment he saw the ultrasound began to recede, back toward me, slowly and inevitably as the tide. I

knew he had been about to say words that I would not be able to forget, or to paint over, or to dismiss as simply a guy-commitment thing,
and I was sure in equal parts that I did and did not want him to finish
saying them. But I'd already crossed off one too many fears to stop
now. "What were you going to say, Vincent?"

"Really, nothing."

"I'm not buying that."

"Okay. It's just that, for sure, in this thing, you've been way, way
ahead of me from the beginning. Even in California, you did sort of . . .
move in on me."

I wanted to die but kill him first.

"I moved in? You invited me in, Vincent. You led me into your room.
You gave me clothes hangers. You cleared a drawer and a bathroom
shelf."

"I wanted to be . . . the right way. I wanted to be considerate."

"You wanted to be considerate by having sex with me twice a day for
a week?" I said.

Vincent raised both hands, leaned back in his chair, and made as if
to ward off a Cape buffalo. "Hold on. No. That's harsh, Sicily. I never
said it was meaningless. It was wonderful. But one day we were shaking hands and the next day you were sitting on my bed looking at my
photo albums. I said I was afraid I followed your lead and I let it get
out of hand. My feelings too. Let's go back to where we were going—
to talk when this is all over, have dinner."

Have *dinner*? When this is *all over*?

"When this is all over? Do you mean, what, in twenty years? If it—
if she survives, this will never be all over for me, Vincent. Even when
you stop paying child support. I sort of expected you to be an insensi-
tive jerk, from what people said."

"What did people say?"

"I hate you, Vincent."

"What?"

"I hate you. You know why I hate you? Because, until I met you, even though I was ugly and even though people shunned me, nobody in my life ever completely got to make me feel ashamed."

Vincent stood up and, through the Vestex, reached for me. I couldn't move or even turn away from him. "Don't," I said. "Don't touch me."

"Sicily," Vincent said, and I could hear in his voice genuine mourning, a note in a minor key that was not rehearsed. "Sweet Sicily. I'm sorry. I'm so sorry. Believe me. Just once, believe me. Just because you were ahead of me, it doesn't mean I won't catch up."

Then, I genuinely hated him. For blindsiding me with a sudden surge of genuine charm, I truly hated him. How could I figure out a way to say that I hated him, convincingly, when a mere change in his inflection could sink my equilibrium like a cloudburst swamps a kite? I needed to think.

Then an armada of nurses swept toward us. "We need to spend a little time with Miss Coyne," one said. "We need to check her vitals because of the preterm labor."

"I understand," Vincent said.

"Not now," I said. "In a moment."

"Okay," the gloved nurse said, with a tight smile across her eyes, the rest of her face invisible. She stood back against the wall to wait, and the others followed suit.

"Please give us a few minutes. He has to leave for California. Please."

"It's fine. Go ahead," said the woman. She studied a clipboard. I had never had such strong homicidal ideation. Neither of us said a thing. Finally, the nurse broke the silence.

"We won't take more than fifteen minutes. Then you can go right back to chatting."

"Can you wait?" I asked Vincent. Whiny and needy and wheedling.

"I have to go," he said. "I have like twenty meetings—"

"Tomorrow. Yes, I know. I know you are busy and important."

"Sicily, this is way too personal to talk out, especially with an audience, for now. Not even nurses are priests." Vincent smiled at the nurses. Their eyes smiled back over their space masks.

"Not even priests are priests," I said, and Vincent grinned.

"You always make me laugh, Sicily. And, yeah, it sucks. We always end up this way."

"'Always' implies a pattern. There's no always."

"Can't we talk? Please?"

"I don't know," I said.

"It's not like I'm the head of a studio or anything. I could postpone things. It would be difficult to rearrange some things, but I could. I could send the plane back, pay for another day. I shouldn't, but I could."

"No, it would be difficult. Just call or something."

"Are you sure, Sicily? Are you really sure? Because I'm an idiot. I don't have to go now."

You did sort of move in on me, I thought. *You've been way, way ahead of me.*

"Just go," I said.

Vincent stood up. He pulled the sweater on over his head in the way guys do only in movies, so that he looked sad and sexy and not at all like a gopher that finally got his head to pop out of a hole, the way most people putting on sweaters look. I held my breath for so long that tiny black phantom fruit flies danced in front of my eyes.

The nurse ducked inside and gently steered my bed away a few feet. Vincent put on his lousy leather coat—I could remember the smell of it against my face—then put both hands against the Vestex wall one last time. That was when I should have said, *You don't have to know. I know for both of us. You were right when you said that I was ahead of you. You will catch up.*

As one nurse put the blood pressure cuff on, I yelled at her, "Just get off me!" and tried to get up.

"Sicily, don't! Don't move. That could be devastating," said the nurse Derry.

"Then give me the phone. Please give me the phone."

Silently, Derry handed the real phone to me. Vincent's card was in a folder on the desk. I pointed and said, "Please give me that. No, just dump it out. Just dump it."

She did. I saw the red-and-green logo. Not until after Christmas had I noticed that Vincent had crossed out the business number and written his own personal number next to the "V." I'd committed every digit to memory, but I didn't dare risk a mistake in the state I was in. "Please read me that number." I dialed it as she did. The phone rang. . . . It rang and rang. It rang more. It rang as though the line was engaged. Finally a voice picked up. "This is Vincent Cappadora. Leave a message."

"No!" I shouted.

"Sicily, you need to quiet down."

I dialed again. The phone rang—and I could hear it ringing. Turning my head, I glanced at the door. There was Vincent's cell phone, whirling on the floor like a child's toy. He'd gotten up to pace, like the expectant father he was, when he learned that *Hey, Dad, it's a girl! It's a girl!*

"That's his cell phone. He dropped it! You have to get him! Please go get him."

"Okay, I will." Derry took off running. The phone kept spinning.

I didn't realize until I felt the tears running down my neck that I was crying, the kind of gulpy, sloppy crying that doesn't make you look vulnerable and pretty but instead leaves you basically a swollen, drooling subhuman with eyes that will look bruised and bleary the whole next day. This was what I had feared. Something inside me had finally given way, and I could no more stop the crumbling, tumbling collapse than I could have kept a building standing by bracing my back against one of the walls.

He would not come back.

He would not come back ever.

Of course he would.

He would come back once in a while.

He would come back when she was born.

He would send checks.

I would send pictures.

I would be good friends with the Cappadoras. Sort of like extended family. We would always be good friends. This was not the way it was supposed to end, with me strapped to a bed and Vincent walking away, his hands in his pockets, unsure of what the girl who always had something funny to say really meant—or meant to him. Happy he had a little girl. Soon my twin mother doves, Marie and Beth, would come up to cradle me.

"Vincent," I said.

"That's okay, honey," said the other nurse, whose name I didn't know. "You've been through a rough time. You go ahead and cry it out."

"I can't," I said. "It's been so long . . ."

"I know how you feel. Sometimes you just have to let it out."

Once every thirteen years.

CHAPTER TWENTY-TWO

The days slipped in and out of each other as spring rolled into Chicago, balled in morning fogs unfurling soft as socks. I lay still and wet the bed like a ninny and stopped caring and grew bigger, bigger, and lolled and yearned for the tiny wing sweep of someone's hair to tickle my cheek as he held me—as she held me. Anyone. Vincent. A civilian. Someone who didn't rustle or smell of rubber and paper or of rubbing alcohol. I longed for the desperate tremor of sexual impact, the near-painful delight of a too-hot bath, the scrape of sand on my hand, the friction of wool or wood or corduroy or the soft, raspy navel of a coneflower. I wanted to hear a voice that was not recorded or muffled. My music was stale, strings of giddy nonsense or syrupy rhyme. All food tasted like pudding and seemed to be the temperature of the inside of my mouth. There was no pleasure in it (how had I forced it down for so many years before the transplant?). My appetite plummeted, and there were times when my aunt spoke to me that I didn't answer at all, just smiled at her in a way I hoped wasn't limp but that I knew was, in fact, practically soppy.

I longed to hear someone, anyone, say Vincent's name.

Eliza now turned up nearly every other day. She brought food to try to tempt me, spicy things and sweets. She brought gossip that she thought I might like. There had been a brawl at the first location of The Old Neighborhood. It had been a party for the son of one of Angelo's friends, who was headed to prison for tax evasion—a little send-off. Someone raised a toast. "To Vito, for all the time they didn't catch you." Someone else broke a bottle. Ben had to leap over the bar like Clint Eastwood and grab a bunch of black silk lapels.

"Oh, wow," I said. "Hey, Eliza. What's up with Vincent?"

"He's been on the road so much. It's constant. Would you believe they're making a sequel to the germ movie?"

"I'd believe anything. Does he talk about me?"

Eliza said, "Not in so many words. Ben says he thinks about you and the baby all the time. Our new family baby. What are you going to name her, Sicily?"

I turned my face away. Once I had uncapped the bottle, I cried like a water fountain in a kids' school, at two different speeds—wistful and truly bereft. "I don't know," I said. "I don't like to think too far ahead. She's not out of the woods yet."

"But every day is a good day."

"Of course it is." I said suddenly, "Eliza, would you and Ben stand godparents for her?"

"Of course," said Eliza. "We would be honored."

"I mean in the real way. The old way. Like if she's sick or if I die. Would you take her and raise her like she was your own? Like she was a Cappadora too?"

"She is a Cappadora, Sicily. She's my family. And so are you."

I thanked Eliza. She said thanks were not necessary. That was good for a half hour of tears every time I thought of it. I tried to think of it as often as I could. Derry the nurse had been right. Once you got the hang of it, it felt better to let it out.

"It won't be long now, Sicily," Aunt Marie told me. "This has to be torture. Sometimes I just fly out of here in the mornings, after one night. It's like the silence has its own sound."

"It's like listening to your own heartbeat inside a conch shell," I said.

"That's just how it is." Aunt Marie had begun to read to me from *Wuthering Heights,* and I, having gone from zero to seventy in one day, crying-wise, cried like crazy through half of that lovely, crazy book, written by someone who had about as much experience of the world minus two men as I did. I cried for Catherine, too proud until it was too late to admit she was freaking coughing out her lung tissue, who knew so much about the mute love she had never experienced that it was supernatural. I cried because Heathcliff was just a self-centered asshole writ large but also kind of like the guy you would want to pull you up onto the black horse. I cried for what that reminded me of and then felt like a saphead for that too. I also cried because beautiful language, like anything else in my battened world, was just too much, a beckoning hand, a train whistle in the night, an aria.

Dr. Setnes came several times a week now. She told me that the little contractions that made a hard shelf of my belly were not the abruption but truly normal and would go on for the rest of the time. She said the baby looked good and active, and her limb length compared with her head size and all that jazz I no longer paid attention to were appropriate to whatever they were appropriate to.

Hollis was all up on the moon about the saddest case in the world, the face transplant of an infant—the face of an identical twin who had died during birth was transplanted to her sister, whose own face had been conjoined to the back of the infant's head. She sat and blatted on to me about how this was a case in which no pre or post anti-rejection regimen would be necessary and that in all likelihood the baby would survive for her expected lifespan, which made me think Hollis believed that I, on the other hand, would not.

Of course, Vincent and I didn't "talk."

We spoke briefly by phone a couple of times, but there was no way to begin the conversation we needed to have. And as his visit receded down the days, the less urgent the conversation itself began to seem. If the baby held on until June, it would be about the time that Beth would complete her year-long saga of the pilgrimage of this changing face. She had refused the Ossum Tate Gallery on behalf of a big main-gallery show at the Art Institute in Chicago, after which the selected photos would tour various smaller galleries and museums. It could not have been more fitting.

The show would open on the anniversary of the Holy Angels fire—coinciding with the spread in *Sense and Sensibility*—and the sale of all first-night reception tickets would go into a fund to pay for fire victims' reconstructive surgery at UIC. I had decided to go back to school after that, keeping this decision even from my aunt Marie, but I felt very good about the way that the whole project would end in a geyser of hometown beneficence, stoked by a dazzling popshot of national attention.

At the end, it would all be right and worth it.

By early May, the nights were the best of times.

I lay watching what Beth called "the landscape channel," which is more or less exactly what it was. The baby curled low between my hip bones. Because I always lay on my side, with piles and piles of pads beneath me, I never had the panicky experience of being nearly unable to breathe. I pretended that I lay on a berth in a train, facing a picture window. I imagined it would feel about the same—an unforgiving mattress, a crackling pillow. But the vistas would make it worthwhile—wharves strung with bobbing lights like small pumpkins, breathless mountain gorges, endless plush wheat fields, Central Park in snow, two New Orleans row houses with lacy metalwork hands interlaced like a lady's lacy gloves. Places I had never been. Places I could go now, except that I would be a single mother. How long had my single-girl period been? Not even a season, which I had wasted on dopey, inevitable self-interrogation about matters that would be revealed when time turned the page to the answer key. As an instructor would say to me later, in the only rebuke I ever got, I was a person who honestly believed there always was more time.

Kit and Anthony had broken up. But Kit had been promoted to chief designer. This meant a move to New York, and although Kit was elated at the thought of a pool of four million men to graze, she was distraught at leaving me behind. Kit had dozens of other friends but, I flattered myself, only one Sicily. I had few, and they had become fewer, oddly. My new face had not made me many new friends, except for Eliza. I would have to join another group, like FFSM (Formerly Faceless Single Moms). It had a vaguely perverse, erotic sound. Perhaps I would found it. On the last day before she moved, Kit came to see me.

"Well," she said. "We've been friends for twenty years, and I thought I would be the one to have a baby first. I thought you would be maid of honor in my wedding, like we promised each other when we were five."

"I will be still. You can buy bridesmaid dresses in size twenty-two," I said.

"Oh, Sicily. You'll piss out twenty pounds overnight when she's born." Kit leaned closer to the intercom. "I think Anthony is gay. I don't think he's out to himself."

"That said," I told her, "I wish I were gay."

"Sissy!"

"Think about it. The food would be better. The house would never stink. The toilet seat would be down and you could borrow the other person's clothes. Probably the sex would be better too. Although I guess for me . . ."

"It don't mean a thing if it ain't got that swing."

"Alas, heterosexuality. The bane of mankind."

Kit cried on my shoulder when she left and I cried as well, mid-level tears. Kit was still a kid in lady's clothing, with a great smoky eye but an inward eye that didn't have the sense not to wear turquoise. I had perforce become a woman with responsibilities. At least, I was doing the run-up. Indeed, I had filled out insurance forms and school applications and drawn a birth announcement and made daily entries in the journal for waiting.

Miss Thing, This is the clubhouse turn. I wish I could promise you a world without confusion and heartaches. I wish I could promise you glamour and fun all the time. The fact is, you're going to be the daughter of a mommy with a demanding job, but it will be interesting to your first-grade class, I promise. And I already love you more than I ever knew it was possible to love anyone, even though you probably weigh about as much as a good Reuben. But you're my girl. And we're out on this together, just us. You were only unplanned. You were never ever unwanted, and you sure won't be unloved. I can't be sure about me. Love, Mommy.

I was watching a really dramatic thunderstorm, pretending I was Catherine or Isabella looking out at the purple crags above the moor, when Derry the nurse brought me a letter. It was still warm to the touch, freshly baked. It was handwritten, with a return address in Beverly Hills.

Had he moved?

Had he actually left that little blue clapboard house? Who slept now in the room where the tree branches bushed the window like fingertips, like a wand?

He hadn't moved. He was just using hotel stationery.

It read:

Dear Sicily,

    I'm not good with words. Actually, I am good with words, but not the serious kind. In high school and in college, I became well known as sort of the local screwup and screw-off. If I had two choices, I would always make the wrong choice. I had a vocation for making bad choices. So I started to do it on purpose. I thought, Screw them. If they were going to think of me as a loser,

I would be a big loser. Screw everybody. Eliza's mother had to get me out of so many stupid things I did that she called in every favor owed to her by anybody else in any police department in America, and she finally said the next time she would let me go to Joliet and play footsie with people who knew what it was like to be really bad and to enjoy it.

Even that did not really change me. I felt like I had such a hard time when I was a kid, I did not owe anybody a thing.

Then I made my kidnapping film, and that was basically all about me too.

It was selfish because I was trying to figure out if I was just some asshole or if other families went though the same stuff my family did when they lost a child. It was the hardest thing I ever did. I had to listen to their grief and care about it. I would forget, hey, I'm the guy who only cares about himself. The film was good and it got a lot of attention and awards, but the important thing was that I learned everything good is hard and there are no short-cuts.

So, the last time I was in Chicago, I was talking to my grandfather, Angelo, who is my father's father.

I was trying to explain why we weren't together—that is, you and me, not my grandfather and me. I was telling him that the world was different now and that a man does not make a lifetime with a woman because she's having his baby. I said that you saw my point about this.

My grandfather sits there for a while and at last he says, "Are you like a professional athlete or something?" I have no idea what he is talking about. He says, "You are going to leave babies all over the country that you made and send money to the mothers?" I kept trying to tell my grandfather that was not the point.

I told him that other than the baby we had nothing in common. He said we must have had something in common, because we made a baby together. He also said, "How much does anyone have in common, and what does that matter ten years from now?"

I just sort of realized that was true. Like, we made love and that made sense at the time, but loving somebody is not the same as having sex with somebody. Not all the things you feel have to make sense, however.

The last thing my grandfather said was, *Uomini mantenere le promesse*, which in Italian means sort of *men keep their promises*.

How I see it now is that I made a promise to you, and I do not want to break it.

You made a promise too and, even though you didn't know you were making it, you are keeping it. My grandfather is first generation and he is very old-fashioned. Maybe I am old-fashioned as well.

What this all boils down to is that I have no idea what I can give you except a person who has made a lot of bad choices. The only thing that is good about that is I know when I am making a bad choice, and it feels like I am making a bad choice now.

When we were together at my house, it felt like I was making a good choice. I insulted you when I said you moved right in. I should have said, It felt like you should move right in. It felt like I was home. Of course, I was home. It was my house. What I mean is, I felt like you were my home.

Please get back to me on this and advise.

Love,
Vincent

P.S. I hope you are not thinking I wrote this because of what my grandfather said. He helped me put into words what I already felt.

P.P.S. I hope you are not upset that I did not say this in a phone call. That would be impossible. This is definitely the longest letter I have ever written, and there is no way on earth I could have actually said these words.

I read it three times.

I wanted to make sure that I was sure of what he meant and that I was sure I wanted what he wanted. But wasn't Angelo exactly right? Whatever stood between us was no more than a slope on a learning curve. It might be harder for a man who'd been single for as long as Vincent had been single (which, I guess, had in some sense been since the day he was born) to get used to a house in which there was a shrieking baby and a half-Irish, half-Italian dominatrix. And yet he was made from those same bricks as I, grown in the same soil—with fully as many identity shifts as I had endured, although his did not show on the outside of his body. We might be like two cactuses fighting for water in one pot. We might grow together like a rose and a briar. It might be an opera, complete with broken glass and sword points. It might be a beach picnic on a Tuesday night.

It would be interesting, in any case. Human life was a dare. You could take it or leave it.

Was I foolish?

Absolutely.

Was I brave?

I like to think so.

When Eliza came by that evening, I asked her if she knew Vincent's home phone number. She reached into the pocket of her monogrammed white lab coat and took out a slip of paper. "Do you know how long I have been carrying this around? Suffice it to say a long time." She gave me the slip of paper and said, "Mornings are better. Do you know something? When Ben asked me to marry him, I said, Let's wait. Let's wait because I'm still a kid. I'm in school. And he said, Okay, we can wait forever. But time is only time. It doesn't change anything."

The next morning, right at the moment of the shift change, I depressed my buzzer. "We'll be right there, Sicily," said a weary voice.

"It's an emergency," I said. That wasn't fair. When I asked for the phone, the nurse on duty pointed out that she had been awake all night. I told her that I had too. I held the phone in both hands and thought, *It's five in the morning in California.* And then I dialed.

A woman answered. She said, "Hi. Uh. Hi."

"Is this Vincent Cappadora's house?"

"Yes but he's asleep right now. Do you want me to wake him? Is it urgent?"

"It's urgent," I said. "But not important." I hung up the phone and lay hugging my child and cursing every sentimental impulse that made me believe in the honor of assholes. But by the following morning, I thought, *What kind of dime-store beauty girl answers the phone at five in the morning?* I had visited Vincent, and although I hadn't awakened on Central Time, someone else might. It could have been one of his cousins. He had at least one girl cousin who lived out there, and three or four altogether. What did it matter now? I was all in. Maybe I wasn't Vincent's best girl, but I lived next door.

To know for sure, I made myself wait for four days.

I filled out more papers, wrote more journal entries, pasted more sonogram pictures into my daughter's book, wished on stars and flipped coins and did other stuff that only people who are in love or crazy do. And then I watched documentaries. I picked out a baptismal outfit, not knowing that Eliza would give me the one that Vincent had worn. Finally, at a civilized hour, nine in the morning, I called again.

The woman who answered this time had an accent. She sounded like a cartoon villain or my old pal and client Dr. Joshi. "I will find him. He is across the street. At the neighbors' house. Who may I tell him is making this call?"

I said, "Skip it."

She said, "Well, does this mean you want to talk to him or you do not want to?"

"I don't want to talk to him anymore. Tell him I said so."

"Tell him that who said so?" A mark, I thought. A naïve dipshit. I made you a promise and I don't want to break it, Sicily. Really? Vincent was right about one thing. He knew his own texture exceedingly well.

"I will say goodbye then. *Spaseba.*"

I said, *"Dob ryy d'en."* There was an audible silence.

"You are Russian?" she said.

"Yes. Vincent is a fugitive. Tell him that we found him now and it's just a matter of time. We're watching the house."

"Nevozmozhnoe."

I had no idea what that meant. But it sounded like some form of refutation. *"Da,"* I said. *"On yest. Dasvidaniya."*

Until next time.

But there would be no next time. What would time matter? It didn't change anything, as Ben Cappadora said.

The phone rang that time. I counted the rings. Eleven.

Then it stopped.

On the morning of May 8, I woke to see my aunt smiling spectrally at me over her mask. "I brought chocolate," she said. "You're getting too thin for a pregnant person."

"They suck your blood, these parasites. I'm not hungry, Auntie."

"Well, you need to eat anyhow. That's what I hear. It's a beautiful day. I wish I could bring you a breath of air. The lilacs will come soon. And then the roses. You'll be out in time for the roses, Sicily." Marie gave me a hard look. "What the hell is wrong with you? You look like someone punched you."

"That's what happened last night. A crazy escaped transplant patient."

"Have you been crying?"

"It's my new second job," I said. "Auntie, it's just biology."

I shifted my position ever so slightly and that's when time ran out, along with enough warm fluid to soak the bed. A contraction so brutal and swift it made me grunt seized my gut, and I grabbed my aunt, who reached around me to the call button.

Within five minutes, I was out of isolation. Assessing my condition came first, someone said. Resterilizing the room would come afterward. The obstetrical resident, a woman so tiny she made Eliza look statuesque, came running in without even a mask, checked me, and paged Dr. Setnes. Dr. Setnes came, wearing blue jeans and Dansko clogs. By the time she thrust her arms into the gown the staffers held out, tapping her foot as they tucked her braids under a paper cap, I was yelling like a three-eleven alarm.

"Sicily," she said, as hands slipped warm clean sheets onto the bed in place of the soaked-through linens, "try not to worry, because we'll get an IV going and administer . . ." She paused as the resident tucked a pillow under my back, then, with every confidence, Dr. Setnes leaned in and began a cursory exam. "We'll administer . . . Nope. Okay. We'll administer surfactant. Because we're going to have a birthday. Let's get Miss Coyne down to a labor and delivery—no, not an operating room. I think just a regular birthing suite will be fine."

And along everyone trotted, the IV bag swinging next to my head like an udder. At the elevator door on three, the neonatologist, Tom Cook, listened to Dr. Setnes describe his patient, who would be born at thirty-one weeks and one day and might be smaller than the expected three pounds because of the effects of maternal medication or an abruption or a combination of the two.

There was every reason to fear that I might hemorrhage. I'd given my own blood, weeks earlier, against that possibility. The cramps were violent by then and I was breathing too hard.

"Sicily, settle down now, long breaths, like the yoga coach taught you," said my aunt. We'd seen precisely one birthing video on the closed-circuit hospital channel. We never got past breathing. But my aunt remembered the power of those long, cleansing breaths. "You're going to hyperventilate, Sicily. Listen to me."

"Something is tearing," I told my aunt. "This isn't how they're supposed to feel. I don't feel waves. Something is tearing me apart."

"It's going very fast," Dr. Setnes said. "But it's not going so fast that we don't have time to think and settle down. And nothing is tearing, Sicily. Do you feel sharp pains in a band across the lower half of your belly, below your navel, on both sides?"

"Yes!" I roared in her face, as though something was about to pop out of my chest and rip off Dr. Setnes's glasses, along with her face. "When is the break?"

"Usually there are intervals of up to two minutes. Do you feel a lessening of the pain between those sharp pains?"

"No!"

"I'm here, Sicily," said Eliza. "I'm right beside you. You're going to have a beautiful baby. My little Charley's baby cousin. And everything will be just fine."

"Hi, Eliza!" I screamed.

"Do you feel as though you need to go to the toilet?" Dr. Setnes said.

"I have no idea." The nurses laid warm blankets across my thighs as I began to shiver.

"Let's have a mirror," said Dr. Setnes, as Eliza and the labor nurses helped position my stockinged feet. What I saw looked nothing like my dainty nether parts. It was blue and engorged and stippled with mess. I decided at that moment I would tell Kit and all the friends I would have one day to send their husbands out of town during the birth.

"Let's not have the mirror," I said, and pain like hot tongs, mindless but precisely aimed, hauled down on my belly.

"No pushing yet," said Dr. Setnes, as though studying a particularly vexing bit of stitchery. "We just want a little more time here." I saw her glance behind her at the big, bright warming bed in the corner, where Dr. Cook and another man—a huge dark-skinned man I would come to know well—waited with the open, soft-kneed, easy stance of tennis players.

The tongs seemed to open, but only for an instant, and then clench harder at me, lower in my belly. Who the hell thought this shit up? Pain was no stranger to me, but this pain was something even I had never experienced—relentless, destructive, personal. There was nowhere to escape. My aunt said, "Try to put yourself out in front of it mentally, Sicily. Try to concentrate on what's happening. Think about progress and that the worst of this is behind you. You're making progress."

"You never did this!"

"I wanted to," Marie said.

I was afraid that if I clenched my teeth harder, I'd break one. "Can't I have something for pain?" I asked. They offered me Tylenol. If I could have gathered enough breath to laugh, I would have.

Eliza told me, "Try to think about the best moment of your life."

"The best moment of my life since about age ten is what got me here," I told Eliza. Still, I pictured that beach. There was a little girl with me, young but tall and skinny. She had done her own hair, with about twenty different barrettes and elastic bands. She looked up at me, with my father's cloudy eyes.

"Then try to concentrate on one thing. Think about me and your aunt and everyone who loves you holding you; plenty of people have gone down this road before and, as scary as it will feel, it is safe. Just hold on to us. Hold on as hard as you can, and before you know it, you will be in a park with a carriage and your daughter and I'll be there with Charley."

So I gave up my body and held on and howled and tears sprang from my eyes, and Eliza was right. There was no going back up that path, but in an amazingly short time, my body gathered itself and, with such propulsive relief as I had not believed possible, I burst her into the world. She was yelling, but so small she was like the rough sketch of a human being.

"Not much there," said Dr. Cook, "but what there is is doing just what it should and looking good."

Cook had his obligations, of course. He who would later describe my child's chances for a normal life like the warnings for a medication to treat migraines, which could result in shingles, acne, bronchitis, seizures, arrhythmia (occasionally serious), uncontrolled bleeding, liver failure, gastrointestinal distress, and death. Since everything else had already happened, it was impossible that these things also could happen, so I exercised Dr. Ahrens's prescription for some everyday denial. I decided she would be fine. She weighed three pounds precisely and she breathed on her own. Her Apgar scores were seven and eight. Not as good as, but better than most kids, even as little as she was.

"Every delivery is a special delivery at UIC," I said. "Right?"

"This one is," said Dr. Cook.

"Every day after this day will be a good day for her," Hollis said. She had materialized from the ventilation system like a genie. "Every day you will cross one catastrophe off the list. She will go from strength to strength."

"I expect that," I said. "I fully expect that." I did fully expect that.

For a moment, just before they whisked her to a receiving bed under warming lights as if she were the main course at a buffet, they let me hold her. She fit in my palm. I saw only that her head was the size of a tangerine, her eyes the color of blueberries, inquisitive and unblinking. I wished Vincent had experienced that moment. Whatever I had construed as an understanding of love or lust or drink, drug, vanity, victory, courage, cowardice—it all disappeared under a great drift of immaculate peace. How had I ever considered ending her? My daughter. Shuddering and covered in glistening slime and dark blood, she was the solstice of my life. She was a little girl who had my father's face. Jamie Coyne's jaw, square as a sugar cube. Maybe she was not mine. I would love her long enough to let her go someday.

But I would always be hers.

Alone for hours, while the NICU poked and assessed her, I gave strong thought to my child's name.

I had always known what it would be, but now that she was here, corporeal, with a presence, I had to give her the chance to claim another name. For half an hour, I called her Natasha, Nat, Natty, Tasha. For an hour I called her Maria—Mimi and Mia for short. I thought of calling her Jamie, short for nothing. I actually flirted with the idea of Elizabeth, but Beth already had enough tributes to her walking around. The primary value of that name was that it would have made Vincent feel guilty.

Abruptly, I sat up and called his number. No one answered from

Russia with love or even from La Jolla with silicone. The machine picked up. I hung up. I called back. He answered then: "Huh . . . hello." I hate it when people answer the phone as though they're drugged. Then again, maybe he was. Why not just sit up and act like a person and realize that people don't call you at dawn to talk about good avocado recipes.

"This is Sicily Coyne," I said and thought, I will say, *The results of our misconception arrived this morning.* Instead, I said, "Vincent, I need . . ."

"Are you okay?"

"Yes, I'm fine. Our baby was born this morning—your daughter."

"It's way too soon! It's, like, not even thirty-two weeks."

Absurdly, my heart turned at his calculation of the weeks. I began to cry, not sobs but soft, salty, unceasing sheets across my cheeks and down onto my neck that soothed me.

"Is she going to die? Is she okay? Sicily? Are you there?"

"Considering how small she is and how far she has to go, she's actually pretty great, Vincent. She's a little red and scary-looking, but I think she'll grow up strong and healthy. I hope so."

"Thank God." It was my turn to wonder if anyone was there. "I'll come right away."

"You can wait. Until she's out of the hospital."

"No. That wouldn't be right."

"There's no protocol for it, Vincent. You know, come when you get around to it." *Shut your fat mouth, Sicily,* I rebuked myself. *Shut your fat stupid mouth.*

But Vincent said only, "Thank you, Sicily."

"It was only polite to call."

"For her, I mean." I did start to cry then, in earnest. It turned out that I had a gift for it.

It was not true that I'd given birth to my daughter so that I could have one living thing I loved in my life stay with me.

Now that I had given birth to her, though, I would have given any-thing in exchange for her to be well and to stay with me. This was way bigger than I'd understood, and I thought that I had understood. It wasn't interesting or a challenge or love or even the right thing. It was the only thing, the whole tortilla.

In the end, I named her Gemma, the combination of Gia and Emma. Her middle name was Marie, of course—not like everyone else on the West Side of Chicago but like one person in particular.

Outside the hospital, there was a park on a path through this little gar-den. I was standing out there, knee-deep in daffodils, convinced that even the smell of cigarette smoke and reheated burritos from the staff tables around me couldn't stanch the triumphant green undercurrent of spring, when a cab pulled into the circle and Vincent got out. He looked at me without recognition and I realized, with a freaky splash in the face of reality, that he was *looking at me*—the way a guy would look at a girl. I'd given birth just three days before, but I had the gift of youth and all those hours at the barre, and my body had snapped back like vinyl to its approximate previous shape. My appraisal of Vincent's appraisal seemed to possess telepathic qualities, because Vincent did a double take and said, "What are you doing out here?"

"Smoking," I said.

"You are?" All the nurses were smoking like religion. Nurses smoke. So do opera singers.

"Come on. I'm the mother of a baby on semi-life support? Please? I'm just standing in the air. I've been zipped inside that building since Christmas. Somebody ripped the zipper open too soon. I'm breathing fresh air, or at least what's in the vicinity. It's May. May flowers. Mother's Day. Funny you should show up. This is the only good thing about it."

"Is she okay?"

"She's pretty okay. I didn't mean big life support. Just a little help."

"Is she pretty?"

"She will be," I said, and thought, *Oh, why?* He had *not* come right away. There's always a flight to Chicago, and he could have been there by the first evening. He'd taken a few meetings first. He'd packed carefully, instead of throwing stuff into a bag like it was an . . . emergency or some once-in-a-lifetime thing. Maybe it wasn't. At least for him. And still, my eyes were starved for the sight of him. I could feel my cheery expression begin to crumple, the way it did before one of my now-customary thirty-minute sobbing sessions. I tried to think of all the other men in Chicago who would consider the job I would have someday as cool and sexy, who would line up to seduce me despite the fact that bits of my face might start to shear off periodically (SM965,900 was still technically experimental, although I would never go back to the standard drug regimen) and that my daughter might have had a class-four cranial bleed and be blind . . . It was a sobering-enough thought to bring me back to standing in the daffodils instead of picking daisies in my mind. He loves me . . . not.

"Can we go in?" Vincent asked.

"In just one minute. I'm going to be inside for a while. Six weeks, they say. Until she weighs five pounds." There might come a time when I would want to go home, for an hour, for a hot bath, for a nap on my own bed. The angelic and exquisite NICU nurses—Walter, whose individual fingers were the circumference of five of his tiny patients' thighs and who had the gentle digital dexterity of a lacemaker; Sabine, who was the size of my car and who carried a fistful of markers and drew pictures of dancing mousies and cartwheeling bunnies on the sides of the hard-plastic Isolettes; Lucy Min, who belted show tunes while she drew blood from a foot the size of a thumb knuckle and replaced blindfolds the size of my pinkie nail.

"Aren't you supposed to be with her?"

"Your mother, your grandparents, and Walter are with her."

"Boyfriend?" He did not look pained, my daughter's dad, at the thought that I might already have a new love. Or maybe I just expected more drama.

"She can't date. She's three days old," I said. I knew what he meant but, for God's sake, exactly when did Vincent think I'd forged this relationship and how? Intercom sex with a passing phlebotomist? "Walter is a neonatal-intensive-care nurse. He's about seven foot twelve and from Montego Bay. She doesn't take up half his palm."

"Gemma Marie Cappadora," he said.

"Coyne," I told him, almost regretfully. "Gemma Marie Coyne."

"Sicily—"

"Yeah, I know. Your name is on her birth certificate. But she has to match me."

Vincent shrugged, but it wasn't a to-hell-with-it shrug, more an attempt to lift away what could not be lifted: regret and rueful thoughts. So much spilled milk—and, yes, I realized with a little jump, as my breasts rose like little loaves in time lapses, I couldn't waste any more time tiptoeing through the tulips, because I had to nurse the baby. For the only time in my life, I rode in an elevator facing another person who was sober.

"Who does she look like?"

"Vincent, she looks like something you would cook with celery and potatoes, and to me, she is the most beautiful thing that ever breathed assisted air. That's the other thing you have to know." We walked out onto the NICU, which had been decorated, a bit frantically, as an orchard. Everyone knew who Vincent was, and we were ushered in without a question. Vincent had the same reaction that everyone had: They flinched in horror and pity. Most of the babies looked like shaved rabbits. Those were the babies who might be okay, preemies like Gemma. The babies to worry about, said Lucy Min, were big plump babies who looked like regular big plump babies, with tight auburn curls or thick sandy feathers. They didn't move or wiggle. Something inside their brains had burst or burned or was never built. They were rosy and beautiful and some of their baby mouths couldn't form a seal to nurse from a bottle, so they were fed through tubes in an incision cut into the wall of their drumlike little tummies. The skinned red babies had IV lines in every vein, brain monitors, more TV screens than a multiplex. And the parents? The parents weren't like me, mostly. They were skinny teens with Scorpio tats and too-black hair. They were forty-something mommies and daddies who'd waited too long—their begging eyes filmed and puffed with lack of sleep. Piles of stuffed animals in hammocks hung from the heated beds, with big, elaborate photos of siblings suspended overhead. Some of those babies were twins achieved with fertility drugs. My Gemma was the anti-fertility-drug babe, forsaken as many times as Jesus by St. Peter, unwanted and adored. Vincent's face was a mirror of pity and horror. I wanted to cradle him. I couldn't see her that way anymore. Gemma Marie Coyne needed CPAP to breathe so that she didn't use up too many calories, yet she was in some sense the envy of the ward, the shining star of the room. I could remove her from her warmer bed and hold her to my breast and feel her tiny mouth engulf my nipple, fierce as a fighting fish. Gemma received nutrients through a nasogastric tube, too. She had lost three ounces, but she flailed so fiercely she had to be sedated lest she outdo herself aerobically. So there were times when I pumped and read and rocked.

It was different for the other parents.

I was only a little afraid for her. I was only a little afraid of her.

The other parents probably had expected perfect. I had expected okay but had gotten not as good as but just one small handhold up the mountain better than. The other parents had not been me.

Pin-neat in her pleated black suit, Rose Cappadora drew Vincent close against her shoulder. Angelo kissed Vincent's cheek. Beth stared at him. "Ma," he said.

She said, "Vincent."

It wasn't his fault. Vincent. Lavender and salt and the brine of his mouth. He loved me. He loved me not. He loved me. He loved me not. The last petal had dropped. If he didn't know how to love me, maybe he would know how to love her. . . . It wasn't his fault.

Walter said, "Man, this is one beautiful girl of yours. This is two beautiful girls you got." Walter gave Vincent hand-washing materials. Taking Vincent's hands in my own, I helped him disinfect. There were cuffed openings in the bed, like little portholes on a small boat in an uncertain sea. Each of us put one hand inside. Gemma shuddered and opened her eyes. Vincent's eyes widened in response, asking me, Would he hurt her? I nodded to tell him it would be okay. She loved to be touched.

Together, with two fingers each, with the tiniest motion of rocking between us, we held our daughter—as an infant—for the first and last time.

CHAPTER TWENTY-THREE

After forty minutes in the Prince's Hall at Navy Pier, holding even such a flyweight as Gemma, Marie Caruso's arms were about to detach at the shoulder, to snap as though attached with rubber bands. Although little, Gemma was not placid. People who mistook her for a baby and goo-gooed her got a rebuke: "Ima big girl, Gemma, please!" Fortunately for Marie, her granddaughter had obligingly slept for nearly an hour and now was graciously humming throughout the mayor's address to the graduates. The tune sounded something like the nursery song that Gemma insisted on calling "Old McDonald's," drawing out the long "zzzzzs" at the end to make sure her mother and Marie understood that the moo-moo here lived under the golden arches. When Gemma tired of singing, she began to call out softly, "Why Mama there?" and then, in what verged alarmingly on a whine, "Wanna coupla cookies, Marie." (Gemma didn't call Marie "Grandma," although she did call Beth "Grandma," as she did Marie's own mother. From listening to Sicily, Gemma called her "Marie" or "Auntie," and Marie was vain enough to be just fine with that. She had all the perks and none of the pejoratives of grandmotherdom.)

Now, she could tell that Sicily heard Gemma's voice, but her niece didn't turn a hair. Except for her chin—and, of course, Emma Cassidy's turned-up nose—Sissy's profile that day was Marie's sister Gia's, down to the pore. Her posture was all Jamie. That slender back in her long-sleeved dress whites would never touch the back of the chair.

Suddenly, with an ache that felt nearly physical, Marie thought of Jamie. Jamie would have been sixty now and trying to avoid retirement. In his body at this moment, there would have been room for nothing but hope and glory. Marie thought of the day after Sicily's track meet, when Jamie uncapped two beers and confided in her that he hoped one day for his little girl to wear the Maltese cross—but he warned Maria not to tell her sister.

Despite her family's holy history, Marie was not especially a believer; still, she couldn't help sending up a mawkish hope that Jamie could see not only Sicily's strong shoulders and her sweet, healed face but also the little girl with the gray eyes and square jaw who so favored Jamie himself.

Marie began to bob back and forth in the time-honored shimmy of motherhood. Although Gemma was and always would be a small-size person, she was not as good as but better than most two-year-olds at all the stuff two-year-olds were supposed to do—running, drawing on faux-marble walls with permanent marker, screaming her ass off when she was denied sticky or sharp-pointed things. If Marie were to set her down, she would be off like a mouse out of a slingshot, even if she had to wriggle her way under the hundreds of folding chairs with the gold-draped seats to grab the back of her mother's legs.

At last, the mayor, whose own nephew was among the candidates being inducted into the Chicago Fire Department, finished blatting on about honor and courage and proud traditions, raised both hands, and began to applaud. Gratefully, Marie shifted Gemma to Pat Cappadora, who, to the toddler's delight, set her on his shoulders. Although no family members had been allowed to pin on the graduates' badges for ten years, that tradition had just been reinstated. Marie began to make her way down a side aisle, along with several dozen other mothers, fathers, and wives, a few of them also wearing the uniforms of firefighters. As she did, Marie tried in vain to smooth the wrinkles Gemma had installed in her new-for-the-occasion linen jacket, which was fractionally larger than six others like it in Marie's closet—fractionally in proportion to the fractional growth of her ass. There was no hope for that.

What the hell.

If Marie was not the proudest woman in Chicago that day, maybe someone else's kid had cured world hunger. Photographers—although not Beth, not that day—followed her progress. Ever so slightly, Marie preened. Normally, a class of graduating firefighters was a class of graduating firefighters—hunky guys and compact women, cute and wholesome and good for one shot on a slow news day. Today, one of the graduates was Captain Jamie Coyne's daughter, who had been the girl with no face and the subject of a much-discussed, gorgeous, disturbing exhibit at the Art Institute. Furthermore, if Marie could admit it, none of the graduates was the adopted daughter of TV legend (that meant you were old) Marie Caruso.

It wasn't as though Marie had approved of any of it. It wasn't as though Sicily had cared. Sicily was stubborn as a boulder, relentless as a hailstorm. "I'm doing this, Auntie," she said. "I was always going to do this. I just didn't know it."

"But your face! How much are you going to push it? You're a fool," Marie said.

"It was my face that let me do what I should have done in the first place."

And that was the last they said of it, for quite a long time. Marie refused to speak to Sicily, hoping it would change Sicily's mind.

For weeks, Marie took Gemma into her arms each morning at the door—before the sitter arrived, when Sicily left for class—without saying a word. For weeks, Sicily kissed Marie's cheek and said, "I love you," and left for Renee Mayerling's class at Merit University, a ninety-minute drive each way. Four hours a day, three days a week, Sicily was in classes, starting when Gemma was four months old. Most weeks she worked a good twenty hours too; she got by with what Vincent sent and, yes, with what Marie chipped in. Between work and school and running and ballet class and studying late and nursing Gemma, Sicily wore probably a size four, Marie guessed, when she had never, not at her skinniest, worn anything smaller than a six. Although Sicily was still just a kid, exhaustion pinched lines in the corners of her mouth. But you had to hand it to her. Because of her previous degree and all of her and Gemma's medical stuff, Sicily placed out of most of the science classes and the human-body-type classes she would be required to take as a rescuer and a paramedic. At night, bouncing Gemma on one of those strong dancer's legs, Sicily would repeat, "Attic ladder: An attic ladder is usually eight to ten feet long and can be folded to . . ."

"Addy laddy," Gemma would say, when she learned to say anything.

"Drafting: The pulling of water from a source other than a pressurized fire hydrant or apparatus . . ."

Sicily got her BS in fire science in just three semesters. When the twelve fire-science grads came in for the ceremony along with thousands of other kids and adults wearing blue caps and gowns, they also wore their firefighter helmets, the silver tassels on top. Sicily's was an old leather-covered helmet, scorched and battered, with a numeral 3 on the front—her father's.

A month later, she had entered the academy. All those years of ballet and running paid off, as Sicily lugged hoses and tripped up three stories with an ease that made strong men cry.

Sicily would be honored today, first in her class. Not that she hadn't had an edge, with her history—a history you wouldn't choose if it wasn't yours already. A lot of these people were the sons and daughters or husbands or wives of firefighters. The department tended to be generational like that, in Chicago perhaps more than anywhere. Sicily also had another mysterious edge, the kind no one questioned. The way that the academy worked, it could take years for your number to come up in a random system of approved graduates. But rookie-firefighter Coyne already had a job at Chicago Engine 88, her father's first outfit—on the ladder, she hoped, once she'd done all her rotations. Search and rescue. And from there on up.

The first time that Marie and Sicily had talked about it, Marie said, "All I want is for you to admit it's nuts."

"I admit that. It would be nuts for anyone else, at least. But you know it's what I'm supposed to do. Doing my medical illustrations paid the bills, but at the end of the day, it was kind of like a cloister, like what Aunt Christina always wished on me. I was hiding in it. Now I want to get out there. Maybe I'm sentimental. Maybe I'm interesting. Why don't you give me the benefit of the doubt?"

"But so much? A bachelor's?"

"Auntie, you know me. I'm aiming to be brass someday. It's not like it was back in the day with my dad. You don't advance just because you're Irish and a brave lad. You have to be smart."

"So this isn't a flirtation. It's a life thing."

"Well, it's always been a life thing. I was always this way. I just wasn't out to myself. For good reason. Before, it was impossible. And now it's no longer impossible. So I have to."

"Why, Sicily? Guilt? Because of your father? Because your baby turned out healthy instead of having a ton of problems?"

"Sure," Sicily said. "That's absolutely part of it. Auntie, there is good guilt and there is bad guilt. It's not only my father or Gemma. It's the kids who died at Holy Angels and the ones who still wish they did. It's Mrs. Cassidy and Emma. It's that piece of trash Neal. It's my chance to give the whole tortilla, and, no, don't look like that! I don't mean dying. I mean, like Aunt Christina says, maybe I was spared for a reason. I also really think it's going to be fun. Fun and hard and active and different every day. People to goof around with and have their back. Not like drawing a good intestinal bypass."

"You don't have to atone, Sicily. That's bullshit."

"Oh, but I do," Sicily said. "If you start a fire, you're responsible for whatever it burns."

"You never started a fire, Sicily," Marie said. Sicily just pressed her lips together and smiled at Marie. That was something Sicily said all the time, and Marie knew that her niece believed it. But she was still not sure exactly what Sicily meant.

The myth was that Sicily would be at real hazard probably half a dozen times in thirty years—far less than the danger she was in every day when she started her car and nosed it out onto Ohio Street. But in fact she would be in danger more often, because of how she was. It had been her nature to take chances: once with the transplant, and again with the evidence that was right here in Marie's arms. Since Sicily had become a parent, though, it was clear to Marie that she would not take a path that involved truly insane jeopardy. Marie would have been furious, personally insulted, if Sicily had done any of this at the expense of Gemma, after going through what she had to have the baby. But Sicily was a smart mom, just adoring enough, just strict enough. Gemma always came first for Sicily, though she didn't let her know it. She allowed Gemma to sleep in bed with her but ignored her tantrums. She let her take Popsicles into the living room but never asked if she "wanted" broccoli. Gemma grew up a little beauty, who could be as ferociously sharp as the meaning of her name and then clamber up on you like a cub, tucking her tiny arms under yours to get closer. Just as Sicily had refused to leave the newborn intensive care for one single hour of Gemma's thirty-one nights (Marie could not escape a visceral image of Gia at Sicily's bedside), Sicily never left her child behind now. For an evening, yes. For a whole night, never. When Sicily and Beth traveled to do lectures or radio interviews about the exhibit or the magazine piece, Gemma came along. At two years old and change, Marie's grandchild had been in more cities than Marie had visited in her first ten years out of college.

Marie took her place on the dais and gazed out at the other family members. Just as at Jamie's funeral, so many of the primary players were here today: Only Martin Coyne, Jamie's father, had died—at the age of ninety-one, falling from a ladder. But there was his mother, Patricia, seemingly aged not a single instant in sixteen years, and his brothers with their wives, and all the Cappadoras except the sister who sang opera—and one other notable exception. There were Renee and Moory and Schmitty and a few others from Jamie's old crew.

Fire Chief Linden Doyle took the microphone from the podium and said, "Now, families and friends, let's meet the graduates. Will the four students who have achieved high honors step forward?" Sicily stood, along with three men. "Thank you. Congratulations and welcome to the fraternity of your brothers and sisters, first in your class, Firefighter Sicily Marie Coyne," said Chief Doyle.

Marie took the badge from his hand and pinned it to Sicily's lapel, where it shined dully, Marie thought—compared with Sicily's eyes.

And so again, Hollis Grigsby thought, as she watched Marie pin on the badge, this young woman who did things her own way—despite the tenuous nature of the bonds that had sometimes kept her tethered to life, or more likely because of them—had done one more. Hollis had not been surprised when she received the invitation to Sicily's graduation and could think of no valid reason why Sicily should not do this work.

Routine use of SM965,900 had allowed Hollis's own work to reach down lower into the age ranks for appropriate candidates for face transplants among young women, and her colleagues around the United States and in Germany had been able to do the same. She knew of three young women who now were expecting babies, although, unlike Sicily, all of them had waited two years after their transplant surgeries to attempt pregnancy.

Only once, at the Chicago opening of the "Face-to-Face" exhibit, had Hollis, whose courage was ever insufficient when it came to personal matters, asked about the father of Sicily's little girl.

"I don't see him," Sicily had said. "It's not that he doesn't care. Vincent's life is there. My life is here. One of us would have to give in and change everything or go back and forth. Maybe that would have been possible once, but . . . he's old now. He's an old guy. He'll be forty in a couple of years." Sicily wasn't even sure that Gemma should see Vincent, at least for an interval—until she was old enough to comprehend a father at a distance. Vincent's brother, Ben, was a spectacular uncle, Sicily said. And Sicily did have a boyfriend, a great one. "Beth says Vincent doesn't have anybody serious," Sicily said. "I guess I'm not that unhappy for him."

"You were always selfish," Hollis had teased.

"Yes, but I'm not sorry. Obviously. Your kid . . . I mean, you know: She's the idea that inspired civilization. And sometimes I think, maybe there are people who are meant to make great babies together. Like born to be mated up just once for that purpose. I'm crazy about Ben. Ben's the closest person on earth genetically to Vincent. But when I see Ben, I guess I feel about the same way Vincent does when he sees Ben. You know?"

"That's biology," Hollis said.

"Exactly what I tell people," Sicily said.

Hollis wished she could stay and celebrate with this hardheaded young woman who had become a friend. Indeed, all Hollis's patients became friends. Pediatric surgeons had loyal patients. Heart-transplant patients were loyal, too. But, in her experience, the longer they had their faces the more likely transplant recipients were to get in touch. They reveled in their restored appearance. They sent cards and emailed photos of things they might never have done—of a father dancing with his daughter at her wedding, of a young Grandma reading to a class of preschoolers, a minister with his first congregation.

Even among all those fine people, Sicily was extraordinary. What had first seemed to be the most extraordinary of her gestures—the documentary art—was shouldered aside by the baby drama. And yet, the art was Sicily's lasting gospel.

A large formal print of one of the black-and-white photos—Sicily leaning over a dreamy-eyed Emma Cassidy, who appeared to be lolling among pillows beneath her pink quilt, held pride of place on a well-lighted wall outside Hollis's conference room. Hollis worried that patients and their families would find it grotesque, like the Beauty and the Beast. Instead they saw it as an affirmation of simple human grandeur, and were comforted.

Hollis needed to go back to the hospital now, for a surgery this afternoon. Turning to leave, she sent her thoughts toward the podium, as she'd mailed a card to Sicily's home days before. As Hollis slipped through the double doors at the back of the auditorium, a slight, fair-haired man held the door for her. He was dressed in a light linen jacket over an open-collared yellow shirt. Hollis almost stopped. Did she know this guy? He seemed to put her in mind of someone. She was, certainly, the kind of person who never forgot a face. But so many people resembled others superficially. It was not until Hollis was on the train, headed for the hospital, wishing, not for the first or fiftieth time, that Chicago could be just ten degrees more forgiving on the cusp of spring, that it popped into her mind why she recognized the man she'd passed at the door of the auditorium.

After she received her badge, Sicily sought Beth out in the crowd. Beth caught Sicily's brief, conspiratorial wink but then noticed how it instantly vanished, like a raindrop from a clean windshield, replaced by a solemn and hyperalert gaze. As someone who knew the palette of Sicily's face probably as well as anyone on earth, Beth was alarmed.

What was it? The other graduates filed past Sicily to accept their handshakes and certificates. For Sicily, they were clearly invisible. Sicily watched a fixed point at the back of the room. Unobtrusively, Beth turned to try to see what Sicily was seeing.

Because of the unaccustomed clothing he wore—sort of church clothes—and because his presence here was as unexpected as . . . well, catching sight of him sitting next to Rosie and Angelo in their dedicated pew at Holy Angels, for a trace instant Beth did not recognize her own son.

Why was Vincent here? Not in Chicago but here, at this place, now? This was pomp but . . . essentially a nonessential ceremony. Just to do a good turn? To wish Sicily well? For the first time in two years?

With a certain uneasiness, Beth thought of the video clip she had sent Vincent a month before—something lasting less than a minute that she'd filmed at a children's party, a fund-raiser for the zoo, which Ben loved. On a rare simultaneous day off, Eliza and Ben had come to the fund-raiser together. The big heated tent was crammed with food tables, a dance floor, and even a tiny petting zoo. An elaborately bored Stella tried to pretend she wasn't enchanted by the newborn lambs and dwarf goats, while sturdy two-and-a-half-year-old Charley chased everything on four feet or wings. Oddly, there had been an old-timey rock 'n' roll band called Nervous Breakdown or Midlife Crisis or something. When they played a samba, Ben and Eliza started to dance, with Charley between them and Stella ruefully, gracefully, on the edges. That was the part Beth had filmed with the video function on her Nikon. Just behind them, to one side, Sicily and her boyfriend, Adam, an actor who was a staple in Chicago theater, began to dance too. Adam scooped Gemma up, and the little girl stroked Adam's cheek while Sicily swayed to the music. But the two of them weren't goofing around. They really danced, bringing the Latin beat down to their hips. Sicily was laughing; her hair, long again, was coming undone from a careful French braid. Adam held Gemma in one arm and caught Sicily around the waist with the other.

Beth regularly sent photos of Gemma to Vincent, snapshots and portraits, with the family and without them.

Never did they include Sicily.

The video clip had been a slipup. At least, Beth hoped it had been a slipup. Was it true that there really were no mistakes? Beth was regularly surprised, in hindsight, to hear how unacquainted she was with her own motives.

Vincent stopped just inside the door of the hall.

He didn't approach his mother or acknowledge her beyond a single taut smile. Beth smiled back but stayed put in the midst of a small huddle of family. Pat had left them to go up to the front with Sicily and Marie, to take a picture of the new firefighter and her little girl. As the last graduates were named and the hall pitched into the throes of hugs and cheers and backslaps, Pat gave Gemma into Sicily's arms—planting a kiss on each of Sicily's cheeks as he did. Marie began snapping photos. At that moment, Beth thought, if this were a movie, Sicily would see Vincent and burst into diamond-pendant tears as she set Gemma down. Whereupon Gemma, guided by instinct like a heat-seeking missile, would run straight to Vincent, who would sweep her into his arms.

In fact, Gemma didn't know Vincent from a parking meter. The only time Vincent had seen his daughter in the flesh, she weighed about as much as a half gallon of milk and wore tiny patches to shield her eyes from the heat or the liver lamps that blared down upon her small, red, half-finished self. Now Sicily did slowly set Gemma down. A brother firefighter hugged Sicily, and Sicily returned the embrace, her eyes watchful over the man's shoulder. When the classmate squatted down to greet Gemma, the little girl stiffened, embedding her face in the sharp crease of Sicily's uniform slacks. There was a moment of awkward familiarity, the guy apologizing and Sicily brushing it off, smiling absently, never, not once, making eye contact with her friend.

Shaking her own eyes away, Beth made her way briskly through the crowd, up to the front. She took Pat's arm, installing herself in a chain between him and Marie. The moment Pat saw Vincent, Beth knew, he would start waving and yelling. She also could tell that the rest of the relatives had by then seen Vincent and were doing their best not to look at him, poised on instinctive red alert to stop Pat from raising a bellow in the form of a hello. They succeeded. Pat barely noticed as Sicily reached down for Gemma's hand and walked toward Vincent.

As Sicily grew near, she held out her hand.

They're going to shake hands? Beth thought.

Well, what else should they do?

Vincent did take Sicily's hand, but carefully, without pressure, he pulled Sicily into a light hug. Beth knew that Sicily could have escaped if she had tried, but she let Vincent hold her, going so far as to let her hands rest, ever so briefly, on his shoulders. Gemma grabbed a firm fistful of her mother's slacks. There was a long beat of silence, during which everyone who knew either of them and had been concentrating on the opposite direction could no longer restrain themselves and turned to stare. Her face flushed, Sicily stepped back, stepped forward again, and then swept Gemma up into her arms. Vincent tried to touch Gemma's nose with his finger and got his hand kicked for his trouble. Instead, while Gemma hid against Sicily's shoulder, he petted her hair, the little girl reaching back to bat at him with one small fist. Beth could see only a slice of Sicily's profile, but whatever Vincent had said when Gemma socked him, as he drew his hand up like a bird's wing in a parody of being injured, made Sicily shrug and grin.

"What the hell?" Pat said. He was perhaps the only person among them who had not yet realized that the guy with the long hair graying in two fingerprints over his ears—Beth noticed this with a shock that squeezed her throat—was his son. Beth heard Pat draw in a breath to call to Vincent.

Forearmed, Beth hushed him. "Don't."

"But it's Vincent."

"No way," Beth said. "I think you're right, Pat. Are you sure?"

Pat squeezed his eyes and brushed off Beth's jest. "Ha-ha, Bethie. I mean, why is he here? Did you invite him?"

"Nope."

"So what's the deal?"

"I don't know," Beth said. "Let's wait until he tells us." They watched as Vincent continued to talk to Sicily, telling her something that she acknowledged minutely, dipping her head, tossing back her hair. Whatever it was, her response didn't savor of a passionate declaration. Vincent raised his hands, palms not quite meeting, then pointing to himself. After a moment, Sicily shrugged.

"You don't think of seeing your kid as a father," Pat said.

"You see your kid as a father every day," Beth replied.

"Well, Ben, sure. Ben's not like Vincent. Ben was always responsible."

"Vincent's responsible."

"You know what I mean."

Beth did, but she wasn't about to let her husband have the point so easily. "People trust Vincent to make movies with millions of dollars. Not even his dollars."

"With family. You don't see Vincent as the type," Pat said. "The family type."

But Vincent was exactly that, Beth realized suddenly, as if she was waking up. Not in this way, not as a father and a husband, at least not until now, if indeed now at all. When he was a child, though . . . Beth might have believed, after thirty years, that she could forget Vincent's famished eyes, turned on his mother and father, and on Ben, all of them, wakeful, willing all of them home. Vincent was exactly that— the family type. He wanted family so much that he was afraid of it. A door stuck open was as useless as one for which everyone had lost the key.

So far as Beth knew, Vincent didn't even own a shirt like this pale-yellow broadcloth. He didn't own one that wasn't emblazoned on the back with a political slogan or the name of an airport. No, that wasn't quite right. There was one other shirt, the kind meant to be worn with a tuxedo.

The hall was emptying, as graduates and their families headed off to restaurant lunches or parties at home. Sicily and Vincent seemed not to notice the relatives waiting to congratulate her, and how few people were left in the hall. Staff had begun to untie the bows and fold the chairs.

Finally, Gemma kicked to be released from her mother's arms and ran toward Beth, colliding hard with her grandmother's knees. Gemma's parents turned away from each other to follow her with their eyes. Sicily absently continued to rock from side to side, as women do, an attitude at odds with her quasi-military garb. Vincent visibly took a breath—they all did the same thing, along with him—and raised both hands to comb through his hair. Then he didn't seem to know what to do with those same hands and looked at his palms as he again began explaining something to Sicily—a monologue, because she wasn't answering, although she did turn back to face him. Resting lightly, her feet in the same dancer's turnout they would assume all her life, Sicily gave Vincent her full and grave attention. When Sicily took a step closer, Eliza did the same thing, and then, simultaneously (unnoticed except by Beth), so did Angelo. They were all crazy, Beth thought—crazy people whose blood was overheated. They all seemed to expect Vincent to fall to one knee in lustrous slo-mo to win Sicily's heart, which was absurd. Grandstanding wasn't Vincent's style. Beth knew that. And yet it also wasn't his style to fly four hours for nothing. Perhaps Vincent was on his way to New York and changed his itinerary, just to stop by? Just to stop by at Navy Pier, a full two-hour drive south of his parents' house on a hunch that the whole group—including his daughter and . . . well, her mother—would be there, just at this moment?

Or perhaps he actually had come, to plight his troth, to try to claim both his girls—only two years too late, in the way Vincent always did everything, just when everyone had given up all hope?

What were the odds of that?

They were statistically impossible.

Acknowledgments

This book would have been impossible without the help and friendship of the firefighters of Southside Station 6, in Madison, Wisconsin—especially Lt. Doug Rohn and Eric Winker, who amend their world every day and who opened that world to me. That is also true of burn surgeon Dr. Lee D. Faucher of the University of Wisconsin, who generously shared his wisdom, and anaplastologists Jane Bahor, of Duke University, and Suzanne Verma, of Baylor College of Dentistry, as well as Andrea Stevenson Won, who makes digital and physical models—all of whom do work that restores not only ears, noses, and fingers, but dignity. My dear friend Dr. Gay McManus Walker kept me honest in a presumptive medical world of tissue transplant and anti-rejection protocols, while Tanya Bolchen and her mom, Jean, led me through five terrible minutes of fire, in which a husband and father died but saved the two-year-old girl in his arms. Tanya's fifteen-year fight to function as a person and a woman is gallantry itself. Christine Gralapp helped me understand the basics of an ancient and changing art—medical illustration. Shawn T. Mason, Ph.D., of Johns Hopkins Burn Center, tried to take this author to the heroic and haunted places where he has spent his career—inside the emotions of burn patients. Friends and photographers John and Virginia Sutherland shared their experiences in making pictures in trauma settings.

My enduring gratitude goes to my editors, Kate Medina and Millicent Bennett, for giving me the green light to go to a fearful place of moral and medical controversy. Face transplant technology is not at the level of proficiency that it is for Sicily Coyne, in part because of the psychological aspects of donorship and recipients, but one day it will be, literally, a saving grace, most especially for people who are burned. Special thanks to Millicent for staying with me until I finally figured out that one scene—leaving me mystified that twenty lines could make such a huge difference. As before, the design and production team at Random House, especially production editor Vincent La Scala, made me look good, with consummate class.

All my children, but especially my firstborn daughter, Francie (who never accepts the easy answer), deserve my thanks for their patience and long thoughts. To my beloved best friends—Jane Gelfman, my agent, and Pamela English, my co-worker—I owe and give gladly my best love and unflinching loyalty, from this morning until the stars fall down.

—January 4, 2011, Madison, Wisconsin

ABOUT THE AUTHOR

JACQUELYN MITCHARD is the *New York Times* best-selling author of the first Oprah's Book Club selection, *The Deep End of the Ocean; No Time to Wave Goodbye;* and fifteen other books for both adults and children. A former syndicated columnist for the *Milwaukee Journal Sentinel,* she is a contributing editor for *Parade,* and her work has appeared in *More, Reader's Digest, Good Housekeeping,* and *Real Simple,* among other publications. She lives in Wisconsin with her husband and seven children.

www.jacquelynmitchard.com

ABOUT THE TYPE

This book was set in Fairfield, the first typeface from the hand of the distinguished American artist and engraver Rudolph Ruzicka (1883–1978). Ruzicka was born in Bohemia and came to America in 1894. He set up his own shop, devoted to wood engraving and printing, in New York in 1913 after a varied career working as a wood engraver, in photoengraving and banknote printing plants, and as an art director and freelance artist. He designed and illustrated many books, and was the creator of a considerable list of individual prints—wood engravings, line engravings on copper, and aquatints.